THE

VELOCITY
OF MONEY

THE
VELOCITY
OF MONEY

A Novel of Wall Street

STEPHEN
RHODES

WILLIAM MORROW AND COMPANY, INC.

NEW YORK

It is the policy of William Morrow and Company, Inc., and its imprints and affiliates, recognizing the importance of preserving what has been written, to print the books we publish on acid-free paper, and we exert our best efforts to that end.

Library of Congress Cataloging-in-Publication Data

Rhodes, Stephen.
    The velocity of money : a novel of Wall Street / Stephen Rhodes.
        p.   cm.
    ISBN 0-688-15538-3
    I. Title.
    PS3568.H66V45   1997
    813'.54—DC21   97-20626
                                                          CIP

Printed in the United States of America

First Edition

1   2   3   4   5   6   7   8   9   10

BOOK DESIGN BY MARGARET HINDERS

For Jamie, with love—your unflagging support, strength and encouragement made this possible

When money is disembodied—removed from any material basis at all—it speeds up, travels farther, faster. When satellites went up, enabling near-the-speed-of-light, round-the-clock world stock trade, they expanded the amount of global money by 5 percent, an effect similar to circulating more money. Digital cash used on a large scale will further accelerate money's velocity. Once completely disembodied, digitized money . . . is as malleable as digitized information.

To the list of things to hack, we may now add finance.

—KEVIN KELLY
Out of Control (1996)

Prologue

DEATH OF A WALL STREET LAWYER
Saturday, November 29

THE NEWLYWEDS FROM BERWICK, PENNSYLVANIA, were having a splendid time in the big city until the Wall Street lawyer fell from the sky and splattered Ordell Coover in blood, brain matter and pink strings of flesh.

The incident occurred on the weekend immediately following Thanksgiving, the busiest three days of the year for New York City's tourist trade. Ordell and Tricia Coover were among the six hundred thousand visitors in town for a long weekend of shopping, sightseeing, burgers at the Harley-Davidson Café and a shot at tickets to Letterman, or the Radio City Christmas Spectacular. It was purely a confluence of unrelated events and nothing more that put them at that particular place at the particular moment in time that L. Thomas W. Bingham exploded at ground zero.

Like most out-of-towners who had never set foot in New York City before, the twenty-six-year-old high school sweethearts harbored an irrational fear of getting jacked at gunpoint by some psycho in a Santa outfit, or something of that nature. Until that moment, the city had defied their backwater expectations. The Coovers discovered that the holiday spirit had magically transformed New York City from a soulless, menacing slice of hell to the world's capital of exuberant Christmas cheer.

Saturday morning: an inch of fresh snow had coated the city in a pristine white shell. Ordell and Tricia emerged from the lobby of the Milford Plaza Hotel into a snowswept urban cityscape right out of a Currier & Ives print.

"It's so beautiful," Tricia said in a Pennsylvania Dutch singsong. "Just like a Christmas card."

They gulped down an Egg McMuffin breakfast on Broadway and indulged in a brief snowball fight amid peals of childlike laughter. Then, arm in arm, the Coovers strolled toward the mise-en-scène of Fifth Avenue. Tricia referred to her copy of *The New York Post Guide to Holiday Lights and Displays*, pointing out the sights along the way. Reaching Fifth, they were enthralled by the dazzling fusion of sights, sounds and scents all around. The limestone edifices of the avenue were bedecked in festive red ribbons, constellations of sparkling lights and rivers of glittering silver tinsel. A dual procession of snow-dusted evergreens lined both sides of the thoroughfare, their branches adorned with swirls of red-green-and-gold lights, silver glass ornaments and cherubic angels. Their nostrils were suffused with the sharp tang of pine needles from the wreaths on one corner, the aroma of roasting chestnuts from the vendors' carts on the next. Sidewalk Santas clanged their bells with stoic urgency; shoppers responded in kind with the musical jangle of silver coins into the pot-bellied kettles. From every storefront, Christmas carols blasted over speakers. Ordell shook his head in awe. Like everything else about the Big Apple, this was an in-your-face Christmas celebration.

The Coovers melded into the stream of shoppers moving along in a deliberate flow. Much to the cheer of the local merchants, most of the pedestrians toted several pastel-hued shopping bags with high-ticket gifts for loved ones. Each retailer had worked long and hard to prepare for the holiday season, resulting in something of a competition to outdo the others in the outrageousness of their decorations. There were pictur-esque displays of jewel-studded figurines, hand-painted drummer boys and trees with origami ornaments. Tricia was especially enthralled by Lord & Taylor's full-motion Toyland exhibit with the mechanized nut-crackers and teddy bears. Ordell favored the nativity scene at St. Patrick's Cathedral, which featured dozens of foot-high terra-cotta figures sculpted in the eighteenth century by European woodworkers.

The capper, of course, was the soaring eighty-five-foot Norway spruce at Rockefeller Center, which had been harvested at a tree farm in Glastonbury, Connecticut, just eight days ago. The Coovers lingered at the railing of the plaza, peering in slack-jawed reverence at the majesty of the thirty thousand multicolored lights blazing in its boughs. Across the plaza, the Harlem Boys Choir performed "Silver Bells" a capella, as skaters in light wool sweaters cut lazy orbs on the shiny ice below.

Trish entwined her arm in Ordell's and rested her head on his shoulder. In that instant, a lifetime of contempt and distrust for big, bad New York City receded from Ordell's world view. Running his fingers through his wife's waist-length chestnut brown hair, Ordell murmured, "Guess maybe New York's not such a godforsaken hellhole after all."

He had spoken too soon.

Once they encountered the Beauty Pageant of Death, things quickly went downhill. Ordell was intrigued by some sort of commotion going on beneath the three-thousand-bulb, twenty-seven-foot illuminated snowflake suspended above Fifth Avenue and Fifty-seventh Street. "Hey, sugarbear, what do you think is goin' on over there?" Ordell asked, steering her toward the vibrant throng.

They pushed their way through the ring of spectators to catch a glimpse of the proceedings. There was a group of militant don't-buy-fur demonstrators staging a parody of a beauty pageant. To their revulsion, the "contestants" were draped in bedsheets drenched in *faux* blood, studded with the skeletal bones of small animals. A sound track of screaming animals shrieked over a fully cranked boom box, as the master of ceremonies—dressed as Death—speed-rapped, "Isn't she lovely, ladies and gentlemen? She's so lovely. So lovely, isn't she? So lovely—"

"Oh my Lord," Tricia gulped, "I'm gon' to be sick."

The emcee disrupted the proceedings to turn his humiliating bullhorn on a passing woman brazen enough to be wearing an actual fur coat.

"Thirty-two animals were sacrificed for your vanity, woman!" his amplified voice boomed out.

"It's not real fur," the fur-enveloped woman yelped pathetically as she scurried away.

"I'd rather be dead than wear fur," the emcee began to chant, joined by the others.

"God, please, can we *go* now, *please*?" Tricia begged, plugging her ears.

Ordell steered his young wife clear of the scene, just got her the hell away from there. They wandered over to Madison Avenue to continue window-shopping, but it was apparent that Tricia—a sucker for a furry animal—was no longer into it. "Those poor furry creatures," she kept mumbling to herself.

The sky turned an ominous gun-metal gray. A hard sleet began falling, stinging their faces. By the time they decided to pack it in and return to the hotel, Ordell had lost his bearings and was uncertain of the direction of their hotel. Yellow cabs glided by, each one of which carried weary shoppers in the backseat. For the next twenty minutes, Ordell and Tricia Coover continued north without luck, until Alejandro Melendez' cab braked to a rocking halt next to them on the corner of Eighty-third and Madison.

Alejandro Melendez of Harding Park in The Bronx was notorious among the other cabbies at the Jenny Cab Company for his hot-blooded temper and his bitter resentment that a hack's license entitled him to an average of just eighty-five pretax dollars per twelve-hour shift. Never enough to feed his family. Melendez was always up for a fight, and always carried a gun.

Ordell Coover stepped off the curb and asked Melendez to bring them to the Milford Plaza off Broadway. Melendez shrugged. What with the bad weather and all the tourists in town, demand for cabs far exceeded their supply and it didn't seem unreasonable to Melendez to expect an extra off-meter premium of, say, ten dollars for the trip downtown. Ordell stated he wasn't born yesterday and the ten bucks smelled to him like rip-off city.

Melendez shrugged once more. "Take it or leave it, *jefe*."

A vigorous argument ensued between the two men through the open window.

Tricia stood on the sidewalk, hugging herself and shivering in the bone-biting chill. Ugh. *That macho thing again.* She'd seen Ordell this way on many occasions and didn't care for this side of him. Tricia turned away from the dispute. She shielded her brow against the sleet and swept her eyes over the crowns of the skyscrapers looming above them. She felt a drunken wash of vertigo as she took in the majesty of the structures. *What would it be like to live on the top floor of a place like this?* she wondered, as she peered up at the penthouse floor of the apartment building directly above them, a luxury complex named the Diplomat. A blur of motion sixty-seven stories above street level caught her eye.

Tricia Coover would later tell police her first impression was that some thoughtless jerk had thrown a large sack of refuse over the side of the balcony. *Shame on whoever would go and do that,* she thought.

In the next instant, though, it occurred to her that the object plummeting to earth was in fact not garbage. It was a *person.*

Coming right at us!

The human form was flailing wildly, nearing ground level at the mind-boggling velocity of one thousand feet per second.

Confusion and panic left Tricia immobilized and unable to speak. She willed herself to shriek only by clenching her fists so tightly, her fingernails broke skin.

Ordell tore himself away from the argument and whirled around. He followed Tricia's line of vision skyward.

Saw what she saw . . .

A wild-eyed man in the final seconds before meeting a violent death, scrabbling desperately in midair, G-forces pulling his face into a taut mask of terror.

Just then, Ordell's self-preservation instinct kicked in, compelling him to push away from the cab with a primal scream. Ordell backpedaled onto the sidewalk. There, the 1989 state wrestling champ of Berwick

High School and part-time volunteer fireman collapsed into a cowering tangle on the sleet-crusted asphalt.

Alejandro Melendez had just closed his hand around the gun beneath his seat when the 173-pound body of Wall Street lawyer Tom Bingham slammed face-first through the top of his yellow sedan. Even as the metal roof gave way like pie tin, the lawyer's head exploded on impact, sending shrapnel of cranial fluid, blood, bone and brain tissue in a 180-degree splatter. Ordell reflexively raised his hands to shield himself from the gore, but to little effect. He barked out in revulsion when he tasted the dead man's blood on his lips—warm and coppery.

A terrible silence followed. Tricia crept past her whimpering husband, toward the imploded vehicle. The dead man's legs were thrusting from the maw in the roof, skewed at impossible angles. She stared at the sight in a catatonic stupor, her brain unable to reconcile reality with what she had just witnessed.

And like zombies drawn to blood, transfixed New Yorkers began to cluster around the grisly scene within the first few minutes.

"Guy turned himself into sidewalk jelly," someone blurted. "*Way* cool."

A Korean shopkeeper in the all-night Smiler's deli down the block had the presence of mind to call 911. Before Detective O'Bannon and the rest of the five-oh's arrived, however, the driver of the white Chevy Corsica across the street casually fired up the engine and dropped the gearshift into drive. The rental car melded unnoticed into the uptown traffic, heading to the Triborough Bridge.

Part I

THE DAY OF THE CONTRARIANS

January 4–30

*Financial crises are the result of the normal
functioning of the economic and business
systems over the course of the business cycle.*

—WOLFSON, 1994

One

AT AN UNGODLY HOUR on the first workday of the New Year, Rick Hansen stirred awake from a vague soft-focus dream about the chocolate-brown Labrador retriever that had accompanied him throughout his childhood. Eleven years had passed since they'd buried her in the woods behind the upstate New York home he'd grown up in, yet he still dreamed of her occasionally.

Rick squinted at the Indiglo blue digits of the clock-radio at bedside: 4:17 A.M. Daylight wouldn't break over the East River for several hours, but further sleep was out of the question. For some time, Hansen contemplated the light and shadows playing on the ceiling. On street level ten stories below, there was the pneumatic grind of a city sanitation truck and the distant whoop-whoop of a car alarm a block away. The surge of excitement hit him at once.

Today was the first day of his new job on Wall Street.

Wall Street. *Wall Street.*

The two words evoked distinct images: power, wealth, stability, tradition, history. Wall Street was the engine, the personification of the fabled American Dream. And here twenty-eight-year-old Rick Hansen found himself waking up to his first day on the job in the Legal Department of a major global investment banking firm: Wolcott, Fulbright & Company.

In the fifties, it was the mailroom of William Morris. During the sixties, it was *Rolling Stone* magazine. The seventies—*Saturday Night Live,* then MTV. During the eighties, it was Drexel Burnham Lambert (at least for a while), then in the early nineties, it was Microsoft. Now it was the late nineties, the homestretch to the millennium, and the place for young professionals to be was once again Wall Street. And beginning today, Hansen would be there, right at the center of the Zeitgeist, baffled by the imponderable confluence of hard work, schooling and luck that had gotten him there.

The Major Leagues.

He rolled onto his side, spooning the sleeping form of his wife, Stephanie. For a lingering moment, Hansen luxuriated in the candied scent of the Pantene shampoo in his wife's shoulder-length honey-blond hair. Stephanie stirred slightly when he kissed the downy nape of her neck. Delicately, he reached over and placed his palm over the modest swell of her belly, reverently caressing the life-form immersed in a warm soup of amniotic fluid within Stephanie's womb.

"Hey, Baby X," Hansen whispered, his lips brushing the tawny skin of Stephanie's exposed belly. "You sleep all right in there?"

To his amazement, the baby-to-be-named-later responded with a series of fluttering thumps, as if to transmit a morning greeting in some tactile variation of Morse code. Rick suppressed the urge to wake his wife with this news flash—she needed the sleep.

He scissor-kicked the bedsheets off to the side and padded to the stuttering shower awaiting him in the prewar bathroom.

———•———

It was 5:04 A.M. when Hansen stepped briskly out of the lobby onto Fifty-fourth Street. There was not another soul in sight. Hansen loved this time of the morning, savoring the illusion of having the entire city all to himself—for a short while at least. With a purposeful stride, he purchased a freshly printed copy of *The Wall Street Journal* from the corner newsstand and walked the four city blocks to the Lexington Avenue station at an ambitious clip.

Descending down the gum-speckled staircase of the station, he was assaulted by the sour stench of fresh vomit. Quickly, he swiped a blue MetroCard along the slot of the turnstile and pushed through, steering clear of the offending islet of someone's hastily regurgitated fast food.

Further belowground, the platform and tunnel possessed all the charm of a mine shaft. It was eerily quiet at that time of the morning, but not entirely devoid of life. A dozen others aimlessly paced the length of the platform, weary from pulling the graveyard shift at the hospital, the newsroom, the power company. Presently, the downtown 4 train careened into the station with the shriek of steel against steel. The doors parted open with a shuddering rumble.

Hansen had his choice of seats, of course, yet he was mildly surprised by the number of other early risers who were, like him, migrating to the southernmost tip of Manhattan to make a living at this otherworldly hour of the morning. Each one was engrossed in the *Journal*'s front-page stories or the *New York Times*'s business section. All wore identical brow-furrowed grimaces, as if deeply troubled by current events. The train gathered speed as it pulled out of the station with the whine of its electric engine and the chaotic bump-rattle-squeal of its forward momentum.

Rick unfurled his copy of the *Journal* and burrowed through the statistical snapshots of the world financial markets in the manner a sports fanatic consumes box scores. The *Journal* devoted most of its editorial pages to a special recap of the wildly stellar year the global markets had just completed.

The U.S. equity markets were on an unprecedented tear, with the Dow Jones Industrial Average racing toward the mind-boggling 10,000 level. Moving in lockstep with the influential American markets, twenty-one of the twenty-five major countries' stock exchanges had experienced significant gains in the previous year.

Seventeen of those exchanges finished the year at record highs.

Thirteen hours ago, the Asian stock markets had closed out their first trading session of the New Year, and the *Journal*'s World Market report on page C-16 indicated that the unbridled optimism of last year's markets was spilling over to the New Year.

In Tokyo, the Nikkei 225 stock index edged higher, supported by the strengthening of the dollar against the yen. Even though the European markets were only just opening at the time the *Journal* was going to print, an upsurge at the open for the FTSE-100 stock index on the London Stock Exchange reflected a buoyant mood among the Brits, who anticipated generally positive corporate earnings for the year. In Frankfurt, the DAX German stock index leapt on the opening bell to 5,230.42, another record. Notably, in Paris, the CAC 40 was the only major equity index to finish with a slight decline, backing off its record high as investors took their profits at year end. The other bourses experiencing gains were those in Mexico City, Sydney, Kuala Lumpur and Zurich. Likewise, stocks soared in Amsterdam, Milan, Madrid, Stockholm, Brussels, Seoul, Taipei and Bangkok.

The wealth of the world was multiplying at an unprecedented rate.

Hansen's eyes drifted away from the relentless parade of graphs and charts and tables and wondered what was in store for the first trading session in the U.S. markets that day. He gazed about the nonoffensive light-gray-cinnamon-and-cream motif of the subway car.

ANAL FISSURES? The advertising placards around the crown of the car commanded his attention with their deeply personal rhetorical questions. ARE YOU CRYING EXCESSIVELY? HOOKED ON COCAINE? MUST YOU SUFFER WITH CHRONIC FOOT PAIN? PREGNANT? DOES YOUR DADDY

TOUCH YOU THE WRONG WAY? OSI ERES VIH POSITIVO? World of pain, he thought. The stock markets were soaring and the human condition was deteriorating.

Rick's train of thought was derailed by the musical trickle of urine streaming from a homeless man's trousers onto the floor. To his horror, a thin tongue of the bodily fluid cut through the filth caked on the linoleum floor and spiked toward his seat. He lifted his new Allen-Edmonds wing tips just in time to avoid contact. When the doors opened at the electric-blue-tiled Wall Street Station, he bolted out of the car and onto the platform, grateful to escape the first commute to his new job with nothing worse than a near-miss.

———•———

It wasn't even five-thirty in the morning by the time Hansen reached the financial district. No reason to languish inside an office building killing time, Rick reasoned. So instead of heading for work, he walked around the Wall Street area as the auroral glow of daybreak leaked over the city.

The first sight he encountered on street level was the tiny, centuries-old graveyard off Rector Street. The ancient tombstones of long-forgotten Dutch settlers were huddled closely together, poking out of the brown grass like crooked teeth.

The graveyard struck Rick as a cautionary symbol. *Look how easily you can get killed on Wall Street.* Then he crossed Rector and entered the asphalt ravine slicing through the imposing limestone and granite canyons of the financial district.

In a few hours, 875,000 workers would converge on the world's most famous chunk of Manhattan real estate, less than half a square mile in size. But while the vast armies of overeducated men and women who worked in the financial district each business day were at that very moment being trucked in by bus, train, ferry and car, it would be hours before they arrived in force. So Hansen had all the time in the world to meander around Wall Street and its environs, taking in its architecture and the ambiance as a tourist might.

A plaque corrected a common misperception Rick had held that Wall Street was so named because the enormous bas-relief buildings looming over the narrow one-way thoroughfare effectively formed a "wall." Instead, the Street had been named after the Wall of New Amsterdam, constructed in 1653 to protect its inhabitants from attack, predating by centuries the edifices that now towered cosmically overhead. The buildings projected a stately aura of integrity and power and confidence. *Old money*, Rick thought, especially when contrasted to the nouveau-riche opulence of the impersonal modern-day glass-and-steel towers of mid-town Manhattan.

Old money, new money, whatever, the place was teeming with it: each day, $1.4 trillion in activity pulsed in the form of electronic blips through the fiber-optic corridors of the handful of financial institutions inhabiting these buildings. Collectively, the companies on Wall Street formed the veritable nerve center of the global economy. Their money was made making money for others, helping the rich get richer. *The way of the world.*

On the next block, Rick passed the venerable New York Stock Exchange building, the monument to capital markets—a white Grecian temple replete with columns, frieze and grand marble steps. It was effortless to imagine the fluted columns as giant gears of commerce that would begin churning mightily once the equity markets opened at nine-thirty. Traveling past the site, he was astounded by its Olympian majesty and resisted a curious temptation to genuflect.

———•———

At a quarter to seven, Rick Hansen entered the brightly lit chrome-mahogany-and-mirrored lobby of the skyscraper located at 44 Wall Street, his new place of employment, and flashed the temporary ID Human Resources had issued him the previous week. The pair of sleepy security guards at the checkpoint barely nodded, waving him through to the elevator bank.

The elevator jetted him at unexpected speed up to the thirty-seventh floor, where he was to report to work. A burnished aluminum sign on the gleaming glass door to his right identified the area within as:

LEGAL, REGULATORY &
COMPLIANCE DEPARTMENT

Hansen keyed into the secured area by swirling the magnetic stripe of his temp ID over the glowing red electric eye, which responded with the leaden mechanical click of the deadbolt. He entered.

His first impression was not a very good one. The common area of the thirty-seventh floor had been carved up into a maze of putty-brown cubicles. This was the telltale sign of a department the bean counters call a "cost-center," that is, a nonrevenue-generating back-office unit whose budget had to be micromanaged to the penny. Shunted off to a poorly lit ghetto of the building, the modular, cookie-cutter work spaces comprising the majority of the LR&C Department were unsuitable even for raising veal.

You're definitely not at a law firm anymore, Hansen reminded himself, winding his way around the back-office ghetto of cubicles.

He was relieved, then, when he came across a modest-sized, glassed-in office with a view that had a small brass nameplate bearing his name. He walked in and shrugged off his overcoat, appraising the respectable view of the Empire State Building. The office barely had enough space to park a VW Beetle in, but—thank Christ—it had a speakerphone, bookshelves and a door to close. All the basic necessities a securities lawyer required to function. Okay, so the desk itself was a clunky hulk of good-enough-for-government, elephant-gray metal, the sort that issued a hollow boom every time your knee banged against its side. A far cry from the elegant teakwood desk he'd had at his old law firm, but hey, this wasn't his old law firm. He'd get by.

Hansen opened the top drawer of the desk. It was barren inside, except for a striking leather-bound agenda for the new year. Flipping through some of its pages, he saw no notations in it. Virgin. *Nice.* There was an intriguing credit-card-sized device tucked in a pocket in the back of the agenda. Rick pulled it out and inspected it. The electronic gadget had a metallic casing and a liquid crystal display similar to that of a cheap calculator. The liquid crystal display had a six-digit number: 098-740. As Hansen watched, the number changed: it was now 915-667. In precisely 120 seconds, a new number replaced that one: 347-672. Hansen replaced the device in the pocket of the three-ring agenda, and set it to the side. He spent the next two hours unloading the books and files that had been messengered over from his law firm the previous week.

———◆———

"Happy New Year, Rick."

Rick looked up from his reading of the *Wolcott Fulbright Equity Desk Procedural Manual* to see his new boss standing in the doorway. "Oh, hey, Mike, good morning and Happy New Year."

Kilmartin adjusted his unremarkable striped rep tie and took a sip of steaming Lipton tea. "What'd you do for New Year's Eve?"

Rick shrugged. "My wife threw a charity fund-raiser with about two hundred of her closest friends. Me, I just sort of put on the black tie and show up. How about yourself, do anything out of the ordinary?"

"Yeah, something *really* out of the ordinary. I went to bed at nine-thirty." Kilmartin shrugged. "When you get to be my age, New Year's Eve is not something you celebrate as much as it's something you endure."

As for age, Mike Kilmartin was just a few years north of forty, a gangly, wire-thin securities lawyer who was thrumming with hyperkinetic activity and looked five years younger than his actual age. He was as pale as an Irishman in the dead of winter customarily would be, in need of a vacation to South Florida, but cursed with a schedule that rarely permitted such indulgence. With his thick, wire-rimmed Oliver Peoples glasses and a hairstyle comprised of an unruly thicket of reddish-brown cowlicks, Kilmartin looked every bit the part of a book-smart securities attorney. Hansen imagined that in years past, Mike Kilmartin was the type cheaters were magnetically drawn to during final examinations, hoping to cop a peek at his answer sheet as he raced through the test.

Kilmartin took a long gulp of tea and asked, "You getting settled in?"

"Yeah, I'd say so." Hansen made a gesture encompassing the stacks of files on the floor. "Got quite a ways to go, but I'm getting there."

Kilmartin smiled at the mess. "Well, if you could pull yourself away for a while, I thought I might take you around to see the Street's premiere equity trading floor. What do you say, can you spare the time?"

"Absolutely," Hansen replied as his hands scrabbled under the stacks of manila folders obscuring his desk. "Let me just find my ID."

Kilmartin smiled. "Oh, Rick? Take that suit jacket off. People around here don't wear them."

Two

FOR SECURITY REASONS, access to the trading floor was highly restricted. To get there, Kilmartin brought Hansen back down to the lobby, then led him to a special express elevator at another bank. The common area was guarded by a triumvirate of no-nonsense security specialists who were a breed apart from the rent-a-cops working the reception desk nearby. An imposing, bull-chested guard narrowed his eyes suspiciously at Hansen's temporary ID pass for what became an unpleasantly long interlude, until Kilmartin intervened to move things along. Eventually, the guards permitted them to swipe the magnetic stripe of their ID cards through the grotto of the electronic security system, creating a computerized record of their entry.

They pushed through the turnstiles and boarded the one-stop-only elevator. Joining them for the journey was a glassy-eyed mailroom grunt pushing a cart brimming with trade summary reports as thick as the Manhattan Yellow Pages and a sleep-deprived young Jamaican trading assistant who knuckleboned her eye sockets vigorously, trying to look alive for the new year. The doors glided shut; with a confident hum of its gears and cables, the elevator surged skyward to the uppermost reaches of 44 Wall, where the firm's equity trading floor was situated above the spires of Lower Manhattan's skyline.

"It may be a royal inconvenience," Kilmartin observed as the digits of the floor numbers spun higher, "but the firm had to impose additional security measures after the bombing of the World Trade Center in '93. Used to be, the firm ignored the whackadoos threatening violence against Wall Street firms in the name of some militant religious dogma. Can't do that these days. Someday they're gonna strike Wall Street, it's only a matter of time." The elevator slowed to a smooth stop. "Our floor."

As they passed through the short corridor toward the trading area, Kilmartin smiled. "An equity trader on the block desk once told me that when he walked onto Wolcott's trading floor for the first time, he felt like he had suited up in pinstripes and taken the field at Yankee Stadium. Said it was like going to the Major Leagues."

When Rick Hansen approached the expanse of the trading floor, he saw for himself what the trader meant . . .

It was one of the most impressive man-made spectacles Rick had ever encountered. In sheer size alone, the equity trading floor was an astounding place, consuming two football fields' worth of prime New York commercial real estate. Not a single square foot was squandered in the design of Wolcott's trading floor; hundreds of two-man trading turrets were arranged to maximize the sheer number of workstations for commission-revenue-generating personnel. Perhaps by way of compensating for the cheek-to-jowl working conditions of the foxholes, the floor boasted accoutrements of a world-class caliber. The entranceway to the trading floor was gilded in oiled fiddleback mahogany panels and jade-tinted St. Sour Patricio marble, with the corporate crest displayed prominently in faux gold. The rich scarlet, no-static, sound-absorbing carpeting was so plush it sucked at the soles of their shoes as they walked the floor. Gleaming brass railings defined the perimeter of the sunken trading pits. The entire area was bathed in a luminous, ice-blue light from the firm's state-of-the-art Zümtobel illumination system.

As a forceful reminder that time was truly money in this universe, banks of six clocks had been installed on each wall, indicating the respective times in the half-dozen key money centers—New York, Chicago, Los Angeles, London, Hong Kong and Tokyo. With a brief glance up from the trading screen, a trader could instantly discern the time in these six zones. (It was utterly unnecessary to do so, however; a strip of digital clocks on the trader's trading screen did precisely the same thing.) Since information was the most highly valued commodity in the trading culture, the firm had invested heavily in the LED "ticker tape" toteboards mounted along the entire length of the southern and northern walls of the trading floor, known among the trading personnel as the Zipper. Glowing numbers and letters over two feet tall rolled fluidly across the black stripe like the headlines at Times Square, reflecting the last reported sales price of equity securities traded on the U.S. exchanges. The Zipper reminded Hansen of a *scoreboard*, which lent an air of competitive gamesmanship to the proceedings and symbolized the quantum leap financial technology had taken since the forties when bubble-domed tickers laboriously cranked out stock quotes in the form of endless paper ribbons. The regulation basketball hoop the equity derivatives group had affixed to the wall next to the Zipper reinforced the impression of stock trading as sport.

"This is incredible," Hansen marveled. "Must've cost the firm a fortune."

"That it did," Kilmartin assured him. "A few years back, the top-brass decreed that Wolcott would join the race to become the world's first truly global financial superpower. As a first step, they decided to build the finest trading floor on the Street. And—this is important—they were willing to *pay* for it." Kilmartin turned his palms upward and gestured expansively. "This is what $147 million gets you."

Hansen whistled. "One hundred forty-seven *million*? "

"You ask me, the firm got its money's worth. Look up at the ceiling, for example. During construction, the ceiling was raised an additional thirty feet to allow the heat to rise. You wouldn't believe how much heat five hundred traders and their equipment throw off during a volatile trading session. And the floors." Kilmartin stamped the floor several times with his heel.

"Hollow."

"Right. They had to lower the floors to accommodate hundreds of miles of fiber-optic cables and copper wiring that feed the computers. Look at each workstation, how many computers do you see?"

Hansen pivoted around, surveying the turrets. "Four or five, I think."

"Some of them have *nine* systems. In the information age, one computer just doesn't cut it. No, you have to have a screen for Bloomberg, Telerate, ADP, Quotron, Reuters, Dow Jones, GLOBEX. All of *them* have to be tied into a single $125,000 Sun SPARCStation IPX. When you realize that each one of the nine or so computers an equity trader has on his trading turret is immeasurably more powerful than the ones NASA used to put Neil Armstrong on the moon, you get a sense of the firepower these guys are armed with."

"I suppose that kind of hardware chews up a hundred-fifty million pretty quickly," Hansen acknowledged.

"Right. And that figure doesn't count the construction of a special disaster recovery area they built somewhere else in the building, which cost millions, as well." Kilmartin grinned. "It ain't cheap keeping up with the Dow Joneses, you know. C'mon, let me show you who does what around the floor."

The lawyers waded into the platoons of men hunkered down in their foxholes, working the phones in the final fifteen minutes before the trading session commenced. Communal energy gushed forth from the trading populace like a supercharged wave of heat from a blast furnace. With the Dow Jones on an unprecedented winning streak, the spirit on the

floor was soaring. It reminded Rick of the party atmosphere that prevailed in the parking lots before a Grateful Dead concert. True to form,
someone tossed a Nerf football fifty yards over the trading floor. When
a trader on the other side of the room made a Hail Mary catch, an
appreciative cheer went up. Hansen was struck by the atmosphere of
camaraderie of the trading floor, fostered in part by the proximity of the
turrets and the communal goal of making money. This was the main
event, Hansen said to himself, the real deal, the big kahuna . . . this was
Wall Street, the fulcrum of the money culture.

They traversed the length of the floor during their walking tour; Kilmartin seemed to know virtually everyone at each turret and the execs
in the fishbowl offices. As he hobnobbed with the traders and sales reps
like an incumbent politician seeking reelection, he introduced Hansen as
the new in-house derivatives counsel.

At the same time, Kilmartin identified each of the distinct business
units to Hansen. "This is the OTC desk, making markets in NASDAQ
issues. That's the block desk, which handles trades of size for institutional
customers, twenty-five thousand shares or more . . . over there is equity
capital markets, and next to it is the syndicate desk. Just beyond that is
risk arbitrage . . . the foreign equities desk . . . and at the far end, program
trading, index arbitrage and equity derivatives, the area of your primary
responsibility." The senior compliance attorney smirked at the rookie
sales and trading counsel. "Derivatives, as you know, are the rocket scientists, the techno-geeks from MIT that could blow up the franchise.
Includes program trading, index arbitrage and financial engineering for
synthetic equities. That's McGeary's group."

"Gil McGeary is a legend." Hansen grinned. In the course of Hansen's seven-round interview process, McGeary canceled at the last minute, begging off due to a market melt-up that apparently couldn't happen
without him. McGeary extricated himself from the face-to-face interview
by popping his head into the conference room and saying, "Hansen, your
CV is excellent, thumbs up from Gil McGeary, welcome to the firm,
I've gotta hop." Then bolted out of the room back to his trading turret
to capture price discrepancies in the roiling marketplace. That was the
sum and substance of Rick Hansen's personal history to date with the
famed derivatives trader.

"Yeah, you could say that. Gil McGeary is one of the best derivatives
traders alive, up there with Jon Najarian or Victor Sperandeo. But be
forewarned—with Gil on your watch, you have to know what you're
doing. He's sharp, he's aggressive, and he's extremely demanding of the
lawyers."

"Danger is my business," Hansen deadpanned.

"And you say that *jokingly*. There's been lots of bad press about derivative products in the last few years. They're not very popular with Congress or among the taxpayers of Orange County these days. It took one lone asshole to blow up Barings Bank with a billion-dollar loss trading Nikkei stock index futures. Between us girls, Magilla McGeary has the capability to destroy this franchise. With the initial public offering of the firm calendared for the spring, management wants him watched. That's why it's imperative you get your arms around their derivatives business *tout de suite*." With a gesture that was more like a non sequitur, Kilmartin clapped him on the shoulder in a comradely fashion. "Whattaya know, the market's opening in thirty seconds."

As if on cue, the white-noise din of the trading floor lulled to a low buzz of anticipation as they awaited the opening bell: the quiet before the storm. As the open drew near, there was a discernible rise in chatter, building to a crescendo as they approached zero hour. Hansen felt his adrenaline surging with those all around him, mood and pitch rising like a fever. Once the sweephands of the perfectly synchronized analog clocks moved into the last five seconds, a few outbursts punctured the lull:

"Let the games begin!" someone yelled.

"Tear the roof off the suckah!" somebody else yelped.

"Get ready to rrrrummmmmmble! "

Then it was 9:30:00 A.M. Eastern Standard Time.

The trading crowd exploded in a spirited *huzzah!*

The first trading day of the new year was under way!

The *Sturm und Drang* broke out with full fury as the floor came alive, crackling with vibrant activity. In the first few minutes, the DJIA spurted up six points to another new record, 9,115. Phones trilled incessantly with institutional customers on the other line, *demanding* insight. *Is the market peaking? Is the inevitable market correction coming soon? Should we buy, sell or hold our long positions?* Rick watched the traders and sales reps—all seemingly in their mid- to late twenties—standing stiff-spined at their turrets, suit jackets off, bounding back and forth in a tight semicircle, like pit bulls tethered to their workstations by the length of their telephone cords. They worked the phones frenetically, stabbing the speed-dial buttons of preferred customers, speaking in rushed, breathless sound bites to convey the heat and energy and drama of the stock market from their front-row-center seats. Overlapping snippets of agitated sales chatter segued in and out of Hansen's earshot:

"Furman Selz has got three hundred thousand to sell, but they're playing cute 'cause they know there's interest on the buy side . . ."

"Sorry, Dan-o, can only show you a little leg on this one."

"Whenever the yield curve undergoes a phase of negative convexity, effectively, you're short gamma, short volatility and you get shorter when the market rallies. You follow?"

"How far you need to go out on that futures hedge? Auggies? You want, I can get you deeces—"

"—listen, the head of the desk at Bankers is gonna go ethnic on me if I go back to him with these numbers. You tryin' to get 'em to do the trade away from us or what?—"

"—you ask me, the straddle is a screaming buy—"

It was an electrifying spectacle, observing the money culture of the trading floor. Hansen would later attempt to describe it to Stephanie as equal parts auction, casino and symphony orchestra. There was the music of deal making, bringing two parties together, meeting of the minds, money exchanging hands. There was the general clatter of time-stamping machines as traders whacked their tickets and tossed them into a wire basket for the sales assistants to run over to the trade entry window. Each trading day was 390 grueling minutes, 23,400 punishing seconds, turbocharged with fear, greed, ambition, adrenaline, endorphins, testosterone, caffeine and muffin-sugar. And Hansen positively loved his first taste of it.

Kilmartin snapped Hansen out of his trance. "C'mon, killer. I want to introduce you to the equity derivatives team." He steered him over to the southern end of the trading floor.

The twenty-two-man Equity Derivative Group was situated next to the picture window with the postcard-worthy view of the New York Harbor, a high sign of the team's contribution to the department's "P&L," or profit and loss statement, the scorecard of a desk's ability to make money. Man for man, Derivatives was the most profitable unit of all at Wolcott Fulbright, with the possible exception of the mergers-and-acquisition prep school pups two floors above.

The overeducated men who made up the Derivatives squadron were primarily young meat cherry-picked from a short list of premiere b-schools, to which Wolcott's Recruitment Committee had donated hundreds of thousands. Perhaps a third of them had been big-time losers in high school—awkward slide-rule geeks who captained the chess team and couldn't scrape up dates to the senior prom. But now the geeks had inherited the earth; most of them earned a larger salary each year than the President of the United States. Still, they scrupulously avoided the in-your-face "asshole consumption" of the 1980s. This breed didn't wear the Audemars Piquet and Vacheron Constantin timepieces that were back in favor; they wore $39.95 Timex Indiglo Ironman Triathalon digital watches. They wore starch-stiffened Hathaway white shirts, with their cuffs rolled to a bunch at the elbow. The only conceits were stylish

European silk ties (Ferragamo, Princess Mara and Hermès, mainly), and seventy-five-dollar haircuts. Work was prayer for the derivatives guys, much more so than the economic spoils of it. The cacophony of clattering time-stamp machines, enthusiastic sales pitches and blurt of fizzy voices over the firm's hoot'n'holler was more than a few decibels higher in intensity and volume than elsewhere on the floor.

Mike Kilmartin broke in on a heated discussion among seven of the traders, and introduced Rick as the new counsel serving the derivatives sales and trading effort. The traders were introduced to Rick by nickname: The Stain, Joe Money, Train Wreck, Eddie Pockets, Zaps, Danny Partridge, Gumby. The nicknames were apparently a mandatory element of the fabric of the trading culture, in the same way they were for professional athletes, military personnel, frat brothers and Mafiosi. Hansen had an irrational flash of worry concerning the nickname they'd eventually tag *him* with.

"Where's McGeary?" Kilmartin asked, peering into the boss' vacant fishbowl office.

"He's at his monthly NAMBLA executive board meeting," Zaps deadpanned, as he whacked a ticket for a Fidelity trade.

The Stain added in a pronounced London School of Economics–influenced dialect, "It was his turn to bring the punch and cookies."

"And the fifth-graders," Danny Partridge chimed in.

Joe Money looked up from the spreadsheet on his Hewlett-Packard 200 LX palmtop and jerked a thumb in the direction of the London Equity Program Trading group. "Actually, he's pricing an off-board basket of garbage stocks for the blueshirts." Joe was referring to their British counterparts, who wore blue shirts to work the way their Yankee counterparts favored white shirts (and were accordingly referred to as "whiteshirts" on the other side of the pond).

"When will he be back?"

"Beats me."

The phone rang and Train Wreck scooped it up. Instead of answering it with the firm's name, he stated the current level of the S&P 500 index. Covering the mouthpiece, he barked out, "Danny Partridge, you got PIMCO holding on eight-seven."

"I'll call 'em back in five, this has to be resolved first," Danny Partridge replied.

"All right," Kilmartin stated. "When McGeary gets back, have him give me a bell."

"Wait a second," said Zaps. "You guys are lawyers—or reasonable facsimiles thereof. Maybe you can resolve this issue for us."

"We'll try."

Zaps' face remained impassive. "Who would you rather do—Betty or Veronica?"

Without hesitation, Rick replied, "Betty, of course."

"Betty!" Danny Partridge groaned. "Why Betty?"

"Veronica always seemed so manipulative, you know? Always playing Archie and Reggie against one another."

"Rich bitch," The Stain agreed, though he was from London.

"Real silver spoon attitude," Train Wreck put in.

"Let's not forget," Kilmartin chipped in, "it was the sexual tension over Veronica Lodge that broke up the Archies. She was the Yoko Ono of the comic pages."

"Aw, you guys have no taste." Danny Partridge waved dismissively. "Betty was one step removed from trailer trash. Always throwing herself at Arch that way. It was despicable."

"Well, despicable or not, it's resolved," Zaps declared. "Betty you fuck, Veronica you marry. Pay up, Danny."

The pronouncement inspired a chorus of victorious whoops from the semicircle of traders; apparently, Hansen's answer had resolved a wager among the traders that Danny Partridge was on the losing end of. Danny Partridge grumbled unhappily, tugging out a wad of bills and thrusting ten dollars apiece to Zaps, The Stain and Train Wreck. Zaps pocketed the ten-spot and raised his noise above the din. "All right, time for the main event: Penelope Pitstop versus Jessica Rabbit. Who wants in?"

The phone bleated again and The Stain scooped it up. "Wolcott. Yeah, you got 'im. Oh, hey, Steve, how was the Rangers game last night? Some finish, eh? Two fights and an overtime, yeah. You stay for the whole thing? Wait, can you stay with me for a sec?" Stainsby covered the mouthpiece. "Hey, it's Soros on the line. Gotta take this, all right?"

"Have Magilla call me," Kilmartin shouted over the din.

The Stain waved by way of acknowledgment and began shooting the shit with the customer.

———•———

On the elevator back up to LR&C, Kilmartin asked his new hire, "So, what'd you think of the daily Darwinian struggle otherwise known as Wolcott Fulbright?"

"Pretty radical change from life at my old law firm."

"Ain't that the truth." Kilmartin chewed his lip thoughtfully. "Sometimes I envy McGeary's crew, their chutzpah and *esprit de corps*. Sometimes I ask myself why I don't make the move to become a trader myself. Then I snap out of it, and realize those guys are the ones out there with their asses on the firing line day after day, taking risks, eating pressure for breakfast. They're like pro athletes—their careers could be over in a heartbeat. And suddenly I don't mind so much making a tenth of what they do, doing what I do." Kilmartin massaged his jaw thoughtfully. "After all, if I wasn't so risk-averse, I would've gone to b-school, not law school."

After the elevator doors opened on the thirty-seventh floor, Kilmartin brought him around to meet the rest of his colleagues in Legal, Regulatory & Compliance.

For the remainder of the day, Rick kept to himself in his office, digesting treatises on derivatives and scouring the data in seven trading runs a courier had dumped on his desk while he was touring the trading floor. At about 8:20 P.M., Rick called it a night, but not before gathering some more reading materials for homework.

As he leaned forward to shut down his PC for the evening, he glanced at the stock ticker window. Turned out the market had churned up 77.34 points on the day, starting the year at another record high.

"Sonuvabitch," Hansen whisper-muttered in awe. *Where she stops, nobody knows.*

He snapped off the power and the colors on the screen collapsed into a small white dot in the center of the darkened screen before disappearing altogether.

Unknown to Rick, and unknown to most users of the Wolcott Fulbright internal computer network as well, an automated notation is created any time an employee accesses the system. A program logs the time spent on the system, the files accessed, the Internet sites the employee visited on company time, and—for a period of sixty calendar days—all of the keystrokes made once access has been gained to the system. The techs in Wolcott's data security department had created the Big Brother surveillance tool to ensure that none of its employees was engaging in any unauthorized copying of sensitive Wolcott documents, disseminating distasteful Polish jokes via e-mail or spending too much time perusing the *Penthouse* home page.

But as with any such monitoring tool, the Wolcott security system was vulnerable to abuse. Rick Hansen couldn't have imagined that his activity could be watched by unseen eyes. Only in the months to come would it even matter to him. And then, it would matter tremendously.

Hansen closed the door to his office and headed home to tell Stephanie how much he loved the first day on his new job.

Three

TWO DAYS LATER, nine financiers of international repute gathered on a luxury motor yacht two miles off the shore of St. Barthélemy's in the South Pacific. Colbert referred to these men as The Contrarians, a mocking reference to the essence of their ambitious scheme.

Colbert had handpicked each one of them, and had done so discriminatingly. Obscene wealth was the threshold consideration, of course; anyone with less than $100 million in liquid net worth was of no use to The Contrarians. On the other hand, it was clear that an allegiance of mega-millionaires who had gone soft living the good life would lead to an even worse result.

The Contrarians, then, were comprised of a different breed entirely. Unlike the garden-variety trust fund babies who ostracized them from their Old Money social circles, none of the Partners had had his fortune handed to him by the deceased scion of a family dynasty.

To a man, they were self-made magnates. They had fire in the belly.

Starting with little or nothing, they had cleverly and vigorously leveraged the three L's of the business world—loopholes, lawyers and lawsuits. They had recruited armies of top-priced legal and accounting mercenaries to cheat, steal and bribe their way to nine-figure wealth. But while the judicial process had proved an efficient vehicle for wealth accumulation for this group, each Contrarian possessed a strident contempt for the applicability of the law to *himself*; each maintained a firm conviction that he would never serve a day of his privileged life in prison, no matter how egregious the crime committed.

Their fortunes had been won in the shadowy worlds of dark commerce. For example, Van der Leun was an industrialist whose profits came primarily as a global arms dealer; Reich was a promoter of dubious stock deals around the world; Zull had stolen controlling interest in a South African company that had uncovered a stunningly lucrative vein of uncut diamonds; Pethers, an Australian lawyer, had embezzled hundreds of millions from the Kuwaiti oil trust during the Gulf War; De Moncheaux laundered billions for the Medellín cocaine cartel. Rules and laws were for *others* to follow; the genetic coding and cultural breeding of these men made it impossible for them to play by the rules. Others followed the rules of society, they did not—this distinction had made them rich beyond comprehension. But not rich enough.

Greed, ego, insecurity, revenge, self-hatred—Colbert was indifferent as to what gave the players the fire in the belly. The accumulation of wealth had to be a constant craving for a Contrarian. For each man in the partnership, every conscious moment had to be devoted to the obsession of attaining the ultimate prize life had to offer . . .

One billion dollars net worth.

A billion dollars—to Colbert, this was not such an impossible objective. It was merely *a thousand* millions. It was likely that some, if not most, of the men gathered about the yacht would attain that goal without this initiative. But such men were innately impatient. When they became Contrarians, Colbert promised to accelerate their ascendancy to this exclusive club of only five hundred men worldwide. For every single dollar invested, they would get at least a hundred back. Colbert knew such men could never decline such an invitation, not the ones he had assembled.

———•———

Of all his yachts, the *Full Acquittal* was Colbert's sentimental favorite. Stem to stern, the ship was a magnificent vessel, a 105-foot Hatteras capable of twenty-five knots top speed. It featured twin MTU engines, Naiad stabilizers and four luxurious madrone burl wood staterooms, which would easily accommodate eight guests. Admittedly, the yacht had been an impulsive purchase, commissioned by Colbert immediately after he had been acquitted by a jury on twenty-seven counts of federal securities fraud and tax evasion in 1991. It was a self-indulgent gift to himself for his savvy, his scrappiness and his acumen. When all was said and done, Colbert was still the best in the game. *Full Acquittal* was an appropriate venue for a clandestine meeting away from prying eyes.

Shortly after 11:00 A.M. local time, Colbert dispatched the first mate to the flybridge to inform the others that the summit was about to commence. He turned the navigation of the vessel over to the four-man crew, then descended to the main stateroom to await the others.

The rest of The Contrarians drifted down the staircase to the fiordipesco marble-gilded cabin of the *Full Acquittal*. Their skin was rosy from several hours of sportfishing in the tropical sun. They jousted good-naturedly with each other, as men of their socioeconomic caliber often do, engaging in one-upmanship over mega-deals and transactions recently completed. There was no mistaking the undertone of intense competitiveness lurking beneath their cordial demeanors.

As the men gathered around the Honduran mahogany conference table, a servant placed pitchers of a little-known brand of sparkling water flown in from the Italian Alps and platters of croissants and fruit spreads beneath the Waterford chandelier suspended from the ceiling. Colbert coolly surveyed the group of men present: Reich, Kuypen, Van der Leun, Jermyn, Lanzaretti, Zull, Pethers and De Moncheaux. *If travesty sank the vessel this very moment, $3 billion in net worth would be swallowed by the sea,* he calculated. Then he smiled to himself: if the initiative followed the Three Rivers Model to the letter, the men would be worth a multiplicity of that sum.

Consulting his Patek-Philippe Calibre '89 tourbillons chronograph, he noted it was precisely 11:30 A.M. *Showtime.* Colbert called the meeting to order.

"Gentlemen, it is my immense privilege to host this, our final summit, before we commence the first leg of our initiative. I'm grateful that each of you was able to rearrange your busy calendars to accommodate this meeting on such short notice. Since the fish are biting, my summary will be brief."

"Hear, hear," boomed Gunter van der Leun, who had landed a shark earlier that morning and was ready for his next prize.

"I called you here today to inform you that all systems are indeed 'go' for our initiative. The papers for the offshore vehicles have been filed in the various tax-friendly jurisdictions we've identified."

"When do we begin using them?" Antar Reich asked.

"Monday morning."

Cheers erupted. The game was about to begin.

"Of course, that means the final installment of your capital commitment is due and payable by wire transfer to our offshore bank on the Isle of Man. No later than Monday morning at ten A.M., New York time, please."

"I was waiting for that part," Gunter van der Leun quipped.

"Time is of the essence, I'm afraid. We're close to finalizing a deal in Baltimore with the Dartmouth Funds Group, and we cannot jeopardize it with a temporary shortfall in seed capital."

The news that they were close to a deal with Dartmouth elicited an approving buzz among The Contrarians. It had seemed impossible, yet Colbert was on the verge of pulling it off.

"Also, as you know," Colbert continued, "the two broker-dealer/ futures vehicles we have established in Los Angeles and Florida have received licenses from the appropriate regulatory authorities and have been properly capitalized with Contrarians' money. They are now ready to execute your derivatives transactions." Colbert gathered up a sheaf of collated photocopies and began passing them around. "The name of the L.A. vehicle is Infinity Technology Securities Company. New York is GoldBridge Capital Advisors. Dieter, Gunter, Dirk and Graham will capitalize their proscribed derivatives transactions through Infinity; Mario, Marty, Antar and Jean-Claude are to use GoldBridge. You'll find the account numbers for your fictitious offshore entities on the pages I have just distributed."

Dieter Kuypen raised an index finger. "The schedule lists transactions up to January twenty-ninth."

"Friday, January twenty-ninth, is when we go live," Colbert replied.

"Why the twenty-ninth, of all days?"

"The model generated by the Three Rivers expert system appears to have factored the so-called January Effect into its calculations. Based upon historical models, it has identified the twenty-ninth as the optimal day to take advantage of any artificial run-ups in the price of broad-based equity indexes."

Zull frowned. "You mean to say that all of our capital is being handed over to a *machine*? I'm still not entirely comfortable with that idea."

"Think of it as a robot trader, Marty," Colbert said soothingly. "A machine that can instantaneously react to any subtle changes in the marketplace. But it goes beyond that, way beyond that. In any event, your capital is at little risk."

"We shall see," Zull harumphed.

"Permit me to explain." Colbert returned to his position at the conference table. "For the initiative to succeed, each order entered is economically offset by an opposite-but-equal transaction by one of your colleagues. It is a zero-sum game, you see . . . since the mirrored orders have the economic impact of canceling each other out, at no time will The Contrarians' initial capital be at risk. But because of the size of each transaction, the Three Rivers expert system creates a self-fulfilling prophecy." Colbert gazed at the blank faces surrounding him at the table and decided to leave well enough alone. "That's all I'll say at this time."

"Have we worked out the bugs in the black-box system?" Dirk Jermyn asked.

"That was my next topic of discussion, Dirk, thank you. Despite the unacceptable results of early beta-testing of the black-box system, I'm delighted to report that the system is up and running, courtesy of our man Stiletto in New York. The results have been flawless. Any attempt on the part of the authorities to trace the source of the trading activity would prove futile."

"That is good news indeed," Antar Reich enthused. "Frankly, I thought the technical problems were insurmountable."

"Me, too," Kuypen stated, shaking his head and grinning.

Van der Leun cut in. "By the way, when will we learn the identity of this mystery man Stiletto?"

"Never. Next question."

The men laughed. Colbert's protection of Stiletto's true identity had become something of a running joke for The Contrarians. All that was known about Stiletto was that he was someone of considerable influence in the U.S. financial community. Stiletto was the invisible hand tugging the levers that would enrich The Contrarians beyond imagination.

"Who came up with that code name, anyway?" Van der Leun muttered under his breath. "*Stiletto*, for bloody Christ's sake. Sounds like something from a Hollywood spy movie."

Jermyn piped up. "I don't mean to be contentious, but I don't understand why we are compelled to stay on the sidelines in this go-round. I mean, what's the harm in placing a few relatively small side bets in the over-the-counter derivatives markets and getting a piece of our investments back?"

This provoked several nods of assent from the others, who were itching to reap immediate profits. It was, of course, a question Colbert had fully anticipated. "Once again, gentlemen, the January initiative is merely a prelude to the main event. As I have explained before, we cannot afford the risk that off-exchange derivatives activity will hit the radarscope of the U.S. authorities and attract scrutiny."

"But we could set it up offshore. In the privately negotiated markets—"

Colbert held up a silencing hand. "I assure you, your reward at the back-end of the first tranche will be spectacular and will validate your patience. But for the time being, you and all members of The Contrarians are prohibited from placing unauthorized off-exchange derivatives transactions prior to the January initiative. Let me make this perfectly clear: *no single one of us may endanger the entire franchise*. Therefore, I must once again demand an assurance from each and every one of you that you will not disregard this directive." His eyes darted around the room, scrutinizing the others to ensure that no one dared violate this tenet.

Graham Pethers, the young Australian embezzler, met Colbert's glare in what seemed to be a contemptuous manner.

"Graham, do you have a problem with that?" Colbert asked sharply.

Graham responded tartly, "With that? No, no I don't."

"Good."

"What perturbs me, quite frankly," Pethers said, drawing the words out, "is that when we signed on, not a word was mentioned about any bloodshed."

Colbert stiffened. "What?" he hissed.

"I believe you heard me. The Wall Street lawyer is dead. Bingaman or whatever his name was. Stiletto's boy-lawyer. We weren't consulted, nor were we informed about his killing even after it was carried out."

Colbert chose his words carefully. "Thomas Bingham was a consultant to this project, yes. And it is true that he took his life by his own hand. He was a deeply troubled individual. Manic depressive and incurably addicted to gambling. While his death was untimely and unfortunate, The Contrarians have progressed to a point where we no longer need to rely upon the expertise of the—"

"*C'mon*, mate," Pethers spat. "With all due respect, do you expect us to believe that this Tom Bingham offed *himself*? *Before* his big payday?"

"That's enough, Graham," Kuypen interjected.

Not an attractive man, Colbert often used his unpleasant features as a weapon. His face could tighten into a stark, cold mask of venomous contempt that could instantly silence a negotiation at the bargaining table. Now, in the wake of a serious allegation that could undermine the confidence of his capital partners on the eve of funding, Colbert glared icily at his inquisitor. His irises had the shiny lifelessness of gleaming black marbles. "What are you suggesting here, Mr. Pethers?"

"I'm not suggesting *anything*. I'm asking for your assurance that Bingham's misfortune was not our—meaning The Contrarians'—doing."

"For the record, The Contrarians cannot be considered responsible for whatever demons drove Bingham to do what he did."

"Would you swear under oath that—"

"*Any further discussions* on this subject must be taken off-line," Colbert spat.

"Off-line it is," Pethers replied evenly.

An iceberg of anger rose within Colbert, as he placed the flats of his hands on the table and leaned toward the group. "From the outset, I have pledged that this initiative will be purely financial in nature." He directed the last comment toward Pethers, who challenged his stare. "I resent any implication that I am not a man of my word."

The men in the room murmured their support of Colbert, their commitment to the initiative. The room lapsed into silence; the rattle of the central air conditioning was the only audible sound.

"Are there any further questions?" Colbert asked finally.

No one dared to venture any.

"Lunch will be served on the upper deck at one P.M.," Colbert said, tersely. "We shall put into port at approximately five P.M. Enjoy your stay."

The men solemnly filed out of the cabin to return to their sportfishing activities. Colbert tilted his chin up and fired a malicious expression, it seemed, toward the Waterford chandelier.

The Japanese-engineered fiber-optic video camera with the half-inch CCD Sony microchip was concealed in a discreet glass thread protruding from the center of the chandelier, completely inconspicuous to the casual observer. The pinhead-sized lens captured Colbert's image in 300,000 pixel resolution and transmitted a 500-line picture of it to Colbert's personal chief of security, who had been videotaping the proceedings for his boss in the aft quarterberth.

Viktor Alexeyev nodded knowingly at the monitor. He'd gotten the message: *Pethers has to be managed from here on out.*

Colbert's expression had told Alexeyev the killing was *not* over, not if the need arose again. But the killing was nothing, a sideshow, a distraction from the central truth. It came down to this and this alone: no one person could be permitted to endanger the entire franchise. No one.

Four

"CARE FOR A SMOKE?"

Those were the first words Gil McGeary had spoken to Rick Hansen since his seven-minute interview. As it happened, it wasn't until the end of the week that Hansen hooked up with the legendary head of Wolcott's equity derivatives desk. Professing volatile trading markets that required his hands-on management, McGeary canceled meeting after meeting with Hansen, until a window of opportunity opened up at nine-fifteen on Friday morning. Even then, McGeary was a good twenty-five minutes late.

On the trading floor, Rick killed time by making notations of "to-do's" in his new leather-bound agenda. When he exhausted that activity, he pulled out the curious metallic card from the back pocket of the agenda, and watched the digits change every 120 seconds.

129-567...
435-778...
099-987...

At around 9:40, Hansen heard a commotion that caused him to look up. It was then he spied the head of the derivatives desk for the first time.

Gil "Magilla" McGeary strode across the trading floor with a majestic aura of braggadocio that enveloped him like body armor. He clutched a bag of yogurt-covered pretzels from the cafeteria in one hand and a sloshing coffee mug that said TYPE A'S HAVE MORE FUN in the other.

At thirty-six years of age, McGeary projected the effortless confidence of the professional athlete he once was, having spent three seasons in Toledo playing Triple-A ball before hanging up his cleats with a not-bad career average of .257. He had the beefy, thick-necked build of an ex-jock who was turning to flab from several years of the good life. His patrician nose had been broken twice in collisions at the plate and both his knees had been blown out and already gone to hell; but he possessed a striking Herculean mane of snow-white hair and a rich, resonant baritone that would leave a network news anchor envious, both of which lent him an intractable air of authority in the jungles of the trading culture. Above all, McGeary was blessed with a mercurial personality that was especially suited to times of excessive market volatility. As a perennial moneymaker for Wolcott Fulbright, McGeary didn't so much walk as swagger; he didn't so much talk as *orate*.

Magilla's minions clamored all around him, competing for his attention as if he were some sort of rock star. The commotion was mother's milk to an ego the size of McGeary's.

The red-haired trader nicknamed Danny Partridge cut in: "Magilla, we won the bid on the Putnam EFP!"

"Oh yeah? Size? Bigger'n a breadbox?"

"Two million shares, done offboard, after-hours on Crossing Session 2."

"How's the price?"

"Six cents a share."

McGeary beamed. "Awright, homey! Way to kick ass and take names!" McGeary extracted a yogurt-pretzel out of the bag. "This calls for a Scoobie-snack. Open up and say ahhh!"

Danny Partridge's mouth yawned open and McGeary underhanded the yogurt pretzel in a high arc. Even from a seated position, Danny Partridge expertly gobbled it out of the air. His colleagues burst into applause, both at the trick and the size of his profitable trade. Danny Partridge basked happily amid the attention, hamming it up with a bow.

Hansen cleared his throat. "Gil?"

McGeary whirled around.

Hansen offered his hand. "Rick Hansen from Legal, Regulatory and Compliance. We had a meeting?"

McGeary said nothing for a while. Instead, his eyes swept over Rick as if sizing him up. "Care for a smoke?"

"Smoke?"

"Yeah, you know. A cee-gar?"

Got to go along to get along, Hansen reasoned, so he replied, "Sure, why not?"

The head trader made a cordial open-palm gesture toward the door of his fishbowl office. "Whyn't you step into my orifice?"

McGeary closed the door, muffling the chaotic sound and fury of the trading floor raging outside. The fishbowl office was modest in size, but all the same a telling badge of privilege, considering many managing directors at Wolcott sat at the same type of open-air turrets as the traders under their command.

McGeary had converted his fishbowl into an impressive emporium of stress toys and pop culture paraphernalia. There were the jock touches— cricket mallet, pool cue, baseball bat, hockey stick, Nerf basketball—and the homage to Gen-X trash-culture kitsch—a Batman lunchbox from the 1973 TV show, Speed Racer sippy-cup, a cookie jar in the shape of Poppin' Fresh, the Pillsbury doughboy. As an undisputed big hitter at the firm, McGeary's wall was adorned with the obligatory needlework sampler embroidered with his own personal credo. McGeary's was: THOSE WHOM THE GODS DESTROY, THEY FIRST MAKE PROUD.

"So, there's a new sheriff in town, and you're it." McGeary circled around behind his desk and muted the sound of the CNBC talking head on his Mitsubishi television set. He then pulled the head off the Poppin' Fresh cookie jar, revealing a thicket of pungent Cuban cigars in a deep chocolate-brown leaf wrapper. "I half expected you to be carrying hand-cuffs, Counselor."

"You must be mistaken," Hansen deadpanned. "I was hired to keep you *out* of handcuffs."

"Good answer," McGeary smirked, as he clipped a cigar neatly with his silver beveling tool. He passed it to Hansen. "I hope by that you don't mean you're gonna put a monkey wrench in all my exotic trading strategies."

"Mike Kilmartin tells me I'm here to help you get your trades done the best way possible."

"Music to my ears." McGeary fired up Hansen's cigar with a chrome Zippo, then lit up his own. The two men breathed out a luxurious mush-room cloud of deep blue smoke. "What do you think?" McGeary in-quired.

"It's good, really good. Smooth."

"Solid smoke, with a hint of spices and nuts, right?"

"Yeah. You can definitely taste the spice."

McGeary used his cigar as a pointer indicating Hansen's cigar. "You see the label on that bad boy?"

Hansen inspected the yellow-and-black band encircling the thirty-eight-ring-gauge chocolate-brown wrapping of his cigar. COHIBA, LA HA-BANA, CUBA, it said. "Yeah?"

"What you are smoking right now, my friend, is a Cohiba Corona Especiale. This is not just an ordinary cigar any Joe Six pack can pick up at Nat Sherman's. Up until 1982, it was one of the three hand-rolled blends available only to Fidel Castro. It's made up of a blend of two Cuban tobacco leaves, ligero and seco, which are moistened and fermented in a top-secret process at the Liguito factory. Then it's hand-rolled by women—and women only."

"Huh," Hansen grunted as he took another draw.

"I think the code name at the factory was Liguito Number Two. Whatever, even now it's forbidden fruit for imperialist Yanquis such as you and me. Must've cost those assholes eight hundred dollars for a box of these puppies."

What assholes? Hansen almost asked, but checked himself in time. Instead, he said, "Where'd you get them? Overseas business trip?"

"A holiday gift from the Risk Management Task Force. Their profound thanks to me for not blowing up the firm with aggressive derivatives trading. Along the way, I guess I picked up six or seven hundred million for the home team, which no doubt helps Wolcott's upcoming initial public offering." McGeary studied the Cohiba appreciatively. "Don't get me wrong—it's a damn fine cigar. But if Bobby Wolcott thinks this is going to suffice in place of a raise in my base salary next year, it's close, but no cigar."

Hansen chuckled. For all of Mike Kilmartin's warnings, Rick was having a good time so far.

For the next few minutes, they pulled on their smokes and engaged in companionable small talk. The subjects were the Knicks' shot at the Eastern Conference title and the futility of New Year's resolutions. Then, abruptly, McGeary's bassoon rasp filled the fishbowl with the tenor of authority. "Hope you made the right career decision, Hansen. This is no law firm, you know."

"That's exactly why I came here. I wanted to escape partnership-track hell."

"Yes, well, you traded one hell for a different one. Shame about your predecessor. Smart guy, but that insider trading problem of his got the best of him, I guess. Can't say I'm completely surprised he snapped."

"My predecessor?"

McGeary tossed him a surprised look. "Tom Bingham?"

"Did he go to another derivatives shop?"

McGeary was all poker-face. "Tommy Bingham killed himself. Jumped off his balcony last Thanksgiving."

Rick recoiled. McGeary had said something about an *insider trading problem.* Hansen made a mental note to tactfully ask Kilmartin about it later.

"Listen, you talk to Kilmartin about that," said McGeary, switching gears. "Since time is money, let me bottom-line you here, Counselor." He set his cigar down and fixed his eyes on Rick's face like twin laser beams. "When this firm wooed me away from Goldmine, Sachs five years ago, I was given $1.3 billion worth of marginable securities and a simple mandate—to make as much money for them as humanly possible. And by every account, Gil McGeary has done a damn good job at that. I've been the firm's top equity producer five years running.

"Now, what does that mean exactly? That means that the muckety-mucks up there in the executive suite cut crazy Magilla McGeary a *lot* of slack. They give me my own little fiefdom here—give me responsibility over two dozen ham'n'eggers and give me *beaucoup* capital to ply my trade. Generally, that means a guy like McGeary has a quote-unquote 'high-risk profile' and must be watched carefully by the bow-tie-type compliance lawyers. Meaning you."

McGeary often referred to himself in the third person, as if he were someone else not present in the room. The high sign of an egomaniac, Rick knew.

"Because of the latitude given to me," McGeary continued, "I've been able to assemble an A-team of quant jocks to concoct some of the most cutting-edge derivative products since Howard Sosin worked at AIG. And you know what I'm most proud of?"

"No."

"I'm most proud of the fact that I didn't hire a single *asshole*. They're all solid, good guys. Don't be fooled by their pee-pee and ca-ca humor; my boys are the thoroughbreds, first-stringers, the Chicago-frigging-Bulls, and I'll put 'em up against any derivatives shop on the Street, bar none. Salomon, Lehman, Morgan—any one of 'em." Here McGeary paused to take a thoughtful puff of his premium stogie. "But as a bow tie, you don't care about that, Hansen. You're wondering: are these propeller-heads capable of blowing up the firm? Destroying the franchise with risky trades or fraudulent activity? Knowing human nature the way I do, I'd be a liar if I told you there was absolutely no way. Let's face the music, there's a lot of pressure on these guys."

Hansen nodded in assent. As a lawyer in private practice at the law firm of Cleary Gottlieb, he had sat in on numerous arbitration cases involving securities brokers who meandered over to the dark side. "The pressure in this business occasionally drives people to do things they're otherwise not capable of doing. Sticking tickets in a desk drawer to cover up a losing trade. Washing fictitious trades through the error account."

McGeary picked up the theme. "Lifting some P&L from another department's books. Forging a Series 24 supervisor's signature to some cancel-and-corrects. Believe me, I'm eyes-open about that shit. But in

Gil McGeary's world, there is no penalty box for that conduct; there's *only the death penalty*. No second chances! Because at the end of the day, *I'm* the one's accountable. *I'm* on the line for a 'failure to supervise' charge from the SEC. And I don't want my momma reading bad things about me on page one of *The Wall Street Journal* simply 'cause some schmoe goes Pete Rose on me, thinks he's bigger than the game itself."

The phone began ringing insistently, but McGeary ignored it. He permitted himself a Cheshire cat smile. "In my nine years in the derivatives game, only one of my guys went over to the dark side. Started washing the bad trades off his books through fictitious entries in the error account. Now, you can ask anyone around here—ask Mike—it was *me* who pushed the NASD to ban the sonuvabitch from the securities business for *life*. Last I heard, the asshole's tending bar at some chicken-wing joint in Buffalo." McGeary sat back in his racing-car chair, looking evenly at Rick. "Joe Jett, Barings, Drexel? Rogue traders who could bring the franchise down before its initial public offering? Uh-uh. *Not* on Magilla McGeary's watch."

Finally, McGeary grabbed the bleating phone. "McGeary. Yeah, you got 'im. Yo, Trader Vic, gonna gimme some color from the floor of the Merc?" McGeary punched out several keystrokes at his computer, and frowned. "Spoos are on the march, huh? Yeah, I see it on the screen . . . it's moved five handles since the open. Spreads look mighty rich to me. Hold a sec—" The head of the derivatives desk covered the mouthpiece. "Look, Rick, I'm gonna have to jump here, all right? Welcome to the firm."

Hansen nodded, stubbed out the smoke and rose to leave. McGeary had already turned away from him and was engrossed in the digits blipping on his computer screen. He was jawboning with the stock index futures broker on the floor of the Chicago Mercantile Exchange: "Vic, bid ninety at twenty, fill or kill. That's right, I'll take the pipe, if I have to. Sometimes you gotta just hold your balls and jump—"

Hansen closed the door behind him when he left.

———•———

On Wall Street, the phone never stopped ringing, or so it seemed. There was always a new derivatives trade pending, a new options account that needed to be opened *right away*, a customer that needed some handholding on a trade strategy or an ISDA Master Agreement. Without the telephone, the derivatives lawyer would be rendered completely useless.

During Rick's first week on the job, Mike Kilmartin had schooled Hansen repeatedly in the fundamental truth about the financial services business: institutional customers were the lifeblood of the bulge-bracket

Wall Street institution. Of course, customers are the lifeblood of *any* business, but nowhere are they worshiped in the same way they are by the major broker-dealers. You're only as good as your customers.

For all the hue and cry on the Street about trading savvy, gut instinct, brass balls and the like, the plain truth of the matter is that Wall Streeters are nothing without institutional customers. Fact: the top 5 percent of your accounts generate 90 percent of your firm's revenues.

Fidelity, Soros, Steinhardt, Kemper, GE Pension, Tiger, Strong. BlackRock, T. Rowe Price, CALPERS, BEA, Moore, TIAA-CREF. Mellon, Brinson, GM Pension, IDS, PIMCO, Scudder. If you are the relationship manager for any one of these A-list accounts at your firm, congratulations, you are a certifiable Big Hitter. Set for life. Another year or two and the coveted title of managing director and all the fuck-you perks appurtenant thereto are yours. Servicing a blue-chip account like Fido or Dreyfus is the fastest sure-fire way to rise to the top of the charts, the head of the class, the cream of the crop on Wall Street.

Problem is, Kilmartin pointed out, the customer knows this and never lets you forget it.

Customer screams. You grovel.

Customer demands. You comply.

Customer complains about a lousy fill. You eat it.

Customer's coming to New York. You arrange second-row center seats for *Phantom*.

Customer concedes that your last trade idea shot out the lights. You ask her to call your boss at bonus time.

Like other people's spouses, all the good customers are already taken by someone else less worthy than you. Worse, the accounts are invariably happy with the coverage they're receiving at your competitor and don't care to switch to your shop, thanks anyway, bye-bye. In practice, it's an exceptionally rare event to coax a top-tier institutional account over to your shop. If you succeed in bringing over a new account that trades "in size," you're Michael Jordan, you're having a power breakfast with your firm's CEO tomorrow.

Customers, at the end of the day, are *everything*.

And the lawyers are there to provide service to the customers, i.e., to get the trade done. Otherwise, there's no need for them, or so the business people would have you believe.

So Hansen found himself spending the better part of the afternoon on the phone, working with a Pennsylvania bank to get a futures agreement into place with some modifications.

"I think we can concede some of the changes you've proposed to the default provisions, Marianne," Hansen said to a lawyer somewhere in the city of Philadelphia, "but I would have to run this last proposed change by the Credit Department. I don't have the authority to modify the set-off provision without their okay."

"Fine. Do that and call me Monday morning," the attorney said. "If you guys sign off on the change, our guys will pull the trigger on trading first thing. Otherwise, I have to go to the business people to see if they can live with that set-off language. I kind of doubt they can."

"I'll come back to you Monday," Hansen said.

"Thanks."

He hung up the phone and made a notation in his leather-bound agenda to contact Scott Mendelsohn, the derivatives contact in Credit, about the changes.

"Richard?"

Hansen looked up and saw a tall, slender woman in the doorway to his office. The first thing that struck him was her professional appearance. A simple string of pearls encircled her neck and her Claiborne finery was crisply pressed.

"I'm Kathleen Oberlin," she said. "I'm supposed to be working for you as your paralegal—"

Hansen leapt up from his roller chair to greet her. "That's great. I'm pleased to have you—"

"—but I won't be. I'm leaving Wolcott Fulbright."

Rick Hansen stood there for a moment, not certain what to say. "That's too bad, Kathleen. I'm starting to get a sense of just how much work needs to get done around this place and I could've used you. Have you taken a position somewhere else?"

"No. I'm just . . . taking some time off. I don't know how much, but it will be a while."

He nodded. Now that he stood near her and had the benefit of closer inspection, he began to surmise that beneath her workday uniform was a woman barely holding herself together. Kathleen's chocolate-brown irises were bloodshot and lifeless, and the raccoon's circles beneath her eyes betrayed a very recent string of sleepless nights. Her long, shoulder-length auburn hair was listless and snarled with split ends. Ordinarily she would have been a striking woman, Hansen realized; now he was gazing upon someone with a deeply troubled soul. He waited for her to fill in the blanks.

"I worked for Tom Bingham, see, and after his death, I was really *really* shaken." Here, she gripped her elbows like she was hugging herself against a sudden chill. She gazed past him, as though staring at an object a thousand miles outside his picture window. Her voice was soft, trance-like. "You may end up hearing some rumors about my relationship with

Tom, but they were nothing more than that—just rumors. It's true, we really were close friends, Tom and I. He was just a great boss, a good rabbi."

"I'm sure he was."

"A place like this—I don't want to bad-mouth it in your first week here, Richard, but it can be brutal place to make a living. Wall Street sucks the life out of you, and that's why so many people are out of the business by their thirties." Kathleen sighed deeply. "With the initial public offering coming up in the spring, the backbiting at Wolcott is at fever pitch." She began absently massaging her temples. "Right now, I just need a long vacation. Maybe a permanent vacation."

Hansen indicated a chair near his desk. "Would you care to sit down? Get a soft drink or coffee or something?"

"No," Kathleen Oberlin said, stepping back from the office into the corridor. "I've got an exit interview with Human Resources in about five minutes. I'm sorry, Richard. Nothing personal, I'm just not up for starting over."

"Understood." They did not shake hands. Rick lowered his voice an octave to convey sincerity. "I have a lot of chits in the favor bank at my old law firm, if you ever decide you want to try something different."

Kathleen Oberlin turned her gaze to the carpet. "Leaving this place is something different. Good luck to you." With that, she walked away, disappearing amid the maze of cubicles in the department.

Five

IN THE GLOOM of the partially lit subterranean facility, the man who insisted on being called "Stiletto" waited anxiously for the call to come. He was not a man well suited to waiting, yet there was nothing he could do to accelerate events. He sat at the unfamiliar desk, toying with the band from his cigar, and puffed away. Smoking helped kill the time, certainly, but Stiletto also took a small measure of satisfaction in his screw-you contempt for the no-smoking edict that had been posted liberally around the facility. Violating the New York City Clean Indoor Air Code, however, was an immaterial transgression compared to the one he was about to commit.

The shrill twitter of the cellphone pierced the quiet of the facility, jolting Stiletto from his reverie. With a sweating palm, he picked up the phone and pressed it to his ear. "Yes."

"Is this line secure?" came the voice on the other end.

"Digitally scrambled. Impossible to eavesdrop."

"I'm now commencing the procedure."

"Fire at will," Stiletto said, hanging up. He swiveled toward the computer monitor, his face eerily aglow with its greenish light.

———•———

On a yacht moored off the west coast of Florida, the Enter key of a 266 MHz Pentium laptop computer was punched. This single keystroke activated an artificial intelligence software program its creator had named LINDA.

LINDA, in turn, transmitted an encoded signal via cellular modem to the SprintLink SONET network. The digital signal was then beamed to the bent-pipe transponder of a solar-powered GM-Hughes low-earth or-bit (LEO) satellite geostationary orbit some 435 miles above the equator. The LEO satellite was equipped to execute 282,000 MIPS, or millions of instructions per second, which enhanced LINDA's digital signal and relayed it back to earth at a frequency of thirty gigahertz (billions of cycles) per second.

Back on earth, an elaborate mesh of fast-packet communicators within the 1,500-mile footprint of the LEO "bird" routed the signal through an Ohio gateway and onto its final destination—Pittsburgh, Pennsylvania.

All of this occurred at the speed of light.

In Pittsburgh, an infinitely more powerful computing system responded to the call from LINDA on the second ring. The respective modems of the laptop and the Pittsburgh system exchanged high-pitched beeps, tones and twitters, all of which were indecipherable to the human ear. This was the "electronic handshake," the process by which two vastly different computing machines established a common data transfer rate, assembly language and other essential protocols. The handshake succeeded, and the two machines engaged in a binary discourse with one another.

CCITT HANDSHAKE	UART 16-BIT 16450
ZMODEM PROTOCOL	ZMODEM OK
DB9 CONNECTOR	DB9 CONNECTOR OK
NO PARITY <ON/OFF>	OFF
USER NAME?	LINDA-1
PASSWORD?	STILETTO

WELCOME TO THE CARNEGIE-MELLON CENTER
FOR SUPERCOMPUTING STUDIES.
ENTER COMMAND NOW.

LINDA issued a brief set of instructions that engaged the "master/slave" mode. This meant that the Pittsburgh supercomputer was now a puppet to the laptop, acting on the whim of a 3.3-pound Pentium computer located 3,500 miles away off the coast of Florida.

Three minutes had passed and LINDA was just getting warmed up.

CD\BACKBONE, LINDA commanded.

With BACKBONE, LINDA had instructed the system to execute its "massively parallel processing" capabilities, a powerful new technology that permitted the Pittsburgh computer to "cluster" together a coalition of nine other equally powerful but geographically dispersed supercomputers scattered at academic sites around the country. Tied together by a nationwide 14,000-mile figure-eight of dedicated fiber-optic circuitry, the Backbone Network Service was not unlike an elite, superfast Internet. Backbone clustered together ten machines into one unified parallel processing system that simultaneously executed numerous number-crunching applications. Whereas the Pittsburgh supercomputer by itself was capable of a speed of four thousand MTOP's—millions of theoretical operations per second, or roughly *four billion* instructions—the Backbone consortium collectively ramped that speed up more than *tenfold*. Within six minutes, the Pittsburgh system had logged on to nine other supercomputers.

At that moment, LINDA had at its disposal the sixth most powerful MPP computing power on the face of the planet.

RUN 3RIVERS, LINDA now commanded.

Instantaneously, the 156 processors in the MPP-connected network began their mind-boggling "data-mining" operations. Nine decades' worth of data for U.S. stocks, bonds, indexes and rates were "mined" by the cluster of systems to search out pockets of logic in the seemingly random movements of the markets. Each system had been delegated a separate application. Urbana-Champaign sought out historical relationships between traditional benchmarks by analyzing the oceans of data pouring into its processors from Bloomberg, S&P Comstock, TeleRate, Reuters, Bonneville, DBC Signal and DataCode. Cornell's IBM SP2 ran monte carlo and lattice models, applying permutation query techniques to the multivariate set of data. U-Penn sifted through two hundred thousand what-if simulations on a real-time basis.

The conclusions drawn from the technical analysis and pattern-spotting of trillions of bits of information were relayed back to the Pittsburgh Cray Superserver 6400 by asynchronous transfer mode (ATM), a devastatingly powerful new network-switching technology. Within two minutes, the cluster of supercomputers was sifting through information at the rate of twenty-four billion floating point operations per second, analyzing it against the if-then parameters of a computerized model called Three Rivers Model 1.

RUN BEACON, said LINDA.

The Pittsburgh system complied by dialing up a Cray EL-94 mini-super in an underground location beneath the streets of downtown New York City.

The New York computer hummed to life.

Stiletto was ready. The screen prompted him for user ID and password. A hunt-and-peck typist, Stiletto methodically tapped out WOL-

FULB03 as the user name. The password—which was known to only a few others—was MUDHENS. Then Stiletto himself punched the Enter key.

He was aware that he'd gone breathless as he watched the screen flicker with activity.

DIALING. PLEASE WAIT.

In due time, the target computer system responded:

WELCOME TO SUPERDOT.

Stiletto let out a long, sour breath. LINDA was now connected to the supercomputer of the New York Stock Exchange. . . . Come Monday morning, when the NYSE opened for trading, the computerized system would begin buying and selling stocks on the New York Stock Exchange according to the dictates of the Three Rivers model.

LINDA, Stiletto said to himself, *I'd like you to meet SuperDOT. Let's see what kind of bastard offspring you two can produce.*

He picked up the cellphone and punched the speed dial. "Done," was all he said before disconnecting.

Afterward, as he stubbed out the cigar, he sat back and let the import of his deed wash over him. He had prepared himself mentally for this moment, expecting a devastating tidal wave of remorse. So he was surprised to feel a vague sense of triumph over the act he had just committed. In a word, it was payback, and payback was sweet.

Stiletto powered down the workstation and exited the facility.

———•———

On his yacht in the Gulf, Colbert closed up his cellphone and felt a grim satisfaction. As promised, Stiletto had done his piece, marrying the Pittsburgh network to the New York Stock Exchange machine. With that, the first leg of The Contrarians' initiative had just gone live.

Even so, Colbert did not permit himself a smile. There was much to be done before January 29. Many loose ends to be tied.

Six

LOWER MANHATTAN
Sunday, January 10

"STEPHANIE, CAN I TELL YOU? You look *so* great."

"I do not. Look at me, I'm eating like a Russian bodybuilder. I cannot prevent myself from eating off other people's plates. Even worse, I've got this bizarro craving for Hamburger Helper."

"That's perfectly normal. You're not just eating for yourself anymore."

"But *Hamburger Helper?*"

"Jenna's absolutely right. You're carrying all out front. You look great."

"Well, thank you. I need to hear that."

"Are you going to find out what it is?"

"We could, if we wanted to. The amnio results came in, but we told the doctor we didn't want to know."

"It's going to be a boy."

"Why do you say that?"

"The way you're carrying. See how it's all out front? It's the baby's male hormones."

"I can't get over how slim you are."

"Oh, let me tell you what I saw on the subway the other day—"

The Sunday morning brunch had been of Stephanie's devising, of course. This was her gift: bringing together a group of disparate people for an occasion of some sort, always with considerable success. The occasion this morning was to celebrate her husband's new job with the investment banking firm of Wolcott Fulbright. So she invited three other young couples from the Upper East Side for brunch—Robbie and Traci Singer, Paul and Jenna Gelbaum, Tim and Lisa Carella. Robbie and Paul had worked with Rick as attorneys at Cleary Gottlieb. Lisa was a colleague of Stephanie's in the promotions department of Sony Records.

Stephanie had selected America, a cavernous yuppie bistro on Eighteenth Street where the decibel level among the weekend patrons brought to mind the acoustics in the Seattle Kingdome. But the food was good and the service reliable, and it was a landmark establishment for young Manhattan professionals to gather, so it was worth making the scene, even if you often had to shout to be heard by your companion across the table.

It was nearing one in the afternoon. The feta cheese omelets and onion bagels had been consumed and the waitress had dutifully refilled their cups with a high-test Sumatra brew three times. The affair was winding down into its comfortable, full-bellied homestretch. The subject of conversation was the Hansens' baby, which was due in March. Like a high school dance, the women gathered in a snuglet on one side of the table, discussing how affirmatively rude New Yorkers had become to pregnant women on the subway.

"Oh, it's horrible, let me tell you. No one gives up their seats anymore. Just the other day, I saw a Rolex-wearing Wall Streeter hide behind his newspaper when he saw a pregnant woman coming near where he was seated. As if she didn't even exist."

"It gets worse than that. I've seen pregnant women get hip-checked to the side with some of these guys going for a seat."

"It's some sort of backlash, I think."

Meanwhile, the guys collected on the other side of the table, focusing on a recent scientific survey that concluded that the men of Manhattan possessed the highest sperm count in the nation.

Paul Gelbaum was saying, "The study said that the New York male has something like 130 million sperm per milliliter, *twice* the amount of a guy from L.A."

"Hey, no surprise there," said Tim Carella. "It takes a little extra testosterone to make it in this town."

Paul asked, "How about you, Hansen? You procreate first time out of the box?"

"Well, it was the first few weeks of trying."

"Attaboy. Like I always say, Cleary Gottlieb produces some pretty potent lawyers."

Robbie Singer clapped Rick on the shoulder. "God bless you guys, Rick, but as for us, I don't think we're ready to give up the spontaneity. Midnight feedings, mini-van in the 'burbs . . . nah, no bid for that just yet. We still have a lot of living to do."

Hansen shrugged. "You'll know when it's the right time. It was right for us."

Robbie spun his fork around. "Yeah, I think I'd rather drive a moped than a mini-van. That's kind of like the official death of cool, you know?"

Paul Gelbaum gave Singer a Clint Eastwood squint. "What *are* you talking about?"

"Mini-vans just don't float my boat."

"So don't get one."

"Yeah, when we go into kiddie mode, I'm gonna talk the woman into a Range Rover."

"Oh, oh, oh!" Stephanie shouted just then.

Rick immediately went into seizure mode. Was this *it*? "Honey?"

"The baby is moving!" she proclaimed.

Instantly, three women's hands searched out a spot on the dome of Stephanie's modestly distended tummy. Each woman closed her eyes as if participating in some communal New Age experience.

"Do you feel it?"

"No, not yet—"

Traci cried out, "Yess! Yes! Is that his leg? Or is it his—"

"Penis?" her husband Robbie offered.

"Robbie!" Tracie scolded. "You're so *warped*."

"Well, theoretically, it could've been." Singer winked conspiratorially at Hansen. "Right, Tripod?"

But Rick was immersed in watching his wife, the center of all this attention. At that moment he realized, *The female is clearly the superior of the species.* Enduring *this*. Inwardly, he shivered, as he once again contemplated the miracle of gestation. He was filled with wonder that this could possibly be the end-result of two people making love. *The ordinary miracle.* Six billion lives on the planet, virtually all of which had been conceived from that single carnal act . . . it boggled the mind.

But here it was, nearly six months into the process, two trimesters down and one to go, yet Hansen still felt maladjusted to this world that promised soiled diapers, Barneymania and, yes, possibly a Chrysler minivan in the suburbs of Connecticut. For crissakes, even the vernacular of childbirth was daunting. Colostrum. Leukorrhea. Episiotomy. Lamaze vs. Bradley. Linea nigra. Eclampsia. Epidurals. Braxton-Hicks. Bloody show. Mucus plug. *What the hell was a mucus plug, anyway?* (He could have blissfully gone his entire lifetime without knowing what that was.)

But if Rick felt like a stranger in a strange land, Stephanie had been a rock-solid presence throughout. Impending motherhood brought out the best in her. At all times, she radiated a maternal glow, exuding a fragile Botticellian frailty that instilled in Hansen protective instincts he never realized he had. *We're going to be a family.* He said it to himself so often, it had become almost a Gregorian chant echoing in his mind.

At once, Stephanie shifted uncomfortably and gently disengaged the hands from her belly. "Sorry, everyone. Got to visit the ladies' room again." Hansen came around to help her out of her seat, and she made her way to the washroom.

As Rick called for the check, Lisa Carella touched his forearm. "Congratulations on your new opportunity."

"Thank you, Lisa."

The attention of the table turned to Rick, as general best wishes and congrats were murmured by all.

"Hometown boy makes good. No more lawyer's hours."

Paul Gelbaum said, "Man, I'm so jealous. How did you get that job?"

My predecessor killed himself, Hansen said to himself. "Headhunter."

Robbie Singer said, "Can you give her my name, please? Or better yet, will you hire me as your assistant? I'm not too proud to fetch a cup of coffee for the boss."

"What do you do there?" Jenna Gelbaum asked.

"I'm the trading practices attorney responsible for the equity derivatives desk at Wolcott, Fulbright and Company."

Rick's new title drew blank gazes from the others.

"On behalf of the rest of the table," Robbie Singer said, "just what the hell are *derivatives?*"

"And please," Tim Carella cautioned, "go easy on us. Try to make it 'Derivatives for Dummies.' " The rest of the group laughed.

Hansen paused, trying to frame a response in plain English. "You know what stocks are?"

Yes, the group said. Each share represents a fractional ownership in a company.

"And you know what bonds are?"

Yes, the group replied. A bond means you're the holder of a debt that a company owes you.

Rick forged ahead. "Derivative products are financial instruments— sometimes simple, often complex—that are so named because they *derive* their value from some other, more basic instrument, like a rate, or a currency, a stock or a bond."

"So derivatives are like stocks and bonds?" Traci Singer asked.

"Well, yes and no. Generally speaking, a derivative is *not* a security that trades on a stock exchange. It's a contractual agreement between two sophisticated investors, each of whom agrees to pay the other a certain value at some point in the future based upon the performance of the underlying financial instrument without actually owning that instrument. Wolcott Fulbright claims it can create twenty-two hundred different types of synthetic instruments for its customers."

Paul Gelbaum whistled. *"Twenty-two hundred* types of derivatives?"

"Well, actually, they're variations on a half-dozen basic categories of derivatives—cash-settled puts, calls, forwards, collars, swaps, futures—"

"Whoa there, killer," Rob Singer pleaded. "Go easy on me. I don't want my head to explode like a character out of *Scanners*. Why wouldn't people rather own the, uh, underlying stock or bond than a derivative instrument?"

"Two reasons: flexibility and leverage."

"Okay, professor, tell me about the flexibility part first."

"Because derivatives are privately negotiated contracts, they often provide custom-tailored solutions to the investment needs of institutional portfolios—"

"How about an example?"

"All right, think of IBM's $15 billion pension plan as this three-hundred-pound dude with no clothes on."

The group laughed.

Rick continued. "Now think of the stock market as the weather outside. Right now, the market's at an all-time high, so the weather's wonderful. This guy can go around bollocks-naked, and he's perfectly comfortable, since it's nice and sunny out. But the guy knows from experience that everything's seasonal. The weather's going to have a downturn sooner or later, it's inevitable. Well, stocks and bonds are standardized securities—they come in one size only and don't fit the naked guy's profile well enough to protect him against a downturn. So the guy covers himself with a series of derivative contracts with others that fit his needs like a custom-tailored suit. When the weather turns bad, meaning, when the market craps out, the guy won't lose too much of the value of his portfolio because his derivatives will *make* money when the rest of his stocks and bonds lose money. It's a strategy they call 'hedging,' as in hedging a bet."

Three tables away, a group of waiters sang "Happy Birthday" and presented a cupcake with a single lit candle in it to someone's mother.

Over the ruckus, Jenna Gelbaum said, "From what I'm hearing, derivatives sound wonderful. So why have they gotten such lousy press over the last couple of years?"

"That would be the leverage factor."

"The leverage factor?"

"Simply put, it means a derivatives player can control a lot of dollars' worth of market exposure with very little down. By comparison, when you buy a stock from your broker at Charles Schwab, you pay for the full value of the securities, or, if you're borrowing on margin, you pay at least half of the value. That's not the case with off-exchange derivatives, especially in the case of so-called 'turbocharged' derivatives. For every dollar you put down, you get twenty to thirty dollars' worth of exposure to the market. Now, in the previous example, if you're hedging your stock portfolio with derivatives, that's good news, because any losses in your derivatives are made up by gains in your stock. But if you're *speculating*, it's like toying with nuclear weapons."

Tim Carella said, "Speculating, meaning placing a naked bet on the direction of the market?"

"Correct. Speculating in derivatives is not much different from placing a bet on the black or the red on the roulette wheel at Atlantic City, because you're betting the market's either going to rise or fall—one or the other. But because of the leverage factor, derivatives investors can lose far more money than they initially put up."

At this point, Stephanie returned from the rest room and chimed in. "And that's what happened to Orange County in California, isn't it?"

Rick nodded. "Yes, exactly, Steph. Essentially, the elected official in charge of the county's money borrowed billions and placed huge derivatives bets that the Federal Reserve was going to leave interest rates untouched in '94, or even cut them. Of course, the Fed ratcheted interest rates up *two hundred* basis points in nine months, the steepest increase in forty years. When the smoke cleared, Orange County was down around two billion dollars."

"Wow. Two *billion*." Lisa Carella shook her head at the sum.

Tim Carella pointed out, "And they're not the only ones who got burned speculating in derivatives. Remember that incident in early '95, when a 225-year-old British bank declared insolvency overnight because of a billion-dollar loss in derivatives?"

"Nick Leeson," Hansen said knowingly.

"A twenty-eight-year-old kid single-handedly brought down one of the most powerful financial institutions in the world by building up huge positions in Japanese stock index futures on the Singapore Futures Exchange."

The check came. As Hansen signed his name to the credit card, he said, "Derivatives are almost totally unregulated by the SEC. Some people believe that because of the size of the market and the lack of oversight, the industry poses a danger to the entire financial market. The Barings incident could have been a catastrophe, except the bank had more than a billion dollars in assets to cover the obligation, so the marketplace didn't panic. But the next time a Barings happens, there may be a domino effect that creates a meltdown of the world economy. At least that's what the doomsayers predict. Still, you can't help but shudder to think what kind of damage a Mike Milken could have inflicted on the American economy if he had these instruments in his arsenal." Rick Hansen trailed off. "Or even the global economy."

This prospect silenced the table. Robbie Singer finally broke the quiet. "Well, good luck in your new job. Sounds like you're going to need it."

———•———

Forty minutes later, back at their apartment on Fifty-fourth Street between First and Second, Stephanie murmured, "All this talk of derivatives has made me horny."

Rick laughed. "A likely story. Maternity has sent your hormones into a state of total flux."

"*Whatever*. Let's just make love."

Next thing that happened, they were in the domain of their bedroom, experiencing those resonating moments of anticipation before making love. When they were unclothed, Stephanie mounted him, the swell of her belly supported by his stomach. She began rocking back and forth—slowly, gently, rhythmically. Since she'd been pregnant, she'd informed him, sex had never been better; something about the increased blood flow to her pelvic area had heightened her sexual response, made it effortless for her to achieve multiple orgasms. Yet while Rick responded to her ardor, he did so uneasily, worried that somehow the baby was aware that Mommy and Daddy were doing the nasty. Rick brushed his fingertips lightly, reverently, against the taut, shiny skin of her belly, then cupped her engorged breasts—God, they were *huge*—and softly pinched her nipples. Stephanie bit her lower lip and hummed softly, rocking back and forth in the same motion for a long while until she abruptly stiffened, then shuddered, in climactic release, her head thrown back in a squinch-eyed ecstasy, her sensuous lips pursed in a pouting O. She abandoned herself to the spiraling bolts of tremors that rippled through her. Rick's thoughts turned to the baby—couldn't help it—wondering how it experienced the orgasmic waves that contracted its mother's birth canal—an instrument serving dual purposes—providing both carnal pleasure and life itself. Taken in this context, it weirded him out.

His thoughts were disrupted by the bright peal of the bedside phone.

"Yeah," he said flatly.

It was McGeary on the other end, hating like hell to bother him on a Sunday, but a new money manager running money on a global scale was inquiring about a massive equity swap structure. Could Rick step through the mechanics of it with McGeary, ensure he was comfortable with it?

The four-way, intercontinental conference call killed the better part of two and a half hours, and really, the rest of the day was shot. Here it was, Hansen's first week on the job, yet his wife was already preparing herself once again to divvy up her husband's waking hours with his mistress—his livelihood. Not for the first time, Stephanie Hansen worried that her soon-to-be-born child would be subjected to a cat's-in-the-cradle father, one so hopelessly addicted to his calling, he would have no time for his family.

For God's sake, she thought, *isn't that the reason he said he was leaving the law firm?*

Seven

"WHERE THE FUCK HAVE YOU BEEN?" The voice snarled at him in a raw fury that chilled Eddie Slamkowski's blood. "I've been ringing this number for *close to an hour*."

Christ on a bike, Slam said to himself. *What's this guy expect from me?* All right, granted, it was 5:57 A.M. Pacific Time, twenty-seven minutes after his agreed-upon start time. Maybe if Stone had set up shop at a Pacific Coast Highway address like Slam had urged, instead of opting for the gloomy, out-of-the-way Kilroy Airport Way digs, Slam could have squeezed in his predawn surfing ritual with Damien and Derf and *still* made it to work at the usual agreed-upon-but-ungodly hour.

But Eddie Slamkowski *needed* this job, so he resorted to the script he'd mentally practiced during his high-speed commute into Long Beach. "Mr. Stone, I'm very sorry, I was delayed by a terrible accident on the PCH. Traffic was backed up for—"

"*Don't* start in with the *excuses!*" Charles Stone thundered at the other end of the line. "That only makes it more *pathetic*."

"But there's still—"

"I'll remind you that the customers I'm bringing to Infinity Technology Securities are among the most coveted offshore accounts in the world. They are world-class hedge funds, foreign banks and the investment arms of sovereign governments—"

"Yes, sir, I know that." Slam certainly did, since *he* was the one who had endured the seemingly endless tedium of filling out the fifty or so new account forms for the customers Charles Stone had signed up for Infinity. And though Eddie had never heard of any of the foreign accounts before, Stone had procured their quarterly audited statements as part of the federally required documentation for new equity futures accounts. Not one of the accounts was worth less than $100 million. It was, to be sure, quite an impressive customer base for a strictly ground-floor start-up operation like Infinity, Slam conceded admiringly. Though Eddie had never met the man face to face, Slam was convinced Stone was one superconnected mojo.

Stone's tirade continued. "*Think*—why would accounts of this caliber do even a *single-lot* trade through an Infinity Securities rather than a Goldman or a Merrill or a JP Morgan? It's one reason and one reason *only*"—at this point, Slamkowski silently mouthed the words as Stone recited his shopworn mantra—"because I have personally promised the *best execution* on the U.S. derivatives exchanges at the *lowest commission rate possible*. And you will make a liar of me if you intend to be habitually late to work each trading day—"

"Mr. Stone, *please*," Slam cut in. "You've put your points up on the board, now let me have the ball."

There was a long pause on the other end. Then: "I'm listening."

"Okay, you're positively right, this is a lousy way to start things off, but let's put this behind us and get on with business. The Chicago markets open in less than thirty minutes and we need to get our customers' market-on-open orders in the hands of the floor brokers ASAP. I'm confident we'll get them the executions at the prices Infinity has promised them."

"All right, fine," Stone huffed, though he was clearly calmer. "When are you transmitting the orders?"

"I modemed them to your fax forty-five minutes ago."

"Right, good. I see them on my screen. I'll e-mail them to the boys in Chicago straightaway."

"You do that. Oh, and Eddie?"

"Yes?"

"As you know, I expect Infinity will be fully automated for robot-trading next month. If I were you, I wouldn't screw up again. You're officially on *probation*."

Before Slam could retort, there was a twitter-chirp that signaled the disconnect of the cellular satellite uplink.

"*Sonuvabitch!*" Slamkowski cursed as he bashed the phone down in anger and humiliation. The wisecrack enraged him. Stone had hired Slamkowski sight unseen for the new technology venture—a fully computerized stock-trading boutique that somehow routed orders over the Internet—and Slam needed this job. He didn't have the luxury to—as Stone put it so patronizingly—screw up. Still, fuck him for playing head chess. On *probation. Kiss off, Chuckie!*

Slamkowski grabbed a pen and a stack of blank order tickets and stepped over to the fax machine. He found the pages awaiting him in the output tray and squinted at them in the semi-darkness. The size of the initial orders took him by surprise:

S&P 500 MARCH FUTURES
All Buys/Market-on-open orders
Discretion as to price up to five ticks above market

AMOUNT	CUSTOMER	STRATEGY
100	Singing Oak Properties/London	BONA FIDE HEDGER
150	Megafund II (Caymans)	BONA FIDE HEDGER
150	Banque de Lyonnais	PASSIVE INDEXER
100	OPM Partners	BONA FIDE HEDGER
150	Hemisphere Bank of Britain	PASSIVE INDEXER

TOTAL=650 CONTRACTS
Allocate to Accounts Accordingly

Slam whistled in awe. *Six hundred fifty* contracts to be executed at the opening with discretion to pay an above-market price, he knew, would move the market significantly higher. A single S&P 500 futures contract based upon Friday's closing price was worth $318,750. Six hundred fifty contracts meant the five accounts collectively would control—he ran the numbers on his Sharp calculator—in excess of $200 million worth of equity index futures. Fortunately for the offshore accounts, the initial margin for the instruments was only $12,000 per contract. In essence, the group of customers controlled $200 million worth of stock index futures for a down payment of about $7,800,000—just 3½ percent.

Slam filled out five order tickets, one for each account, and whacked them in the time-stamping machine. Then he picked up the phone and dialed the floor of the Chicago Mercantile Exchange. His heart began trip-hammering as he waited to be connected to the trading pit he once called home.

A familiar voice answered with the Friday's closing price of the March S&P futures contract. "Nine hundred and thirty-seven dollars and forty-six cents."

It was Vic! Slam's voice warbled. "Trader Vic?"

"You got 'im."

"This's Slamkowski."

A disbelieving pause. "Slammer, that *really* you?"

"Live and in living color."

"Suh-lammer!" Trader Vic turned to his fellow traders. "Guys, it's the Slam-man!"

Over the boisterous turbulence of the trading pit, he heard Swanky Frankie's voice yelp out, "Slammmmuh!"

Slamkowski's spirits soared with joy. The bastards hadn't forgotten him after all.

"Slam, you dirty dog, how's the love life in Southern Cal?"

Slamkowski pshawed. "You kiddin' me? Gettin' chicks in Southern Cal?"

"Yeah . . . ?"

"It's like clubbin' seals."

"Clubbin' seals?" Trader Vic howled. "That's *classic*! As for me, don't ask, I'm so hard-up, Angela Lansbury gives me a pocket full a wood. Hey, stay with me a sec—"

Trader Vic put him on hold for a minute. When he returned, he sounded rushed. "Hey, Eddie, really great to chat, but I gots to jump. You come back to Chicago, come to the floor, we'll do Cactus."

"Not so fast," Slam said gleefully. "You didn't think I called just to shoot the shit, didyuh?"

"Well, I—"

"Got some orders for you to execute."

Trader Vic's astonished voice came floating back to him. "You back in the game, Slammer?"

"Yeah," Slam gloated. "Back, and better'n ever."

God, it felt good to say that again. Slammer was *back*.

———●———

The Infinity orders were transcribed, time-stamped and run over to the sunken pits where the S&P futures were traded by a gold-jacketed runner named Swanky Frankie DiMarco. Swanky thrust the Infinity order cards into the hands of Andy Studd, a floor broker in the pit who worked with Trader Vic's firm. Because Infinity's buy orders gave some upside discretion as to price, Studd put these cards at the top of his "deck"—giving Infinity priority over other customers seeking to purchase March futures contracts.

At 8:30 A.M., Chicago time, the bell rang, signifying the opening of the trading session. The pit erupted in its daily pandemonium. Studd pushed, jostled and elbowed his way into the chaotic crush of brightly jacketed brokers and traders crammed into the sunken ellipsis of the trading pit, much as he would to get closer to the stage at a Who concert. Shouting and waving vigorously to get a selling broker's attention, Studd signaled his desire to buy by thumping the palm of his hand repeatedly against his chest. A selling broker emerged out of the crowd, making the opposite motion, pushing his open palm away from his body energetically. The bizarre mating ritual commenced. Studd indicated quantity— sixty-five contracts—first holding his signaling hand near his head, then extending just his index finger horizontally (symbolizing "six") and then vertically extending five fingers. Similar signals were then exchanged to set the price, indicating that the trades were to be done slightly above the prevailing market price. Essentially, they were conducting a one-on-one auction. The two men indicated to one another that the trade was "done." A blue-jacketed observer positioned on the catwalk above the pit recorded the transaction into the CME's computerized price reporting system, which informed market participants around the world that a sixty-five-contract trade in the March index futures had moved the market five ticks. Thus, the trades were executed without a single, intelligible spoken word passing between Studd and the contra-broker.

Infinity was "done" within three minutes of the open.

Trader Vic relayed the fills to Eddie Slamkowski in Long Beach, California. "Wham-bam, thank you, Slam. You're *done* at fifty-five."

"Done at fifty-five," Slam acknowledged.

"Slam? Good to hear your voice again."

"You'll hear it again real soon." Slam hung up. Gratified, he time-stamped the order tickets a third time. Then he called the 1-700 number of Charles Stone's voice mailbox to confirm the customer fills. Replacing the phone on the hook, Slamkowski said to himself, *Stone will be pleased we got the orders off. At least he fucking better be.*

Eddie Slamkowski was right; Stone would be pleased. But what Slam couldn't have known was his unwitting complicity in setting into motion a complex financial scheme that would, in time, stagger the imagination of Wall Street.

Eight

KATHLEEN OBERLIN WAS OBLIVIOUS to the cosmic clock that had begun ticking down the final minutes of her life, giving her less than twelve minutes to live.

It was 4:32 P.M. She'd been sitting there in the front seat of her Saab in the parking lot of Stew Leonard's famed dairy store in Norwalk, Connecticut, for about twenty minutes. Just staring at her image in the rearview mirror.

God, she looked terrible!

The purplish-black bags under her eyes, skin drained of color. She was, admittedly, a woman beaten to emotional submission by a senseless tragedy. Six weeks had passed, yet the plague of depression still engulfed her, with no signs of letting up. Kathleen wasn't sleeping at night. She tossed and turned, sifting through even the most minute of the details of the previous eight months to make some sense out of it all. She needed the truth.

It was a suicide, the cops had said.

"The hell it was," she murmured defiantly to the mirror.

The detective's name was O'Bannon. He had been sensitive enough for a hardened cop, recognizing that the deceased was Kathleen's boss. Over brackish coffee at the precinct, O'Bannon spent forty-five minutes with her, patiently discussing the case.

It doesn't make any sense, she said.

The act of suicide rarely does make sense to those left behind, he replied.

But he didn't leave a note of any kind.

Contrary to popular belief, O'Bannon said, *notes are left behind only twenty percent of the time.*

O'Bannon emphasized that at the outset of any such investigation, the

NYPD approached the task with the same skepticism Kathleen had. Apparent suicides were always treated like homicide cases; the evidence was allowed to speak for itself. In this case, there was no trace evidence suggesting a struggle or sign of forced entry.

In fact, the evidence collected by the attendant officers strongly indicated the opposite. The medicolegal autopsy showed he had a belly full of vodka, suggesting a suicide victim working up the courage to take his own life. Also, a prescription vial found in his medicine cabinet showed he was being treated for manic-depressive illness. No surprise to Kathleen, who had been with Tom during the ups and downs of his condition. A well-worn copy of *Final Exit* had been found on his bedside stand. And the cops had turned up evidence of a so-called "motivating factor"—a statement from his corporate American Express card that detailed cash advances of almost $12,000 in Atlantic City taken over a period of three weekends. (No preset spending limits on that AmEx Corporate Card, as Tommy had discovered.) Surely, once that came to light to his superiors at Wolcott Fulbright, Bingham's career there was over. It was likely his license to practice law would be revoked as a result of it.

Kathleen took this all in. Then she admitted to O'Bannon, *Tommy Bingham and I were involved.*

O'Bannon expression remained flat. *I figured as much*, he'd said.

Tommy Bingham did not kill himself, she assured him.

She believed the statement she'd made to the New York City detective, but she couldn't entirely be certain of it.

For Tommy's life had not exactly been an open book. How many times had he implied to her that he led something of a double-life? By day, he played his role as the conservative, white-shoe securities attorney at Wolcott. Then there was another, darker side to Tommy Bingham. Something else entirely, a counterlife. He often alluded to some scheme of international proportions with sinister secrets hinted at but never shared with her. And there were the bizarre rumors sweeping Tommy's final days . . . his involvement in insider trading . . .

Rap, rap!

A green-shirted parking lot attendant knocked on her window, startling her.

"Is everything all right, ma'am?" he asked.

She nodded.

"All right then," he said, kindly. "If you're done with that space, we sure could use it, thanks."

Kathleen waved him away dismissively and started her car. Pulling out of the lot onto the Post Road, she dry-swallowed another dose of serotonin. She was popping them like breath mints these days. If the only way to suppress the constant anguish was by chemical means, then so be it.

Kathleen turned off from the Post Road, onto the on-ramp to Interstate 95 from Exit 16. She merged with the traffic heading south toward the home she and her husband had in Stamford.

In time, the drug took the edge off her despair. Her thoughts returned to Tommy.

Tom Bingham had been manic-depressive; he had delusions of grandeur. But above all, Tommy had been addicted to secrets and intrigue. Now it was becoming apparent just how addicted he was. In another life, he clearly would have been a spy, or a secret agent of some sort—anything but a stressed-out, caffeine-addled securities lawyer on Wall Street.

Had he been murdered?

If so, why? She'd asked herself that question every waking hour since November and still, the answer was as unattainable now as it was back then. Murder? That was as senseless as suicide.

At that instant, a white Oldsmobile Cutlass pulled even with her in the passing lane. It was now traveling at precisely the same speed as her Saab—sixty-two miles per hour. She glanced over at the driver. Two men inside. The man behind the wheel stared at her. As if committing her face to memory. And the passenger—a young man with an ugly face that bordered on deformity. When he bared his yellowed teeth in a grimacing smile, a mortal chill rippled through her. Instinctively, she pumped the brake, slowing her Saab by fifteen miles per hour. The Cutlass shot past her.

Something urged her to pull over *now*. A service stop loomed ahead within the cone of her vision. The bright, primary-colored logos of McDonald's and Mobil brought a peculiar comfort to her. Refuge. Without signaling, she maneuvered her Saab into the right lane, cutting off a red commercial van with the words BEACON SERVICES. The van blasted its horn, but she ignored it, focusing only on getting off the interstate, gritting her teeth in anticipation of an impact that did not happen.

Once she hit the off-ramp at forty miles per hour, an inexplicable feeling of relief flooded over her.

C'mon, Kathleen. Pull yourself together, girl.

At the same time, a muffled explosion rocked the vehicle from its undercarriage. Before Kathleen could react, a geyser of flame spurted up through the floorboard in the backseat. A spasm of primal fear jagged through Kathleen as she realized she was about to die. She screamed. The gas tank ruptured in a fiery explosion, incinerating Kathleen, silencing her screams. Her death came mercifully fast.

Motorists watched in helpless terror as the rolling firebomb appeared to be headed directly for a bank of Mobil gas pumps. In the last seventy-five yards, however, it veered off onto a grassy median, where it came to a rest without posing further threat. Its shell was reduced to a blazing hunk of molten metal spewing superheated flames. An oily smoke roiled out of its carcass, blackening the sky. The intensity of the heat kept would-be rescuers at bay, although there was no rescue to perform.

Already almost a mile away, Viktor Alexeyev pocketed the remote control. "Dead?" he asked.

"No question," Gagarov the Gargoyle responded in Russian, as he craned around to view the carnage.

Alexeyev nodded, certain his companion's report was accurate. Maybe a dozen times in the last ten years, he'd activated KGB-designed spike-concussion bombs, just like that one. The devices had never failed him. Continuing south toward New York City, he turned up the classical station and absently took a swallow from his Styrofoam cup of McDonald's coffee. An expression of repulsion contorted his face.

"What is it?" the Gargoyle asked.

Alexeyev cursed bitterly, opened the window and tossed the cup of liquid out onto the interstate.

"I *despise* cold coffee," he replied.

Nine

IN A MULTIMEDIA-EQUIPPED CONFERENCE FACILITY called the New Delhi Room, the lights went down and Mike Kilmartin kicked off his slide presentation. It was just for an audience of three; then again, it was a very important and influential audience of three—the firm's Risk Management Task Force.

Showtime, he said to himself as the opening slide clacked into position.

The first visual was nothing more than stark white Helvetica letters against a stop-sign-red background. Kilmartin read aloud from it: "First Capital Advisors—$128 million."

Kerchunk. The carousel on the projector lurched forward a notch and the next slide dropped into place. "Kidder, Peabody—$350 million in losses."

Kerchunk. "Onto the billion-dollar club. Daiwa Bank, $1.5 *billion*." *Kerchunk*. "Barings Bank, $1.4 billion." *Kerchunk*. "Orange County, California, $1.7 billion." *Kerchunk*. "Sumitomo Bank, $1.8 billion." *Kerchunk*. "Metallgesellschaft Bank, $2.2 billion."

Mike Kilmartin stepped forward a few steps to pose the rhetorical question to the elite audience of three. "What do these events have in common?" He thumbed the remote device of the slide projector—*kerchunk*—and the next visual summed it all up:

DERIVATIVES AND THE
ROGUE TRADER PHENOMENON:
AN OVERVIEW OF FRANCHISE RISK

"Each of these catastrophic losses was caused by a single trader abusing derivative instruments. This phenomenon has occurred on such a frequent basis in this decade that the term 'rogue trader' has leapt into the everyday lexicon of the general public."

Fifteen feet away, one of the members of the task force cleared his throat preemptively. "Uh, Mike?"

"Yes, Irv?" Kilmartin squinted in the semidarkness at Irv Siegel, the managing director for fixed-income risk management. "Do you have a question?"

"Uh, Mike, do you mind if we dispense with the dog-and-pony show? I'd rather we just kind of hash out this 'rogue trader' thing informally. Face-to-face."

"Not at all," Kilmartin said. He was actually quite relieved at the suggestion. Mike was far more at home with a session of Q&A, rather than going through the formality of a prepared text. A slide show for an audience of three? Definitely overkill. Then again, it had been the suggestion of one of the three task force members now present in the New Delhi Room, Bobby Wolcott. *Yet another brilliant idea, Bobby*, Kilmartin thought acidly, as he turned to the woman from Corporate Presentations and said, "Hit the lights, Ann."

Blotches of colors flashed in Kilmartin's eyes in protest at the sudden brilliance. When his vision adjusted, he turned to the three managing directors sitting around the conference table. All had been specially hand-picked for the blue-ribbon Risk Management Task Force by Max Schomburg, the mercurial Chief Executive Officer of Wolcott, Fulbright & Company.

According to a Schomburg memo distributed on goldenrod paper throughout the firm in December, "The purpose of the task force is to perform 'autopsies' on catastrophic trading disasters at other global investment financial houses, in the hope that the franchise could avoid a similar fate prior to the firm's initial public offering next spring." Cynics at the firm noted that Schomburg's memo didn't seem to mind if a rogue trader sank the firm *after* the firm went public. If all went well with the IPO, the cynics wagged, Max Schomburg would stand to add around $125 million to his personal net worth.

The task force, then, was formed to protect the golden goose until it was spun off. The Risk Management Task Force, in turn, called upon the day-to-day head of Legal, Regulatory & Compliance issues, Mike Kilmartin, to make a presentation on the possibility that such a rogue trader could blow up the firm.

"What about it, Mike?" Irv Siegel asked. "Could it happen here?"

"Yes. It could happen at any firm, including ours."

Alan Milgrim frowned. "A rogue trader could be in our midst at this very minute, is that what you're saying?"

"Yes, Alan, that's right. There's no reason to believe there is, but it's entirely feasible. Bottom line is that if a trader has evil in his heart, has the trading authority without adequate supervision, a Barings-like event *could happen* in our shop."

The men shifted uncomfortably in their seats, chewing over this piece of information. *What do you want from me?* Kilmartin wondered. A unequivocal declaration that all was hunky-dory, so they could file some sanitized, happy-ass, Mickey Mouse executive summary with Max Schomburg that *it couldn't happen here?* Sorry, boys, ain't gonna do it. Kilmartin would be doing a disservice to the firm if he candy-coated the hard realities. Worse than that, he wouldn't be doing his job.

Kilmartin pulled out a roller chair and took a seat at the conference table with the managing directors of the task force. "Before we hit the panic button though, it's crucial to stress that 99.9 percent of the traders and salespeople at this firm are good, honest people. On a percentage basis, gentlemen? There's far more corruption in the New York City Police Department than there is on Wall Street. I've been in this business going on twelve years. The MBAs we hire at Wolcott recognize it is an immense privilege to have a seat on the trading floor at a global investment bank of this caliber. They know there's roughly a thousand freshly minted Ivy Leaguers who would gladly swap a testicle for that seat on the trading floor. *Our people want to abide by the rules.* The last thing a producer wants is to screw up some technical regulation that ends his career faster than you can say 'Michael Milken.' "

"You look at this firm's Form B-D," Irv Siegel pointed out. "Wolcott has a relatively clean slate on the regulatory front vis-à-vis our peer group in the bulge-bracket category." The Form B-D was the annual filing required of all broker-dealers that detailed all material fines, sanctions and penalties imposed upon it by the regulators.

"That's right. So the trick of it is, finding that needle in the haystack, the asshole who's gonna bring the franchise to its knees."

"The number of blowups at major firms in the last five, six years has been appalling," Milgrim stated flatly.

"No denying that. Of the ten rogue trader incidents in the last six years, four of them destroyed the firms that failed to detect them. Kidder, Barings, Drexel. All were killed off by a single superstar trader who was rewarded for breaking the rules. I've heard rumors of other rogue traders at our competitors that haven't been publicized. Our *major* competitors."

Siegel persisted. "So why the increase all of a sudden?"

"Several factors are at play, Irv, some new, some old. Here's what's new: the computerization of money. Computers and telecommunications have made it easier to gamble millions with just a few clicks of the mouse.

THE VELOCITY OF MONEY 65

Also, globalization of the business has made it exceedingly difficult for a financial institution to gets its arms around the risky activity in far-flung regions."

"That's what happened at Barings Bank," Milgrim said. "The London management didn't have any meaningful oversight over Leeson's activities in Singapore."

"Right. The other new factor in the equation is derivatives. Derivatives in the hands of traders are like nukes. If used properly, they're beneficial—like nuclear power. If abused, they're more like nuclear weapons—they will completely blow up the firm. And some believe they could cripple the entire global financial system."

Irv Siegel frowned. "Derivatives. I cringe when I think of twenty-two-years-olds on the trading turrets playing with those."

Kilmartin nodded. "That's the other potential problem. The Street is going through a period of infatuation with youth. These youngsters understand the new financial technologies and the math that goes along with them. But the offshoot of that is that we're literally trusting *kids* with billions of dollars in risk capital. Some are so green, they haven't yet developed a moral compass."

Milgrim shook his head. "So they begin to panic when they lose money, stick their trade tickets in the drawer, transfer the losses to a secret account and pray nobody in the back office finds out."

"The pressure of our business is tremendous. That pressure has a way of pushing people into harder, different versions of themselves. Traders can find themselves in uncharted territory, doing the unthinkable. That's a consistent factor in Barings, Kidder, First Capital."

Bobby Wolcott cleared his throat and spoke up. "I hope I'm not coming completely out of left field on this one, Mike, but isn't that why we pay you boys the big bucks in the Legal Department? For crissakes, isn't it *your job* to ensure that a rogue-trader blowup on the order of Barings doesn't happen at Wolcott?"

Mike Kilmartin's eyebrows shot up. He touched his chest with his fingertips. "Bob, the Legal department is *not* the greed police. Nor are we an insurance policy against unauthorized trading activity. All we can do is advise senior management on how to minimize the risk of it happening here."

Milgrim held up a placating palm. Eyeing Bobby Wolcott warily, he said, "No one here is saying that you're going to prevent the problem. We're looking to you people in Legal for advice. So—advise us. What should we tell Schomburg the firm ought to be doing?"

"This task force is a solid first step, but upper management and the senior supervisors have to reinforce a corporate culture that doesn't tolerate any star trader going off the reservation, exceeding trading limits in risky, leveraged instruments." Kilmartin handed out a bullet-point summary of proposed initiatives the firm could undertake. "The securities industry is probably the only industry in this country that imposes *statutory liability* on managers for 'failure to supervise' the people on their watch. That may not be fair, but that's reality. That needs to be communicated to all line supervisors."

Milgrim ticked off the points on the memo. "Enhanced written procedures, regular review of the error accounts, an in-person briefing to the troops by Schomburg. All that's doable."

Bobby Wolcott frowned as he read through it. "You suggest a head count increase in the back-office control functions?"

"As it stands, Bob, the business unit controllers are woefully understaffed after the last round of cuts. If there's a manpower deficit in those areas, you increase your risks of failing to detect improper activity. That's the unvarnished truth." Kilmartin couldn't help thinking that on Bobby W.'s *base salary* alone, the firm could hire ten bean counters to scrutinize trading reports on a real-time basis.

"What about this one?" Irv Siegel said. "You recommend an immediate review of the activity of the firm's top traders?"

"Nobody questions the star trader when he's making money for the firm. Star traders become rogue traders only when they lose tens of millions of dollars and no one uncovers it in time. The tendency at financial shops like ours is to give star traders tremendous latitude. We need to start with a list of the firm's top ten producers, pull them into a room, look them in the eye and ask them if they have any secrets we need to know about."

A glimmer of amusement crossed Irv Siegel's face. He turned to Alan Milgrim. "Two words for you, Alan: Gil McGeary."

Milgrim shook his head and smiled knowingly. "After this debriefing, I'm walking down there personally to eyeball his P&L reports."

Mike Kilmartin looked at his audience of three and felt a modicum of gratification. The Risk Management Task Force had gotten religion, and hopefully the sum and substance of it would be conveyed to Schomburg. Maybe now they understood that Wolcott Fulbright's hard-won reputation had taken decades to establish, but could be destroyed overnight with just a few clicks of the mouse by one rogue trader.

From the back of the room came a woman's voice. "Michael?"

Kilmartin tilted his head at Ann Brady, the audiovisual aide who had just popped back into the room. "Yes, Ann?"

"Your secretary said it's urgent and can't wait."

"Excuse me," Mike said, snagging the telephone on the conference table. "Yes, Felicity, I've only got a few seconds here."

When Felicity tearfully informed him about Kathleen Oberlin's accident, Mike Kilmartin pinched the bridge of his nose and wailed softly, "Oh, Christ, no."

With that, the dog-and-pony show came to an abrupt end.

Ten

THE FIRST FEW WIRE TRANSFERS came out of the Swiss accounts. Modest sums in the amount of a few million dollars were transferred to London, San Francisco, Baltimore, New York, Hong Kong, Abu Dhabi. The money was largely for balance sheet purposes, that is, to make non-existent shell companies appear to be viable legal entities.

One of the transfers, in the amount of 2.5 million U.S. dollars, was earmarked for a numbered account in the Cayman Islands established for the benefit of Stiletto. It was partial remuneration for Stiletto's contribution to the initiative, the first of four equal payments. By Colbert's devising, the account was restricted from any withdrawals until the day after the scheme's successful conclusion.

That morning at 9:07 A.M. Pacific Standard Time, the first wave of money flooded into the primary account of Infinity Technology Securities' Wells Fargo Bank account in Los Angeles. The funds would be used to feed the insatiable LINDA, with its hunger for millions in investment capital. January 29 was rapidly approaching and the money needed to be in place. All was on schedule. In fact, it was a bit ahead of schedule.

———•———

Early that afternoon, Hansen gathered up his leather agenda and walked down the hall to discuss some to-do's with Mike Kilmartin. The door to Mike's corner office was open, so Hansen craned his neck inside tentatively. Kilmartin was at his desk, but there was someone else in his office with him. Both Kilmartin and the man in the chair facing his desk stopped chatting and turned toward Rick.

"I didn't mean to interrupt," Hansen said.

Kilmartin waved Rick in. "It's all right, Rick, we were just finishing up."

"Is this the guy you were telling me about?" the man asked.

"The very same," Kilmartin said. "Rick Hansen, this is Detective Dan O'Bannon of the New York City Police Department."

Hansen stepped into his boss's office and took the seat next to O'Bannon. Definitely a cop—the $175 poly-blend Bancroft suit was a dead giveaway. In his mid-forties, Hansen guessed, though cop-years were worse than dog-years, so you could never be sure. The man's fleshy-jowled face was a road map of worry lines, a reflection of the collective stresses and shocks of two decades in urban law enforcement. The cop's hulking build was what some might describe uncharitably as like a fire-plug. O'Bannon's eyes were moist, as if he'd been weeping; Hansen figured it to be a sign of hard drinking. The detective's thinning sandy brown hair had been combed recklessly over his balding pate. Yet for all of these physical debits, Rick regarded the man before him as a superior being. The police were the thin blue line that protected him and his wife from the chaos that would surely overtake Manhattan without them.

O'Bannon pulled out a stained handkerchief and musically cleared his sinuses. "So your boss tells me you graduated from Fordham Law."

Hansen nodded. "Five years ago."

"Day school or night?"

"Day."

"I'm in the night program," the cop said. "My last semester. I graduate in May." O'Bannon took a swill of coffee from the Styrofoam cup. "Great school. You ever have Perillo for contracts?"

"No, I had Yorio."

"Yorio was brilliant, they say." O'Bannon nodded. "So was Perillo. He wrote the textbook, you know."

"Yeah." Hansen looked at Kilmartin. He didn't quite get what was going on.

Kilmartin filled him in. "Detective O'Bannon came by to ask a few questions concerning Kathleen Oberlin," he said somberly.

Hansen nodded. Half the department had attended her funeral over the weekend.

"Mind you, it's not my turf," O'Bannon said. "The Oberlin case is being handled by the Connecticut State Troopers. I'd barely closed the file on the Bingham investigation when a drinking buddy of mine tips me that Mrs. Oberlin was killed in an accident on I-95. And it was kind of strange that she'd worked for Tom Bingham, who, as you know, committed suicide."

Kilmartin fell silent. He seemed to stare at an inkblot on his desk.

"Anyway," O'Bannon coughed, "you can never be too careful when these sorts of coincidences occur, so I'm just doing my due diligence here."

Hansen was stunned. "The police think this is . . . a murder? A *double* murder?"

The detective held up his palms. "Whoa, hold the phone, I didn't say that. Is there any evidence of foul play here? None whatsoever. I mean, Kathleen Oberlin was killed in a freak accident when the gas tank of her car exploded on I-95. If you're looking for a murderer, look to the car company. Still, as I was discussing with your boss, Oberlin admitted to me she was sexually involved with Bingham and she was married, so that means you can't entirely rule out the jealous husband factor. I mean, if my wife was doodling some other guy, I would . . ." O'Bannon trailed off, shrugged. "Anyway, it doesn't fit the crime-of-passion profile. But we're interviewing Mr. Oberlin again this afternoon, see what happens." O'Bannon rose from his chair. "There is one thing I learned by coming by this morning."

Kilmartin asked, "Yeah?"

"The coffee they serve you guys on Wall Street? It's as bad as stationhouse coffee." O'Bannon chugged the dregs of the liquid, made a sour face. "Worse, actually."

O'Bannon thanked them for their time, handed each a business card and trudged out of the office.

After he was gone, Kilmartin stared off into space. After a moment, he said, "Close the door."

Hansen complied and took the seat O'Bannon had occupied.

Kilmartin's voice was hoarse. "Well, that explains why Kathleen'd taken Tom's death so hard. I guess I should have suspected that Tom and Kathleen were having an affair. Not that it's any of my business, but—look, these are Kilmartin's rules—but you don't shit where you eat, right? I mean, Tom was divorced, so it's really his business, but Kathleen was married and—it's just not good form." Mike's voice trailed off. "Just goes to show that people possess secrets. But everybody has one. Bingham had two."

"Two?"

"Just before Tom's death, some evidence came to light that he may have been involved in insider trading activity."

"Huh," Hansen pushed a hand through his hair, stared off into space in thought. "Really?"

"It seems he acted alone, trading in only a single stock that was on our restricted list in some numbered account at a broker-dealer in Canada. Very very sloppy. Even though Tom's . . . uh, passed away, the head honchos around here are very nervous about how the regulators are going to respond. Internal Audit completed an initial report on it. I'll have Felicity lend you a copy, if you'd care to see it."

"I would," Hansen said. "So do you think there's anything to what the detective says?"

"What, that there's foul play here? God, no. Just a freak thing. A coincidence. Tom Bingham acted alone on the trade. It was just a couple thousand shares. Just enough to drive him to take his own life, I guess."

"What was going on with Tom? Why would he . . . do something like that?"

"You mean trade on inside information? I honestly don't know." Kilmartin crossed his arms and stared at the surface of his desk. "Tom had been with the firm for four years, doing what I think was a fine job. I'd always given him stellar reviews, pushed for raises for him every year. But in the last year, something about Tom changed. I can't tell you exactly what, but he began to withdraw. He isolated himself, sat behind closed doors all day long. After a while, the only phone calls he would take were those from Gil McGeary. I don't know. It was weird how he suddenly transformed into this privacy freak before my very eyes. I still can't explain it."

Rick Hansen nodded. Everything he thought of saying in response to this was inappropriate. Instead, he changed the subject. "You ever see one of these?" he asked, withdrawing the metallic card from the back pocket of the leather agenda.

Kilmartin glanced at it curiously. "What is it?"

"Some device I found in Tom's office." Rick handed it to his boss. "There's an six-digit number that changes every two minutes. And that's all the thing seems to do."

Kilmartin scrutinized it, then grunted. He flipped it over to inspect it for markings, and found none. "Damned if I know. Maybe you should just turn it in to Security. I'll bet they'd know what it's for." Mike handed it back to Rick. "Say, I'm sorry to have to kick you out of my office, but I've got a follow-up lunch meeting with Siegel, Milgrim and Wolcott tomorrow to discuss the firm's global risk management policies. I've got a lot of spadework to do between now and then."

For the rest of the day, Mike Kilmartin's door was closed, the same way he said Tom Bingham's was. His secretary, Felicity, was instructed to hold all calls, and no one was permitted to see him. When Rick Hansen left the office for the day at eight-thirty that evening, he cast a sidelong glance at his boss through the front window-wall of his corner office. Though Mike Kilmartin's green banker's lamp was still blazing, and the papers were strewn before him on the desk, Mike appeared to be sitting there, doing nothing at all. Just thinking.

Eleven

IT WAS THE NATIONAL OBSESSION. Everybody was talking about it, *everybody*. It had become the *thing* of the moment, like gourmet coffee bars, or Rollerblading or the Internet. It was featured on sitcom plots, the dust jackets of bestsellers, mainstream magazines. The media was happily complicit in fueling the obsession, creating new cable channels devoted entirely to the subject.

All across the country, it was the hot topic at the church socials, the PTA meetings and pickup bars. They talked about it in the beauty parlor, at the bowling alley and on the golf course. It drove the small talk at baby showers, cocktail parties and bridge games at retirement communities. It became the common denominator linking the cabdriver with the bank president, the wheat farmer with the architect, the housewife with the computer engineer. Your mother didn't want to discuss her health, no, she wanted to talk about *it*.

The stock market: everybody wanted a piece of the action.

For the academic studies had proven it time and time again. The stock market was the winnable lottery, the financial rotisserie league, the slow-motion sure thing to a million-dollar nest egg. Passbook savings accounts and their 2.75 percent annual interest were for out-of-touch losers and 'fraidy-cat octogenarians. As for residential real estate, the spectacular twentyfold gains your parents scored for owning the four-bedroom Tudor you grew up in were unattainable for your generation. The Social Security system was a taxpayer-screwing pyramid scheme, doomed to run dry by the millennium. *Hey, you want to live in a box and eat Gravy Train during your golden years, be my guest. Me, I'm riding the stock market to a retirement villa in the Italian Riviera. I'm taking control.*

Six million Americans owned stock in the fifties; nowadays, *sixty million*

Americans were shareholders. The stock market had single-handedly cured Americans' global reputation as piss-poor savers. A groundswell of $4.5 trillion pushed the stock market to successive new summits. The Dow Jones was setting a new high every other day, and the reporters' clichés were played out already. Of late, the media was no longer dazzled by the new highs. An oligopoly of ten equity mutual fund companies were largely responsible for the near religious fervor the average American now possessed for stocks, and the fund managers were quasi-celebrities treated accordingly by the media. Finally, what scholars (and stockbrokers) had been saying all along had finally burrowed its way into the national psyche and had become a mantra. *Over time, investments in a diversified stock portfolio will historically outperform all other investments.*

Which was not to say that gains were guaranteed. Pundits climbed on top of their soapboxes, warning that if investors maintained their unrealistically high expectations of unabated gains, they could become instantly disillusioned and dump equity holdings during market down cycles. The "lemming effect" this time around could be devastating and far-reaching, they warned.

But with stocks continuing their breathtaking ascension to ever-greater heights (pushed higher by an infusion from overseas investors wanting their own piece of the action), no one paid much heed to the indications that the market was overheating. Small investors were fully caught up in the frenzy of wealth multiplication. Nobody wanted to miss out. Circulation numbers for *Barron's* skyrocketed. Elderly widows had taken to pulling money out of FDIC-insured CDs and bank accounts, transferring the entirety of their nest eggs to high-octane mutual funds at Fidelity and T. Rowe Price. The retirees were lining up at Charles Schwab locations around the country, waiting in line for fifteen minutes for their turn at the Quotron to see how IBM and Microsoft were doing; once apprised of the latest bid/asks, they moved briskly to the back of the line for the chance to see if they were up *fifteen minutes after that*. Average Joes were taking cash advances against their credit cards and boasting to their brothers-in-law that they too were "playing the market." It wasn't about "fundamentals," it was all about "the greater fool theory"—the expectation that there's a greater fool out there willing to pay more for that stock than you did. Publicly held corporations were trading cards to be flipped in the short run for short-term gain. And everybody wanted to be in the game.

But the euphoria had gone on far too long; everyone knew it. So what happened on January 29 surprised no one. Still, no one was quite prepared for its ferocity.

On the morning of the day that would soon be known as Freefall Friday, the market appeared to be taking a breather before resuming its unstoppable climb.

Morning trading was lackluster. By quarter past eleven, the Dow was just about dead-even at 9,368, up twelve points from Thursday's close. Only 58 million shares had exchanged hands on the Big Board.

At Wolcott Fulbright, the equity trading floor was relatively sedate. The traders caught themselves dreaming of packed-powder conditions at their rented slope-side condos at Stratton, Killington and Mad River Glen. Julian Stainsby started a game of liar's poker amid the lull on the equity derivatives desk. The secretaries and trading assistants busied themselves with an electronic chain letter from the Singapore office that obligated them to e-mail seven copies to other Wolcott employees or risk dire misfortune. It had been rumored that poor Kathleen Oberlin, a former paralegal in the LR&C Department, had broken the chain while she was on personal leave and look at what had happened to *her*. That morning, over eight hundred copies were dispatched through Wolcott Fulbright's global e-mail system via an Internet gateway.

At 11:17 A.M., Danny Partridge leapt up from his turret and announced he was taking orders for lunch a half-hour earlier than usual. As always, the derivatives crew was badly divided as to whether it would be Tex-Mex or Thai food or soul food shipped in from Sylvia's of Harlem. In the end, it was decided that a run to Smiler's deli would be an adequate compromise. Even then, the traders fussed over the particulars of their sandwiches—mayo or mustard, hard roll or multigrain, Snapple or Fruitopia, don't forget the pickle—

Joe Money was the last to place his order. Joe appeared to be staring deeply enough into his computer screen to read the future. Danny said, "What about you, Money-man? What'll you have?"

"Shit!" Joe Money suddenly exclaimed.

"On a hard roll or rye bread?" Danny Partridge quipped.

The traders looked over at the engrossed Joe Monetti and chortled. "A naked Elle MacPhearson on a silver platter couldn't tear that guy away from his Bloomberg," Train Wreck joked.

"Knock it off!" Joe yelled, waving for silence. "Something's going on in the market."

Without exception, the traders' smiles vanished.

"What is it?" Stainsby asked.

"The Dow spiked down sixty points. Just like that."

The traders' thank-God-it's-Friday jocularity was gone. They gathered around the color monitor of Joe's Sun SPARCStation.

"Sixty points is nothing," Zappia scoffed. "Not even two thirds of a percent. Just a hiccup."

"A *hiccup?*" Joe Money responded. "Market doesn't just shed sixty points in an eyeblink unless something's behind it."

He no sooner finished his sentence when the numbers on the screen for individual stock prices blinked an urgent red. All the stocks on the monitor downticked in unison.

"Whoa! You *see* that?"

"Yeah—price declines across the board."

"All in component stocks of the Dow Jones Industrial Average," Joe Money observed.

"The Dow's down *seventy-eight.*"

"What's the news? Is there any news?" The impulse to seek out the rationale behind such a market move was second nature to seasoned equity traders. Joe Money toggled his mouse, positioned it over the Dow Jones News icon. He double-clicked the mouse and the News window blipped open on the right corner of the screen. The headlines streaming up the monitor were eye-boggling:

11:23   DJN—Mobil (MOB) Sell Imbalance: 246,700 Shrs
11:23   DJN—Ford (F) Sell Imbalance: 220,400 Shrs
11:23   DJN—Amer Express (AXP) Sell Imbalance: 170,000 Shrs
11:24   DJN—Disney (DIS) Sell Imbalance: 314,500 Shrs
11:24   DJN—Exxon (XON) Sell Imbalance: 275,200 Shrs
11:24   DJN—AT&T (T) Sell Imbalance: 300,100 Shrs
11:24   DJN—General Elec (GE) Sell Imbalance: 323,000 Shrs
11:24   DJN—Intl Bus Mach (IBM) Sell Imbalance: 312,500 Shrs

"Sonuvabitch," The Stain mumbled. "Could be a massive selloff."

"Hey," Danny Partridge said, "shouldn't somebody should bring Magilla into the loop?"

Hunched over the computer in his fishbowl, McGeary was already all over it.

———•———

11:32 A.M. The DJIA stood at 9,281, down eighty-seven points.

Gil McGeary had sunk enough years in this business to sense that this market movement would gather broad-based momentum rapidly. The market was overbought, had been for weeks, and at the first hint of profit taking, smart money could be headed for the exits. It would be followed in short order by mutual fund and pension monies, then the flight of offshore capital, then the little-guy investor. It was what the finance professors at the University of Chicago had called the cascading market scenario.

But now was not the time to act rashly. Now was the time to remain clearheaded and unemotional. McGeary fired up his program trading system. He began building large "baskets" of sell orders that included each stock of the Standard & Poor's 500 Stock Index. Since McGeary had control over $3 billion worth of the firm's equity capital, he had to be in a state of preparedness in case the market ratcheted down another fifty ticks. As the computer automatically constructed the baskets of securities to be sold via SuperDOT, the stock exchange's gateway for programmed trading orders, McGeary hit the speed dial for the Legal, Regulatory & Compliance Department.

"Rick Hansen."

"You best get up here," McGeary barked to the lawyer. "We've just gone into 80-A mode and I've got a shitload of stock to blow out of inventory." McGeary disconnected, and returned to the task at hand.

Downstairs, Hansen wheeled around in his desk chair and flipped on his Bloomberg terminal. Astounding! The market was plummeting in what seemed to be a straight line. Hansen grabbed the *Rulebook* of the New York Stock Exchange from his bookshelf and sprinted for the elevator. Feeling the heft of the *Rulebook* tucked under his arm, he felt something like a Bible-toting priest called upon to pray at the bedside of a severely injured bull market.

———◆———

11:40 A.M. The Dow was down 102 points.

At 20 Broad Street, dozens of poly-blend jacketed specialists collected on the sidewalk outside the New York Stock Exchange for a communal nicotine fix. For the unshaved floor personnel, catching a smoke with their outer-borough brethren was a thrice-a-day ritual. Conti, the Philip Morris specialist from the market-making firm of Corcoran & Corcoran, and his pal Katz, the Chrysler specialist from Bear, Stearns, stared at a group of blond French girls with backpacks. The girls were among about a hundred tourists standing in the long line of visitors awaiting a tour through the observation gallery of the exchange. One of the French girls realized the specialists were staring at her. She blushed, broke into a flustered smile and began whispering to her companions.

"Ooo-la-la," the Philip Morris specialist leered. "I'd *love* to print that trade."

"She *is* fine," the Chrysler specialist agreed. "Why don't you strike up a conversation? Offer to take her and her friends to Planet Hollywood to meet Arnold or something."

"My wife would not be psyched about that."

"So," the Chrysler specialist shrugged with a smirk, "you don't bring your wife, and she don't get to meet Arnold."

In the next instant, a senior-level specialist for IBM appeared from inside. "Hey, you nicotine freaks! Better crush out *those* butts and get *your* butts back to your goddamn posts! Market's in freefall."

After a brief flurry of consternation, the specialists crushed out their cigarettes en masse and poured through the revolving doors, to join the chaos already building on the exchange floor.

The tourists in the line witnessed the activity with openmouthed awe. "It is true," the French schoolgirl named Thérèse Baingot declared to her companions. "Wall Street is an exciting place to visit!"

———•———

11:51 A.M. In Long Beach, California, it was 8:51 A.M. The industrial average was now down 112 points.

Eddie Slamkowski had CNBC on the tube, *The Money Wheel* giving a tick-by-tick description of the market decline. In Lake Worth, Florida, Slam's father was watching the same show and fretting about his retirement portfolio. "Should I call my broker at Schwab and have him cash me out?" he asked his son.

"Dad, the worst thing you can do is panic. Sheep get *slaughtered*. Look, seventy points is barely one percent of the market's entire value." The other line rang. "Dad, I gotta go. Yeah, I'll come back to you soon's I can." Eddie punched up line two. Not surprisingly, it was Stone.

"Liquidate everything at the market," Stone commanded.

Slam was stunned. Infinity's thirty-two offshore customers had sizable long positions in blue-chip equities. Liquidation of those holdings would certainly drive the market down further. Not only that, but some of Infinity's customers who had bought at recent highs would almost certainly take a loss.

"Everything?" Slam asked.

"*Everything*. Now, repeat what I just said."

"Sell everything at market."

"Good boy. Now *do it*." As was his trademark, Stone clicked off without so much as a good-bye.

Before Eddie called the execution broker on the floor of the NYSE, he rang his father back. His father was on call-waiting with Schwab customer service in San Fran. "Dad, get out now," he told him. "Sell as much as you can."

———•———

11:59 A.M. Market down 142 points.

Gil McGeary gathered his boys around the perimeter outside his office. Hansen arrived on the floor in time to catch McGeary's chalk-talk. McGeary had a pumpkin-orange basketball tucked under his arm: the coach in the heat of the big game.

"Okay, this is gonna be as short 'n' sweet as I can make it. This is the World Series, fellas. We must emphasize to our customers that it's not the time to push the panic button, not just yet. This could simply be the correction we've been expecting all along, a backlash to the January Effect. As market professionals, the best favor we can do our customers is to keep our heads clear, tune out any unfounded market rumors. Remember that, in a falling market, some of the best trades are the ones you don't make. Now, let's work the phones, keep our customers on top of things. Danny, I want you to plug into the whisper circuit, get some skinny on what's driving this market down."

"Will do."

"That's it." McGeary wheeled around and tossed the basketball toward the Zipper. It banked in off the wall, into the net for two points. His squadron hooted and cheered. "All right, kick ass, trade smart, and have fun."

With that, the group went into Swiss Army mode and dispersed to their respective turrets. They punched their speed-dial buttons and began burning up the lines to their best institutional customers. McGeary turned to a pretty young trading assistant named Staci Hanover, who'd graduated *summa cum laude* from Bard College the previous May. He pressed three hundreds into the palms of her immaculately manicured hands. "Get these guys some deli," he growled. "I can't have them risking firm capital on an empty stomach."

"It's as good as taken care of, Gil," she replied smartly.

"Good." He turned to Hansen. "Counselor, you come with me right now."

They entered McGeary's fishbowl. The head trader dropped down into his $3,499 Recaro leather race-car-driver's seat. He jogged the mouse and the screen saver disappeared, revealing the execution screen for program trading over the SuperDOT system. "Lemme bottom line you. I've got $450 million worth of customer and proprietary sell orders in the pipeline. If I don't execute 'em now, the firm stands to lose millions. Your mission, should you choose to accept it, is to make an executive decision as to whether execution of these orders *right now* is going to violate any stock exchange rules on program trading."

Hansen took a breath and said, "Let's consult the good book." Rick cracked open the NYSE *Rulebook*, turning to the complicated text of Rule 80-A, the so-called "circuit-breaker," which prohibited certain types of program trading during periods of extreme market volatility. The firm was obliged to follow the rule to the letter to avoid major regulatory problems.

"There's no time for *reading*," McGeary snapped. "I've got to know right now—*can I do this trade?*"

Walking the tightrope without a net could get you killed. The image of decayed tombstones in the nearby graveyard on Rector Street flashed in Hansen's mind. "Is this trade related to index arbitrage?"

"No. Straight sells. Can I do this trade?"

"Are you selling the securities short?"

"No, they're coming out of my long account. Can I do this trade, Counselor, yes or no?"

"Gil, I'm not gonna sign off on this trade until you answer every question satisfactorily."

"Richard," McGeary said calmly, "if I don't fire these trades off right now, my P&L is gonna ride this subway train straight to hell. You will be accountable."

Hansen was unnerved by the implication. "Where's the spix right now?" Spix was slang for SPX, the ticker symbol for the Standard & Poor's 500 Stock Index.

McGeary's eyes flicked to the screen. "Down thirteen and a half handles and dropping fast."

One thing was certain. Once the S&P cash index—the "spix"—dropped fifteen points from the day's opening level, McGeary would be frozen out from any program trades in S&P securities by virtue of stock exchange rules meant to slow steep declines. In that sense, Gil McGeary was right—it was either now or never for the trade.

Sometimes you gotta grab your balls and jump.

"Do the trade," Rick said.

Gil McGeary hit the green Go key of his keyboard. Instantly, $450 million worth of sell orders, 10 million shares, of blue-chip stocks raced through the telephone lines to the specialists' books on the floor of the New York Stock Exchange. Within minutes, the Dow Jones Industrial Average tumbled past the psychologically important down-100 barrier. The "sidecar" rule was triggered, preventing any further program trading for at least five minutes. Hansen felt his stomach clench into a knot. *Was that the right decision?*

12:30 P.M. The first hour of bloodshed had elapsed. The market was down 176. Volume in that hour alone had been 97.3 million shares.

The next sixty minutes were just as punishing. The thin filament of investor confidence that had held the market in place finally snapped. The resistance level crumbled beneath the weight of the sell orders pouring in from around the world. The Dow was now dropping at a rate of three points a minute.

On the equity trading floor of Wolcott, the tenor of the traders had gone from kinetic to frantic. Sales reps bounded around the perimeters of their workstations, sleeves rolled up, sweating half-moons of perspiration through their Brooks Brothers shirts. No longer did they soft-pedal the market break to their institutional customers as a "profit-taking scenario," "pullback," "price-spike" or "correction." Their voices were hoarse from urging customers to pull the trigger *now*.

"It's turned into a *bloodbath*. Get out now."

"—mutual fund–fueled meltdown—"

"—the lemming effect has set in. Capture those profits now, or kiss 'em bye-bye."

"—a freakin' freefall—"

"—could be Black Monday all over again—"

This ritual was being repeated on trading floors all over Wall Street. As a result, the market spiraled lower and lower.

At 1:45 P.M., the Dow was 250 points below its opening level and the Board of Governors of the New York Stock Exchange declared a halt in the trading of equities on all U.S. exchanges. The Chicago Mercantile Exchange, American Stock Exchange and Chicago Board Options Exchange immediately followed suit. The markets would remain closed for sixty minutes, a "cooling off" period that had been devised as another circuit-breaker after the 1987 market crash. The sixty-minute time-out had never been implemented. Until now.

The financial markets held their collective breaths as the clock ticked away the minutes, waiting for the markets to reopen at 2:45 P.M. EST.

The Chairman of the New York Stock Exchange peered down from the window of his sixth-floor office. He snorted in disgust at the news trucks jamming Broad Street below. Reporters scrambled to position themselves against the backdrop of the exchange building. It galled the Chairman to witness the media circus unfolding in his backyard, using the venerable edifice of the Big Board to lend an air of legitimacy to asinine tabloid sound bites that only incited panic-selling among the nation's small investors. Vultures. He could envision the headlines in tomorrow's papers. DOWN JONES! SHOCK MARKET! STANDARD & POOR-ER! The media was so pathetically predictable.

The Chairman's secretary cracked the door open enough to crane her head inside. "The others're waiting on the hot line."

The Chairman nodded. "Hold all other calls for at least thirty minutes."

When she was gone, the Chairman gazed at the hot line for a short while before picking up. Installed shortly after the '87 crash, it had been used only four times: the mini-crash of '89, the Gulf War, a 130-point decline in one hour in 1995. And now. The Big Board was going to be under the microscope and it wasn't going to be pleasant. He sighed and joined the conference call.

Roll call was taken. All told, twelve participants were on the line, including executives from the American Stock Exchange, the Merc, CBOE. Also present were senior-level officials from the SEC, the CFTC, the Fed and the Treasury. The Chairman cleared his throat and got right to the point. "Let me just state at the outset that this market event, as it stands right now, poses no systemic risk to the financial system. We have every confidence that this is a long overdue correction in the equity markets that could very well reverse itself in the final hour of trading."

"Walter, do we know what's driving this downturn? Is it portfolio insurance?" the Commissioner of the CFTC asked.

"Preliminary indications tell us it's program trading."

"Not *that* again," someone complained.

"Index arbitrage?" queried an official from Market Regulation at the SEC.

"No. There's not enough buying activity on the futures side to indicate index arbitrage."

"Are the hedge funds ganging up to force prices down? Soros, Steinhardt? Or hot money, maybe?" "Hot money" referred to the big currency players who had tremendous influence over the global economy.

The Chairman took a breath. "Not that I'm aware of, but again, we won't have a complete picture until the member firms turn in their Daily Program Trading Reports."

"When will that happen?"

"Trade date plus two. That means Tuesday."

The Chairman's counterpart from the AMEX chimed in, "If we know that program trades are causing the declines, shouldn't you guys just prevent them from trading for the rest of the session?"

"Come again?" Had he heard that right?

"I said, should we cut off the program traders completely? Close off SuperDOT, and permit phone orders only."

The Chairman bristled at the suggestion. "One, legitimate institutional customer orders done strictly on an agency basis are not to be disadvantaged simply because they are executed by computer rather than phone line. Two, the phone clerks are already backlogged with sell orders and can't keep up with the phones. Three, the program traders have a tendency to come into a declining market and reverse the momentum if given enough time. And number four, quite frankly, even if I had the authority to restrict the program traders, I wouldn't do it."

The Commissioner of the CFTC jumped in. "So, all right, where do we take it from here? Do we shut down the markets for the rest of the day, make it business-as-usual on Monday?"

"I disagree," the SEC official stated. "The circuit-breaker rule provides that we reopen after one hour. I say we do that."

"I'm with Mary," said the Chairman of the Merc. "This cool-down period's probably thrown some sand in the gears. Besides—dare I ask—how much more damage can be done in the final hour and a quarter? Not much more, I *hope*."

———•———

In fact, there was much more damage to be done. And the suspension in trading did nothing to cool investor panic. If anything, it was magnified.

When the markets reopened for business, the pent-up demand to sell blasted through the pipeline. The orders to liquidate poured in from around the globe: hot money, overseas investors, institutions, teachers' pensions, small investors, and, especially, from mutual fund managers who needed cash for the massive redemption requests that would inevitably come from their shaken investors. Attempts by well-intentioned program traders to stabilize the market were blown away by the market's downward momentum. Like trying to scale the sheer face of a mountain during an avalanche.

Price quotations were delayed five minutes, then ten minutes, then fifteen minutes. The specialists were on the verge of running out of cash. After the Toronto Stock Exchange declared it was closing down its trading session a half-hour early, the President called the SEC to find out what the hell was being done here in the United States.

Mercifully, the closing bell clanged at 4:00 P.M., sounding like the final gong of a bloody prizefight. When the carnage ended, the market had lost 616 points, the worst single-day loss since Black Monday of 1987. After all was said and done, more than $570 billion worth of shareholder wealth had been erased in just under five hours.

In Pittsburgh, Professor Howard Gammage had canceled his Friday afternoon class so he could witness history in the making. And now, as he watched the coverage of the carnage on CNBC on the twenty-inch color television in his modest Squirrel Hill living room, Gammage pounded the armrest of his chair in elation. *Goddamn*. LINDA had performed just as advertised. *I'm rich*, he said to himself. Then he said it aloud: "I'm fucking rich." Perhaps now was as good a time as any to seek payment of his consulting fees. And maybe a little additional success bonus while he was at it . . .

Twelve

EARLY THAT EVENING and well into the night, the fluorescent lights blazed in hundreds of conference rooms at financial service firms throughout the country—especially in New York, Chicago, Washington and San Francisco. The subject of these ad-hoc meetings was virtually the same: Freefall Friday—what was the damage and what would happen when trading resumed on Monday morning?

In the Buenos Aires Conference Room on the fifty-fifth floor of the 44 Wall building, the members of Wolcott Fulbright's Risk Management Task Force circled the wagons, calling upon two dozen personnel from the firm's key middle- and back-office units to provide impact snapshots of the market break. The meeting was jointly run by Irving Siegel and Alan Milgrim of the task force. Even Bobby Wolcott managed to make this particular Friday night meeting, breaking off his "prior obligation with some politicos" in Washington, D.C., where Wolcott kept an apartment. Wolcott was fooling no one—it was widely known that Wolcott's D.C. mistress was Alyssa Sumner, a lobbyist engaged by the firm to influence pending congressional legislation.

The meeting was grinding on. In attendance for this round were Mendelsohn from Credit, Pascarella from Operations, Welch from Risk Management, Chi from Systems, Kilmartin and Hansen from Legal. Hansen felt ill at ease among this crowd—the kid at the grown-ups' table. His game plan was to keep his yap shut throughout the proceedings, to prevent himself from saying something stupid.

"Max Schomburg has asked us to parse through this market event as best we can, people," Alan Milgrim stated. "McGeary?"

McGeary swallowed a mouthful of Chinese food before responding. "Yeah?"

"Market lost over 600 points today, more than Black Monday in 1987. But back then, the Dow was around 2250, whereas it's four times that level today. Big picture, are we overreacting somewhat?"

"Two thoughts," McGeary said. "You're right. A 600-point drop today represents about six, seven percent of the Dow. Back in eighty-seven, the market lost 508 points and that was twenty-two percent of the overall market value. But what troubles me in this case was the velocity of the meltdown. The decline started at eleven-thirty and gained speed over the next four hours. People forget that Black Monday was actually preceded by a record 109-point drop in the Dow on the previous Friday. That was around five, six percent also. This feels more like the prelude to the main event."

Several of the people in the room reacted visibly.

"Are you saying the market is going to crater even further on Monday?" Siegel asked.

McGeary shrugged. "Who knows? You find somebody who can predict Monday's market, send him my way, wouldja? He's got a job for life in my unit."

It was late on a Friday night and Milgrim was in no mood for humor. "What is this I've heard about a visit from Securities and Exchange Commission on our program trading activity?"

Mike Kilmartin cleared his throat and spoke up. "Members of Market Regulation have requested an opportunity to speak with Gil sometime next week, yes."

"Actually, I've heard they *insisted* on such a meeting."

"Why are they so insistent?" Siegel asked.

"My understanding? They're looking into all program trading activity executed during the market break. My contacts at Morgan Stanley and Nomura tell me they're meeting with Market Reg next week, too. My sense is that it's more exploratory than accusatory, at least at this stage."

"Do we have any legal exposure? Did we perhaps violate Rule 80-A or 80-B?"

McGeary spoke before either Kilmartin or Hansen could. "None that I'm aware of, Alan. In fact"—McGeary made an open-palm gesture indicating Hansen—"I insisted on having the firm's derivatives counsel at my side when I pushed the button, just to be certain we crossed the *t*'s and dotted the *i*'s."

An alarm went off in Hansen's head. He realized the son-of-a-bitch had just made a shrewd political maneuver before the task force at Hansen's expense. Right now, McGeary was looking like a hero for acting decisively in the midst of pandemonium. But just in case there was a regulatory train wreck on this one, it would be blame-the-lawyer time.

In effect, McGeary had just retained all the upside of the act, while divesting himself of the downside.

Alan Milgrim turned his glare on Hansen. "As you're no doubt aware, computer-guided program trading was considered the primary villain for the meltdown on Black Monday. Seems to me it could be made a convenient scapegoat in this case as well. Also, Congress has always been interested in the role computers play in market volatility. This franchise can ill-afford to make enemies in Washington, not with our IPO coming to market. Bob, Irv and I should be jointly kept in the loop on all developments with the stock exchange in connection with this."

Hansen nodded and said in a small voice, "Sure."

Kilmartin added, "Legal will 'cc' you on all memos."

"Good," Milgrim and Wolcott said at once.

Siegel whirled around to a fidgeting Scott Mendelsohn, the number two in Credit, who was flipping randomly through an exposure report the girth of the Manhattan Yellow Pages. "Now, Scott, where does the firm stand with customer short exposure at this very moment?"

———•———

The meeting wound up around 12:40 A.M. Most of the attendees called private radio cars for the trips home to Connecticut, Westchester and Long Island at around a hundred-twenty bucks a throw. Hansen, wanting to clear his head, declined the door-to-door transportation, which struck him as excessive for just a trip uptown. Anyway, he preferred to walk a bit, let the crisp winter air clear his head.

The financial district was eerily quiet at that time of the morning. *Lifeless. A lunar landscape*, Hansen thought, as he walked in solitude along Wall Street. A news box already had the morning edition of the *New York Post*. FREEFALL FRIDAY, the headline screamed. Hansen dropped fifty cents into the slot and pulled out a copy. *Suitable for framing*, he mused.

On the corner of Church Street, he noticed the light was on in the window of a modest shoe repair shop. He was drawn to it. Peering inside, he saw a reed-thin man with wild gray hair and a weathered face. Hansen figured the man was in his late fifties. He imagined the shoemaker was an ethnic who probably spoke broken English, heavily accented by his mother tongue. The shoemaker had a mustache that signified his second-generation European ethnicity and an oily sheen of sweat on his skin. Half-lens glasses were perched on the tip of his patrician nose. His nimble fingers worked confidently at the task at hand, as he plied a humble trade that had been insulated from the technological boon that had revolutionized so many other businesses.

The shoemaker was hunched over his workbench, working through the night to repair the wing-tip shoes of Wall Street executives. Watching the shoemaker risking his fingers with sharp implements in dim light to put food on the table for his family gave Rick a sting of guilt. Rick was half this man's age and he was using his graduate school–fortified brain to participate in the massive wealth transfers that the financial community did so well. The shoemaker and the securities lawyer—they were at opposite ends of a spectrum.

As the man worked in the dim light, he seemed blissfully uninformed about the magnitude of the afternoon's freefall in the stock market. But even if the shoemaker didn't realize it, his life would be affected by the shockwaves. If the markets continued to drop indefinitely, Wall Streeters would be terminated by the thousands. The shoemaker's client base would shrink commensurately. Indeed, if the value of the stocks continued to plunge, the confidence in the economy could quickly evaporate. A ripple effect might plunge the country into a recession. Then the shoemaker and his family would truly feel the effects of the market break. What happened on Wall Street affected what happened on Main Street. There was no denying that.

Suddenly, the shoemaker looked up from his labor and caught Rick staring at him. Hansen moved away quickly, and headed for the subway entrance near the graveyard.

———•———

At home, Stephanie was asleep on the couch. The television was tuned to *CNN Headline News*. Freefall Friday this, Freefall Friday that, *yada, yada, yada*. Hansen aimed the remote at the set and snapped it off. He kissed Stephanie lightly on the cheek, waking her.

"What time is it?" she asked dazedly.

"It's late, Stephanie," he said softly. "How are you and Baby X doing?"

"Baby X is fine. It's Mommy who's falling apart. I've got a nagging backache, leg cramps, an itchy abdomen, a urinary infection and a bizarre craving for pork rinds."

"Should I run out and get you something?"

She smiled. "That's sweet, but the doorman already made a junk food run for me." She pointed to the spent, crumpled bags surrounding the couch. "I've been watching the news reports. How are *you* doing?"

"Fine. A little wired."

"I can imagine. You coming to bed?"

"I need to wind down a little. I'll be right behind you."

"Don't be long." Stephanie lifted herself from the couch and lumbered off to the bedroom. Hansen went to the bathroom to brush his teeth and had just squirted out a small ribbon of toothpaste when it occurred to him that he had forgotten to jot a notation of an eight A.M. meeting with Kilmartin on Monday into his page-a-day diary.

Yawning, he returned to the kitchen and extracted the leather-bound business agenda from his briefcase. He opened it and flipped through the pages, looking for Monday, February 1. Past Thursday, Friday, Saturday, Sunday . . .

A handwritten entry he hadn't seen before caught his eye. He thumbed back a few pages to the Saturday, January 30, page. Bingham must have scrawled it in there shortly before he . . . Hansen peered at it:

"JAN'Y EFFECT" (TRM1)
Fri. Jan. 29
6.5% to 8% drop in DJIA
Call Gammage Sat. / 361-5212

Hansen blinked, not comprehending the significance of the notation. Then it hit him. *No, it couldn't be, could it?* Hansen raced over to the kitchen area, retrieved the *Post* from the countertop. Turned to its ink-smeared business section, past the hysteria of the headlines, to the stock tables. Market Monitor.

He did the calculations on the newsprint.

On Freefall Friday, the Dow had dropped 7.5 percent from Thursday's close. Solidly within the range indicated in the Bingham notation.

The young lawyer couldn't believe his eyes. *Did Bingham write these numbers or was it written in by someone else today?* No, the agenda had been in Hansen's possession all day long.

So, if these figures were entered into the agenda by Tom Bingham's own hand, then the dead bastard had accomplished an absolutely impossible feat . . .

He had predicted the occurrence of Freefall Friday . . . *nearly two months before it happened!*

Part II

THE ULTIMATE
KILLER APP

January 31–February 19

*As a result of normal market behavior and the
extraordinarily robust financial structure
inherited from World War II,
the periodic triggering of a financial crisis
is well-nigh certain.*

— MINSKY, 1977

Thirteen

OVER A WEEKEND that found millions of Americans reeling from the devastating losses of Freefall Friday, the group of elite financiers who called themselves The Contrarians gathered in a lavish ballroom in the Ritz-Carlton ski resort in Aspen, Colorado.

Unlike most Americans, these men had cause to celebrate.

The requisite cigar orgy kicked off the festivities. A panoply of cedar boxes was arranged neatly on a linen-lined serving table in the Mill Street meeting room with a view of the village square. No matter that most of the selections were illegal Cuban imports; senseless customs law did not prevent men of this echelon from enjoying the spoils of victory. Not surprisingly, the offerings tended toward the expensive (twenty to fifty dollars a smoke): Hoyo de Monterrey Double Coronas, Macanudo Vintage No. VII, Paul Garmirian Gourmet, Romeo y Julieta Churchill, Ramon Allones Gigantes. Faced with such daunting selections, each partner took five or six at a time, hoarding their choices for later. Ten minutes into the event, a blue-gray gauze of smoke rose like a ghost above the celebrants.

The selection of single-malt Scotch was the province of Colbert himself, who had raided his private collection for the occasion. The Partners spent a half hour debating the color, nose, body, palate and finish of the Craggenmore 1976 Gordon and MacPhail versus the Glenmorangie 1972 single-barrel vintage. The Springback West Highland 1966 and the sixteen-year-old Macallan ended up a dead heat for the consensus favorite.

A white-gloved wait staff appeared from nowhere and cordially ushered the men to their seats, as dinner was about to be served. A procession of exotic delicacies then began, seemingly without end. The appetizers included asparagus spears wrapped in rare filet mignon; smoked gravlax on toast points; belon oysters on the half shell. A lobster cake in a rich orange-butter sauce was singularly exquisite. The main course was the *pièce de résistance*: tournedos of Charolais beef with shiitake mushrooms in a red wine sauce, served with a potato and arugula risotto. Dessert was a strawberry torte with chocolate sorbet.

Their sophisticated palates sated, they contentedly puffed their sixty-ring gauge smokes and swirled snifters of brandy. The Partners spoke to one another in any of several languages, reflecting their international sensibilities. They marveled at the ski conditions at nearby Snowmass, and one-upped each other with outrageously ambitious business ventures. They tiptoed around the subject that had brought them all together this last time; that was Colbert's province and no one wished to steal his thunder.

Colbert himself sat at the head of the table, and gazed around at the other members sitting in their down-filled lounge chairs. There was more in store for his business partners. As a bookend to the event, an escort awaited each Contrarian when he retired to his suite for the evening. Not the local genetic garbage for these men. No, Colbert had flown in a bevy of aspiring actress/models from an elite brothel in Beverly Hills that catered to studio executives and bad-boy movie stars. Smart girls—ones who had Keogh retirement accounts in Fidelity Magellan and were on a first-name basis with the staff at Georgette Klinger. Girls who consumed Pat Conroy novels and European films in their spare time. Girls who were studied professionals in the art of the male orgasm, and whose beauty entitled them to a few hours with one of the men in this ballroom. Of course, it wasn't compulsory for a Contrarian to have some company for the night, but it was there for the taking. The choice to have sex with a beautiful woman was purely his own. Colbert provided it as another modest reward for participation in the venture.

All in all, this was a celebration worthy of a room of such men, each of whom was severely afflicted with a god-complex. *No apologies, there,* Colbert thought. They *were* gods. The men in this room had collected as one and moved the biggest stock market in the world.

As the plates were cleared by the wait staff, Colbert turned toward the striking platinum-blond woman waiting in a corner of the room. He nodded, a cue to her that it was now time. She moved toward the group with a self-assured luminescence that caused the Partners to fall quiet. It wasn't just that the woman was stunningly attractive, a statuesque sex goddess. It was more her outfit, a black translucent Dolce & Gabbana number that revealed she was wearing lace panties, but no bra. She swirled around the table, handing each Contrarian a simple Crane paper envelope bearing his name. This was a very different sort of mail call.

Antar Reich was the first to open his envelope. "Oh my God," he blurted involuntarily.

"What is it?" Dieter Kuypen said. When he opened his, he too invoked the name of a deity.

They held in their hands a partnership statement accounting for their profits to date. For each unit purchased, the return on investment for the first five months was 2,200 percent! But as astounding as this sum was, it was potentially mere pocket change. If all went as planned, Colbert promised a return of five hundred dollars for each dollar put up.

Colbert silently watched the Partners respond to the numbers. It was a most gratifying sight, and he permitted himself a rare smile. Then he nodded again at the blonde. She left the facility and closed the giant oakwood doors of the ballroom behind her. The only ones remaining there were Contrarians.

At this point, Colbert rose from the table and strode up to the podium. The men turned toward him and stood up as one. They applauded him vigorously. Colbert leaned into the microphone.

"Gentlemen." His amplified voice boomed out throughout the meeting facility. "They said . . . it couldn't be done. They said . . . it was *impossible*. They said . . . the markets are too big, you can't move them. *They* were wrong. Because you, gentlemen, through your faith and your financing, made it happen. I give you the event that will go down in history as . . . *Freefall Friday*."

On that cue, darkness blanketed those in the enormous room as Colbert stepped aside. Six television screens positioned in a 180-degree arc flickered to life.

For the next fourteen minutes, the Partners were treated to a video replay of the world reaction to Freefall Friday. The video production had been prepared in a frenzied twenty-four-hour period by a Texas media company Colbert controlled. It began with the CNN logo. The booming baritone of James Earl Jones: "*This is CNN.*" Then came the parade of talking heads and splashy graphics, one after another, describing the events that had stunned every American with hard-earned dollars invested in stocks or mutual funds. Brokaw, Rather and Jennings. Lead story on all the networks. Jennings: "Late day carnage on Wall Street . . . and when it ended, the stock market sustained the biggest single-day drop since Black Monday, 1987." Segments followed on what it meant to Main Street, U.S.A. . . . The pundits opined, experts on both sides of the fence. "This could be the signal that we're at the beginning of a protracted give-back in the Dow," said the First Boston economist. "At most, it's a temporary blip on the upward march of the equity markets," countered chief economist Roslynn Blum at the firm of Wolcott Fulbright. A bow-tied finance professor from Princeton University asked rhetorically, "Once more, the age-old question—is it time for gun control on Wall Street again?" CNN's Lou Dobbs sounded the alarms on his nightly *Moneyline* program. "Perhaps it's time for small investors to prepare themselves for the coming storm in the equities markets." . . . A shot of three dozen miserable investors from all walks of life, hanging out in the World Trade Center branch of Charles Schwab, watching the electronic ticker provide a minute-by-minute account of the Dow's spectacular crash and burn. Several sound bites followed that likened the markets to storms, earthquakes, wars and other disasters . . . The White House press secretary read a brief prepared statement: "The President has asked his Chief of Staff to look into the precipitous drop . . ." Then a montage of screaming front-page headlines from the respected daily publications—*The New York Times, Barron's, The Wall Street Journal*—with news radio reports in voice-over. The video concluded with a sweating, bespectacled official of the stock exchange sounding the closing bell of the bloody trading session and a freeze frame.

Fade to black.

Stark red capital letters faded in:

FREEFALL FRIDAY, JANUARY 29.
−7.6%

That graphic dissolved, giving way to another, more ominous graphic:

FRIDAY, MARCH 19.
−50%

The reaction to this was an exuberant admixture of gasps, cheers and curses.

THE DAY OF THE CONTRARIANS IS COMING.

Fade to black. The End.

The lights came up and, after a bedazzled pause, The Contrarians, to a man, clapped forcefully, and cheered loudly.

Colbert returned to his place behind the podium.

"You did this!" he boomed. "*You* created this!" (In Colbert's mind, of course, he had actually been the one who had pulled it off. The rest of the partners were merely passive investors.) "The academicians said it couldn't be done. They said that the markets were purely resistant to a concentrated force. *The Contrarians* proved them wrong."

Dieter Kuypen and Antar Reich drunkenly yelped and cheered.

"The black-box technology worked to perfection. The decline was at the high end of the predicted range. The pieces are almost in place for the final leg of our initiative. The articles on the Middle Eastern money have been planted with the financial media, and we expect intense interest from the dealers. On both coasts, our trading functionalities are virtually ready to switch over to full remote control mode. And, finally, I expect to clinch a deal on the Dartmouth Funds in the next few days, which will instantly enhance our leverage by a factor of twenty.

"For security purposes, this is the last time we will meet as a group until our venture is completed. From here on out, as always, the key to the initiative will be your discretion. Pursuant to our partnership agreement, you must remain circumspect about the details of the operation until its conclusion. After that, I don't give a damn, because I'll be in the Alps of Switzerland without a forwarding address." The Contrarians roared. "Next-door neighbor to me, probably," laughed Van der Leun.

Colbert sensed it was time to conclude the proceedings. "Gentlemen, I thank you for your faith in the initiative thus far, and expect you feel the same sense of gratification as I have in the success of our plan to date. We will speak again on Saturday, March twentieth."

Colbert stepped away from the dais, a cue that led the men to rise as one, pounding their hands together. They paid homage to the visionary before them.

———◆———

In the course of the next thirty minutes of this nearly perfect night, each Contrarian in attendance approached Colbert to convey his gratitude. Each of them: Dieter, Gunter, Dirk, Mario, Marty, Antar, and Jean-Claude. Colbert received each partner, accepted his accolades coolly, and thanked each one personally for his faith in the initiative. Then when Colbert was alone, his thoughts turned to the dissident partner.

Graham Pethers.

Pethers was a problem. The messages he had been leaving on Colbert's international voice mail system were becoming increasingly shrill and disturbing. Pethers wanted to pull out, demanding an immediate return of capital. He wanted to know the truth about Colbert's activities in the name of "security." Worse, he was providing not-so-veiled threats about contacting the authorities. What did that mean? The FBI? The SEC?

Yes, Colbert had long suspected he had made a mistake in judgment in inviting Pethers to join The Contrarians. But the Australian barrister had laundered billions of dollars looted by insiders to the Kuwaiti oil trust during the confusion of the Gulf War. Pethers was cut from the same cloth as the others, Colbert had no doubt. But now the Aussie bastard was drawing an ethical bright line between destroying the global equities markets and killing off an inconsequential pawn to ensure the secrecy of the plan. Eliminating Bingham, while distasteful, was a necessary course of action. Now, due to his irrational conscience, Graham Pethers was placing himself in harm's way just as Bingham had done before him.

"Are you ready?"

Colbert looked up and saw the blond woman standing over him, beaming seductively. Laura Jennings was the madam presiding over the Beverly Hills brothel whose girls had populated the junket. The Aspen event had added considerably to Jennings's personal bank account, and Colbert had the pleasure of her company that evening at no additional charge. "That was some blowout you hosted there, Mr. Stone. Business associates of yours?"

"Partners," Colbert replied tonelessly.

"You know how to treat your people right." She was simply trying to be conversational, but the inquiry annoyed Colbert. "What line of work are you in?"

Colbert held her gaze and smiled. "I could tell you, but then I'd have to kill you."

The smile was meant to be disarming, meant to convey this man was simply joking. Still, Laura Jennings shuddered inwardly, believing the words were not completely a joke. The subject was avoided for the rest of the evening.

Fourteen

IN THE END, Rick Hansen didn't so much make a decision to pursue the truth to the mystery Tom Bingham left behind as yield to a compulsion to resolve it.

For Rick, the query became a living thing the instant he discovered the cryptic notation in the leather agenda inherited from his dead predecessor. *How could it be?* One autumn day at least two months before, while Tom Bingham still drew breath, he picked up a Bic ballpoint and penned a note to himself. The note appeared to predict the mini-crash of the stock market—on the day it happened *and* within a few percentage points.

And who is this guy Gammage? Rick Hansen lay awake all night as Friday became Saturday, flipping around in tangled bedsheets, tormenting himself with the puzzle. Mike Kilmartin had told him that Bingham had probably killed himself because he feared he was about to be discovered as an insider trader. An Internal Audit probe conducted after his death confirmed his secret holdings in a company whose stock was restricted because of pending deal announcements. So was this notation somehow indicative of a continuation of his misdeeds? Was it possible that Bingham had inside information on Friday's market break? No, that was clearly impossible; there was no single event that had created the mini-crash. Moreover, there was no way to obtain inside information on a broad-based stock market decline, because no such inside information existed.

Okay, fair enough. But ruling out that possibility still left Hansen with an equally preposterous theory.

Tom Bingham had predicted Freefall Friday. The day of it, the extent of the decline.

Stephanie laughed the next morning when her sleep-deprived husband posed the question to her over breakfast. "Someone else put it in your datebook," she said, "either as a joke or just some reminder of a historical event."

Hansen shook his head. "No. The book was in my possession all day."

"Well, whatever. I wouldn't let it ruin your weekend, honey."

But of course the weekend was ruined for Rick; he was distracted by the question, obsessed with the illogical annotation that glared back at him defiantly from the leather agenda. During a Saturday afternoon phone conversation, Hansen had tried it out on Paul Gelbaum, who also snickered at the notion of someone predicting a stock market crash. "Stone cold impossible." Hansen later bounced it off his other former colleague, Robbie Singer. "Nostrodamus himself couldn't pull that off," he said doubtfully. Stephanie rolled her eyes on Sunday morning when Hansen even queried his father. "Everyone knows that's impossible," Hansen's dad scoffed. "But just in case it's true, is there any way I can invest with this guy? Sounds like he could've saved me some money Friday."

It was unanimous. Such a prediction was simply not possible. So Rick Hansen stayed up until midnight on Sunday evening, staring at the handwriting on the Saturday, January 30, agenda page. *Then what the hell does it mean? And who the hell is Gammage?*

———•———

Monday morning came as quickly as it always does.

Rick arrived at work at 7:45 A.M., shrugged out of his trench coat, and checked his voice mail for urgent messages. Three messages, all concerning pending legal documentation, none especially urgent. Good. He rolled up his shirtsleeves and got busy.

He drew the leather agenda out of his briefcase and turned to the January 30 page. Then he opened the first drawer of the stainless-steel filing cabinets in the office, which contained manila file folders previously created by Tom Bingham. Quickly, efficiently, Rick searched for rough drafts of previous memos, handwritten notes in the margins of word-processed documents—anything that contained a sample of Bingham's penmanship. Five documents were located and withdrawn from the files: three word-processed memos with revisions in Bingham's own hand, a cover note written out in pen and a message slip the lawyer had filled out to remind himself of an upcoming appointment.

Hansen brought the papers to the desk, laying them next to the leather agenda.

Though Hansen was no expert, he was almost immediately convinced that Tom Bingham was the author of the notation in the agenda.

The "G" in Gammage was consistent with the capital "G" in a Bingham writing sample with the words "Government bonds." The word "Call" in the agenda was an exact replica of the word in a handwritten line "200 IBM 150 call options at 12½." The letter formations, the slant, the flow, the style—all were consistent between the samples and the datebook entry. The clincher was Bingham's apparent disposition toward the same Bic blue-ink ball-point that sometimes left gobs on the tops of 'o's and 'i's. Bingham was the author of the notation, no doubt about it.

Everyone else was wrong. The sonuvabitch *had* predicted Freefall Friday.

———•———

Distractedly, Hansen worked the phone and pushed some paper, earning his keep. But he obsessively kept an eye on the time, like a clock-watching school kid waiting for the 3:15 P.M. bell. When eight-thirty came around, Hansen rose and emerged from his office. He mumbled a greeting to Cliff Weiner, the temp secretary who had been assigned to him in the wake of Kathleen's departure.

"Good morning, Mr. Hansen." Cliff put an extra cheerfulness into his greeting; he was a "floating temp" who was eager to become a full-timer in the department and get some medical benefits for once. "You've gotten a few calls already."

"I've got a special project this morning that's going to keep me tied up. If any call is truly urgent, patch it through. Otherwise hold all calls until ten-thirty, okay?"

"Sure thing, Mr. Hansen."

Hansen strode purposefully down the hall toward Mike Kilmartin's office. Mike was not yet at work, which was out of step with his early-bird standard. Kilmartin's secretary, Felicity Robbins, had just arrived at her workstation outside Mike's corner office. Felicity was a large, doughy woman in her early thirties, whose size was offset by a unpleasant face and wheat-colored hair. She was rumored to be a third-generation heiress to a Texas oil fortune who had burned through a trust fund partying at Studio 54 in the eighties, and now she had to suffer the indignities of a nine-to-five job. As Rick approached, Felicity was in the process of getting settled in for the workday, tucking a tri-folded *Times* into her black glove-leather Bottega Veneta bag. "Good morning, Rick."

"Morning, Felicity. How was your weekend?"

"Wonderful. Yours?"

"Busy. Where's Mike?"

"He's at an ISDA documentation task force meeting at JP Morgan until eleven." ISDA was the International Swaps and Derivatives Association, the trade group for the derivatives industry. "Should I let him know you dropped by?"

"Maybe you can help me. Last week Mike said I could see a report written up by Internal Audit on Tom Bingham. I'm looking for a copy."

Felicity's demeanor cooled immediately. "That's a confidential memo, Rick."

"I know. I won't share it with anyone."

She eyed him warily. "By that, I mean it's privileged."

"Attorney-client privilege, right? I'm an attorney, so no problem, my looking at it won't invalidate the privilege."

"I don't know if Mike would want that passed around, Rick. It's on a need-to-know basis."

"Felicity, I need to know."

"Uh huh. Well, maybe he should be the one to make that determination."

On Wall Street, a secretary often improperly assumes the power and authority vested in her principal. In a sense, the secretary sees herself as an extension of her boss, and becomes unnecessarily confrontational with the professionals down the reporting line. At the end of the day, however, Rick Hansen didn't report to his boss's secretary, and didn't have to play this game of chess. Tiring of the thrust and parry, he gripped the edge of Felicity's workstation and leaned in closer. "Felicity, Mike and I have already had extensive conversations about what Tom did. Now, I know the memo contains some ugly family secrets, but I'm part of the family now. The point is, I have a reason for wanting to know the contents of that report—a reason I'm not at liberty to go into now—and I don't want to shlep down to Internal Audit to get a copy. My hunch is that the memo is an open secret. But if you can *honestly* tell me that no one else in the LR and C secretarial pool has read the Bingham memo, then just say so and I'll go away until Mike himself tells you I can read it."

Felicity flushed an arterial red. Cora Ann Stewart, another secretary, who had been listening in on the conversation, turned her head and pretended to be involved in finalizing her boss's travel vouchers. She, too, was blushing.

Hansen knew then he had Felicity Robbins dead to rights; the whole freaking department had gawked at that memo.

"I'll bring it to your office," she said.

Ten minutes later, Felicity Robbins showed up at Rick's office with a twenty-four-page photocopy still warm from the machine. "Please don't make any copies."

"I won't."

"And bring that copy back to me when you're finished. Within an hour, please?"

"That's fine. And thank you, Felicity."

Backing out of his office, she asked, "Do you want the door opened or closed?"

"Closed, thanks."

Felicity complied. Alone with the document, Hansen tore into it.

———————●———————

The stock market whipsawed in the early part of the morning session. Continued pessimism drove the market down sixty-four points at the opening bell. But the market promptly rebounded, and by 10:07 A.M., it had gained back all it had lost at the open and then some. Electronic trading kicked in with a flurry of buying activity, spurred by bottom fishers and bargain hunters speculating that the market break on Friday was irrationally driven panic selling. By ten-thirty, the market had climbed 112.45 points, recapturing nearly a fifth of Freefall Friday's losses.

Gil McGeary patrolled the equity trading floor with an autocratic presence. That morning, the derivatives desk head was afflicted with a sudden toothache in one of his molars, and he was chewing on ice cubes to numb the pain. McGeary feared dentists, and would do anything to avoid them. *Pain's not so bad anymore,* he assured himself.

Strolling down the narrow aisles between the trading turrets, McGeary's survey of the activity on the floor was gratifying. Money was being made. The phones were jangling insistently with customers expressing buy interest. The equity derivatives guys worked the electronic doughnuts with newfound optimism and energy.

"Yeah, it's hard to get a rope around it, but it seems to have the makings of a snapback rally. The wheels aren't coming off this market just yet—"

"Would somebody pick up the lights, please? That customer's been on freakin' perma-hold all morning—"

"—I'd charge a buck and a hey a half-turn for the EFP—I know, I know, you're losing money on it but you make it up positioning the basket and guaranteeing the customer VWAP."

"Look, we offer a more robust structure for that type of trade than Goldman. Truth is, we mow Goldman's grass on that line of business."

"That's right, Sam, there's a lot of edge to that trade, if you got the stomach for it. The market just now's a meat grinder."

" 'leven teenie bid, five eighths for 'em all—wait, stay with me—jussa-second—yo! Would somebody pleeeease pick up line oh-thirty-two. Wassamatter, Danny Partridge, you got gator arms?"

Gil picked up the line himself. He recognized the voice of a despised headhunter who was attempting to pick off one of his guys for a big-noise position at Salomon. McGeary said, "Don't even think about it, Althea," dropping her with a stab of the red kill button. McGeary's squadron was brimming with top-tick talent, which made guys like Joe Money and Julian Stainsby choice targets for executive recruiters, the vultures who tried to snatch away his impact players for the competition. McGeary compensated his people as highly as he possibly could, but sometimes Milgrim, the global head of equity, chintzed out at year's end. It wasn't unheard of for Gil to dip into his own pocket to bring a sales guy or trader up, at least a little. It was largely symbolic, but still, it shouldn't be that way. If paychecks were the report cards of life, you had to ensure that the guys at the head of the class got the straight A's they deserved—otherwise they'd go somewhere else to get those kinds of grades. This should not even be an issue, McGeary ranted to himself. The trader was getting fed up fighting the muckety-mucks and had long suspected that he, along with several others, would get royally screwed when the firm went public in a few months. McGeary's plan to protect himself was already under way; hey, he was just looking out for number one.

McGeary had a more immediate problem at hand.

His program trading volume on Friday was massive, his biggest ever. McGeary had been in the business long enough to know that the regulators were putting his activity under a microscope *at this very instant.* They had to be; his trades directly contributed to Friday's downdraft. Some fifteen-year careerist from the SEC would be calling Kilmartin soon to arrange for a little Q&A session, he just knew it. And even though he had faced regulators before, even though the new trading practices attorney, Hansen, had blessed the trades, this time Gil Mc-Geary really had something to be anxious about.

It'll be all right, he assured himself. *Just paint the right picture and they won't touch you.*

McGeary tipped the cup of ice, filled his mouth and disappeared behind the closed door of his fishbowl office.

———•———

ATTORNEY-CLIENT PRIVILEGE—
ON THE ADVICE OF OUTSIDE COUNSEL
THIS IS A NONDISCOVERABLE LEGAL DOCUMENT—
NOT FOR GENERAL DISTRIBUTION UNDER ANY CIRCUMSTANCES

TO: Distribution List
FM: Internal Audit Task Force
RE: Certain Trading Activity of Thomas Bingham

EXECUTIVE SUMMARY

At the request of the firm's Risk Management Task Force, the
Internal Audit Department was asked to conduct a review of the
stock trading activity of Thomas Bingham ("Bingham"), a trading
practices attorney in the Legal, Regulatory & Compliance
(LR&C) Department of the firm. Bingham committed suicide last
month on November 29. After his death, police turned over
records obtained from Bingham's residence. Upon a review by
Alan Milgrim of the firm's Risk Management Task Force, it
appeared that Bingham maintained an unauthorized securities
trading account at a small Toronto broker-dealer named
Dominion Securities.

After a two-week inquiry, it is the determination of the
Internal Audit Department that Bingham illegally profited from
the improper use of inside information by purchasing equity
securities in a company that was on the firm's restricted-from-
trading sheets ("Restricted List").

The company was TeleDisc Satellite, a communications
company that was acquired by Montefore Media in a deal
structured by the Investment Banking Department ("IBD") of the
firm. As a trading practices attorney, Bingham routinely had daily
access to the Restricted List, and would have been in a position
to know the company was a takeout target. The profit from this
investment was $24,570.

Hansen placed the memo on his desk and massaged his eyes. He was
stunned at the brazenness of Bingham's act. Obviously, only a privileged
few at the firm would have access to the Restricted List, so Bingham's
trading activity would have been under constant scrutiny by the firm.

Wall Street firms were tenacious about ferreting out insider trading, hiring teams of outside investigators to conduct ongoing surveillance for employee accounts away from the firm. It was something they undertook with the utmost seriousness and expense. For Bingham to conduct his illicit trading in *Canada*, of all places—he was virtually asking to be caught.

The rest of the memo gave detailed descriptions of the trading activity, and the firm's prompt liquidation of the illicit holdings. It concluded with a section on how the proceeds were immediately turned over to an escrow account in the name of the Securities & Exchange Commission. Wolcott Fulbright's CEO, Max Schomburg, was negotiating with the SEC to settle out the matter with a minimum of adverse publicity. Tom Bingham was a bad apple.

Which left Rick Hansen more intrigued than ever. He opened the door to his office and called Cliff Weiner inside.

"Here I come," Cliff said in singsong.

"Cliff, do you know Bingham's old password?"

"You mean the password to get access to his computer files?"

"Yeah." Hansen tried to sound casual about breaking into his predecessor's computer files, but the act wasn't necessary. The temp wasn't about to question his new boss' business purpose for looking into a dead man's hard drive.

"Sure. Try 'MAMBOTHING.' "

" 'Mambo thing'? Mambo as in the music?"

"Right. All caps, no space between the words."

Rick carefully typed this in. "Was he a fan of mambo music?"

"Actually, Tom was a jazz fan." Cliff smiled. "MAMBOTHING is an anagram of Tom Bingham."

Hansen scrambled the letters in his head. "You're right. It is."

Seconds later, the system responded LOGIN SUCCESSFUL.

"You're in," beamed Cliff Weiner. "God bless the technology people. They haven't gotten around to shutting off access yet."

"How about that," Hansen mused. "Say, Cliff?"

"Yes?"

"How did you know Tom's password?"

"No biggie," Cliff replied. "He called me once from a business trip in Hong Kong and asked me to log in for him. He wanted me to bring up a memo on equity swaps, or something like that. Knowing Tom, I figured he wouldn't remember to change it after I got in." Cliff lingered at the doorway. "Is there anything else you need?"

"Yes. Can you bring me all of his expense vouchers for the last year?"

"Yes, sir, right away." Cliff Weiner saluted. This irritated Hansen, an indication the temp was feeling a bit too chummy under the circumstances. But all was forgiven when before parting Cliff said, "By the by, he used the same password for his voice mail."

———•———

Within the next few minutes, Rick Hansen mouse-clicked his way through the various windows necessary to get to the screen containing the directory of Tom Bingham's files, which had a default name of MY DOCUMENTS. In the directory, there were 243 files in total, most of which appeared to be business-related. They were listed first by numerical order, then arranged alphabetically.

The first five files in Bingham's system blipped up in the window:

144A Transactions
15-a6 Compliance
1998 Bed & Breakfast Transactions, London →U.S.
1998 Chicago Mercantile Exchange Review of Books & Records
3RiversModelOne

Rick opened the files serially, pulling up one, closing it out, opening up the next. The first four were clearly legal memoranda related to Tom Bingham's day-to-day business as a trading practices lawyer at the firm. Mostly, they were procedures related to properly handling a certain sophisticated transaction, directed to key business people. Purely ordinary work product of a lawyer in Bingham's position.

The fifth file, "3RiversModelOne," was a very different animal. When Hansen clicked on this icon, the monitor flickered and filled with gibberish:

```
>AHREF="#1"<1.>\A<
°N²¤¶»PÀ³¥ÍPGPµ{¦¡ª°¥\‾à¤P‍Í¥Ðè»k²£¥Î̦ Û¤vª°¤½¶}'c
FP˙p¤HÆ_°f<°T®■¸Ñ±K<BR>PGPT®■ÄÒ¤P¤{ÀÒ<BR>="#0000C0">²£¥Î̦Û¤vª°¤½¶}¥P
"p¤HÆN° f<\>■\A><P>"Í¥Î_"Ó³t«×¤]¶V°C¡C±µ¤U"Ó«K¬O¬°¦¹ ¹Æ_°f©R¦W¡APGP
©Ò■e²{ª°µe−±¬°¦¡G<P>¤W−z¥¦°Ø¤è¦¦³£¥Ï¥H■¹¦ "¥[±Kª°°Ê■@¦CPGP
±N·¦²£¥Ï¤@−ÓÀÉ¦W¬Û¦¦P¦ÿ°ÆÀÉ¦W;¬°É¦A³o−ÓÀÉ¦N¬O¥[±K»á°ÀÉ®×¦F−
Y±z̦µw°D¤¤¤w¦s¦b³o−ÓÀÉ®×¦APGP·¦°Ý±z−n»\¦L©Ï−«ü©w¤@−ÓÀÉ¦W¦
C°Ê■@■¦¦"«á¦A«K¥ï¦Î±z»Ý−n¥H¦q¤1¶1¥6©ÎÄ¦ ü¤è¦ ¡°e¥X¦C̦ b³d ³¤@
Â̦I−nª·¸Nª°¬O¦A−Y±z"Í¥Îª°°Ñ¼Æ¦A»h²£¥Î̦°¥[±KÀÉ®×¬O¶³q¤°¦rÀÉ®
```

The attorney rested his chin in the cup of his palm, contemplating the meaningless characters. Must have been some technical glitch that converted the text of "3RiversModelOne" into an indecipherable mish-mosh. He considered contacting the troubleshooters in the Systems Technology group to see if the bug could be corrected, but thought better of it. He had hundreds of Bingham's files to peruse, but decided he'd do his sleuthing on his own time.

One last thing, he decided, picking up his phone. He punched up the firm's internal operator. "Is there a Gammage who works at the firm?" he asked the woman who answered.

A few keyboard clicks echoed in the background as the operator searched the computerized directory for the surname. "No Gammages," she reported. "I have a Gambrell in Sydney Operations. Is that who you're looking for?"

"No. You know what, never mind. Can I have the number for Roslynn Blum in the Economists Department?"

———◆———

"Is it *what?*" Roslynn Blum shot back at him over the line. "Could you repeat the question?"

"Um, I know this may sound like an odd question, uh, but I was wondering if the experts considered it possible to, uh, predict a stock market crash like the one we had on Friday, you know?" Even as he heard himself saying the words, Hansen couldn't believe he was talking to the firm's $750,000-a-year chief economist about this.

"Who is this, again?"

"Rick Hansen from Legal."

Blum sighed irritably. "Listen, Rick. There's a camera crew from Bloomberg Business News setting up in my office to do a sound bite on the market. Would you mind terribly if I came back to you on this?" Blum clapped down the phone on Rick without asking for his extension.

That's that, Hansen figured. *Congratulations, Hansen, you just made an ass of yourself with the firm's superstar economist.* He felt a sting of humiliation for the inspired chutzpah that led him to ring up her up with the question. *What were you thinking?* He turned to confront the mountainous in-box that was threatening to topple over from lack of attention. Still, as the day bled away, Hansen couldn't push the Bingham enigma out of his mind.

———◆———

At 3:59 P.M. Eastern Standard Time, the Chairman of the New York Stock Exchange climbed up to the top of the balcony overlooking the floor of the stock exchange and at precisely 4:00 P.M. personally sounded the closing bell to end Monday's trading session. He did so with a considerable measure of relief. There was no nuclear meltdown of the American equities markets as many doomsday pundits had predicted, thanks in part to substantial program trading activity on the buy side from foreign and institutional buyers. Monday's stock market closed up 137.67 points.

The headline on the front page of the New York *Daily News* the next morning trumpeted: DOW ABOUT THAT! FOREIGN INVESTORS PROVE DOOMSAYERS WRONG, PROPELLING DOW TO 138-POINT REBOUND FROM FREEFALL FRIDAY. Similar sentiments were splashed across front pages all around the country. Investors were suddenly optimistic. Maybe this was not the end of history's longest bull market after all, but rather a long-awaited *buying opportunity*. Once again, fear had given way to greed; it was that kind of market.

Fifteen

"PARK OVER THERE," an irritated Alexeyev barked in Russian.

The Gargoyle maneuvered the rented U-Haul into a spot against the curb and cut the engine. The Gargoyle refused to speak English, although he'd been trained to speak it fluently. "What now?" he asked, drumming the steering wheel impatiently.

"Hold on." Alexeyev pinched the tiny bottle of clear fluid between his thumb and forefinger. Then he pushed the short needle of the syringe into the rubber seal of the bottle's top, filled the chamber with the drug, squeezed the excess air out with a push of the plunger. He secreted the needle behind the clip of a brown clipboard. Tucking the clipboard underneath his arm, he turned to his young apprentice. "Okay. Let's go."

They disembarked from the van. The walk to the professor's house was about 100 yards, in the direction of the nearby college campus. The professor lived on the 5100 block of Beeler Street in the quiet residential neighborhood of Squirrel Hill, an enclave of modest homes owned by academicians who taught at the local universities. Squirrel Hill. There were no Squirrel Hills in Russia, Alexeyev thought.

The men came to the steps leading to the professor's home. "This is it," Alexeyev said quietly.

The Gargoyle tilted his head up toward the three-bedroom stone house perched at the top of a steep hill. He mutter-cursed in Russian at the challenge of the incline facing them.

Alexeyev hissed him into silence and led the way up the steps. *Easy for him*, the Gargoyle thought. *I've got the duffel bag*. All Alexeyev had was a clipboard, syringe, book, a pistol and the device he called a HERF gun.

In time, they reached the top and stood on the porch of the modest house. Alexeyev rang the doorbell.

From within, the muffled sound of footfalls on a creaking hardwood floor, coming closer. The door opened.

Howard Gammage peered out at the two men in suits. His eyes squinted against the midday winter sun. "May I help you?"

Alexeyev sized up the American who stood before him. In appearance, he was no different than expected. Gammage was a big teddy bear of a man, collecting the bulky jacket of flab characteristic of many middle-aged, tenured professors whose daily routine included college cafeteria food and a largely sedentary livelihood. He possessed the stereotypical symbols of the academician, the owl's-eye reading glasses and the bushy salt-and-pepper beard favored among scholars. Alexeyev detected the fresh reek of marijuana smoke from inside, heard the faint strains of classical music. An American professor relaxing in his home one winter afternoon between classes. Perhaps grading students' papers.

"Yes," Alexeyev said at length. "Please look at this."

Alexeyev handed the book to the professor. Gammage was so bewildered by the demand, he failed to notice his visitors wore plastic gloves. He turned the book over in his hands, squinting at it, trying to comprehend what this was all about. It was a hardcover book. Gammage recoiled in vague disgust when he read the title. *The Breathless Orgasm.*

"You've definitely got the wrong house, fellas—" Gammage began to hand the book back to his visitors. But before he could do so, Alexeyev's left hand shot up and grabbed the right side of the professor's face, palming Gammage's bearded fat cheek in a tight claw. In the same motion, the needle materialized in Alexeyev's right hand, positioned in his fist like a dagger. With a vicious strike, he jammed the short needle into the professor's neck, piercing through the meat of his neck and penetrating the carotid artery. In the instant before the shocked man instinctively jerked away from the attack, Alexeyev thumbed the plunger forcefully, emptying 1 milligram of a muscle relaxant named succinylcholine into his bloodstream.

With a savage scream, Gammage twisted backward forcefully, enough to tear the syringe out of the assassin's grasp. In a surreal interlude, Gammage pranced around the foyer in a wild-eyed spasm, his hands scrabbling about his collar until he could yank the dangling syringe out of his neck.

"Close the door," Alexeyev snapped, breaking the Gargoyle's trance.

Gammage was reeling with shock, stepping backward from his attackers. "What is it you want?" he whispered in mortal fear.

Alexeyev did not respond to the question. Instead, he stooped over and retrieved the syringe, palming it into his suit jacket pocket. He instructed the Gargoyle to keep a gun trained on the professor until the drug took effect. Succinylcholine required eighty-five seconds. Only thirty had passed so far.

Alexeyev pushed past his victim and strode around the modest home, searching out the area necessary to finish off the job. Killing, of course, was the simple part. Far more difficult was making several related killings appear utterly unrelated. That was the art to what he did as a professional "suicider." While he may have had the benefit of geographic dispersity of Colbert's victims, his professional standards dictated that he not need-lessly provide any clues that would assist a law enforcement computer in piecing them together.

In the professor's bedroom, Alexeyev located a walk-in closet with a bar. *Good,* he said to himself, clearing a space for the setup. He placed the clothes carefully on Gammage's bed.

He then returned to the living area. Gammage's prone form was splayed on the hardwood floor, paralyzed from the heavy dose of the muscle-relaxant drug. The Gargoyle still had his gun trained on the pro-fessor. *Needlessly,* Alexeyev noted.

"What do you want me to do?" the Gargoyle asked.

"Drag him to the bedroom."

Howard Gammage was barely able to breathe, let alone resist his at-tackers.

In the bedroom, Alexeyev pulled the nylon rope from the duffel and looped it over the bar in the walk-in closet. It was important that they do it while Gammage was still alive, so the succinylcholine could break down in his bloodstream without leaving a trace for the coroner. Alex-eyev handed his apprentice the other end of the rope. "You know what to do from here?"

The Gargoyle nodded.

Alexeyev went about the house searching for any evidence linking the professor to Colbert. There were two hot spots in the house—the living room and the office. In the office, Alexeyev found a copy of the brutish fax transmission the professor recently sent to Colbert, which read in part: *I believe I've been a patient partner throughout our relationship, and that I have in good faith held up my end of the bargain. However, your next in-stallment of $150,000 is over a month past due. I'm afraid I must remind you of the options I have at my disposal to collect on what is due me, if it comes to that . . .* Alexeyev trained the HERF gun on the PC and pushed the but-ton, nuking the magnetic properties of the computer's memory. A HERF gun was a high-energy radio frequency device that completely disabled the hard drive, preventing any high-tech investigator from resurrecting deleted files with recovery utility software. Alexeyev then set about collecting boxes of papers, creating a heap in the middle of the hardwood floor in the living area.

Ten minutes later, the Gargoyle came in and informed him, "He's done."

Alexeyev went in to check on his protégé's handiwork. Inside the closet, Gammage's corpse was positioned on his knees, the nylon rope in a noose around his neck. The other end, looped over the bar, was wound around Gammage's right hand. The professor's trousers and undershorts had been yanked into a tangled heap around his ankles, and his left hand had been cupped around his exposed genitalia. The Gargoyle had strewn several homoerotic pornographic magazines around Gammage's cone of vision, as if his last images in this world had been of scrapping, well-built and well-endowed young men before he accidentally choked himself to death in the throes of ecstasy.

Auto-erotic asphyxiation. That was what the bizarre sexual practice had come to be known as among American law enforcement officials. It had first been described to a skeptical Alexeyev two years ago by a colonel recently retired from the KGB. As the colonel described it, the so-called asphyxiophile placed a noose around his neck, and, by regulating the pressure of the rope, gradually cut off the flow of blood to his brain while perusing pornographic materials. Eventually, he teetered on the verge of blacking out, spots exploding before his eyes. Once the asphyxiophile passed into an altered state of consciousness known as a "fugue state," he would release the choking device and begin masturbating. The result would be an incredibly intense sexual release. Sometimes the asphyxiophile would lose control and go to the extreme, the colonel chuckled, pushing the envelope of the fugue state and literally choking himself to death.

"It is not possible that someone would do that to himself," Alexeyev scoffed. "Not even in America."

But it was, the colonel had assured him. In fact, it was so prevalent in the United States that at least a thousand AEA deaths were reported every year. To fortify his claims, the colonel produced a copy of the pamphlet federal officials had disseminated to coroners, pathologists and police departments on how to recognize the telltale signs of an asphyxiophile's death. Alexeyev peered at the publication with keen interest.

The possibilities were self-apparent to the thinking man's killer. As a cover to murder, it was ingenious. Humiliated family members surviving the victim would ask that the investigation be brought to a quick conclusion for fear that the details would leak out to the press and embarrass the surviving siblings and parents. As long as the murderer set up the death in a way that fit neatly under the checklist of the AEA profile provided to law enforcement officials, local police officers were only too happy to quietly close the case as an accidental, self-inflicted death.

———•———

Alexeyev nodded at the condition of the corpse. The Gargoyle's work was acceptable. Cautious not to smudge the professor's fingerprints, Alexeyev then planted a copy of an underground how-to manual on autoerotic asphyxiation, *The Breathless Orgasm*, in the top drawer of the professor's nightstand. A ground ball to the law enforcement officers who would ultimately investigate the grisly demise of Professor Howard Gammage.

They carried four boxes of files out to the U-Haul. Within the hour, they had destroyed the documents by drenching them in gasoline and taking a match to them. It was done in an industrial section near the Monongahela River, where few would see what they were doing. Those who might witness it either wouldn't care, or weren't in a position to do anything about it.

They were moving south on Liberty toward the Fort Pitt Bridge when Alexeyev pulled out the digital cellular and made the call to Colbert. "It's Viktor, calling from Pittsburgh. Our job is complete."

"Good. Now I'd like to talk to you about your next full-time assignment, which you need to step up into immediately. It concerns—"

—*Graham Pethers*, Alexeyev said to himself knowingly in the instant before Colbert uttered the name.

Sixteen

MANHATTAN

Friday, February 5

HANSEN STARED AT THE PAPERS before him in the unmarked manila folder. The inconsistency made no sense.

Two mornings before, Rick asked Cliff Weiner to retrieve the last twelve months' worth of Tom Bingham's T&E vouchers. Cliff had dutifully done so, providing the spearmint-colored statements for his American Express Corporate Card account in one manila folder, all other expenses in another.

Hansen spread out the AmEx statements on the left-hand side of his blotter. Then he opened the other folder and withdrew the various internal receipts for temporary secretary services and yellow carbon copies of car service vouchers. These were arranged on the right.

Then he began reconciling the records against one another.

The tale told by the American Express bills was a disheartening one. They reflected a lawyer slipping irreversibly into the maw of irresistible temptation and self-destruction. According to the string of charges on the AmEx bill, in the last two months of his life, Tom Bingham was hopelessly addicted to insider trading and gambling jags. Three trips to Toronto, consistent with his insider trading activity. Also, there were numerous cash advance charges taken in Atlantic City, the Foxwoods casino in Connecticut, Merv Griffin's Paradise Island casino-resort. A weekend junket in Reno. Rooms booked at the casino. All on the guy's corporate account. In a six-week span, the charges each weekend grew more and more outrageous, from $550 in the first week of last October to $7,800 the weekend before he committed suicide. It was a pathetic road map of one man's downward spiral to self-destruction.

Until you looked at the other receipts.

On four of those weekends, Tom Bingham had signed off on time cards for his temp secretary, C. Weiner. The time cards showed C. Weiner worked seven- or eight-hour days on Saturdays for Bingham. It could very well have been that Bingham had a temp slaving away over the weekend to make himself look good while he was actually off on a gambling jag in Paradise Island on the largess of his employer, then he backdated his signature on Monday morning when he came in for work.

He called Cliff into his office.

"Are these accurate?" Hansen asked, showing him the time slips.

Cliff nervously fingered his mustache. "Yeah. I think so. I mean, Tom signed off on them, right? I was working for him on those weekends, okay? They're all legitimate hours, I mean, do you have a problem with those hours?"

"No. Not at all. But his AmEx bills say he was in Atlantic City on three of the weekends he worked."

"Well, Mr. Bingham was known around here as something of a workaholic and he worked a lot of weekends. I would not've been here if Mr. Bingham wasn't," Cliff asserted in a prissy tone. "He signed the time sheets, didn't he?"

"He did. But as far as you know, he wasn't racing off to the blackjack table in Atlantic City these particular weekends?"

"What Mr. Bingham did on his own time was none of my business."

"I appreciate that," Rick said. "But did he mention anything about gambling while you were working with him?"

"No. Not a word. Thing about Mr. Bingham? He was all business, all the time."

With that, Hansen dismissed the temp. He returned to scrutinizing the audit trail.

Which story did you believe? The AmEx bills painted the picture of an out-of-control gambleholic. On the other hand, the internal receipts told the story of a workaholic lawyer whose workload more often than not spilled over into the weekend.

As he puzzled over the latest curve ball, the phone rang. "Rick Hansen," he said automatically.

"Richard?" the woman's voice asked.

"Speaking."

"Richard, it's Roslynn Blum, returning your call from Monday. I apologize for being so brusque before," she purred with her most winning Wellesley charm. "Coast-to-coast television interview, bad hair day. Lethal combination, you understand."

"We've all been there," Rick said charitably.

"As it happens, I've been up to my ass in alligators until today. If you have some time, why don't you come up to my office and we'll talk."

"See you in five minutes."

———— • ————

Wall Street was most assuredly a world of intense pressure, not for the fainthearted or the ulcer-prone. The five-days-a-week whipsawing of the financial markets and the requirement to profit from it led directly to fistfights and health problems. Even the most high-throttle stress-junkies couldn't stave off permanent burnout by the age of thirty.

In decades past, women as a gender were perceived by the men in power as ill-equipped for this environment. This world frequently brought out the testosterone-driven caveman in its players, and women tended not to cuss convincingly, smoke cigars, nor have the right type of genitals to scratch. Women filed discrimination suits when terminated. Also, in the face of inhuman pressure, women might cry—a career-killing weakness.

Roslynn Blum was an example of the brave new politically correct gender-blind meritocracy that Wall Street has magically become in the nineties. Well educated, driven and brilliant, Roslynn ascended to the post of chief economist at Wolcott Fulbright while retaining a sense of her own identity and style. She was frequently sought out by the financial press as a pundit of current market trends, considered in the same super-star peer group as Metz at Oppenheimer, Wien at Morgan Stanley or Joseph-Cohen at Goldman Sachs. Having gracefully turned forty in December, she was often described by her colleagues at Wolcott as "well put together" and "stylish." She had rose-tinted Sally Jessy Raphael–type glasses, curly black hair spiced with locks of gray and an intelligent face that had the sheen of a weekly facial at La Casa de Vida natural holistic health spa in Gramercy Park. Today, she was dressed in a pastel Tahari outfit, Ferragamo shoes and her trademark Barbara Bush pearls from Tiffany.

Her spacious corner office was an oasis of femininity amid the Iron John motif of Wolcott Fulbright's headquarters in the 44 Wall Street tower. Whereas Wolcott's common space was heavily accented toward dark woods, money greens and scarlet reds, pictures of seafaring clipper ships and fox-hunting scenes, and manly chrome accents, Roslynn's office emphasized human touches. In contrast to the boy-toys of some of her male counterparts at the firm, Roslynn's space was adorned with artwork and pictures of her family in silver frames. The signed prints by Hal Larsen, Shonto Bagay, R C Gorman and Dalhart Windberg had a distinctively Southwestern flair in common, all of them depicting Native Americans amid colorful landscapes of mountains and deserts.

"Have you ever been?" Roslynn Blum asked Hansen as he admired the pictures.

"I'm sorry, where?"

"Santa Fe, New Mexico," she said. "That's where I collected these works."

"No, never have."

"Santa Fe is one of the most amazing places on the planet," Roslynn said wistfully. "You stand in the middle of the town and the Sangre de Cristo Mountains just rise up all around you. Cochití Lake, the Nambé Indian Reservation, Angel Fire—some of the most beautiful natural spectacles in this country."

"Sounds wonderful," Rick said.

"When I cross the finish line of this rat race, I'm buying a one-way ticket out there."

Hansen nodded. "Thanks for squeezing me in, Roslynn. I'll make it as brief as possible."

"So the question before the house, as I understand it, is whether it is possible for one to predict the stock market? Well, it'd *better* be, otherwise I'm out of a job." Her laugh was positively ebullient. "By the way, what's this for, anyway?"

Thinking quick, Hansen replied, "There's a special project under way in the equity derivatives unit to determine whether movements in the stock market are in any way predictable and if so, how?" That he could fib so smoothly to a senior employee of his new firm took him by surprise.

"The short answer, sadly, is no. It's an absolute impossibility to predict the movement of the stock market with any degree of accuracy. But, believe you me, it isn't for lack of trying. Rocket scientists have for decades tried to work up a system to predict the direction of the markets, but by its very nature, the stock market is unpredictable. Investors want to believe the markets are predictable. Look at the proliferation of newsletters and the financial talk shows. It's ridiculous, if you ask me, the way the pundits are turning the financial markets into a big casino or one giant horse race. My advice? Buy and hold, buy and hold, buy and hold. The only thing that's certain is that over time, the stock market will eventually go higher."

"So, based upon your perspective, the financial markets are by nature unpredictable?"

"Absolutely. Vast sums have been spent to devise formulas and models that attempt to predict movements in indexes and securities. Time after time, models that succeed in the bullish markets fail miserably when the markets turn bearish. Are you at all familiar with the efficient-market theory?"

"I know about it, but I'm not an expert on it."

"It's the cornerstone of modern economic theory, Rick. It means that in theory any advantageous inefficiency in the marketplace would be exploited by players until it disappears entirely. The markets are fundamentally unpredictable because they are only moved by unexpected news."

"So then, the only way to beat the market is to receive that unexpected news faster than other investors. Like the insider trading cases, where people trade on takeover and merger information before it's widely known?"

"Right. Current prices already reflect all the available information about the stock. Only unpredictable news can cause a change in prices, and since unpredictable news is unpredictable, price changes are also unpredictable. It's a 'random walk' in which each price change is unaffected by its predecessor and the system has no memory. All the old news is already assimilated into the prices in the marketplace. Most markets are moved by random bits of news; therefore, the markets can only move randomly. Markets are *reactive*, you see. It's what Professor Burton Malkiel calls 'the random walk' theorem."

"I see." Hansen stroked his jaw thoughtfully. "Well, I'll pass the bad news along to our equity derivatives guys. Roslynn, thank you for your time."

"Not at all. I happen to love kibitzing about the subject."

With that, the meeting was over and Hansen left Roslynn Blum's office.

———————•———————

"Mr. Kilmartin was looking for you. Sounded important."

Hansen sifted through the messages Cliff Weiner had just handed him. "Did he say what it was about?"

"No, but he said to meet him and Mr. McGeary in his office once you got back."

Hansen race-walked to Mike's corner office. When Hansen walked in, he found Kilmartin hunched over his speakerphone, his hands clasped contemplatively as if in prayerful repose. Gil McGeary was there as well. The trader paced the room vigorously, rotating a pair of jade-green Chinese meditation balls in his right hand. The balls emitted soft chimes as they rolled in repetitive figure-eights in the trader's palm.

"Okay, Bob, I'm with you on that, at least," Kilmartin said in a voice of exaggerated volume, loud enough to be picked up by the starfish-shaped speakerphone on his desk. He stabbed the mute button and said to Hansen, "The SEC is coming in first thing Monday morning to ask us about the program trades Gil made last Friday."

"The SEC?" Hansen looked over at McGeary. The derivatives trader gazed back vacantly at Hansen. "I thought they were coming this week. Is that them on the phone?"

"No. It's the Risk Management Task Force. Wolcott, Milgrim and Irv." Kilmartin punched the mute button again, reverting the call back to a two-way conversation.

"—you understand what I'm saying here?" Bob Wolcott's fizzy voice blurted over the box. "We're, uh, trying to ramp up revenues wherever we can, you know, so we can paint the prettiest picture possible for the public offering."

The patience in Kilmartin's voice was beginning to fray. "I appreciate that, Bob, but what I'm trying to understand here is, what's the economic rationale behind these trades?"

"Your mistake here, Mike, is thinking like a lawyer in this situation. No offense meant—"

"None taken, Bob, but that still leaves my question unanswered. What is the economic purpose of the trades?"

"Mike?" A new voice came over the speaker. "Mike, this is Alan Milgrim."

"Hello, Alan."

"Hello. The thing is, we don't know the economic rationale of the trading, because it's not our customers trading."

"Not our customers? Now I'm really confused."

"This should clarify everything. Bob and I had a sit-down with Gil this morning to discuss the size of the trades. The truth is, we don't know the economic rationale for the trading because they're all offshore customer trades that flow through us from another broker."

"Right," McGeary chipped in. "This broker, Infinity Technology Securities, simply uses our connectivity to the exchange to enter the program trades for their own customers."

Alan Milgrim said, "We're just kind of like an electronic gateway for those orders and we act like a tollbooth clerk. For that, I guess, we get what? Three pennies per share?"

Bob Wolcott confirmed it. "Right, three pennies per share."

"Three pennies for the order flow, which, as you can see from their volume, adds up quickly."

Kilmartin tilted his chin up and contemplated the ceiling. "But I don't understand—"

Wolcott cut him off. "There's nothing to understand here, Mike. This arrangement was approved by Schomburg himself."

"Okay, that's fine, Bob. Then I guess that's the firm's position, that's what Gil's supposed to say to the SEC on Monday. These are customer trades, but not our customers."

"That's right, that's the firm's position."

"Very well. After we ring off, Gil, Rick and I will huddle and strategize on this thing."

Wolcott said, "You, Gil and who?"

"Rick, Rick Hansen. The new lawyer who joined us in January."

"The replacement for Tom Bingham?" Alan Milgrim asked.

"Yes. Anything else?"

"No, that's all. Keep us in the loop, and let us know of any developments at all. Cheers."

After the call was concluded, there was a brief period of silence among the three men. Mike Kilmartin stared at his speakerphone as if he was trying to digest what had just come out of it. Kilmartin looked up at McGeary. "Did anybody think to run this by LR&C?"

McGeary shrugged. "If we stopped to pick up the phone and advise the lawyers of every piece of business we were doing, this shop would come to a grinding halt."

"Still," Kilmartin persisted. "Letting someone else use our SuperDOT line, that has broader implications to the firm."

"Take it up with Risk Management. They seem to think it's a business decision."

Kilmartin shook his head. "Well, that's neither here nor there. We need to get you up to speed for Monday morning." Kilmartin pulled out some files from his cabinet. "Apparently, they're sending Don Neufeld over to run the Q&A. Neufeld's the number two in the New York office's Market Reg division, a tenacious son of a gun, smart guy. I've got a few files on some of the cases he's brought against member firms. Now, let's not rush to judgment; Don told me they're talking to about a dozen different firms about their activity last Friday. Still, we can't be too careful, especially with this order flow thing. By the way, Felicity can bring you something to drink, if you want. Coffee, soda, water?"

"I'm good," McGeary said. "But I need to hit the head before we rock 'n' roll."

"I second that emotion," Hansen said.

Hansen led the way to the washroom.

———•———

At first, Hansen and McGeary said nothing to one another while at the urinals. This wasn't good. Something undefinable had changed in their relationship since the previous week. Conversation was strained and businesslike, very unlike his first week at the firm where they had shared Fidel Castro–endorsed contraband in the trader's office and speed-rapped about the vagaries of the business. Now gaps of silence characterized their one-on-ones. Hansen finished his business at the urinal, flushed and zipped up. He sidled over to the bank of sinks and washed his hands.

"Counselor?"

Hands dripping, Hansen turned toward him. "Yeah?"

"Sometimes it takes me a while to get going," the managing director said. "You mind leaving the water running? It helps."

Without another word, the attorney flipped the faucet back on. *Who would've thought a big hitter like McGeary would be pee-shy?* Hansen asked himself.

"There we go," McGeary said, as he finally got going. In something of a non sequitur, he casually inquired, "So, Rick, what'd you think of the report?"

"What report?"

"The report about Tom Bingham's insider trading activity?"

Hansen was stunned. "How did you know I saw that?"

"A little birdie in your department told me."

"Who?"

"I never name my sources, Counselor. Never." Hansen didn't care for the gamesmanship, but McGeary was already charging ahead to the next line of questioning. "What'd you think of the guy who used to do your job? Sorry piece of shit, wasn't he?"

"You're in a better position to make that judgment. Tom used to work closely with you, didn't he?"

McGeary completed answering Mother Nature's call before answering Rick's question. It seemed to Hansen he was framing his response carefully. "I think it's fair to say he was wired differently than you and me. Good lawyer, smart and decisive. But I think his ambition got the best of him and that's what killed him in the end." McGeary was going to say something else, but held his tongue.

Rick took this in, tried to discern what was behind McGeary's words. Then he said, "This is going to sound completely off the wall, but is it possible to predict a stock market crash like Freefall Friday, several months before it happens?"

McGeary's answer was not what Hansen expected. "There's a tiny movement among some traders who believe that 'chaos theory' and artificial intelligence may provide a way of predicting general market trends. I know Joe Money believes in the Elliott Wave theory, for example. But my personal belief is that predicting stock market crashes is probably not technically feasible."

"And what if I told you that Tom Bingham wrote down a prediction of Freefall Friday and guessed the day it would happen?"

"Is that really 'what if,' or did it actually happen?"

"It actually happened."

"Two things come to mind. One, I'd say you're full of crap, because like most lawyers, Tom was utterly gripless when it came to real trading. And two, whether he did or not shouldn't be your concern."

"Why not?"

"Why not?" McGeary dried his hands with a paper towel and approached Hansen with a serious expression. "Because the SEC is coming Monday and my Irish ass is on the line. Right now, Gil McGeary should be your number-one concern, Counselor, not whether your dead predecessor was the Amazing Kreskin. Now, let's get back to the festivities, shall we?"

McGeary did a slam-dunk of the balled-up paper towel into the brimming refuse basket and rambled out of the washroom. Rick watched the door swinging back and forth with a loud, dry squeaking. The lawyer thought, *Yeah, you know, he's absolutely right.*

Seventeen

MANHATTAN
FORT WORTH, TEXAS
Monday, February 8

"AT THIS TIME, I intend to open the record."

Donald Neufeld's words broke the tense presession silence in the Antwerp Conference Room of Wolcott Fulbright's offices, startling the young vanilla-skinned, redheaded stenographer who had been staring openly at Rick Hansen. The stenographer promptly snapped into a stiff-backed, professional demeanor. "I'm ready," she said, her fingers poised over the twenty-two phonetic keys of the stenotype machine.

"Are you ready, Mike?" Neufeld asked.

"We're ready, Don," Kilmartin replied.

From that point on, the pretty stenographer fixed her vision sightlessly at a painting on the wall, her fingers quietly clacking out a phonetic transcription of the proceedings. Depressing as many as six keys simultaneously, she generated a phonetic record of the following proceeding at a speed of 250 words a minute.

> MR. NEUFELD: *My name is Donald Neufeld. I'm a senior counsel on the New York staff of the Market Regulation Division of the Securities & Exchange Commission. With me today is Mary Reilley, vice president of the division, and Rhonda Barrimore, assistant counsel to the division. Mr. McGeary, I would like to read you a statement at this time.*
>
> MR. McGEARY: *Shoot.*
>
> MR. NEUFELD: *Any statement you make during the course of an investigation constitutes a statement to the commission. You may be fined, censured, suspended or barred if you are adjudged to have intentionally made a misstatement during this proceeding. Do you understand that, Mr. McGeary?*

MR. McGEARY: Yes, I do.

MR. NEUFELD: You have the right to be represented by counsel. Are you represented by counsel today?

MR. McGEARY: I am.

MR. NEUFELD: Would counsel please state their names for the record?

MR. KILMARTIN: I am Michael Kilmartin, Associate General Counsel for the firm of Wolcott, Fulbright & Company.

MR. HANSEN: Richard Hansen, Assistant Vice President and Trading Counsel to the Equity Derivatives Group of Wolcott, Fulbright & Company.

MR. NEUFELD: This proceeding is being stenographically recorded in its entirety. A verbatim transcription will be provided to you within ten days of this proceeding. It is very important that you understand the questions we are asking you today. If you do not understand a particular question, please tell us and we will gladly repeat the question. Do you understand that?

MR. McGEARY: I do.

MR. NEUFELD: Please state your full name for the record.

MR. McGEARY: Gilbert Scott McGeary.

MR. NEUFELD: What is your home address?

MR. McGEARY: 9 Whispering Pines Road, Greenwich, Connecticut.

MR. NEUFELD: Are you married?

MR. McGEARY: Yes, I am. Two kids.

MR. NEUFELD: Please review for us, briefly, your employment history.

MR. McGEARY: For three years, I was first baseman and clean-up hitter for the Toledo Mud Hens in the International League, a farm club to the—

MR. NEUFELD: I'm sorry. Let me clarify the previous question. Securities-related employment history only, please.

MR. McGEARY: Okay, sure. Four years in the equity derivatives group of Goldman, Sachs. Five years with Wolcott as a managing director and head of equity derivatives desk.

MR. NEUFELD: As head of the desk, how many people report to you?

MR. McGEARY: Somewhere between twenty-three and twenty-seven, I think.

MR. NEUFELD: You don't know how many people report to you?

MR. McGEARY: Head count is a moving target in this business, so I'm never certain.

MR. NEUFELD: Okay. Mr. McGeary, what was the basis for your sending $2.7 billion worth of stock index–related sell orders down to the *floor on the exchange through SuperDOT on the morning of Friday, January 29?*

MR. McGEARY: *Sorry. Would you repeat the question?*

MR. NEUFELD: *Certainly. What was your investment strategy for entering sell orders through SuperDOT representing a face value of $2.7 billion?*

MR. McGEARY: *Whoa. Wait a minute, time out. Can we go off the record?*

MR. NEUFELD: *We will take a short recess at the request of the respondent.*

"We are now off the record," Neufeld announced.

"Okay," McGeary said. "We're not being transcribed now?"

"No," said Neufeld. "We're off the record."

"Not all those customer orders were mine."

"They're not?" Neufeld frowned. "According to the stock exchange's records, you're responsible for this activity."

"All I'm saying is that I didn't put down that many orders through the program trading systems. Sure, I put down a shitload of orders, but not *billions* of dollars' worth. Half a billion, tops."

Kilmartin blanched at the obscenity before officials from the SEC. "Don, I think we would like some time to confer privately with Mr. McGeary before we resume the proceedings."

"That's fine," Neufeld replied. "Fifteen minutes?"

"That should be enough, thank you."

Minutes later, the three Wolcott employees conferred in a small pantry away from the conference room. They spoke in hushed tones, yet their voices reverberated softly off the tile walls.

Kilmartin asked, "Now what were you saying out there?"

"Just like I told Neufeld, those weren't my trades." As he spoke, McGeary helped himself to a Styrofoam cup of coffee. "You want some?"

Hansen and Kilmartin shook their heads no. Hansen asked, "What about the orders you and I sent to the floor on Friday morning?"

"Like I said, those amounted to only about four, five hundred million dollars. That's one *sixth* of what they said I executed."

Kilmartin frowned. "Who else at the firm is authorized to enter trades through the firm's program trading systems?"

"Beats the hell out of me. I thought I was the only game in town. But that's not my worry."

"I guess it's not."

"I mean, if those are not Gil McGeary's customers' trades, then I am off the hook. Right?"

Mike Kilmartin massaged his nose contemplatively. "I think that's right."

"Whoopee." McGeary gulped his coffee happily. "Can I go back upstairs and trade now?"

———•———

Colbert was on a business trip to Fort Worth, Texas, anxiously awaiting the call in his suite in the Four Seasons. The financier had systematically looted an insurance company he controlled over the last three years and he was working with the lawyers in an attempt to force the company into bankruptcy protection. The creditors were screaming bloody murder, the bankruptcy judge was a card-carrying member of the Old Boy Network and the whole thing was turning into a shitstorm. Besides, he had David Rosenberg and Dartmouth to contend with on Wednesday. He wasn't in the mood for a delay in the report from New York.

When the satellite uplink finally occurred and his digital phone twittered, he picked up immediately. "Yes."

"It's me," Stiletto said.

"You're a half-hour later than scheduled."

"I got pulled into a meeting. It happens, you know."

Colbert suppressed his anxiety. "How did it go?"

"I think they're satisfied for now. We informed them that they were all customer trades and that they were done by a third-party broker-dealer simply using our electronic trading access lines for a fee."

"That was good enough?"

"As long as they're all customer orders, it is. There's no law against foreign institutions selling their stock, either by computer or by telephone, even if it results in a decline in the market."

"Unless the activity is fraudulent, or fictitious," Colbert reminded him.

"Of course," Stiletto said. "But Infinity's books and records display legitimate activity by offshore customers that are fully capitalized, legal entities. Your records do show that, right?"

"Yes. The records Bingham had us create are meticulous."

"I thought so. Also, Infinity is not a member of the exchange, and your so-called 'customers' are all foreign, so there is little the regulators can do except ask the question. The question has been asked and answered."

"Good. I trust your judgment."

Stiletto continued, "It also helps that the vast majority of sell orders were spread around with dealers primarily outside the U.S. There's nothing out there to tie the activity to LINDA. Sure, ours was a big trade, and it moved the market, but you have to look at it in context. On an average trading day, this firm processes nineteen thousand customer and firm trades, worth around thirty billion billions. On Freefall Friday, the volume of Wolcott's equity trades was more than twice that number. You see what I mean?"

"Yes, yes, I do. What about internally? Are our friends in Internal Audit asking any questions?"

"Well, not Internal Audit so much. Legal's not happy about it. Kilmartin, as usual. There's also a new lawyer that was hired to replace Bingham and he's very curious about Tommy's Canadian trades."

"Is that right? What's this lawyer's name?"

"Hansen. Richard Hansen. Goes by the name Rick."

"Is it possible Kilmartin or Hansen could detect the trading?"

"No. It's concealed in a dormant test account that hasn't been used in six years. No one at the firm even knows of its existence. Not even Kilmartin could find it."

"That lawyer in Bingham's shoes could cause us problems," Colbert said. "We should be prepared to take decisive action, if the need arises."

Stiletto cursed in exasperation. "Jesus H. Christ, just what we need, another death in the Legal Department. The police are not going to disregard the coincidence of a *third* death in the department."

"All I meant was that we could reactivate the surveillance mechanisms we had in place to monitor Kilmartin's and Bingham's activities. It would be no effort at all. In fact, we should be watching Kilmartin anyway. Anything could happen in six weeks. Maybe your security people could loan us a set of Hansen's fingerprints so we could perform a little due diligence, just to be on the safe side."

"You're a paranoia junkie." Stiletto snorted in amusement.

You are one to talk, my friend, Colbert said to himself in an unspoken retort. The insistence on this bullshit code name Stiletto, even on the secure, scrambled satellite cellular system—*that* was the epitome of paranoia.

Stiletto said, "Send one of your goons to Reception at close of business Monday. It'll be waiting there under the usual name."

"Good. On a more personal note, if I may, where's your head these days?"

"My head?"

"Yes. Is your head still in the game?"

"Yes, of course it is. Why wouldn't you think so?"

"We go back a number of years, you and I," Colbert said, enjoying himself. Stiletto never squandered a chance to remind Colbert how he had helped him build his first fortune. Colbert was all too happy now to turn the tables. "So I tell you this as a friend. You know they are going to screw you in the public offering. They've all but told you this. Despite all you've done for the organization, the revenue you've generated, this is how it ends for you at Wolcott Fulbright, this is their way—"

"Okay, okay." Stiletto cut him off. "There's no need for you to *manipulate* me," he said dryly. "I'm fully committed to seeing this thing through. You should know that by now."

Colbert smiled. "I do, but I'm the type that needs reassurance every once in a while. The paranoia junkie, remember? On a different subject, that professor of ours bought the farm in Pennsylvania the other day."

Stiletto was silent for a moment. "Well, he had to go, didn't he?" There was another silence. "That couldn't happen to me, could it? I mean, like I said, my head's in the game, I'm fully committed to this thing."

Colbert grinned as he sidestepped the question. "Stiletto, the next wire transfer should hit your account on Monday morning. Please confirm upon receipt. Good night." Colbert rang off and laughed. No, he could foresee no reason to kill Stiletto, it would serve no purpose. But why should he clue him in on that? *Now who's the paranoia junkie?*

Eighteen

"THIS IS THE FINAL VERSION of the press release." Debbie Diamond opened her Coach leather portfolio and withdrew copies of the two-page blurb. She slid them to her clients on the other side of the conference table. "Of course, this would have to be vetted by Stone's lawyers, but this draft incorporates all of your modifications."

"Let's have a look," David Rosenberg said. Rosenberg produced an index card from his breast pocket and began line-by-lining the press release. A few words into the first paragraph, and he was already scribbling in some fresh changes to the text. Debbie looked at him and in her mind, she chided him affectionately. *David, David, David. Even to the end, so maddeningly detail-oriented. So . . . anal!*

The press release announced that the Board of Directors had approved the sale of the Dartmouth Funds Group, a moderate-sized family of seven mutual funds holding assets of $13 billion. David Rosenberg, thirty-eight, and Kendra Price, thirty-five, were stepping down from day-to-day management, effective at a date to be announced. If all went well in this morning's conference call, the Dartmouth Group would be sold to GoldBridge Capital Advisors, LLC, a Florida-based money management firm, for $274 million. The going rate for fund assets was $1 for every $50 under management. GoldBridge had offered a slight premium above the market, with incentive bonuses meant to accelerate the transaction. David and Kendra's personal could be up to $127 million. Not a bad payday for just over three years' worth of work.

As Kendra and David silently read over the piece, Debbie strolled over to the picture window. She gazed out at the flat line infinity of the horizon beyond Baltimore's Inner Harbor and silently contemplated the fortune of her star clients. Clearly, Dartmouth had been the benefactor of a historically unprecedented stock market boom, one that had lavishly rewarded those with vision and an appetite for risk. David Rosenberg and Kendra Price had both. Three and a half years ago—before they were even married to one another—the two were rising-star fund managers at Fidelity in Boston, whose equity funds were ranked in the top 20 percent of the Morningstar rankings. Shortly after management of the coveted Magellan Fund went to Rosenberg's rival, Jeff Vinik, David and Kendra combined forces and engaged a small leverage buyout firm to help them ferret out opportunities to purchase the assets of funds that were either financially floundering or in regulatory hot water with the SEC. The quiltwork result was the Baltimore-based Dartmouth Group, which in three short years had jumped from $3.5 billion in assets to $13 billion.

Debbie had been the outside attorney for the start-up mutual fund venture. She was a so-called "40 Act" practitioner, meaning she specialized in the arcane area of securities law relating to mutual funds and investments advisers. The meat and potatoes for Debbie and her two junior lawyers at the Baltimore law firm of Tresser & Greyrock entailed pushing a lot of regulatory papers out the door to Washington and Rockville, Maryland (to the SEC and the NASD, respectively). With the ascendancy of the mutual fund industry, Debbie's billables had soared in the last five years, and she found herself turning away work. Yet this was the first time she was involved in handling the sale of a mutual fund family to another party. Truthfully, she felt out of her element, but at the end of the day, she would see it through.

It amazed Debbie Diamond that you could actually "sell" a family of mutuals funds to another party. After all, mutual funds were nothing more than other people's money, weren't they? But the deal was progressing at a velocity that left Debbie unsettled. Suddenly, it was the bottom of the ninth inning and the deal just might get closed that morning. The dueling control-freak male egos of David Rosenberg and Charles Stone diminished the lawyer's role in this transaction from an active negotiator to a mere paper-producer. Oddly, Stone never had legal counsel participating on his speakerphone when he talked, and on more than one occasion he referred to lawyers as "bottom-feeders." If he was purposely trying to alienate Debbie Diamond from the deal, Stone had succeeded.

Kendra Price tilted her head and bit her lower lip. "I think it's an improvement over the previous version, don't you, David?"

Rosenberg shrugged. "Yeah, it gets our history at Fidelity right this time." He drummed his fingers on the conference room table. "I would still like to see you use my idea for the headline, 'ROSENBERG AND PRICE CASH OUT BIG TIME.' "

"Oh, stop it, you," Kendra said, playfully. Kendra was elated over the deal; it was as if she had been breathing helium instead of the recirculated air of the conference room.

Junior lawyer Claire Hollingsworth angled her head into the room. "Hi, guys."

"Hello, Claire," Kendra said brightly.

"It's Mr. Stone. Shall I swing him into the conference room?"

"Please," Debbie Diamond said officiously, feeling a jolt of deal nerves.

"It's showtime at the Apollo," Rosenberg muttered. His placid demeanor was betrayed by his jaw muscles, which were twitching uncontrollably.

Seconds later, Charles Stone hooked up on the ProCom SoundStation speakerphone. David said, "Good morning, Charles. How's the weather in London?"

Stone's voice was terse. "If it's all the same to you, Mr. Rosenberg, I'd prefer to dispense with the weather and get to business."

Rosenberg's eyebrows climbed his head in mock hurt. "Be my guest."

"What do we need to close the deal *right now*? The number is acceptable, I know that much."

"Yes. The number is not at issue."

"Then tell me how we make this deal happen."

David Rosenberg made an open-palm gesture to his wife and business partner, indicating it was her turn. Kendra cleared her throat and spoke into the honeycomb grill of the speakerphone. "Hello, Mr. Stone, this is Kendra Price speaking."

"Yes, Ms. Price."

"We'd like to be retained as consultants for a period of six months."

"Consultants?"

"Yes, for a . . . a reasonable time so we can ease the transition for our fundholders."

Stone's voice was flat. "You're demanding the right to stay on and have investment discretion for half a year."

"That's correct," Kendra said.

"If you deduct $35 million from the purchase price, I might consider it."

"What?" Kendra blurted in shock. "You mean you'd *deduct* $35 million for our services?"

"That's right, Ms. Price. Yes, granted, you and Mr. Rosenberg have attained solid returns for your investors over the last three years. But with all due respect, this bull market could make gurus out of chimps throwing darts at the stock tables."

"That's not right," Debbie Diamond said in defense of her clients.

"Yes it is." David Rosenberg contradicted his lawyer with a smile. He was actually *amused* by Stone's outrageous put-down.

Stone continued, "We have invested millions developing a computer-driven strategy that employs artificial intelligence and fuzzy logic in trading decisions. We believe the market is due for another downturn that will make Freefall Friday look like an ice cream social. Our team is confident our 'black-box' technology will provide better, dispassionate decisions for investors, particularly in down markets."

Rosenberg stabbed the mute button and gloated at his wife. "See, I told you he wouldn't go for that."

Kendra stuck her tongue out at him, not unaffectionately.

"Are you still there?" Stone asked, impatiently.

Rosenberg opened up the microphone. "Okay, Charles, we can live without that."

"Fine. Next item?"

It was Debbie's turn. "Well, honestly, we're concerned with the aggressiveness of your time frame for taking over the funds—"

"Who is this, the lawyer?"

"Yes." Debbie was put off by his tone of condescension.

"And your concerns are what, exactly, Ms. Diamond?"

"There are certain regulatory filings we would need to effect a change of control. We would have an SEC problem if we ignored that—"

"That's an incorrect statement according to my legal counsel, Ms. Diamond. The SEC problem would be *ours*, not yours."

"Still," Debbie maintained, "there are papers to be filed."

"My lawyers have already drawn up the amended Form N-1A Registration Statement. That should allay your concerns under the Investment Company Act of 1940, right?"

"Yes, but—"

"Once we come to an agreement in principle, my counsel will hand-deliver the N-1A to the Commission."

"Still, we need time to notify our shareholders of the change of control."

"GoldBridge will be responsible for that."

"We've already prepared a press release for the financial media, which we'll include with the February statements."

"That's unacceptable," Stone said. "To do that prematurely might trigger massive fund redemptions. We would want a period of three months to build a track record before announcing."

Debbie Diamond said, "I'm not certain we can live with that."

"Neither can GoldBridge, Ms. Diamond. That would be a deal-breaker, unless you want to indemnify us for the risk that investors pull out of the fund."

David Rosenberg leaned forward and jumped in before Debbie could counter. "Listen, Charles, we're all reasonable people here. We can live with sixty days' notification, but I can't see pushing it back any further."

"I can do better than that. How about March 31, which is six weeks away?" Stone asked.

"Even better."

"Then we're done?"

"I think we're done," David Rosenberg said.

"Congratulations," Charles Stone said.

———•———

Shortly thereafter, the chilled champagne was flowing into the clear plastic cups. Twenty people from the law firm packed the conference room to toast the now-fabulously-wealthy clients they were about to lose. Deb Diamond's junior associates, Claire Hollingsworth and Rosemary Coogan, and the paralegals and the secretaries were all there, of course. Managing Partner Bill Tresser showed up to kiss the ring of the Dartmouth duo. Even the mailroom guys sneaked in for a cup of bubbly. And though everyone was elated the deal was sealed, no one was more so than the usually low-key David Rosenberg. Debbie Diamond noticed that Kendra was surprisingly downbeat.

Later, she overheard the heated exchange between the two in a corner of the conference room that unmasked her angst.

Kendra said, "You couldn't wait to pull the trigger."

David replied, "C'mon, sweetheart, it was time to close."

"GoldBridge takes control of the funds next *Monday*. The investors have a right to know—"

"Kendra, that deal point was a *dealbreaker*. Besides, it's only a few weeks we're talking about here."

Kendra Price stared at the bubbles spiralling up from the bottom of her cup of champagne. "Still, our investors have the right—"

"No, Kendra," David Rosenberg firmly corrected his partner both in business and holy matrimony. "They're not ours anymore. They're *GoldBridge's* investors now. Get used to it."

Nineteen

"RICK, YOU'VE GOT TO BE KIDDING. You can't possibly be that indispensable to the firm."

"What can I say, Steph?" Rick Hansen looked across the table at his wife and spread his hands helplessly. "The work's piling up faster than I can keep up with it. I've got to go in and do some mop-up work."

"So you're going to leave your pregnant wife on a Saturday and go in to the office?" Stephanie Hansen pouted theatrically.

Rick kept his voice low so the other people having brunch at Madison Café couldn't engage in the favorite pastime of New Yorkers—eavesdropping. "Do you think I want to go in on a *Saturday*? It's not a choice. I *have* to."

"I know. But that doesn't mean I have to like it."

"It'll only be a few hours," he promised.

"Right. On the believability scale that's right up there with the check is in the mail," she smirked.

Rick found himself staring at his wife. Stephanie Hansen was certainly what some on Wall Street would refer to as a trophy wife, an elegant creature of grace and intelligence, passion and compassion. She possessed an unexpectedly exotic sensuality for her born-and-bred-in-Briarcliff-Manor pedigree—a shimmering lioness' mane of honey-blond hair, ocean-blue eyes and sensual pouting lips that left him mesmerized whenever she spoke. But he loved her for her mind too. Stephanie was an incorrigible romantic, the type of woman who clung steadfastly to the hope that all would be forgiven between Carly Simon and James Taylor so they could get back together and begin recording duets like "Mockingbird" again. He knew she secretly maintained a journal in which she meticulously recorded anecdotes of how ordinary singles met and fell in love in modern-day Manhattan, which she hoped would be published one day.

The story of the couple's first encounter four years before was worthy of inclusion in her book.

At that time, Stephanie Bloomfield was the chairperson of a seventy-five-dollar-a-plate benefit for the Hale House, a Harlem-based charity for victims of pediatric AIDS. Richard Hansen, a first-year associate out of Fordham Law School, was roped into volunteering for the steering committee of the fund-raiser by a junior partner at his firm, who'd known the charity to be a favorite of a valued client. The client happened to be Stephanie's boss in the promotions division of Sony Records' jazz label. The instant Rick and Stephanie met, a bright wobble of sexual energy passed between the two. She would later describe it to her friend Traci as "spontaneous combustion."

The sold-out event was held at the Puck Building on a rainy Saturday night in September. Throughout the course of that evening, Rick and Stephanie found themselves unable to resist the mysterious chemistry that drew them to one another like lonely moths drawn to a warm light. The breezy effortlessness of their give-and-take was refreshing to Stephanie, who until then had endured an aggravating string of vainglorious blind dates who monopolized conversation with self-possessed speeches studded with *I*'s and *me*'s. Not only did Rick take a genuine interest in what *she* had to say, he asked for her opinion on what *he* had to say.

Rick and Stephanie swizzled French champagne and danced to Motown most of the night. As the evening steadily depleted, their discourse ventured into ever more intimate regions: family dynamics, misspent childhoods, abandoned dreams and the treacheries of single life in Manhattan. The more they talked, the more they realized they were, in many ways, yin-yang opposites of the other. She was humanitarian, while he was capitalistic. She was artistic, he was financial. She was West Village and he was Upper East Side. They were a promising match, they sensed, in that each one provided the puzzle pieces missing in the other's existence.

The party ended, a rousing success by all measures. Rick and Stephanie ignored the fact that they inhabited opposite corners of the island, sharing a cab home from the Puck Building. Even at 2:30 A.M., the lights of the city that never sleeps were fully ablaze, casting a gleam on the rain-slicked streets. A steady drizzle drummed upon the roof of the taxicab. Rick's hand sought out Stephanie's hand, and she didn't resist. They lapsed into a companionable silence, savoring the elation brought on by an unexpectedly promising start in the urban mating ritual.

They kissed in the backseat outside Stephanie's building on Jane Street for several minutes until the cabdriver scowled impatiently and bleated his horn.

After their first two dates, Stephanie surprised Rick at work with a call wishing him a happy twenty-fifth birthday. (To this day, Rick still had no clue as to how she figured out when it was.)

On their fourth date, they dined at Windows on the World, consumed two bottles of De Boeuf Merlot and returned to Stephanie's studio apartment. There, they ritualistically undressed one another in the pale autumn moonlight, taking each step slowly, as if unwrapping a series of gifts. Making love for the first time was indeed a five-star event, supercharged with pent-up passion and an urgent, mutual desire to forge into the frontier of sexual intimacy.

Within the year, Rick proposed to her on bended knee at the top of the Eiffel Tower. It was an offer Stephanie couldn't refuse.

Two years after that, on the Fourth of July weekend at a bed-and-breakfast in the Berkshires, Rick made his young wife weep with joy when he whispered to her his desire to make a baby with her.

Three weeks of trying. Then they were expecting.

Seven months later and, well, here they were.

"Hey, the baby's moving," Stephanie said suddenly, jolting Rick back to reality. "Want to feel a kick?"

"Sure," Rick said, moving around to her side of the table to cop a feel of Baby X.

As soon as he got there, she not-so-playfully kicked him in the shin.

"Ouch, Stephanie," Rick protested. "That really hurts."

"So does loneliness," she replied.

———•———

Everyone in the business world has a horror story involving a temporary worker. Rick Hansen just happened to have more than his share. At the two law firms where he'd worked before joining Wolcott, he'd gained a reputation as a lightning rod for wacky temps. First, there was the unemployed opera singer who practiced her chops in the ladies' washroom. The acupuncture dude who was caught downloading sensitive client information onto floppy disks. The Grateful Deadhead groupie who was doing bong-hits in the conference room one night was now permanently part of the firm's folklore.

Cliff Weiner was okay, as far as temps went. His nuttiness factor certainly clocked in well above average, but he always got the work done and that was 90 percent of the battle. Yet Cliff Weiner was cut from strictly "temporary" cloth and had positively no shot at scoring a full-time support position at a conservative mecca of global finance like Wolcott Fulbright. It wasn't simply that Wolcott preferred to hire trim, smart women fresh out of college for those positions; it was also that Cliff Weiner and his ilk possessed not a clue about the unwritten code of Wall Street Corporate Culture and didn't care to understand it. His preferred hairstyle was too funky for the taste of the firm, his dress too "East Village," his demeanor too flip, his attitude too lackadaisical. If plopped down on a trading floor, the business people would slice him and dice him like a pack of piranhas. As a temporary support person who knew just enough Microsoft Word to slip by, Cliff Weiner bounced around from assignment to assignment without any possibility of full-time hire. The arrangement worked for both parties satisfactorily, though Cliff made no secret of his desire to settle down and be attached to just one principal.

The phone rang. The pizza Rick ordered had arrived. Hansen swung his feet off the desk, walked out of his office and met the sullen deliveryman with the bristly facial hair from Ray Bari's at the security checkpoint, paid for the pizza and walked it over to the workstation where Cliff Weiner was situated.

Cliff Weiner was chattering on the phone, which he had been doing passionately since he settled in at the workstation shortly after 9:15 A.M. But as long as the work was getting done, Hansen didn't particularly mind (it was, after all, a Saturday). When Hansen arrived at Weiner's work area with the steaming box of cheese pizza with mushrooms balanced on his fingertips, the temp appeared to be busy at the keyboard. Drawing closer, however, he realized Weiner was actually playing Solitaire for Windows, using the mouse to move virtual playing cards rather than text. Hansen shook his head. By building Solitaire and Mine Sweeper into the Windows operating software, Bill Gates had probably cost American businesses a half-billion hours in lost productivity every year.

"I'm not here to lie to you, *girlfriend*!" Cliff Weiner cheerfully said to the party at the other end of the line. "My roomie owes me three months' worth of back rent! . . . Well, of course I've confronted her about it. I said to the little bitch, 'Honey, you make a lot more money than me, stripping for those horny businessmen at that sleazy strip club of yours off Broadway. Where's all that money go, up your nose?' . . . Wait, wait, I'm getting to that . . . so she goes, 'Would you be willing to take it in trade,' and I go, 'Honey, what on earth is *that* supposed to mean?' And she goes, can she screw me for the value of the back rent? Is she barking up the wrong tree or what?" At that point, Cliff noticed Hansen standing nearby with lunch. "Whoops, gotta go, girrrrlfriend." Cliff promptly slammed the phone down. He clasped his hands together, as if in delight, whirled around to face Rick, saying, "Is it really lunchtime already? Good Lord in His infinite wisdom, I am famished!"

Over the next twenty minutes in the conference room, Hansen learned a great deal more than he needed to know about his talkative temp. Cliff Weiner had an uncanny knack for monopolizing conversation and Hansen, having consorted with attorneys over the better part of the last decade, had been acquainted with some world-class windbags in his time. Cliff was a contender for the crown.

Accordingly, it came as no surprise that Cliff Weiner was, in fact, a SAG/AFTRA-card-carrying *actor*. His self-christened stage name was actually "Cliff Chances" ("As in take a *chance* on a me," the actor-temp trilled). He proudly showed off his T-shirt, which said, WILL DO SUMMER STOCK FOR FOOD. Everything about him pronounced, *I am an actor*. The exaggerated gestures, affected mannerisms and, above all, the voice—their sum personified the contradictory persona of the prototypical struggling New York City actor—hopelessly in love with himself and at the same time despising his daily failure to attain the fame he so richly deserved. Weiner was short—skinny and pale with white-blond eyelashes, eyebrows and facial hair. He sported a hip retro-haircut calculated to make his straw-colored hair as fashionable as possible, a sort of Albino-chic. He compensated for his physical shortcomings and insecurities by projecting himself to the world in an in-your-face manner; he was a relentlessly perky bundle of energy.

"I *love* acting because it gives you an opportunity to reinvent yourself," he announced around a mouthful of pizza. "At all times, you are another person, even if you are not on a stage or before a camera. Of course, as a career, acting pays palm reader's wages. I detest that 'starving artist' persona, so I do *this* during daylight hours." He made a face of distaste for his role as a temp. "But I can't complain. Wall Street's not so bad. I get to work with nice people like you. I can't exactly sell my body to pay for head shots and voice lessons. And I'm lucky enough to be a working actor by night."

"Are you in something I would know?" Hansen asked politely.

"Actually, I'm an understudy for an off-off-off-off Broadway musical called *Schoolhouse Rock—Live!*"

"*Schoolhouse Rock?* You mean, based on the Saturday morning cartoons?"

"One and the same! You know, those three-minute cartoons ABC wedged in between *Fat Albert* and *Hong Kong Phooey? 'I'm just a Bill/yeah, only a Bill/and I'm sitting here on Capitol Hill/Well, it's a long, long journey/ to the Capitol City/It's a long, long wait while I'm sitting in Committee/But I know I'll be law someday/At least I hope and I pray that I will/But today*

I'm still just a Bill!" Once he finished, Weiner had a good laugh over his own over-the-top hambone performance. "Enough about you, let's talk about me, why don't we? What is your story, anyway, Mr. Wall Street Lawyer?"

"Actually, if you don't mind," Hansen said, "let's talk about Tom Bingham's story."

Weiner shook his head in pity. "God rest his soul. I don't mean to speak ill of the dead, but I can't say I'm entirely shocked that Tom took the Nestea plunge."

"Why's that?"

"The guy was wired to detonate. I mean, he was like an alarm clock wound too tightly."

"A lot of people on Wall Street are driven."

"True, but Tom was different. One minute he was Prince Charming. The next he was Mr. Screaming-Foaming-at-the-Mouth-Mental-Patient-Man. Tough guy to please. Not like you."

"So you're not surprised that Tom took his own life?"

Cliff Weiner paused and contemplated the ceiling. "Well, no. He didn't seem *despondent* if that's what you mean. The guy was *agitated*. Always on top of me to make certain I was doing what he'd told me. Taskmaster, and *nasty* about it. Mr. Bingham seemed like he was under constant pressure, which I guess he was, otherwise he wouldn't have been working every weekend."

"What was he working on?"

"He never told me. But you ask me, I think it was a book."

Hansen leaned forward. "A book? What sort of book?"

"I'm a dummy when it comes to this stuff, you have to forgive me, but I think it was a history of stock market crashes. He mostly had me inputting long passages he'd highlighted in dozens of books."

"Stock market crashes?"

"Yeah."

"What about them?"

"Like studies of how the stock market crash of 1987 happened, how it could happen again."

Hansen tipped back in his chair. Was that what this was all about? A book on stock market crashes? Had Bingham done his research so thoroughly that he had created a system that predicted stock market crashes? Like Freefall Friday? "Did all of that material get saved somewhere?"

"Lord, yes."

"Is it here, on this floor?"

"God, no. I archived it the last time I was here, the week before

Thanksgiving. I could print you out a list of all the files I sent there, if you want. It's on the system under the Legal Temp 6 password."

"That'd be terrific," Hansen said.

"You know, if you really want to get the dirty lowdown on the man, you ought to consider talking to his ex-wife."

"You did say Bingham was married?"

"Yes, but not happily." Weiner dipped into the box and scooped up the last triangle of pizza. He held it aloft. "You mind?"

"Not at all. I've had my fill."

Cliff Weiner produced a yellow Lands' End canvas duffel from beneath his chair, into which Hansen expected the part-time actor to insert the pizza. But to his amazement, when Weiner unzipped the bag, the furry white head of a three-year-old Shih-Tzu toy dog blossomed from the opening. The dog yipped happily at the sight of the light and Weiner cooed to it in gooey baby talk. Weiner pushed clots of cheese and tomato sauce to the Shih-Tzu's snout, the dog responded with happy darts of his little pink tongue that picked Weiner's fingertips clean.

"This little fella's name is Peaches," Weiner burbled in baby talk. "My best friend in the entire world."

Rick Hansen didn't doubt it for a minute.

Twenty

VIKTOR ALEXEYEV ENTERED the River Room restaurant at the Savoy Hotel at precisely 8:00 A.M. In his left hand, he clutched a thick manila envelope. He located Colbert at a secluded table with an enviable view of the Thames River churning powerfully below. Alexeyev absently adjusted his tie and made his way over to his employer.

"Good morning," Colbert said.

"Morning," Alexeyev said. He made no effort to shake hands with Colbert; his employer harbored a intense phobia for germs. Colbert's aversion had become something of a running joke between Alexeyev and his operatives.

Alexeyev took the chair opposite Colbert and spread the cloth napkin over his lap. Instantly, a formal British waiter swirled about the table, placing a glass of water within Alexeyev's reach. Without consulting the menu, the Russian security expert ordered runny fried eggs, potatoes and black coffee.

Once the waiter disappeared, Colbert got right to business. "I'm concerned about Pethers."

"You should be."

"Is that the surveillance tape?" Colbert inclined his head toward the manila envelope.

"Yes."

"I'd like to see it."

"You mean, now?"

"Yes." Colbert brought his attaché case up to his lap, unhooked the latches and produced a Sony CCD mini-video cassette player, which operated on lithium-ion batteries.

Alexeyev unsealed the envelope and handed the tape across the table. After loading it, Colbert cupped his hands around the screen to prevent the ambient light from diminishing the resolution of the picture. It was also meant to prevent a waiter from glimpsing the footage.

Colbert recoiled at the first image. The body of Professor Howard Gammage dangling from a length of rope in his bedroom closet in some quiet residential neighborhood in Pittsburgh. The corpse's nearly naked form glowed an unearthly alabaster, as if radioactive. Alexeyev's camera lingered on him for a surreal length of time, as though titillated by the lifelessness of the subject.

"Jesus Christ, enough already." Colbert made no effort to conceal his disgust. He fast-forwarded the video, skipping through the scenes shot in Gammage's home—the various angles of the dead man's corpse (*three* in total), and the documents that Alexeyev and his associate recovered from the professor's home, then destroyed. As the tape sped forward, Colbert realized that this was not the original master tape, but a copy dubbed from a different format. Uneasily, he realized the vulnerability of having Alexeyev control that original, but—

Suddenly, a bar of static rolled up on the screen, indicating a sequence of a different time and place. Graham Pethers's lanky figure filled the 3-inch liquid crystal screen. The picture quality was not good, its resolution compromised by its clandestine nature. But it was unmistakably Pethers. A date and time stamp at the top indicated the tape was made over the weekend of February 6.

Colbert exhaled. "Tell me what's going on."

"Kravchenko and Chernigov undertook twenty-four-hour surveillance of the target on Monday, as per your request." Alexeyev paused to light a cigarette. There was something oddly feminine in the way he held it, Colbert thought. "On Friday, Dmitri tailed him to Newark Airport. Do you see his companion on the screen yet? He should be coming into the picture right around now."

"Yes, I see him now," Colbert said. The camera bobbled a bit as it captured a youngish-looking American with a mustache and an Adidas overnight bag coming up to Pethers. He and the Australian attorney clinched in a passionate embrace. "Who is this?"

"We learned through electronic surveillance that this is a lover. The credit card receipts we've obtained identify him as a man named Mark Erwin. We're doing a background check on him right now. Did you know the target was homosexual?"

"No, I didn't." Colbert smiled a little as he drank in the image on the screen. There were two vulnerabilities for the price of one. Pethers's sexual proclivity was one avenue; the other was to threaten the safety of his gay lover. This was good. "Where did they go?"

"Las Vegas, for a gambling trip. Or so it seemed." For the next few minutes, Viktor Alexeyev detailed the itinerary of the pair's three-day gambling weekend in Vegas. After a while, Colbert cut him off abruptly, "Frankly, I don't give a damn whether Pethers saw Siegfried and Roy. What I want to know, Viktor, is whether you found any additional vulnerabilities?"

Viktor Alexeyev sighed. With Colbert, it was always about *vulnerabilities*. "No. But something else you need to know about. Allow me." Alexeyev took the videocassette recorder and forwarded to a segment later in the tape. "On Sunday, Kravchenko tailed Pethers from the hotel. Pethers left his boyfriend behind to go to this exhibition, which I believe was the purpose of the trip." Parenthetically, he said, "This is Kravchenko's camerawork, please pardon its amateurishness." Colbert stared at the image of Pethers alighting from a cab, heading into the Las Vegas Convention Center. The sign indicated something called a "Gun, Knife and Military Show" was being held. For Colbert, Alexeyev's narrative faded to a hush as he watched Graham Pethers strolling through the huge expanse of the Expo Center, peering with interest at the pistols. Before Colbert's own eyes, the perceived threat had become real.

Then there was a shot of Pethers leaving the facility with a beer-bellied man of Native American descent. The man had a ponytail and unruly facial hair. Ponytail carried a duffel bag. Colbert leaned forward with interest, as he watched the two men step into a white Dodge pickup truck. "What are they doing?" Colbert asked.

"Here you see the man handing Pethers two weapons. The first one is a 9mm Glock 17L TacStar. The additional device he is affixing to the barrel is a LaserAim integral laser sight, best of its kind. The second one"—here, Alexeyev froze the frame showing the transaction—"is an Israeli-made FN Herstal P90 Personal Defense Weapon. A high-tech submachine gun. Very compact, and very lethal. The target paid the man with fifteen hundred-dollar bills."

Colbert rubbed his jaw thoughtfully. "He bought those when?"

"Two Sundays ago, February seventh."

"I see." Colbert looked at the frozen frame for some time. "You think he is arming himself to go to war with me?"

"You could draw such a conclusion, yes. He knows you have ordered others killed and he fears for his own life."

"As my personal security consultant, how do you think I should respond to the threat of a disenchanted business partner purchasing lethal weapons?"

Alexeyev shrugged. "Eliminate the threat. But it is up to you."

Breakfast was served and the men commenced the wordless routine of consuming their meals. The clatter of fine silverware against bone china and the murmured chorus of casual conversation filled the silence.

Colbert spoke at last. "Intensify your surveillance efforts on Pethers. By that, I mean electronic devices picking up all conversation, devices capturing outgoing facsimiles. Track his movements at all times. If he picks his nose, I want to know about it."

Alexeyev shrugged again. "Of course. It is already being done."

"Surveillance operations are being conducted on all of the Partners, I presume."

"Yes, of course."

Colbert nodded in apparent satisfaction. "On to new business then. I would like to resume surveillance on the lawyer in the New York headquarters."

"You mean Kilmartin."

"Yes, Mike Kilmartin. I'd be especially eager to hear of any *new* vulnerabilities."

"It will be done."

"And there's another attorney, a new hire, who has been hired to replace Bingham."

"Yes, we know. Richard Hansen."

Colbert wanted to know how he knew that, but it was bad form to ask. Like asking a magician the secret behind his magic trick. He suspected it had come from the tap on Stiletto's phone lines. "Stiletto will provide you with a set of his fingerprints, which will be waiting for you at the usual location. By week's end, I want to know the vulnerabilities of both subjects. After that, I'll decide to what extent we should monitor the new lawyer's activities."

"My friend, your demands are consuming a lot of resources," Alexeyev cautioned. "The bill for services is getting large."

"Not a concern. The cost of security was factored into the cost of each partnership unit," Colbert replied. Left unspoken was the paradox of partnership money being used to ensure the Partners themselves stayed in line. It was not Alexeyev's concern, not as long as TCI Investigations and Security Services got paid. And it always did, at least so far.

On the flight back to the States, Alexeyev briefly considered the nature of his business relationship with Colbert. It was not simple to define, symbiotic in many ways. On the other hand, Viktor always dropped everything to attend to every whim of Colbert's, no matter how insignificant the request. True, the Russian was annoyed that he had to round-trip it to London for a forty-five-minute meeting with Colbert that could have been conducted by telephone just as productively.

But Alexeyev was not in a position to decline such a meeting. It was like the old Russian proverb, *A cat always knows whose meat it eats.* In Alexeyev's case, it was Colbert's meat.

Twenty-one

CHELSEA AREA, MANHATTAN
Wednesday, February 17

AFTER FIELDING THE USUAL CADRE of phone calls, Hansen stepped out of the office at around 11:00. He told Cliff it was an early lunch. He caught the 1 train at Rector Street, rode it ten stops uptown and got off at the Twenty-eighth Street station. When he climbed to the surface, he found that the weather had turned atrocious. A stop-start wind cut through his trench coat, a fine sleet whipped against his face. Hunching in against the wind, he walked two blocks south, turning right at the Fashion Institute of Technology onto Twenty-sixth Street.

Chelsea Television Studios was located in a rough-and-tumble neighborhood, but the weather was too miserable for even the local toughs to be hanging out. A story-high banner proclaimed the facility to be home to *The Maury Povich Show*. A replica of Maury's crow-footed, beaming mug flapped animatedly in the wind.

He approached the purple-haired receptionist behind the vestibule. "My name is Rick Hansen. I'm here for an appointment with Elena Bingham."

Her chipper reply: "I'll let her know you're here, sir. Please have a seat." With that, the frazzled receptionist returned to the phones, which were blubbering off the hook three at a time. In an impossibly upbeat tone, she rapid-fire-answered the calls one after the other. "Chelsea Studios. I'm - sorry - but - Mr. - Bregman - is - in - a - meeting - I'll - put - you - through - to - his - voice - mail - thank - you." Click. "Chelsea Studios. I'm-sorry-but-Mr.-Rand-is-in-a-meeting-I'll-put-you-through-to-his voice - mail - thank - you." Click. "Chelsea Studios . . ."

An aspiring actress, Hansen guessed. *Trying to stay close to the action, maybe hoping to get discovered.* During the ten-minute wait in the pleasant, black-marble-and-chrome reception area, Rick inspected the myriad of autographed stills of Maury Povich on the walls and perused the back issues of *Post-Production Digest*. He was halfway through a positive review of the new state-of-the-art digital Ikegami HK studio cameras when the double doors from the production facility burst open.

"Richard?" a woman called out.

Hansen placed the trade publication back on the table and stepped forward. "Elena?"

"Yes."

"I'm Rick Hansen."

"Hello, Elena Bingham." They shook hands. Her palm was stress-sweaty, but her grip was firm and confident. Hansen gulped in a prompt first impression of Tom Bingham's ex-wife. Elena Bingham was slightly above her optimal weight, but in a way that lent her an indelible air of I'm-in-charge authority. She was done up in an Ann Taylor navy blue pantsuit and strategically conservative jewelry that emphatically set her apart from the technical crew. Elena had intelligent brown eyes behind trendy cat's-eyes glasses and highly moussed black curly hair that fell about her padded shoulders.

"I hope I'm not coming around at a bad time," Rick said.

"Oh, you definitely are." Elena smiled tightly and spoke in the machine-gun staccato of a super-stressed, type-A television producer. "Our LD has blown out three two-thousand-watt bulbs, I've learned that our on-air talent has none, and the Styrofoam setpiece with the logo of our new show dislodged and bonked our guest on the head. This is a very bad time, which makes it a very good time for us to speak. I've got about twenty minutes of downtime, so come up to the set and let's chat."

Elena punched in the security code of the double doors and led the way down a surprisingly dim corridor. Highly caffeinated video-production types bounded about the hallways like pinballs, rushing cartridges from one editing room to another. "If I'd known freelancing was gonna be like this, I never would've taken the buyout offer from Cap Cities."

"What do you do?" Hansen asked amiably.

"I'm an associate producer for my own production company, which essentially means I take any shoot offered to me." They rounded a corner and ascended a staircase that had a reddish glow from the lights indicating tapings-in-progress. Her voice echoed in the stairwell. "Today, we're on a ten-hour shoot for a pilot called *Your Money Tonite*. The backers have envisioned it as kind of like *Money Magazine* come to life. They're hoping MSNBC will pick it up. But the way this shoot-from-hell's going, not even the New York Sanitation Department would want to pick it up. It's almost enough to make me go into infomercials."

At the top of the stairs, Elena led him through the black double doors of Studio B and on to the set of *Your Money Tonite*. He was instantly hit by a chill; the air conditioning had been cranked up—no doubt to compensate for the heat thrown off by the thicket of multicolored, two-thousand-watt Arri spotlights suspended from the elevated ceiling like brilliant lollipops. The cloying smell of wood pulp filled the air, emanating from the freshly constructed sets. Fascinated by the process of creating a television show, Hansen craned his neck around, taking in the activity of the crew. As Elena had told him, the production was on downtime, with most of the crew members swilling coffee and discussing the new production facility CNBC had constructed in Secaucus. Four members of the crew were working with chicken wire and duct tape to cobble the blue-and-gold Styrofoam *Your Money Tonite* logo back into one piece. *No business like show business*, Hansen thought.

Elena Bingham took him into a nondescript Green Room that had no green to it. But it did have comfortable leather seats, a black statuette of a comic gargoyle and a mini-fridge stocked with spring waters and soda. She popped open two bottles of Naya and handed Hansen one. Rick sat down, staring at the gargoyle—the creature's expression reminded him of something or someone. He couldn't quite place it.

"So, Mr. Hansen," Elena Bingham said, "you wanted to talk to me about Tom."

Hansen said, "Thanks for agreeing to meet with me. I hope this isn't painful."

"My therapist actually thinks it's good therapy to talk it out," Elena said, coolly sipping her Naya from a plastic cup. "So what the hell, go ahead."

"I've got the job Tom used to have at Wolcott Fulbright."

"My condolences."

"The police ruled his death as, uh, self-inflicted, but there's some things that defy logic."

Elena leaned in. "Your theory is that my ex-husband did not commit suicide?"

Hansen drew back. "I'm not certain." Hansen briefed her on the discrepancies in Bingham's business records, the freak accident that killed his paralegal and the notation in the agenda.

"Kathleen Oberlin." Elena narrowed her eyes as she spoke the name. "She was fucking Tom, you know."

Hansen hesitated. "Yes, Elena. I knew that." He changed the subject. "The notation in the datebook refers to someone named Gammage. Had you ever heard him mention Gammage?"

"No."

"Were you aware of enemies Tom might have had?"

"Yes," she said with a straight face. "Himself."

"Himself?"

"Tom Bingham was a severe manic-depressive, Rick. Bipolar. Do you know what that is?"

"That's—a mood thing, I think. Has to do with swings in moods."

"That's right," Elena said, her tone becoming clinically quiet. "It's not a terribly uncommon ailment. Maybe one percent of the population has it. Tom used to call it his 'brilliant madness.' One of his quirks was a big-time superstition of the color red. Tom used to never permit anything red in the apartment."

"Was he on medication for it?"

"Oh yes. Lithonate, which is a lithium-based drug, and sometimes amitriptyline. Sometimes they were effective, sometimes they weren't. It killed our marriage."

"Tom's condition?"

"Absolutely," Elena said. "Tom was intense, very intense. He had this shell of privacy that no one could penetrate, not even me. Secret bank accounts and credit cards under assumed names. A hidden P.O. box. He had this whole secret life thing going. Bipolar or not, whatever, I finally got tired of the rages, the spending jags and the promiscuity. I finally hired an attorney and got out of a bad situation. Thank Christ we did not have kids." Elena Bingham lit a cigarette.

"So Tom was depressed all the time?"

"No, that's the misconception about manic-depression. When Tom wasn't depressed, he was absolutely ecstatic, dancing on the ceiling. He had delusions of grandeur, as they say, a belief he was invincible. Then, of course, it would come crashing down and he would be in a dark mood for days on end. I used to think Tom had just two faces—a happy face and a sad face. Nothing in-between."

"Did Tom ever talk about taking his own life?"

Elena mulled this over. "Not that I can recall. But that doesn't mean anything. Bipolars dream about death all the time. It's part of the chemical disorder. They say it doesn't take much to push one over the edge. Maybe this last time out, his make-a-million scheme went bust and I wasn't there to be his nursemaid. He kept saying this time his ship *really* was coming in, that he was going to be a multimillionaire by the spring. Tom Bingham's ship was coming in, all right, but the ship happened to be the *Titanic*." Elena Bingham sat back in her chair and exhaled. "I'm sorry, that wasn't very nice, was it?"

"You mentioned make-a-million schemes."

"Get-rich-quick schemes—lottery tickets, stock tips, ideas for inventions. A bestseller he was going to write. In the months after I left him, he would call me a dozen times a day to tell me what a mistake I had made leaving him. My own therapist actually thinks it was the 'false euphoria' a bipolar often experiences before making the decision to commit suicide."

"And he said this to you when?"

"Just before he died. October, November, I think."

"Could it have been the insider trading scheme he was talking about?"

"Probably, though he never really told me what he was cooking up." Elena's features crunched into a frown. "Tom had an addictive personality, you see, and gambling scared the daylights out of him. He *loved* the intense high of winning, and hated the feeling of losing. A sure thing was probably too good to pass up, even if it was illegal."

Hansen stared at the gargoyle in the corner. Macauley Culkin in *Home Alone*, he realized, the scene where he slaps the aftershave onto his cheeks. That's what the figurine reminded him of. "You know about Freefall Friday?"

"The recent stock market crash? Sure."

"What would you say if I told you that before his death, your ex-husband predicted the mini-crash of the stock market?"

She shrugged. "He was always predicting the stock market would crash. It was bound to happen."

"*To the day* and within a few percentage points?"

"Not only is that impossible, but it's doubly impossible. Tom Bingham couldn't even balance a checkbook, let alone guess the market."

Hansen was deflated. The suicide theory was beginning to make sense. This was a guy poised for a fall. Literally speaking. He thanked Elena Bingham for her time and returned to work.

———•———

The Gargoyle entered the lobby a few minutes after Hansen had left the building. He walked up to the ridiculous receptionist with the purple hair and metal stud embedded in her tongue. "I was supposed to meet my partner Richard Hansen here for a meeting, but traffic was murder."

The receptionist held up a single finger, meaning *hold your horses, wouldja?* "Chelsea Studios . . . please hold . . . Chelsea Studios . . . she's not in right now . . ."

While the woman was distracted, the Gargoyle helped himself to the sign-in book. A few lines from the bottom was the name of the target: R. HANSEN, in at 11:25 A.M. Time out: 12:05. Visiting: ELENA BINGHAM. *The ex-wife*, he noted. That was all the information needed, so he turned around and left before the woman could form a better mental impression of his facial features.

Outside, the Gargoyle buttoned up against the chill, and headed north to the TCI office. He felt a surge of satisfaction: his surveillance of the target had already yielded something tangible. This news couldn't wait. He called his boss on the cellphone, pulling Alexeyev out of a meeting with Chernigov.

"The target just spoke to Bingham's ex-wife for twenty-five minutes," the Gargoyle informed Alexeyev. "What would you like me to do next?"

"Come back to the office and we'll discuss that with Ilyutovich."

Twenty-two

DRAMATICALLY AND UNPREDICTABLY, the world had changed vastly in the decade preceding the arrival of the millennium. Gone were the lethal hostilities between the great nations that had epitomized the twentieth century. Superpower countries were no longer enemies. The first domino was tipped when Communist Russia imploded, impoverished by the costs of the Cold War. Then, in a telegenic rock 'n' roll event witnessed by the world, East Germans and West Germans took sledgehammers to the Berlin Wall, reuniting the two countries as one. The Iron Curtain had been lifted, and consequently, vast numbers of men found themselves obsolete.

Those in the espionage trade were particularly impacted. Ill-equipped for careers outside the arena of intrigue, these men gravitated toward the shadow worlds that could call upon their expertise: industrial espionage, arms dealings, black market operations, heroin distribution networks.

Some former KGB agents thrived in this wealth-driven New World Order. The skill-sets they had obtained as spies and assassins were in demand by a cartel of international financiers whose limitless appetite for power was matched only by a more consuming obsession of wealth multiplication.

———●———

At his superior's request, the Gargoyle returned to the office of TCI Investigations and Security Services (otherwise known as TCI-ISS, or simply, T-Siss). The security firm occupied the entire third floor of a brownstone building in a quiet mixed-purpose neighborhood on West Fifty-sixth Street off the Avenue of the Americas.

The Gargoyle stepped off the elevator into the common area. It was occupied by about a half-dozen Russian-American men. All of the men were on the phones, mostly speaking in a Russian dialect. The New York office of TCI had twelve "specialists" and was expected to double in size by year's end. Gargoyle nodded his greetings at the investigators as he walked toward Alexeyev's office. This group of men worked for Ilyutovich, the "I" in TCI, who was otherwise known as the Shovel for his ability to dig up dirt on targets.

The Gargoyle rapped on Viktor Alexeyev's door. Alexeyev beckoned for him to come in. Ilyutovich was already there, discussing the ongoing surveillance of The Contrarians. The Gargoyle closed the door behind him and the three men took seats at the circular conference table by the window. Alexeyev took a long gulp of scalding coffee, as hot as he could stand it.

"Let's see what we have so far on the other lawyer." Alexeyev spoke in Russian, drawing up three categories on the top sheet of his legal pad. In the first category of Alexeyev's "system" was the background information, the "soft" stuff. Using no more than a telephone and a computer, the Shovel had requested, obtained and digested seventy-six different reports available on the American lawyer named Richard Hansen. It was all accomplished within forty-eight hours, and a similar search could be conducted on any person in the United States at a moment's notice. "What have you been able to dig up so far on the new target, Sergei? Does he have any tax problems we can exploit? Failure to file?"

"No. He has always filed on a timely basis."

"No tax liens against him?"

"Nothing there."

"Any civil, criminal proceedings against him?"

"A speeding ticket in 1991 in Dryden, New York. Fine of eighty-five dollars, paid."

Alexeyev snorted contemptuously at that. "Has any disciplinary action been taken against him by the state bar association for misconduct as a lawyer?"

"No."

"Has there ever been a complaint lodged against him by a client of his law firms?"

"Nothing shows up."

"Divorced?"

"No, still married, first time. Three years."

"What do his credit reports tell you?"

"He has student loans outstanding of $21,975 and $1,765 in credit card debt."

Alexeyev made a note on his pad. "What does he own?"

"Nothing. No real estate, no automobiles."

"Has he ever been evicted from a residence?"

"No."

"Does have any bad business debt, either that he owes, or is owed him?"

"No."

"Bankruptcies, either personal or for a business he owned or controlled?"

"No, he's clean there."

"You ran it for all fifty states?"

"Of course."

"Let me have the file."

Ilyutovich pushed the HANSEN file folder across the table to Alexeyev. The Russian security consultant sifted through photocopies of Hansen's documentation. Voter registration files, telephone numbers, employment history records, driving history, vehicles searched by DOB, litigation searches, medical records, bank account and asset search, mutual fund and brokerage accounts by SSN, and casino cheating records in Nevada and New Jersey. The man was extraordinarily *ordinary*.

Ilyutovich sighed. "He was not a bad tenant, dishonest student or cheating husband. He's in good health. No glaring vulnerabilities, at least not from the soft search."

Alexeyev paused to scribble another note in the first category. Then he turned to the Gargoyle. "What about your initial surveillance?"

"The fingerprints provided nothing," the Gargoyle said. "He has no record of troubles in the securities industry or in his legal practice. We will conduct a background check with the people who know him, under the guise of a background check for his new employer. I should have some additional results by the end of the week."

Alexeyev nodded. "You said he met with Bingham's ex-wife this afternoon."

"Yes. He has a curiosity concerning the death of Bingham. Computer records show he has attempted to access Bingham's files on numerous occasions."

Alexeyev was alarmed. "Those files still exist?"

"Not to worry. They are encrypted."

"I don't care. Destroy them."

The Gargoyle nodded, almost imperceptibly.

"So what do we have?" Alexeyev said. "I'm hearing nothing. This target, he is like grabbing smoke."

The Gargoyle stared out the window. "There is a vulnerability we could exploit if necessary."

"Yes?"

"His wife, she's pregnant."

Finally, a vulnerability. Colbert would be pleased. Then again, no, he would demand more, much more. The financier would rage that the hundreds of thousands he was investing in security were being squandered. It was a good vulnerability, but it was only a starting point. With that, it was agreed TCI would step up surveillance on Richard Hansen, effective immediately.

Twenty-three

"SILK NOOSE," DERF COMPLAINED as he tugged at the tie encircling his neck. "Like, so when do we get the two-point-two kids and the mini-van?"

This had Damien cracking up, which only added to Eddie Slamkowski's irritation. Slam hissed, "Show a little respect, Derf. You have to wear a tie to access the floor. Those are the rules."

"Rules," Derf snipped. "Rules weren't designed for surfers."

"These rules apply to *everybody*. Just be glad I lent you grommets the only Jerry Garcia ties I own."

"Big deal. The Dead sells out to Corporate America. That's what this tie means."

"Listen, in forty minutes you'll be knocking back a few cold ones. In the meantime, just chill." Slamkowski sighed. "This has to do with making a living, okay?"

Damien and Derf fell silent. Even D&D understood the importance of *making a living*. To them, making a living was a necessary evil, what you had to do in order to afford surf time.

"Cool, dude," Damien said. "We're cool."

Slamkowski turned to the pretty girl behind the reception area on the second floor of the Chicago Mercantile Exchange and said, "Would you mind paging him again?"

Her amplified voice boomed over the thirty-five thousand square feet of the Merc's two trading floors. "Vic Insalata, please meet your guests in the reception area."

This was a business trip, actually, one that arose at Charles Stone's insistence. Just for grins, Slamkowski had brought Damien and Derf along for the ride, thinking they'd get a kick out of seeing where Slam had once worked in the days before he became a rock-bitten surf god just like them. Now, standing at the security desk, he was having second thoughts. *Rules weren't designed for surfers.* In the belly of the mighty Merc, Damien and Derf's rock-bitten coolness was irrelevant; they were just a couple of coppertoned slackers who couldn't last thirty seconds in the pits . . .

"Suh-lammmmmmmmmer!"

As one, they turned to the source of the booming voice, the swaggering figure of Victor Insalata. The half-Irish, half-Italian floor broker approached the reception area in the standard-issue mustard-colored floor jacket of the Merc's equity futures traders, his arms extended out for a bear hug. Slam nearly sobbed at seeing his old comrade-in-arms, and choked off his emotion as they embraced in a manly sort of way.

"What's up with the rock star haircut?" Trader Vic joshed, grabbing one of Slam's locks in mock disapproval. Vic cast a glance at Damien and Derf. "Guess that's the style among the in crowd, huh?"

Slam quickly made the introductions. "Vic Insalata, this is Damien Dalton and Derf Perry, friends of mine from California."

"Dirt, did you say?" Vic said, squinting.

"Derf," Derf corrected him. "As in Fred spelled backwards."

"Uh-huh." Slam knew Vic was yanking Derf's chain, making him repeat his own wacky nickname for Vic's twisted amusement. Vic always was a vicious bastard. *Apparently, still is.* Some things never change.

Trader Vic clapped his hands and barked out, "Well, Damien and Derf, you ever been to the Merc floor before?"

Damien and Derf shook their heads.

"Well, let's get right to it then."

They rode the escalator to the so-called lower trading floor on the third level, where the equity futures trading pits were located. The sustained roar of the trading crowd was building as they approached—like a jetliner preparing for takeoff. Slamkowski experienced a Pavlovian reaction to the unseen bedlam: the thrill juices started flowing once again in anticipation of the trading orgy that awaited. The difference this time was that he was coming in on a visitor's pass, not a floor badge. *How could I have let this happen?* Slamkowski interrogated himself harshly, not for the first time.

The contingent arrived on the third floor, walked by the coat check area, through the turnstiles, past the stone-faced security guard and on to the vast trading floor.

A blast of nostalgic energy hit Slamkowski once he reentered this lost world of his.

"You remember this, bro?" Vic asked.

"Same as it ever was," Slam whispered.

Indeed it was: the usual freewheeling chaos that was the Chicago Mercantile Exchange. A world unlike any other, virtually indescribable to the uninitiated. Airplane-hangar huge, the Merc's equity floor is a world of controlled chaos, an assault on the senses. The racket is constant, even in quiet markets, with general hubbub punctuated by frantic shouts, burbling telephones and the PA system asking certain floor personnel to report to the reception area.

Slam's excitement built as they threaded their way around the mazelike layout of the black, rubberized floor of the Merc's equity futures facility. As always, the floor was ankle-deep in a river of paper garbage—cardboard trading cards, candy wrappers, the sports section of the *Chicago Sun-Times*. Everything competed for your attention on the floor: from the frenetic activity in the pits to the winking gas-plasma-lit toteboards that lined the entire wall space of the trading floor. Some of the traders began nudging one another when they recognized Slam. A brief chant went up: "Slammmmuh! Slammmmuh!" Slam waved back like a visiting dignitary. In this boiling sea of testosterone, there was the occasional female specimen, running cards for Bache or phone-clerking at Nomura. *Pearls before swine.* Slam brazenly locked eyes with the women, not one of whom shied away from his gaze. A light-skinned black girl in a deck holder's jacket stared at Slamkowski while sucking on a lollipop. She raised a single eyebrow—a nonverbal that promised Slam he could print that trade if he wanted to. The exchange caused a heated rush of blood to his groin. *Look at this*, he thought. *Thirty seconds on the floor and I'm already sprouting a chubby.*

God, I miss this place.

Meanwhile, Damien and Derf swiveled around, slack-jaw mute, having unexpectedly stumbled into a most excellent adventure. "Bizarro world, dude," was all Damien could manage.

"Damien, bro, I believe we've crash-landed on Planet Stress," Derf said in singsong.

Vic whispered to Slam, "Now which one did you say is Beavis, and which one is Butt-head?" With a chuckle, Vic steered his guests clear of the hysteria of the trading pit to the booth of Insalata & Company. The booth was essentially three feet of working space with zero privacy and no chairs. It had space for eight computer screens, a laptop running a live Reuters feed, a timeclock and a bank of phones. The timeclock and one of the phones had been bashed up in the heat of battle, viciously enough that Vic had to patch the handset back together with silver-gray duct tape. Other than a few Polaroids of Vic's family and a panoply of essential health aids, Insalata's pod was identical to the three-foot-wide pods of all the other futures floor brokers.

"What're you looking at?" Vic asked.

"Your medicine cabinet," Slamkowski said nostalgically, indicating Vic's battery of health aids. "Mine was bigger."

"Yeah, so I remember." Trader Vic chuckled, wriggling into his wireless headset. "Not big enough, though."

"Ouch. You're killing me, big guy."

Futures floor personnel were the health care insurer's nightmare category. Life on the trading floor was fraught with everyday hazards: paper cuts, hearing loss, ballpoint pen lacerations, eyestrain from squinting at the computer screens and the toteboards, foot problems from running the equivalent of about three miles a day. Stress, heart attacks, burnout—all had felled many a superstar trader. Each day's futures trading session was 24,300 seconds in duration, a day fraught with cursing, phone bashing, spitting, slugging, kicking, fistfighting. The 1,300 people working on the equity futures floor of the Merc were a fraternity of extroverts, and tempers often flared.

The trading pit itself was a stop-sign-shaped hole in the floor, comprising about sixty-five square feet in all. It had descending tiers (just like Dante's Inferno, Slam used to joke), in which three hundred gold-jacketed brokers and traders jostled one another, competing for a tiny ambit of standing room. (Slam had heard a rumor last year that someone in the Euros pit had tried to "sell" his highly visible two-foot-by-two-foot position in the pit for $500,000 until the Merc floor officials got wind of it and killed the deal. Positioning was everything in this business.)

The action in the last half-hour of trading had turned frenzied, and the trading crowd reflected the emotions of the market, becoming a blur of windmilling arms. Amid the barks and shouts reverberating among the personnel in the booths and the brokers in the pit, Slam noted the majority were chewing gum or sucking Life Savers candy. Slam knew from firsthand experience that this was to keep the saliva flowing, and in turn, the vocal cords lubricated. Cotton mouth was a nemesis—often the difference between getting filled and getting squat.

"Now then," Trader Vic said, "the reason we are gathered here today is because after Freefall Friday, your boss wants assurances that Insalata & Company gets S&P futures fills as good and as fast as the majors."

"Stone wants better than the majors."

"Some tough guy, that boss of yours. Okay, better than the majors. You go back to Mr. Stone and tell him Trader Vic is the best in the business. Let me prove it to you. Did you know we're now wired to the

TOPS system?" The Trade Order Processing System—or TOPS—was the Merc's electronic order routing system. "Let's say your pals here, Damien and Nerf, decide one day to quit surfing and start up a big-ass hedge fund."

"It's Derf," Derf corrected him.

"Okay, sorry, Damien and *Dirt* start up a $100 million hedge fund. D&D Partners. You or Mr. Stone get a call from D&D saying they need some portfolio insurance because the market's crapping out on the cash side and they're gonna get smoked."

"Right," said Slam.

"This is how that technology affects you." From a cubbyhole under the work space of the pod, Trader Vic pulled out a handheld Fujitsu Stylistic 1000 computer with a light pencil attached to it and handed it to Slamkowski. The device resembled an Etch-A-Sketch screen. "Say D&D calls in an order to you at Infinity, bidding fifty at a hund-o. Go ahead and write that in on this screen with the light pencil."

Slamkowski touched the stylus to the surface of the touch-sensitive screen. Instantly, the backlit screen lit up: WELCOME TO TOPS/ CUBS. An electronic version of a blank trade ticket flashed up. Slam filled it out with the price, quantity and the particular S&P futures contract.

"Now tap the Enter icon," Trader Vic instructed.

Slam did so. The supertwist LCD screen winked.

"Now watch this." Trader Vic pointed to the screen of his own laptop. Instantaneously, the terms of the order flashed up on Insalata's desktop computer. "See that?"

"Yeah." Slam was amazed. "How'd it do that?"

"It's routed over the Internet, electronically through CUBS." CUBS stood for CME Universal Broker Station. "See, even if you're in California, your order is instantly transmitted to us on the floor as soon as you hit the Enter icon. You can use the light pen, the keyboard, or it can be entered automatically by computer. But wait, it gets better. Now, used to be, I would flash that order in to Andy Studd over there, our guy with top-step access for the front-month contract? That's old hat. Watch this." Vic jabbed a button on his telephone console and said into the mike of the headset, "Say, Andy, wave hello to our visitors from Cali."

In the next instant, Andy Studd, the Insalata broker on the top step of the futures trading pit, whipped around and waved to the booth.

"The Merc just signed off on the two-way wireless headsets. With that and TOPS, Andy will be working your boss' order within five seconds of the time you hit the Enter key. There's no runner, no clerk, no hand signals. As soon as your order hits up on my screen, I just transmit the order verbally to Andy, who's got top-step access, Andy flashes it into the pit, and—*voilà*—you're done."

"Amazing," Slamkowski conceded.

"Confirmation of the fill is electronically transmitted to the customer workstation in under twenty seconds. So do me a favor. Go back to your guy Stone and tell him Wolcott Fulbright's using us. In fact, Gil McGeary's my biggest customer. Tell Stone that the new technology has leveled the playing field between us little guys and the big New York trading houses. You do that for me, okay?"

"I'll do that. Stone's gonna love this." Privately, Slam worried, *With automated executions, will Charlie Stone even need me around anymore?*

"All right, fellas, if you'll excuse me for about thirty seconds, I've got a job to do here," Vic Insalata said abruptly, as he glanced at a digital clock suspended above the trading pit. He stabbed the trigger of his microphone, and spoke into it. "To the beloved customers of Insalata and Company, greetings from the Windy City. It's exactly three-fourteen-thirty and we at the Merc are in closing range mode." With that, Trader Vic began reciting the market pricing activity with the feverish babble of an announcer calling a horserace. "Okay, folks, the current market is 60 bid . . . 60 bid . . . half bid at 70 . . . 60's trading . . . 65 to 70, 70's trading, 75 trading, 80 offer . . . Refco's buying into it with fifteen seconds to go—80, 85 . . . volume's starting to pick up . . . 70 bid at 90. 70 bid at 90. PaineWebber's buying 'em here, along with Cargill, FIMAT's selling into it, 80 bid at 90. Ten seconds left . . . even bid at 90 . . . even bid . . . half-offer, half-offer. Support at 90! 90 offer by the locals! 90, 95 . . . 90, 95 . . . and we . . . are . . . *closed!*"

At the sound of the closing bell, the floor brokers and traders let out a cheer. Trading cards flew through the air like confetti at a ticker-tape parade. The floor personnel gratefully yanked down their Looney-Tunes-character ties, high-fived their colleagues and began filing for the exits, while some floor traders lingered behind to finish off the order ticket compliance of trades executed in the closing seconds. Through it all, Damien and Derf stared at the proceedings in wide-eyed amazement, utterly unable to comprehend what had transpired over the last half-hour.

"We are closed!" Trader Vic Insalata repeated triumphantly, tearing the headset from his scalp. "Let's get drunk."

"Now there's something," Derf said happily, "we can relate to."

———•———

Like the futures markets themselves, the Cactus Bar was big, brash and boisterous. The motif was best described as kitchen-sink kitsch: with its hodgepodge of NFL logos, inflatable crocodiles, palm fronds, multi-colored Japanese paper lanterns, plastic sharks, surfboards, ceiling fans, women's undergarments and Nixon memorabilia ("NIXON: NOW MORE THAN EVER"), it was equal parts tropical, Western and sports bar. There were signs admonishing the clientele DON'T DRINK AND TRADE. Cactus' frat party atmosphere and exposed-navel waitresses were big hits with the traders from the nearby Board of Trade and the Merc. By 3:30 P.M. Chicago time, the two wide-open drinking areas were packed with hyped-up futures floor professionals looking to unwind from the stress of trading with a few longnecks and some camaraderie.

Naturally, all this crowd could talk about was the *futures* business, so all-consuming was their profession. The customers at Cactus generally gathered to discuss their killer day-trades, or commiserate about being on the other side of killer day-trades. They jawboned about their brethren's sexual exploits, divorces, career advancement. Occasionally, there would be an off-the-wall change of subject such as *How's the family?* But that was an unusual digression.

That particular afternoon, the sudden reappearance of legendary S&P futures trader Eddie "the Slammer" Slamkowski on the floor of the Merc was the buzz of the bar. The novelty of this event gave way, however, to the instant notoriety of the pair of beer-guzzling surfer-dudes from Southern California who accompanied the Slammer on his return to the trading floor. These guys, Damien and Doofus, or something like that, had ditched their ties and resorted to more traditional surfer garb: body-clinging message T-shirts. Damien's shirt said, IF JESUS COULD WALK ON WATER, IMAGINE HOW HE'D SURF. Derf's had a cartoon of a sloe-eyed alien with the single word BELIEVE. D&D were stating their case for the existence of alien life on the planet Earth. Two dozen patrons in gold, scarlet and blue floor jackets gathered around Damien and Derf at the bar, captivated by their every word.

Swankie Frankie DeMarco handed the surfers another round of Coronas and said, "Just so I'm sure I've got this straight, fellas. The aliens are among us *right now*."

"That's right, dude," Derf replied.

"See, they're so far advanced," the one named Damien chimed in, "they exist in a totally different dimension than the one we inhabit. But, like, they're here, observing us."

"Here? Right now?" a Euros trader asked. "They're here at Cactus?"

"Don't know, dude," Derf said. "Could be."

"Then why hasn't the government stepped in to protect us?"

Derf chuckled riotously. "Like, dude, hello? Wake up and smell the Kona blend. The government is afraid of, like, mass hysteria. Imagine if, like, all of a sudden, there's a page-one headline that says, yo! there's an alien mothership hiding behind the dark side of the moon. The country would freak."

"Yeah, that's why the government and the media have conspired to keep it secret since Roswell," Damien said.

A runner from EDF Man shook his head. "I can only imagine the impression they have of earthlings if they saw the action in the S&P pits today."

"You guys ever been abducted?" a phone clerk from Pru called out.

Damien became pensive. "No, but I think it'd be cool."

Andy Studd nodded and deadpanned, "Incidentally, what planet did you guys say you're from?"

The traders exploded in humiliating laughter.

Derf began a slow burn. "Like, are you dudes making fun of us or what?"

It was at that point that Trader Vic Insalata grabbed Eddie Slamkowski under the armpit and steered him away from the crowd. Near the rest room, he clapped both hands on his friend's shoulders and said, "Slammer, let's talk."

Eddie shrugged. "So, talk."

"You happy doing what you're doing these days?"

"Yeah," Slamkowski responded weakly. "Surf a little, trade a little. It's good."

"Bullshit," Insalata fired back, searching his friend's eyes. "What are you doing with these slackers, Slam? This is not you, not really. You've got a fire in the belly, bro. You're not a *surfer*. You're *The Slammer*, one of the best S and P guys there is in the business."

Was, he thought sadly. Was *in the business.*

After a silence, Slamkowski sighed. "What do you want me to say, Vic? You want me to say this guy Stone is a hard-on beyond belief? You want me to admit I've never met the guy before, he's just some asshole screaming at me on a telephone? You want to hear me say I'm miserable being an order-taker on the buy-side? What do you want me to say?"

"What I want you to say," Trader Vic Insalata said, "is that you'll come back to Chicago and work for me."

So there it was. Out on the table. And it was a bombshell that blew Eddie Slamkowski away. Trader Vic Insalata was offering him a job. *That* came out of left field.

"Vic, I've kind of committed to the West Coast—"

"More bullshit. Where you gonna be in five years doing what you're doing now? George Hamilton with the bank account of a poet. You don't fool me for a second. Back on the floor, I saw that look in your eyes.

You're one of us; you *need* to trade, you asshole, and you know it. So let's flush all the bullshit down the toilet and put it on the table—would you come back to Chicago and work for Insalata and Company?"

Slamkowski exhaled heavily. "Jesus, Vic, I'm blown away. But really, I need some time to think about it."

Trader Vic Insalata smiled knowingly. "Of course. Take all the time you need." Vic cast a scornful glance at Damien and Derf in the center of the pack of taunting traders. "Call me as soon as you decide to get a life."

Twenty-four

MANHATTAN
Friday, February 19

STILETTO WAS NOT KEEN on the idea, but in the end what choice did he have? He reluctantly agreed to the Gargoyle's after-hours maneuvers at 44 Wall, but cautioned Colbert. "For crissakes, there will be people working on deals, even at that time of night. Be fucking careful."

Colbert assured him that these were professionals who had already performed this ritual in 44 Wall before. Besides, this was now a necessary course of action.

"It absolutely *is* necessary," Stiletto agreed. "But that doesn't mean I like the idea of your thugs parading around the offices. Incidentally, there's one condition."

"What would that be?"

"Tell them to stay the hell away from *my* office."

——•——

The coffee-colored uniform was utterly generic except for the legend emblazoned across the back—44 Wall, it said, in huge Helvetica bold letters, much in the current style of federal law enforcement windbreakers or satin rap-artist softball jackets. Unlike feds and rap stars, however, the people wearing the 44 Wall uniforms occupied the bottom rung of the minimum-wage scale. The building maintenance company servicing 44 Wall would have paid their crew far less than $4.70 an hour, if doing so didn't violate federal labor laws. It was classic supply and demand: there was an endless supply of non-English-speaking immigrants who would gratefully empty wastebaskets for half that wage.

The Gargoyle arrived at 44 Wall at three-thirty that morning. Once in the lobby, he immediately removed his down-filled parka so the first impression passersby would form of him was as a uniformed worker.

A trio of bleary-eyed investment bankers staggered out of the turn-stiles as he approached. The Gargoyle was mildly surprised at their youthful appearance, judging them to be in their early twenties. Having emerged from a late-night negotiating marathon, the bankers' weariness made them almost appear . . . drunk. Their ties were tugged down, their Alan Flusser suits were rumpled. They badly needed showers and shaves. The Russian caught a few fragments of their conversation as they passed.

"—scum-sucking lawyers are going to kill the whole deal, they keep up like this. I mean, do they really think our guys are going to indemnify them for the REIT tax risk?"

"Even the Cravath guys couldn't believe the hair on that guy Breitbart, raising a red-button issue like that at *this* stage of the game. Guys, this is the asset-backed deal from hell."

"Hey, look on the bright side. Everybody gets to go home, get three or four hours of sleep, a shower. I don't know about you, but after three nights of this, that to me is like a freaking tropical vacation—"

The young men in their twenties floated past the Gargoyle, paying him no attention as they pushed through the revolving door to the black radio cars waiting to take them uptown. The Gargoyle once again mar-veled at the power of the menial worker's uniform. To the bankers, the Gargoyle was just another drone who cleaned their urinals, an invisible man whose existence didn't even register on the radar scopes of their consciousness.

The Gargoyle gave a short wave to the security guard on duty. The greeting was not returned. The Russian passed the plastic magnetic-striped ID card through the electronic reader at the security turnstile. The mechanism flashed a green light and clicked, and he entered the building.

<hr />

Within twenty minutes, he completed his work in Kilmartin's office. Then, he headed to the young attorney's office three doors down the hall.

The floor plan provided by Stiletto proved to be unnecessary. The Gargoyle had a working familiarity with the floor since Alexeyev had brought him along when Bingham's office was wired back in September. The Gargoyle himself did Kilmartin's office in early November. Ac-cordingly, he moved with the confidence of someone who knew what he was doing.

The nameplate identified the occupant as RICHARD HANSEN. Warily, the Gargoyle peered up at the ceiling. He saw his reflection in the spher-ical lens of the security camera twenty feet away. Alexeyev said that Stiletto would ensure the surveillance cameras were disabled for the night. Anyone reviewing the videotapes would see nothing but static, Stiletto promised. *Better not be a screwup*, he thought. He was distrustful of leaving such details to others.

The Russian unlocked the office door with the same master key provided to other maintenance workers. He stepped inside.

The fluorescent lights flickered on. The office spaces of Wolcott Fulbright had been modernized with motion sensors. The sensor automatically turned the lights on when someone walked in. The lights would go off if no motion was detected for thirty minutes. The Gargoyle was impressed with the simple, practical application of that technology. But the motion-sensitive lights were quaint technology compared to the high-tech gadgetry he was about to deploy.

The Gargoyle scanned the office, mentally parsing it up into distinct communication stations.

The phone.

He disconnected it from the feed wire, pulled off its hard-plastic casing, and began disemboweling the device. Within minutes, he inserted a transmitter microphone that would beam a digital signal of the attorney's calls to a Teac reel-to-reel tape recorder secreted in a room in the Millenium Hotel less than a mile away. Next, he implanted a device to record all of the outgoing numbers Richard Hansen punched up on the keypad, by tonal range of each key. A third mechanism used the phone company's own "caller ID" technology to capture the phone numbers of all incoming callers.

The phone was crucial to surveillance of the lawyer, so nothing was left to chance.

Next, the computer. The Gargoyle was no computer wizard, but he had been trained to perform effective investigations of recent PC use. Using a software utility created by Ilyutovich, he was able to discern the last 150 files accessed by Hansen. Forty-five of those had been files originally created by Bingham. Over the next twenty minutes, Gagarov used a software utility called *Nullfile* that not only "deleted" the files of Bingham and Hansen, but "wiped" them from hard-drive memory. This was, in effect, electronic shredding: the documents were now completely irretrievable.

Then the Gargoyle cut off the power to the lawyer's PC and removed the casing. He replaced the shielded, coaxial cables from the machine to the monitor with unshielded connectors. He installed a booster device inside the computer that would enhance "leaking" of the electromagnetic signals emanating from Hansen's computer. Then he swapped Hansen's coffee-stained keyboard with a replacement equipped for low-frequency transmission of the user's keystrokes to a remote location. Initially, the target might notice the difference in the touch and feel of the keys. Once he got used to it, however, he'd probably not give it a second thought. With that, Hansen's machine had been modified to be highly susceptible to TEMPEST—transient electromagnetic pulse emanation surveillance technology. It is not widely known that the electron gun that feeds a computer screen leaks electromagnetic waves that are tantamount to a radio broadcast of the user's activity. An eavesdropper in a van a mile away can monitor all keystrokes of a particular user with a $20,000 video signal monitoring device called DataScan.

The fax machine.

Before opening it up, the Gargoyle did some due diligence. He pushed a combination of buttons (which emitted a disconcertingly loud series of peeps). The fax immediately whirred to life. A single sheet of paper skidded into the receiving tray. The Gargoyle reviewed it. It was a listing of the last hundred outgoing faxes, the number of pages, the recipient's fax number, and whether all pages had been successfully transmitted. Next: a listing of the most recent hundred *incoming* faxes, some of which actually stated the identities of the senders. SULLIVAN & CROMWELL, LEHMAN BROTHERS LEGAL DEPT., AMERICAN STOCK EXCHANGE, DEUTSCHE MORGAN GRENFELL—all had sent faxes to Hansen within the last two weeks. Both reports would go to Ilyutovich later that morning.

Then the Gargoyle unplugged the machine and implanted a sixteen-megabit imaging card that captured up to five hundred pages of digital images.

The fish-eye fiber-optic surveillance camera was concealed in the casing of a fire sprinkler. The sprinkler was inserted into the ceiling panel directly above Hansen's desk. The Gargoyle spliced a wire from the socket to juice the camera. The twelve-volt camera would provide a 380-line color picture with a low grainy, distorted view of the tops of the heads of anyone in the office, emphasizing the balding areas of those on camera. The resolution of the picture was a far cry from broadcast caliber, but it did not matter. As long as participants in meetings could be identified by Stiletto, that was good enough. The omnidirectional microphone he secreted in the light fixture was smaller than a dime, but would pick up conversations clearly from up to twenty-five feet away.

It was nearly 4:30 A.M. when the Gargoyle stealthily exited the target's work space, locking the door behind him. The Russian made his way through the cubicles of the common area, his mind already racing ahead. Later, he would wire a similar surveillance setup in the target's apartment while the wife was out at a scheduled doctor's appointment. . . .

When the doors opened to the elevator, the Gargoyle encountered a Nicaraguan security guard. The guard was apparently on his way down to another floor, ostensibly to conduct his nocturnal rounds. The guard had a pack of unfiltered Camel cigarettes at the ready, and the Gargoyle suspected he was more likely sneaking off for a smoke break than a security check.

As the Gargoyle entered the elevator car, the security guard nodded cordially to him. It was the first time anyone had acknowledged his existence since he arrived at 44 Wall. The Gargoyle nodded back, wordlessly staring up at the lighted indicator until they reached the lobby.

Exiting the building, he mutter-cursed to himself. It would have been cleaner to have slipped out completely unnoticed. But what could he do? That was simply the professional courtesy one low-paid uniformed worker exhibited to another in this marble-and-chrome world of unspeakable wealth.

The risk of discovery was negligible, he convinced himself. He put the encounter out of his mind.

Twenty-five

MANHATTAN

Friday, February 19

THE STOCK MARKET'S powerful recovery continued apace.

When the closing bell was sounded at 4 P.M. that Friday, the Dow Jones Industrial Average was up 107 points on the day, and 262 points for the week.

The DJIA now needed just 86 points to draw even with its all-time record set on January 28, the day before Freefall Friday.

No doubt, the snapback from the mini-crash cheered investors. Pundits were wondering whether the 7 percent decline was just an extreme example of *profit taking*. The new take on Freefall Friday was that it was no catastrophe, it had simply presented a *buying opportunity* for a bunch of overpriced stocks. Hey, maybe there was still life in this aging bull market, still a chance to score some *big money*.

Otherwise, one of the truisms of investing is that there's more anxiety being *out* of a bull market than being *in* one. People had money to invest and it had to go somewhere. Foreign money, especially, was pushing the indicators back in the direction of the market's peak.

Just weeks after the scare, individual investors were coming back into the game in a big way.

●

Rick Hansen anxiously paced in a tight circle behind the chair in his office, hands in pocket, absently jangling the change. "How's it looking? Not good, I bet."

"I'll know better in another minute," Monica Chi said, peering intently at the screen of Rick's PC.

Hansen fell silent and gazed out the window, feeling powerless and frustrated. The lawyer's computer had gone completely haywire. Every time he tried to access any of his files, the screen invariably looked like this:

```
111111111111111111111111111111111111111111111111111
111111111111111111111111111111111111111111111111111
111111111111111111111111111111111111111111111111111
111111111111111111111111111111111111111111111111111
111111111111111111111111111111111111111111111111111
111111111111111111111111111111111111111111111111111
```

Nothing but the numeral 1 filling the screen, as if someone had taken the trouble to open all of his files and replace every character with a 1. The glitch had also afflicted all of Tom Bingham's files, even the ones that were gibberish, like "3RiversModelOne." Every file under the passwords of Hansen and Bingham had been converted to pages of 1s.

The sexy twenty-six-year-old Asian troubleshooter from Systems was tall and slim, with long legs and breasts that reminded Rick of ice-cream scoops. Her gleaming blue-black hair had been cropped into a retro-fashionable pixie, and an aura of freesia-scented shampoo surrounded her. A huge Motorola alphanumeric message beeper rode her hip.

"Bad news," she said at last.

Hansen put the flat of his palms on the surface of the desk and leaned in next to her. "Give it to me."

"From what I can tell, you seem to be the only one at the firm who's been wiped," Monica said. "You and Tom Bingham, that is."

"*Wiped?* What does that mean?"

"Well, ordinarily, when files are deleted on a computer, the file itself is not actually deleted from the hard drive."

"It's not?" Hansen was confused.

"No, not immediately. The 'delete' command simply removes the directory entry that permits you access to that file. Ultimately, your file will be overwritten by other files and then it is erased from the hard drive. But for some time, the file is still retrievable by using software like Norton Utilities. Are you following?"

"Yes."

"Your files and those of Tom were not simply deleted, they were wiped. That means all the characters in those files were physically *over-written* and replaced with the digit 1. It's precisely the same procedure used by the Department of Defense to remove any traces of top-secret documents from their computer systems."

"You're saying all these files are now irretrievable?"

"I'm afraid so."

"Someone had to do this, right? I mean, someone had to target these particular files and wipe them out."

Monica exhaled. "Well, yes. Someone had to activate a program like *Nullfile* to accomplish this."

"Someone got into my locked office," Hansen said. "I think they switched my keyboard with another."

Monica Chi peered at the keyboard through her oval-shaped glasses. "No, I think it was done by someone in Systems Technology. They intended to clear all of Bingham's files since he's . . . no longer with the firm. Maybe yours were deactivated accidentally."

"Systems wipes inactive files?"

"No. But maybe there's a new procedure. I'm going to check into it. I'm sorry I couldn't be more helpful, Richard." She stood up from the chair and collected her knapsack of diagnostic tools.

"Before you go?"

"Sure."

Rick opened a manila folder and brought up a copy of a page of the gibberish he had printed out from one of Tom Bingham's files. "This was some of the data garbage I was getting when I accessed some of Tom's old files. Is it some sort of glitch that causes this?"

Monica Chi's mouth opened as she looked at it. "No. This is PGP."

"Excuse me?"

Monica's dark-chocolate eyes met his. "PGP. It stands for 'pretty good privacy.' " She pointed to the seemingly illogical lines of characters on the page. "It's an algorithm-based encryption program that scrambles computerized documents."

"You mean to say that Tom Bingham encrypted some of his word processing files?"

"Yes. And with PGP, no less."

Hansen squinted at her. "I'm sorry, what's the significance of this PGP?"

"It was a program created in 1991 by a cyber-hacker in Colorado, and distributed worldwide over the Internet." She spoke in a light accent that softened hard consonants, which Rick found terribly attractive. "He created the program in response to concerns that the government was able to eavesdrop on computer-to-computer communications. The U.S. government was very unhappy about the popularity of PGP among terrorists and industrial spies and tried to prosecute the creator. Unsuccessfully." Monica tapped the page with her finger. "It's impossible to crack without the key code." She made the last statement with an unmistakable tone of admiration.

"You guys in Systems keep the key code?"

"Oh no, never," Monica replied. "The key code is created at random by the user. In fact, PGP is not in use at the firm as far as I know. Systems certainly does not make it available."

"Why would Bingham want to encrypt his interoffice memos?" Hansen asked the question more to himself than to Monica. "And why only some of his files? I mean, if he made the decision to encrypt his work product, why not go all the way, encode everything?"

"Beats me," Monica shrugged. Then she frowned. "Wasn't he rumored to be involved in insider trading or something like that? I thought I had heard something about that."

"Maybe," Hansen conceded.

Then he realized: Perhaps Monica Chi was right. Bingham's illicit insider trading activities—that was a plausible explanation for encrypting documents. Perhaps there was a co-conspirator in the insider trading scheme, one who was now trying to cover his tracks. *One who might be willing to kill his partner to conceal the crime?* Hansen speculated.

By way of exit, Monica Chi said, "I've got to go down to see Gil McGeary in equity derivatives at five."

"Thanks for all your help, Monica."

"Yo, either of you guys Hammonds?" Rick and Monica turned to the sound of the voice at the doorway. A messenger was slouched against the doorjamb of Hansen's office. "Are you Hammonds?" he asked again.

"I'm Hansen," Rick said. "Does it say Hansen?"

The messenger was a skinny white kid dressed in a hodgepodge of loose-fitting, conspicuously-logoed merchandise: Nautica, Fila, Tommy Hilfiger. He sported a wirebrush buzz cut and a humiliating stab at facial hair. A set of Coby digital headphones were looped around his neck like an Olympic medal, the tuneless bass-and-rhythm thrash of the late Notorious B.I.G. rapping prophetically about the thug life that would ultimately do him in. The kid had cranberry-sized acne embedded in his skin and he absently picked at it as he squinted at the rumpled routing slip. "Nope," he finally said with full conviction. "Says it right here. Hammonds."

Hansen looked at Monica and smiled helplessly. "You've found him. Where do I sign?"

Monica mouthed a good-bye and edged out of the office sideways, through the narrow egress permitted by the steel cart stacked with archive boxes. The messenger gaped at her with openmouthed desire as she slipped by. "You're gonna have to sign for 'em, chief," he muttered absently.

"That's what I just said, hoss." Hansen overturned the loose papers on his desk in search of a pen.

"Where do you want 'em put?"

"Can you bring them in here?"

The messenger sized up the room. "I could, but there's twenty-six boxes in all."

Hansen's eyebrows climbed his forehead in surprise. "Twenty-six?" He came around his desk to get a glimpse at the payload and noticed yet another messenger standing behind this one, with another fully loaded handcart of cardboard boxes. Signing the routing slip, he said, "Put 'em in the War Room, I guess."

"Right, chief." The messenger nodded, shoved the receipt in his back pocket and hiked the headphones back over his ears, resuming his visit to the straight-outta-Compton gangstah-rap underworld.

———◆———

The War Room's colorful nickname was well deserved. A small, out-of-the-way, oddly shaped room next door to the copying machines, it was deemed too undesirable to be utilized as an office, and instead had been deployed as a secluded outpost and dumpsite for documentation. Whenever the storm clouds gathered on largely meritless litigation against the deep-pocketed Wolcott, the War Room was occupied round the clock by litigation lawyers, witnesses and paralegals girding up for courtroom battle. True to its moniker, it looked as though it'd been through a war; it had in fact been through several wars. The room was hopelessly cluttered with papers and memoranda from lawsuits long ago filed, resolved and forgotten. Mounds of paper were stacked up on the coffee-stained sea-green carpeting. Yellow Post-it notes scrawled with obscure case captions were stuck on top of other archive boxes, seemingly without forethought. In its center was a small, round table with a glossy Formica surface, with a telephone, some empty Redweld and accordion folders, paper clips, spent staples, a block chisel point marker and a putty-colored Scotch tape dispenser. The War Room's claustrophobic atmosphere was made even more so by the twelve hulking flesh-toned file cabinets that consumed all available wall space.

Hansen entered the gloomy solitude of the War Room and closed the door. The room was eerily silent, except for the constant whoosh of the forced-air heating duct and the barely perceptible buzz of the fluorescent lights. The messengers had arranged the twenty-six archive boxes in a six-stack horseshoe configuration. The boxes themselves were the standard-issue oatmeal-colored corrugated-board squares. The logotype of Silver River Business Archives, the third-party archive provider from The Bronx, was branded prominently in navy-blue ink on the sides of the boxes. They were secured by the same type of plastic bands used to bundle newspapers in a crosshatch style that put Hansen in mind of gift-wrapping. He studied the boxes for a deliberate moment, then drew in a deep breath of air, heavy with the sweet tang of damp wood pulp.

Here goes nothing, he said to himself.

He approached the first stack of four, shifted the top box onto the Formica table. This box seemed surprisingly light to Hansen.

> Client Box Number: 288403
> Principal: T. Bingham.
> Department: Legal
> Client Code—00164/WFC

The plastic strap popped off with a satisfying burst. Hansen pulled the top off, cast it to the side, peered in at the contents. And learned why it was so light.

It was jammed with Patagonia skiwear, woolen shawl-collar sweaters from Paul Stuart and Eddie Bauer, leather gloves, hooded Harvard University sweatshirts.

The sonuvabitch archived his winter wardrobe! Hansen said to himself in disbelief. *And stuck the firm with the expense!*

As Hansen made a notation in his spiral notebook, he shook his head at one New Yorker's innovative solution to the storage problem endemic to living in cramped Manhattan apartments.

The second, third and fourth boxes Hansen perused contained even more of Bingham's winter wear. The fifth was something different—it was stuffed with a neatly folded collection of cotton golf shirts. Hansen groaned at the sight. What's next?

At least the next three archive boxes contained files related to Bingham's job. The file folders had titles like EXCHANGE-FOR-THE-PHYSICALS ("EFP"), PAINTING THE TAPE, STOCK PARKING CASE LAW, and BED & BREAKFAST TRADES WITH U.K. AFFILIATE. Again, he noted the contents of the files on his notepad and shifted the boxes off to the side. Red herrings.

Boxes nine and ten were brimming with personal papers going back as far as six years. He scribbled down the contents on his notepad: Bingham's tax returns for the last four years, Harvard Law School memorabilia, credit card receipts, grad school loan documents, canceled checks.

One document in particular caught his eye. It was a fully executed lease on a $576-a-month rent-stabilized one-bedroom apartment on the tenth floor of 410 Central Park West, an exclusive address on the Upper West Side. A rent-stabilized apartment overlooking Central Park for less than six bills? *New Yorkers would be willing to kill for that*, Hansen thought to himself. *It's like courtside season tickets to the Knicks. You never let it go.*

He made a mental note that the lease didn't expire for another ten months, yet Tom Bingham had moved to that second residence, a penthouse on Madison Avenue. Generally speaking, once New Yorkers got their claws on a rent-stabilized property, death (or perhaps winning the Lotto) was the only way to separate them from it. He wondered if Bingham had held on to it even after purchasing the two-bedroom penthouse. He made a mental note to contact Elena Bingham about it.

Boxes 11 and 12 and 13 were jammed with additional copies of the Wolcott Fulbright *Compliance Manual for Equity Sales & Trading*, three-ring binders thick with mind-boggling procedures for the sales and trading personnel. Box 14 was Bingham's complete sets of Topps and Upper Deck baseball trading cards, from 1980 to the present, enshrouded in airtight plastic, apparently being preserved for investment purposes.

Finally, with Box 15, Hansen hit the mother lode.

———•———

The good stuff filled eight boxes in all.

It was an extraordinary collection of scholarly books, articles and treatises. All on a single subject. *Financial Crises*. Their causes, their effects. The general subject of financial crises was divided into eight subtopics, each of which was designated its own archive box for materials.

1. CRASHES, PANICS, CRUNCHES—ECONOMIC
THEORY
2. CRASHES, PANICS, CRUNCHES—CAUSE & EFFECT
3. THE CRASH OF 1929
4. THE CRASH OF 1987
5. MOB PSYCHOLOGY/IRRATIONALITY OF INVESTORS
6. ELECTRONIC TRADING/PORTFOLIO INSURANCE
7. SPECULATIVE DERIVATIVE INSTRUMENTS
8. THE CRASH NEXT TIME

The literature had been culled from a variety of sources: books purchased at the Barnes & Noble Annex on Fifth Avenue or the Strand, the city's famous used-book bookstore. Several of the scholarly tomes had been stolen outright from the Solomon Library at the New York University School of Business. There were photocopies of journal articles and NEXIS printouts of old news clippings neatly arranged and filed in each box by the ever-diligent Cliff Weiner.

Hansen took the time to count the books stored in the archive boxes. Eighty-two in all, including Allman & Sametz's *Financial Crises* (1977), Kindleberger's *Manias, Panics and Crashes* (1978), Mackay's *Some Extraor-*

THE VELOCITY OF MONEY 175

dinary Popular Delusions and the Madness of Crowds, first published in 1841. He spotted a dog-eared copy of the 1994 Second Edition of Martin Wolfson's watershed treatise, *Financial Crises: Understanding the Postwar U.S. Experience* in the fifth box. The books themselves had been pored over thoroughly by an obsessed Bingham, who had highlighted, paper-clipped and marked significant passages with message slips and bent corners. It was apparent that Bingham had spent literally hundreds of hours compiling these materials up until his death, and was clearly possessed by the analytics of dramatic stock market declines.

So what? a voice inside his head skeptically harumphed at the find. *Isn't all this consistent with a guy who happens to be writing a book on the subject of stock market crashes?*

True, he conceded to the dissident voice in his head. But, he parried, *what in these boxes permitted Bingham to become expert enough to forecast a mini-crash of the stock market on a random day so far off in the future?*

There was no apparent answer for that burning question.

So Hansen rolled up his shirtsleeves and plunged into the first of the boxes, the one captioned FINANCIAL CRISES—CRASHES, PANICS, CRUNCHES—ECONOMIC THEORY. In minutes, the lawyer came upon the collection of four microcassettes labeled THE STOCK MARKET CRASH NEXT TIME. Tom Bingham had dictated them himself.

———•———

"Okay, Cliff, let's start with the title of this document. All capitals, 'AMERICAN FINANCIAL CRISES—THE STOCK MARKET CRASH NEXT TIME.' "

Hansen stared at the Pearlcorder on the table. To listen to the disembodied voice of the man who was now dead was eerie and unsettling.

"Header, 'Executive Summary.' Okay, first paragraph. 'You have retained my services to verify certain claims made to you by a third-party consultant on the causes and effects of significant stock market declines. In the course of doing so, I have studied the facts and circumstances concerning the following historically significant financial crises.' Okay, Cliff, put the following in bullets:

- Holland's tulip futures collapse (1634)
- London's South Seas Company Stock Collapse (1720)
- France's "Mississippi Bubble" (1917)
- U.S. Panic of 1873
- Panic of 1893
- Panic of 1907
- Crash of 1929

• Credit Crunch of 1966
• Crunch of 1973–74
• Silver futures collapse of 1980
• Crisis of 1982
• Black Monday Crash of 1987
• Panic of 1995

" 'In all cases, the factors leading up to the panic, crunch, crisis, bubble or crash were consistent. (1) a period of speculative excess . . . (2) a maturity of a business cycle involving a sustained upsurge in prosperity . . . (3) a wildly overvalued stock or commodities market . . . (4) an external factor that undermined investor confidence . . . (5) a panicked "rush to the exits" by the market as a whole—the so-called "lemming effect" . . . and finally (6) a spectacular decline driven more by greed and fear than by a rational assessment of the situation.

" 'Time after time, history has doomed the stock market to repeat its cycles without exception.' Cliff, put the following in bold, italics and underline. 'Stock market crashes are natural and inevitable after periods of sustained and overreaching economic growth.'

"New paragraph. 'Now, there has been no greater speculative binge in the history of the American economy than there has been in the last ten years. A major stock market meltdown is never a matter of "if," but "when." The factors are in place for the next stock market crash to occur *at any time now.*

" 'According to history, the proper shove could turn a modest market sell-off into a panic that would plunge the American stock markets into the abyss. Possible result: forty to fifty percent decline in DJIA. A recession lasting seventeen to twenty months. And in the absolute best-case scenario, a possible economic depression.' "

Hansen reacted as he heard this: *absolute best-case scenario?*

"Okay, Cliff, final paragraph for this document. 'Conclusion, I am pleased to report that my own research has largely confirmed the rather bold claims submitted by Professor Gammage. His initiative appears feasible, at least conceptually. Now, my own position in New York makes me uniquely qualified to assist in bringing this project to fruition. Of course, I would need to have the benefit of your long-term view of my remuneration before signing on. Respectfully submitted, L. Thomas W. Bingham, Esq.' Okay, Cliff, that's the end of this tape."

An undefinable chill raced up Hansen's spine, as the recording of Bingham's voice dropped off and there was nothing but the hiss of blank tape.

Gammage—that was the name in Bingham's datebook! In this "executive summary," Bingham had agreed with this Professor Gammage's academic theory that a stock market crash was imminent. But just who was the summary prepared for, if not this Professor Gammage? And who was the anonymous beneficiary of the memo? Bingham wasn't writing a book, he was angling for some consulting job. At a hedge fund, possibly? Some group of investors? Did it tie in with his insider trading activities somehow?

One thing was certain. The factors leading up to Bingham's impossible prediction of Freefall Friday were clearly present in the stock market right now. Rampant speculation . . . peak of business cycle . . . over-bought stock market. The notion of a derivatives crisis or electronic trading scenario triggering a massive stock market decline—well, that was pure speculation, impossible to predict. Wasn't it? If so, then how the hell did he predict Freefall Friday?

The Bingham-Gammage analysis was horrifying. In the memo he had dictated, Bingham had predicted a devastating 40 to 50 percent decline in the value of the Dow Jones Industrial Average. And as long as a twenty-month recession to follow. Or even a *depression*.

Oddly, Bingham had called it a *best-case scenario*.

As if Bingham and the people behind the "initiative" were not just predicting a major market meltdown, but almost *hoping* for one to happen.

All this left Hansen more confused than ever. What kind of person would root for a major stock market crash?

Part III

THE GIANT,
UNSEEN ASTEROID

February 20–March 12

Derivatives are hypersophisticated computer-generated instruments that use the public's massive bet on securities to create a parallel universe of side bets and speculative mutations so vast they function like some giant, unseen asteroid—they influence the market's movements with a powerful and dimly understood gravitational pull. And if they wobble out of orbit, they could conceivably come crashing into the sphere of day-to-day investments with cataclysmic effects.

—JOHN GREENWALD, *TIME* MAGAZINE, 1995

Twenty-six

THE PANELIST FROM HONEYWELL droned on about firewalls and the kid next to him tuned out. Blah, blah, blah, widely dispersed computer networks need security firewalls. *No shit, Sherlock.*

Bored, the kid looked out over the audience that would soon be his. Its members were vastly different from the kid. He guessed their median age to be, what?—forty, forty-two? Their faces were humorless, their eyes were dulled. Their bellies had retained much of the red meat that had passed through their alimentary canals over the last four decades. They wore shiny shoes. They were chief information officers of Fortune 100 companies, computer security specialists, law enforcement officials and Department of Defense grunts. They were killing a sacred Saturday morning in Tyson's Corner, Virginia, because they took their jobs *very seriously*, and they wished to ensure they did not lose them.

The kid's name was Freddie Zaraghi, but the audience would not know him by that. Instead, he would be introduced at the Sixth Annual Digital Information Integrity Institute's Computer Security Symposium at the Sheraton Premier Hotel simply as "Thrush." Unlike the members of the audience, Freddie was young and brash, and his appearance was calculated to effect a certain . . . image. He was Turkish-American, darkly handsome with the carefully trimmed Fu Manchu facial hair that was in vogue among computer wonks of late. He was dressed head to toe in black (like a digital ninja warrior), black jeans and a black nylon turtleneck peeled back from his jaw. He had brand-new black Nike sneakers, a cool haircut and an attitude. Perhaps this crowd would initially feel contempt for Thrush, but at the same time it coveted the inner workings of his mind. The dynamic was really no different from that of the cynical Madison Avenue types eager to get inside the heads of Generation Xers.

Zaraghi's participation in the symposium was really about money. Candidly, ever since Gammage screwed him over, the kid needed the money. That's why on a chilly Saturday morning in freaking Tyson's Corner, Virginia, he was playing a prophet of doom named Thrush.

The windbag panelist from Honeywell finally concluded his stupor-inducing speech on firewalls at ten-forty-five, fifteen minutes past his allotted time. Graciously, the moderator of the panel said, "Thank you for the update, Karl-Heinz, that was most . . . thorough."

The moderator then turned to the kid. A self-amused smirk pulled at the corners of his cheesy mustache as he spoke in his dry, ironic monotone. "In the tradition of Madonna and Prince, and other single-monikered rock stars, the final speaker of the panel is a young man from Detroit who refers to himself only as Thrush. Thrush comes to us from the 'dark side of genius,' if you will. At age eleven, Thrush hacked into the city of Detroit's 911 system and replaced the recorded greeting with the voice of *Star Trek*'s Mr. Spock saying, 'Live Long and Prosper.' "

This drew mild chuckles from a few members of the audience. But the majority of this crowd was not amused by such schoolboy pranks, since their continued employment depended on preventing such intrusions. Still, Thrush was grateful for a few chuckles; it would definitely not pay to have this crowd completely despise him.

The moderator continued. "While at Carnegie-Mellon University two years ago, Thrush was arrested by the Secret Service in the federal sting operation code-named Operation Sun Devil, for penetrating the electronic switching systems of the Bell network in the Midwest. The charges were dropped when Thrush assisted law enforcement officials in the prosecution of other criminal hackers." (The audience murmured knowingly about Operation Sun Devil; in fact, some of the Feds involved in the sting were probably in the audience right now, Thrush figured.) "After leaving Carnegie-Mellon, Thrush single-handedly developed a highly advanced system for Wall Street firms to electronically access the securities markets, utilizing artificial intelligence and data-mining technology to perform robot-trading—patent pending, I might add. Thrush is now a freelance computer security consultant to corporations, law enforcement officials and federal agencies. It is our privilege to have him with us this morning to discuss the topic, 'Information Superhighway or Road to Ruin?' Ladies and gentlemen—Thrush."

After the sporadic applause subsided, Thrush folded his arms casually and leaned close enough to the microphone that his lips brushed up against the cool metal. His voice boomed out throughout the room:

"Let's play a game."

"Let's say it's exactly two years from today's date. That would make it a Monday. It's a February morning that seems to be like all others. You go to the bathroom to shower. You turn on the news radio station.

"You first hear of the tragic disaster in Los Angeles the night before. A privately owned Cessna smashed into a New York–bound 747 airliner just as it was taking off, causing both planes to crash. All told, two hundred sixty-seven people are dead. Investigators debriefing the air-traffic controllers are stunned to learn that their screens gave them misinformation about the positioning of the planes. The investigation is continuing . . .

"You're on your way to work, car radio on. A northbound Amtrak passenger train from Newark, New Jersey, to Boston has slammed head-on into a southbound freight train carrying a load of new cars to Miami. Fifty-four people are dead, hundreds injured. A federal official who has asked not to be named believes that the East Coast rail control system has been penetrated by outside intruders, who intentionally rerouted the trains to their collision course. You're thinking, Monday mornings are a bitch, but this one's a doozy . . .

"You get to work, where you happen to have a TV set. You tune in to CNN to get live updates on the two tragedies. Ten minutes into the broadcast, the anchor disappears, only to be replaced by a photograph of Saddam Hussein. Off-camera, a male voice says, cryptically, 'Alaska, ten o'clock.' The anchor returns, disoriented that someone has hijacked the satellite feed of the global news network . . .

"Sure enough, at ten A.M. Eastern Time, there comes a report that the computer-controlled mechanism of the Alaska pipeline has failed. Millions of gallons of raw crude oil are spilling uncontrollably onto the frozen tundra. In short order, the spill bursts into flames and the huge black smoke clouds over that state become an ecological disaster on a scale of the oil fires in Kuwait during the Gulf War . . .

"The hits keep on coming.

"The Culpeper Switch in Virginia, which controls all federal fund transfers, has been attacked by unknown intruders. All along the Southeast corridor, citizens trying to access their money through ATM machines find they have no funds in their accounts. A panic erupts and people converge on the banks trying to withdraw their funds. The Federal Reserve permits the banks to shut down for the afternoon to avert a meltdown of the South's economy . . .

"An electric grid goes out in the Chicago metropolitan area, and the city goes into blackout. With temperatures plunging below ten degrees, many of the poor and elderly are literally freezing to death. Frantic workers are not able to repair the software that controls the power grid. They confess their fears to the press that a hacker has irreversibly corrupted the system . . .

"In New York, the computers of the NASDAQ securities market have been mysteriously disabled. No one is able to enter buy or sell orders. There is mass panic as investors come to believe they cannot sell their holdings. The NASDAQ 100 index loses a third of its value in a single day . . .

"The electronic switching systems of the Washington, D.C., phone network go out, making long-distance and local calls impossible. Ninety percent of the Department of Defense computers, reliant on the outside phone networks, are now unable to communicate with one another, paralyzing the nation's military forces . . .

"The worst-case scenario has become reality. A faceless enemy has drawn the United States into the first 'information war' of the twenty-first century. An electronic Pearl Harbor is going down and the enemy has never set foot on American soil. Someone has to notify the President.

"In fact, the President has already been briefed. He is informed that the unseen 'information terrorists' have taken control of the Big Blue Cube in Moffett Field, Mountain View, California, and disabled the global positioning satellite system. Now comes word from Intelligence that computer intruders have just penetrated the super-secret Worldwide Military Command and Control Systems, the WWMCCS, and they must be stopped *now, Mr. President, now!*

"The President takes decisive action. He bombs the living shit out of Saddam Hussein's palace and other strategic sites with a bunch of smart bombs. Oops, hold the phone, Mr. President, it's the CIA calling with bad news.

"Turns out it ain't Saddam behind this. The cyber-terrorists just wanted you to think that. Ha, ha . . . *fooled ya* . . .

"The President turns to his intelligence people. Who is the enemy? A bunch of acne-skinned sixteen-year-old phrackers out of Peoria? Dutch computer anarchists just out for kicks? U.S.–trained Third World cyber-terrorists? Guess what—you may never know, because this attack occurred over untraceable satellite cellphones. War in the twenty-first century means no front line, no enemy to shoot, no 'theater of operation.'

"And if you think I'm just pitching a far-fetched movie script to Bruce Willis' people, tell you what. Keep your bombs and bullets. Give me a group of ten hackers with the same level of experience and skills as mine, and I will bring this country to its knees in thirty days.

"Here it is, people, short and sweet: we have ceded control of this country's infrastructure to the robots. Whoever controls the robots controls us."

At this point, the kid simply sat back, reveling in the dead silence that followed. Once the theatrical pause elapsed, he leaned back into the microphone. "Now, let's talk about arming yourselves against the bad guys."

Twenty-seven

Manhattan
Monday, February 22

THE BUZZWORD ON WALL STREET that year was "globalization."

For the major players in the wealth multiplication game, that single word was synonymous with *survival*. The century was drawing to a close, and the borders dividing nations were dissolving. Fully globalized corporations insisted that the providers of their financial services likewise be able to step up to the plate in any developed (and developing) region. Globalization was the new wave for the strong, the possible death knell for the weak.

Of course, globalization was obscenely expensive, and not everyone had the dough to step up to the plate. As for Merrill, Goldman and Morgan Stanley/Dean Witter—well, it was a foregone conclusion that they were already feeding at the trough. The other wannabes—Wolcott Fulbright and about twenty other financial houses around the globe— were burning through boatloads of cash, trying to buy themselves one of the three or four remaining seats at the table. That year, Deutsche Bank (Germany), ING-Barings (Denmark), UBS Securities (Switzerland), NatWest (Britain) and CIBC-Wood Gundy (Canada) had charged into the United States, buying up key pieces of Wall Street money-making machines, guaranteeing seven-figure compensation and a global empire to proven superstars.

Though Wolcott was clearly a dark horse among those attempting to stake out a truly global presence, it was making measurable strides, particularly in the areas of derivatives and emerging markets instruments. Assuming its upcoming initial public offering was even moderately successful, it would have the liquid capital necessary to make the final rounds of the global financial supermarket sweepstakes. The firm's CEO, Max Schomburg, was utilizing every resource in his arsenal to ensure the success of the public offering and, therefore, the future of the firm.

A textbook illustration of Wolcott's global attitude unspooled each Monday morning at 7:15 A.M. in the so-called Kuala Lumpur Room of the firm's New York headquarters. As a constant reminder of the firm's initiative to conquer the world, Max Schomburg had decreed that the thirty-two conference rooms in 44 Wall Street would be named after all the far-flung outposts Wolcott either had or would have throughout the world.

The twenty-one men and women groggily grasped for the gelatinous fruit-jelly danishes and aspirin-bitter black coffee in the center of the enormous circular table dominating the Kuala Lumpur Room. Between bites of the sugary pastries, they discussed their adventures over the weekend at their Killington ski houses. Those stuck in Manhattan enthused about the Japanese restaurants they patronized on Saturday night. To an outsider, the intriguing thing about this group was its *diversity*— they represented a veritable United Nations of talent. Sanjeev, Cynthia, Trevor, Helmut, Genghis, Chaim, Bin Bong Yam, Jason, Girish, Chatri, Strobe and Joe sat cheek-by-jowl in the conference room, battling over the pastries. Wall Street firms like Wolcott Fulbright were the ultimate meritocracies: as long as you could make money for the firm, there would be a space waiting for you on the trading floor.

At precisely 7:14 A.M., Julian Stainsby entered the room with a spiral notebook in hand. He jabbed the button on the speakerphone and punched up the conference call operator. Once the operator connected all parties around the globe, Stainsby cleared his throat and conducted the roll call in his disarmingly proper English accent. "London, can you hear me?"

"Plain as a bell."

"Sydney?" Stainsby called out.

"We're here."

"Tokyo?"

"Yes, Tokyo's here." The voice in Tokyo was suffused with the snap-crackle-pop of a bad connection. "We're going to redial in, see if we can't improve our connection some."

"Okay," Stainsby said. "I've got Toronto, Chicago, San Fran and Boston in the U.S. and everyone who's gonna be here in New York is here. Gil's tied up with a piece of business on the desk, so at the last minute, he asked me to fill in this morning and I—"

An annoyed voice burst forth from the starfish-shaped speakerphone: "Hey, New York, what gives? You forgot Hong Kong. What are we, chopped liver?"

Whoops, Julian mouthed silently to the others in the Kuala Lumpur Room. He responded in a contrite tone, "*Terribly* sorry for the oversight, Hong Kong. This is usually Magilla's show, and it's my first go-round—"

"Look, mate," Hong Kong rasped in over the box, "I know we've been handed back over to the Communists, but for God's sake, we're people too."

In conference rooms located in four other major cities of global significance, powerful young people shared a chuckle at Stainsby's expense.

"Right, Hong Kong, won't happen again," Julian said, twisting his wedding band anxiously. His mind was elsewhere, on the hot deal McGeary was working. "Seeing that the market activity is fast and furious, let's get right to it. Hong Kong, let's give you the honors."

According to the Hong Kong report, investors were obsessed with the snap-back rally in the American markets after Freefall Friday. "The slope of the normalized smile has become steeper as the demand for out-of-the-money puts comprising portfolio insurance has increased. All our customers want to talk about is getting back into the U.S. stock market game."

In Tokyo, where Japanese stocks of the Nikkei continued their swoon, "major institutional investor inquiry is heavily skewed toward exposure in the rebounding U.S. equity markets, primarily through derivatives."

In London, the talk of Europe was the sustained "melt-up" in the U.S. stock market. "We see asset allocation managers jumping aboard the train, even as it moves out of the station. We're putting some of our customers into a steep-term structure of the S&P 500, as the increased demand for put protection has pushed implied volatilities to fourteen percent."

In Sydney, Australian investors wanted another taste of American stocks as well. "With the S&P 500's steady upward climb from the depths of Freefall Friday, front month at-the-money vols have fallen, it's no longer overpriced. We say, sell long-dated volatility, buy short-dated volatility. Buy and sell straddles delta-neutral."

Julian himself provided the New York report. "In New York, our equity customers are back in a big way. There's a lot of play in S&P index calls, betting on a continued rally. Based on the demand we're seeing from our Priority A institutional customers, this is no dead-cat bounce, folks. Despite Freefall Friday's attempt to spoil the party, the bubble hasn't burst yet."

"I don't know about you *gaijin*," Tokyo said. "Your markets seem to defy all logic."

Stainsby silently retorted, *Look who's talking*. "That's it, people. Thanks." With that, Stainsby stabbed the disconnect button on the starfish, concluding the morning research call. The attendees filed out of the Kuala Lumpur Room, heading back to their posts on the trading floor to field the fevered inquiries from their customers.

———————●———————

Rick Hansen caught Joseph Monetti coming out of the morning call. "Hey, good morning, Joe, got a few minutes?"

Joe turned to Rick with a deer-in-the-headlights look. Hansen thought, odd this guy is nicknamed Joe Money, because nothing about him suggests money. He was almost sickly thin, with ungainly limbs that moved with marionette awkwardness. His facial features called to mind an abandoned mongrel puppy, with black curly hair and deep-set circles beneath dark, sad-sack eyes. Those eyes caromed constantly around the room in an energetic attempt to avoid eye contact with the person to whom he was speaking. But no denying it, the guy enjoyed a reputation on the floor as a brilliant quant jock whose derivatives structures were almost poetic in their simplicity and creativity. (McGeary referred to him as *"scary-smart."*) Despite the high-water-pants style, Monetti was widely regarded as a go-to resource at the firm.

Joe Money consulted his Timex Ironman Triathlon watch. "I've got a meeting with Gil McGeary in about five minutes."

"This will take two."

"Is this about predicting the market with chaos theory?" Joe Money asked.

Hansen was startled. "How did you know that?"

"Magilla said you'd be asking about it. Also, Roslynn Blum mentioned it to me, said you were looking into creating a system for the desk."

Whoa. The little white lie he'd told Blum had come back to bite him in the ass, he realized. He was about to fumble over some lame reponse, but Monetti saved him. "Personally, I think that's an awesome idea."

"You do?"

"Absolutely. Truth is, chaos theory is probably the most exciting advance in the science of physics in over forty years. It's the first time in three decades that academicians are returning to the intellectual forefront of the financial marketplace. As I see it, the chaologists can no longer be ignored."

Hansen shuffled from one foot to the other. "What exactly is chaos theory, anyway?"

"The bedrock of chaos is that many highly complex, nonlinear systems appear on their face to behave randomly, when in reality, they react in a semi-orderly manner under their own set of rules."

"Example?"

"The weather, the economy. Rioting crowds. But perhaps the most chaotic, nonlinear system of all is the stock market."

"Go on."

Monetti stared at the carpet and absently massaged his ear between thumb and forefinger. "Conventional wisdom has always held that these systems are, by their very nature, no-way-around-it unpredictable. Chaos theory blows that wisdom out of the water. Chaos is *not* the same as randomness."

Hansen nodded encouragingly.

"Chaologists concede that the behavior of any complex system is un-predictable very far out into the future; there are just too many variables changing constantly. But—and this is the key to applying chaos theory—in the short term, the behavior of these systems contains pockets of pre-dictability hidden beneath the white noise of thousands if not millions of variables, not discernible by any amount of human analysis. Chaotic systems move to their own self-generated signal, like the clapping of an audience that begins with one set of hands clapping and eventually be-comes a harmonious, single, nonlinear system. Therefore, assuming you have access to the proper computational resources, you can predict broad-based market movements in the short term."

Hansen frowned in concentration. "You're saying that chaos theory permits a short-term prediction of the markets?"

"It's possible, if you have enough computing power. But some black-box ventures—D. B. Shaw, or the Prediction Company come to mind—claim that chaos theory is only accurate within a band of fifteen to sixty days."

Hansen grunted. Tom Bingham had probably predicted the mini-crash just within that band. Still, he was skeptical that anyone could predict the market with the accuracy Bingham seemed to exhibit. . . .

He was about to ask Monetti about that when a chime indicated the arrival of the down elevator. Joseph Monetti said, "Hey, I got to go. Let's talk further if you're really interested in setting up a black-box system." Then he extricated himself from the conversation and disap-peared into the herd of people packed into the elevator car.

———●———

When Joe Money got back to the trading floor, it turned out McGeary himself was delayed ten minutes. The desk head finished up his call and poked his head out of the fishbowl. "Stain! Joe Money!"

The men turned around.

"My office," McGeary growled, waving them in.

When they were seated at the small round table in the corner of McGeary's office, The Stain said, "What's up?"

"Have you seen this yet?" McGeary asked, waving a copy of *Derivatives Letter* in front of them.

"How could we?" Stainsby pointed out, playfully. "You're the first one on the distribution list and you sit on it forever."

"Well, here." He tossed it on the table. "Consider it distributed."

Stainsby and Monetti positioned the newsletter in front of them. *Derivatives Letter* was a weekly trade publication distributed to subscribers by facsimile every Monday morning. *DL* was notorious for being heavily laced with gossip about hirings and firings in the very fluid derivatives sales and trading community. The *Letter*'s price tag was exceedingly steep—an eye-popping $1,795 a year. The green-eyeshade types at the majors were appalled that an anemic twelve-page weekly scandal sheet fetched the same price as a *dozen* annual subscriptions to the daily *Wall Street Journal*. But the business units retorted that a single lead gleaned from the *Letter* could pay for itself in an eye blink. The article McGeary had circled in red was a case in point:

MIDEAST PETRODOLLARS HUNT OUT MEGA U.S. EQUITY DERIVATIVES PLAYS

Multibillion-dollar pools of oil-generated cash are reportedly eyeing the U.S. equity markets for significant synthetic S&P 500 plays, according to Charles Stone, whose fledging Boca Raton–based investment firm GoldBridge Capital Advisors has discretion over the funds. The assets are apparently those of extremely wealthy Middle Eastern sheiks intrigued by the impressive broad-based rally of American stocks since the January 29 market break (known as "Freefall Friday" among the mainstream press).

The investment partnership formed by Stone plans to shop the business to a variety of New York–based derivatives houses "that are not intimidated by equity options and swaps with a billion-dollar notional amount" featuring "a short lifespan." Stone indicated that his clients were willing to pay "a premium in fees" to the firm willing to broker a string of successive mega-deals for GoldBridge.

Julian looked up after finishing the piece. "Looks tasty, boss. Am I to presume that you want us to pitch the business?"

"No need. Gil McGeary's already been there, done that, and guess what, ladies, we're finalists in the beauty contest. This fellow Stone's in town next week and he's gonna come to the firm for a dog-and-pony show."

"So far, so good," Stainsby said. "What are these hot-tub sheiks into?"

"Juicy stuff. They say it's hedging activity, but I wouldn't rule out the possibility that they're taking a view of the market. Then again, these guys are no proverbial Belgian dentists, either." A "Belgian dentist" was the financial community's slang for an unsophisticated rube who had no business dealing in derivatives. "Suitability is not at issue with this customer. We're gonna need the lawyers upstairs to structure these trades, that is, if we get the business. There's restructuring potential here, as well, rolling to deferred months. And, as it says in *Derivatives Rag*, the notional amounts will be hee-yuge." McGeary's eyes rested on a somber-looking Joe Monetti. "Hey, Money, what's up with the long face? Why you rainin' on my parade?"

"I dunno. It's Middle East money." Joe's shrug was more of a twitch. "Sheiks, especially, are notoriously difficult. It's gonna be an uphill sell with the folks in Credit. And probably with the lawyers too."

"Screw Credit and the lawyers. If we don't do the business with GoldBridge, Goldman will. You know why Goldman cleans our clocks every freaking time? Because they know when to take measured risks. If Max Schomburg really, truly wants to ramp this boutique up to a global franchise on the par with Goldman and Morgan, this is *exactly* the kind of trade he needs to get behind. This GoldBridge deal is a marquee trade, Joe."

Monetti held up his hands defensively. "Gil, wait, I'm on your team, remember? I'm just anticipating the roadblocks to the business is all."

McGeary smiled fiercely. "Right, I know, I know. I've got the same broken record of Scott Mendelsohn's voice playing in my head right now. 'Gil, this is Wolcott Fulbright. We are not Goldman. Nor are we Merrill, nor are we First Boston. Nor will we ever be.' "

Stainsby and Monetti laughed at their boss's dead-on impression of the number-two officer in the Credit Department. The products devised by the Equity Derivatives Group were becoming ever more sophisticated. Not surprisingly, Mendelsohn was becoming more and more a "Dr. No." But the firm did not make money turning business away, especially multibillion-dollar accounts with global implications. Hey, Scott Mendelsohn and the rest of his cohorts in the Credit Department *couldn't get paid* if McGeary and his team didn't do trades. Nor would the upcoming IPO be a success with such a no-can-do attitude. Therefore, Scott M. better have a goddamned good reason to put a monkey wrench in this piece of business, that is, if Wolcott was fortunate enough to get it.

"I promise you, if we win the beauty contest with Stone, we *will* do business with this account." At this point, Gil McGeary leaned forward and flashed a brilliant, cryptic smile. "You guys let me worry about Credit. When I have to, I can be very persuasive."

Stainsby and Monetti knew from experience that in McGeary's world, "persuasive" did not necessarily mean "charming."

Twenty-eight

LONG BEACH, CALIFORNIA
Wednesday, February 24

EDDIE SLAMKOWSKI HAD GOTTEN IN extra early that morning. He waited for the phone to ring with Charles Stone on the other end. As soon as that happened, Slamkowski would submit his one week's notice to a boss he'd never met.

Perhaps it was inevitable that he would return to Chicago. Just the year before, Eddie had been a broker on the floor of the Chicago Mercantile Exchange, a nine-year veteran with a reputation for his savvy and verve in the rough-and-tumble world of the S&P stock index futures trading pits. He recalled the fateful afternoon, not much unlike any other, where he was screaming in the pits to get a twenty-lot order filled for the account of a large Swiss bank. Next thing he remembered was blanking out, and waking to find himself tits-up in the S&P pit, a forest of undulating legs roiling around him.

The on-premises doctor said it was a stress attack combined with a godawful lunch of Polish sausage on white bread from a sidewalk vendor on Wacker Drive. The different types of ailments that could befall a floor trader were legion, and the doctor recommended a sabbatical. Slam, on the rebound from a bad breakup of a two-year relationship, craved a change of scenery. Doctor's orders were his ticket to justify taking a year off from the business.

Slam impulsively handed over the keys to his coveted brownstone at 1500 East Lakeshore to Andy Studd, his ex-colleague on the floor of the Merc. Packed the Lexus 400 SE sport coupe with essentials, put the rest in storage. Drove all night to Huntington Beach, California, a place he'd heard a Merc arb clerk drunkenly rave about one night at the Cactus Bar. Slam rented a shoebox of an efficiency apartment three blocks from the beach and, the following morning, went shopping for a radical new lifestyle. He blew $550 on a six-foot Tom Peterson Spyder/Fireball Fish longboard, Billabong surfer's gear and a concoction called Mr. Zogs Original Sexwax. He was determined to master the sport in record time.

Watching the sun rise over Huntington Beach each morning became a soothing, Zen-like experience for Slam. It was there he encountered a pair of stubble-chinned, leather-skinned Aussie surf-gods named Damien and Derf. D&D were amused enough by the pale-skinned half-Italian/half-Pole's war stories from the Merc to agree to teach him full-monty surfing in the tradition of worldwide surf idol Kelly Slater. As Derf put it, they intended to "get you stoked out of your gourd, mate."

Eddie Slamkowski's first weeks at tube-riding were disastrous. Time and time again, the twelve-foot swells "skunked" him, mercilessly spitting him and his board onto the shore. The time Slam got "chinned by the fin," Damien and Derf clutched their cobbled washboard stomachs and dropped to the sand in convulsive laughter. Derf began calling him "shark biscuit," the ultimate insult of the surfing culture. Damien tactfully attempted to dissuade Slam from further indignity. "Like, you don't have to do this to yourself, dude."

But surfing had already gotten under Slamkowski's skin, spiked his blood with adrenaline. The no-luck sucker from the Midwest surfed ten hours a day over the course of a fortnight, sticking to it until he was able to carve through the peeling, 150-yard barrels like a seasoned pro. Without even realizing it, he found himself discussing the fine art of busting a nose manual and a one-foot backside air-180 with the hard-core extremers. With Pygmalion-like pride, D&D proclaimed the Slammer a rock-bitten, hard-bodied, fin-flying surf-god. ("Dude, you no longer suck!") To complete the makeover, Slam pumped iron relentlessly, tanned his skin to a deep chocolate-brown and let his hair grow to his shoulders.

As much as he found himself craving the gonzo of futures and securities, he had become an inhabitant of the world of Damien and Derf. Quitting the surfer's lifestyle cold turkey was not an option. Eddie Slamkowski contacted several headhunters in Southern Cal to ferret out possible opportunities within driving distance of the beach. But the few recruiters who looked at his résumé assured him his was a hopeless cause: There was no huge demand for an individual with his skill-set unless he was willing to relocate to San Francisco, which he wasn't.

Then, seemingly out of nowhere, Charles Stone surfaced. Curiously, Slam never met Stone, as Stone was always "too busy" with overseas meetings to interview him personally. The entire hiring process was conducted through the headhunter. Sight unseen, Stone offered up a one-year package at $72,500 per annum with a bonus that would bring him to a buck thirty-five, all in. Not terrible. The offer contained a six-month noncompete clause, but Slam would have happily forked over his left nut for the opportunity, which permitted him to retain his long mane of surfer locks. Still, Infinity Securities was far from Slam's dream job. Eddie Slamkowski *was* Infinity, acting as its sole order-taker and back-office troglodyte.

The phone rang. Slam answered it brightly: "Infinity Securities."

"It's Infinity *Technology* Securities," Stone corrected him tersely.

"Uh, right. Good morning, Mr. Stone."

"Did the orders from our European customers hit the system yet?"

"Yes, they did. Everything's cool."

"Fine. And they're cued up to go to the exchanges?"

"Yes, of course. Say, Mr. Stone?" Slamkowski rushed the words so he wouldn't get cut off again. "Mr. Stone, I'm giving notice. I'm going back to Chicago, as early as next week."

There was dead silence. Then Stone erupted in fury: *"You can't do this to me! You've made a commitment!"*

Slamkowski was blown away by his employer's irrational response. He expected resistance, certainly, but not the choking rage that emanated from his phone. "Wait a second, Mr. Stone—"

"I gave you an opportunity when no one else would. I made you the office manager of my flagship branch. I've put you at the center of . . . a cutting-edge technology that will change the markets forever—"

Slam suppressed a smile. Now the guy was going overboard. "Charles," he said, "yes, thank you for the opportunity. I have learned a great deal in my short stint here. But your technology is so good, your systems so automated, I don't even know why you need a guy like Eddie Slamkowski around."

Charles Stone's response came without hesitation. "I need you around to ensure that all goes according to plan."

Slamkowski frowned. *What the hell does that mean?*

Stone calmed down. "Ed, listen to me. You underestimate your role a great deal. You're imperative to the functioning of all the systems. You're a conductor leading a highly skilled but potentially out-of-tune orchestra. I need you there."

"I appreciate that, Mr. Stone, but as I said, but I intend to go back to Chicago."

"In that case, I want to thank you for your contribution in getting this start-up venture off the ground and sincerely wish you the best of luck in your future endeavors. At the same time, however, I also want to make you an offer I hope you can't refuse."

In the next breath, Charles Stone offered Eddie Slamkowski his entire year's bonus payout—$52,500—if he stayed with Infinity through the end of April, rather than leave next week. Free money, Stone said, just for another two months' service. Eddie Slamkowski gasped, swallowed hard, then jumped all over it. How could he not?

Stone had been right; the generous payout was something Eddie Slamkowski didn't refuse. In the end, when it was far too late to reverse events, Slamkowski would desperately wish he had.

Twenty-nine

"BASICALLY, IT'S BIG BROTHER, you know what I mean?"

Wolcott Fulbright's chief of security, Al Bancroft, was fast-forwarding the firm's surveillance videocassette for the night of February 18–19. Bancroft was a barrel-chested tough guy on crutches. The security chief had slipped off the roof of his Staten Island home the previous weekend while trying to sweep off some fresh snow. His broken leg was bent back in a plaster cast the shape of a backward L.

"There's not much that gets by this system," Bancroft said, patting the casing of his Panasonic WV-5470 time-lapse video surveillance setup. "Each surveillance quadrant records sixteen cameras simultaneously. Since the machine captures a black-and-white still image every four seconds, I can squeeze forty-eight hours of activity onto each tape. That means I've got forty calendar days of surveillance at my fingertips at any given time, you know what I mean?"

"I know what you mean." Rick Hansen nodded and rubbed his arms briskly. It was unusually chilly in the security control room.

"We're almost there. Now, you think someone tampered with the computer in your office?"

"No, I *know* someone tampered with it. All my files were deleted and replaced with numbers."

"Huh. You fill out a Security Incident Report?"

"Yes."

"Good. We should have a record of that, you know what I mean?"

"Right, I know what you mean," Hansen said, staring at the blizzard of static on the video monitor.

"Okay," Bancroft said. "We're here." He thumbed the remote control, which allowed the tape to play at normal speed.

The date appeared at the top of the screen. The screen was diced up into sixteen distinct cubes—four rows of four images. Each image had a ghostly white label of its origin:

NORTH HALL	NORTH E HALL	SOUTH HALL	SOUTH W HALL
SECTOR A-1	SECTOR A-2	SECTOR A-3	SECTOR A-4
SECTOR B-1	SECTOR B-2	SECTOR B-3	SECTOR B-4
SECTOR C-1	SECTOR C-2	SECTOR C-3	SECTOR C-4

Though the images were in stark black-and-white, Hansen recognized the cubicles and the common areas of the LR&C Department. The running time was 12:03:33 A.M. on February 19.

"Basically, as you can see, the floor is empty," Bancroft said. "No activity in any of the sectors. Let's skip ahead."

On fast-forward mode, the videotape advanced from midnight to 1:00 A.M. in a matter of seconds. There was no discernible activity during that hour. Then, unexpectedly, all sixteen images from the LR&C Department suddenly flickered to black, then to snow. The labels on each image changed.

CAM FAIL	CAM FAIL	CAM FAIL	CAM FAIL
CAM FAIL	CAM FAIL	CAM FAIL	CAM FAIL
CAM FAIL	CAM FAIL	CAM FAIL	CAM FAIL
CAM FAIL	CAM FAIL	CAM FAIL	CAM FAIL

"Well, blow me in Macy's window," Bancroft mumbled in disbelief. "That's a first."

"What happened?"

"The entire surveillance quadrant failed. Not just one camera, but all sixteen."

"The entire system?" Hansen tilted his head in curiosity.

Bancroft remained mute as the tape spun forward. Suddenly, when the tape reached 06:42:37 A.M. on the morning of February 19, the sixteen images came back on-screen.

"What does that mean?" Hansen asked.

"It means someone futzed with the equipment," Bancroft fumed. "Maybe not intentionally, maybe there was a short in the cord and it got jiggled. But basically, it means we have no visual record of the comings and goings of anyone on your floor that night. Ain't that weird?"

Hansen gazed at the ceiling, as if in search of divine intervention. It came to him then. "The sixteen images didn't include surveillance of the elevators."

"No," Bancroft replied. "The cameras of the elevators are all wired into a separate surveillance quadrant."

"Could we view *that* tape? Would we be able to see if anyone got off on the thirty-seventh floor during those hours?"

Bancroft answered, "It's a definite maybe."

The security chief ejected the videocassette, thumbed through the others, inserted another tape. Within ten minutes, Bancroft captured the blurred-but-distinguishable still image of a swarthy man in a janitorial services outfit stepping out of an elevator onto Hansen's floor at 03:32: 47 A.M. Bancroft said, "Maybe that's your man. Aside from the uniform, he doesn't look like a janitor, does he?"

"Mmm. No, not really. Also, you think about it, three-thirty in the morning is an odd time to be emptying the trash bins, isn't it?"

"And since when do you need a big-ass toolkit like that to take out the garbage?" Bancroft hit a button on his Mitsubishi video-capture printer to make a hard copy of the swarthy man from the time-lapse surveillance video. "I'll check this guy out with the shift supervisor and let you know what he says."

"Mind if I have a copy of that?" Hansen asked. The lawyer didn't exactly know what he would do with the shiny printout, but then, you never knew when it might come in handy.

———◆———

Late in the afternoon, Paul Gelbaum phoned Hansen. "I just had the strangest phone conversation."

"Oh yeah?" Hansen was distracted by the complicated schematic of a synthetic equity-linked debt structure that Joe Monetti had dreamed up.

"Yeah. Funny thing is, the call was about you."

The seriousness in Gelbaum's voice caused Rick's blood to run cold. "What about me?"

"I had just gotten back from lunch when this dude named Ron Dalinger calls me. Claimed he was from a firm called General Investigative Services and was doing a background check on you."

"Oh, right." Hansen shrugged. "That must be the outside firm hired by Wolcott to do routine background checks on new employees."

"Yeah, well, believe me, this was anything but routine. This was a background check straight out of the Twilight Zone. I mean, this guy Dalinger started with normal questions, like how long I'd known you, how were we acquainted, yada yada. Then the questions got progressively weirder and weirder. I actually had to write them down so I wouldn't forget them . . . let me see . . ." There was a shuffling of papers on the other end of the line as Gelbaum tried to put his hands on the notes.

"Oh, yeah, here we go. Here's some typical examples. 'Did Rick Hansen ever cheat in an exam? Get anyone pregnant? Sleep with a teacher? Experiment with homosexuality?' "

"They asked you *that*?"

" '—ever cheat on his taxes? Have any hidden health problems? Owe anybody a large sum of money?' I mean, I couldn't believe the hair on this guy. Finally, I said I had to take another call, and could I call him right back? Naturally, he refused to give me his number. And guess what?"

"There's no listing for General Investigative Services in the Manhattan directory."

"Correct. What do you make of that?"

"I don't know," Hansen said. He wanted to downplay it, so he said lightly, "Of course, you told him I was the Mother Teresa of lawyers."

"Right, a true Boy Scout," Gelbaum laughed. "Basically, I lied out of my ass for you. Hey, what are friends for, right?" After a chuckle, his voice turned serious again. "All kidding aside, Rick, it was really weird. Not like they were doing a background check, as much as they were digging up dirt on you."

Troubled, Rick hung up. Then he dialed up Al Bancroft in Security. The security chief answered on one ring. "Bancroft."

"Hey, this is Hansen again. Does the firm use a vendor named General Investigative Services to conduct background checks on employees?"

"No. We have an exclusive contract with Donnelly. They're the best in the business."

After concluding the call with Bancroft, Rick Hansen stared at the phone, lost in thought. Someone was trying to dig up some dirt on him, and they weren't exactly being subtle about it. It occurred to him then that maybe the indiscretion was intentional. Perhaps they *wanted* him to know they were looking into him. The troubling question was *who?*

Thirty

MANHATTAN

Friday, February 26

THE RAW MEAT FROM Columbia Business School gathered in the Harold J. Fulbright Room. Forty-six young men and women, confident and nervous at the same time, instinctively clustered into the study-group cliques they'd established at school, and gasped at the opulence of their surroundings. With its 360-degree views of the city and New Jersey, silver-plated fixtures and marble-checkerboard floor, the Fulbright Room was a showplace for a firm that so aggressively wooed the brightest MBAs minted at the finest Ivy League b-schools.

But while the all-black string quartet playing Pachelbel's *Canon* was impressive, the Chardonnay perfectly chilled and the sushi hors d'oeuvres divine, it took a lot more than great catering to sign up a Columbia MBA for next year's training class at Wolcott Fulbright. The young men and women in this room were hot commodities and, worse, *they knew it*. The starting salaries for the Columbia b-school grads in this room averaged $100,480. To repeat: *averaged. For starters.* Only Harvard and Stanford grads made more ($102,630 and $100,800, on average). And let's face it, fine firm that Wolcott Fulbright was, it was not quite M-G-M caliber (Merrill-Goldman-Morgan). No, it was more in the peer group of, say, Donaldson Lufkin and Jenrette. Like DLJ, Wolcott was a mighty, up-and-coming global firm that was roaring up the league tables, yes, but it didn't quite yet have the cachet of a Goldman Sachs. The Goldman brand name got you laid at an Upper East Side singles bar like American Trash.

Max Schomburg recognized this. Also, he recognized that in light of its globalization and the expansion envisioned after the impending public offering, Wolcott Fulbright needed 127 new bodies to populate its trading floors and investment banking suites and it needed them right away. The machine was hungry and it needed feeding.

The competition was fierce. There were only a handful of top-tier business schools, an oligopoly that included Harvard, Stanford, Amos Tuck–Dartmouth, Wharton, Kellogg-Northwestern, Chicago, Sloan-MIT, Darden-UVA, Michigan, Fuqua-Duke.

So Max Schomburg himself rolled up the shirtsleeves and personally called each of the targeted MBA candidates to invite him/her to the firm for cocktails to tell the exciting story of Wolcott, Fulbright & Company. Such an invite was not easily declined by the Ivy Leaguers. A personal call from Mighty Max? This was pretty seductive stuff for a twenty-three-year-old who had yet to work a single day in the so-called Real World. Why, just a half a decade ago, some of these kids were mere seniors in high school, faces studded with acne, sitting in their suburban bedrooms with Stone Temple Pilots cranked full blast, fantasizing over the Women of Melrose Place calendar on the door to their rooms.

Now look at them—they could call Dad collect and tell him that Max Schomburg and a bunch of managing directors at Wolcott Fulbright were ringing them up to go out for drinks.

And so each one of the men who came to the Harold J. Fulbright Room that evening dressed in the only business suit he owned, with his benign rep stripe tie that wasn't too flashy and never fell out of fashion. Each woman was dressed in a sensible outfit from Barneys. Collectively, they were a sparkling group of young men and women, culled mainly from that upper half-percent of New England WASP and Jewish privilege. However, their contingent included the occasional union laborer's son or janitor's daughter, proof positive that an Ivy League MBA was one of the last great societal equalizers in America. Bright-eyed and sleek-jawed, the recruits' arteries had not yet been polluted by years' worth of $39.95 filet mignon at Smith & Wollensky. They still possessed washboard stomachs and shiny hair so meticulously moussed it crackled to the touch. The ambition that churned in their bellies had a nuclear intensity, yet the cynicism in these youngsters was embryonic, virginal. They were raw meat, fresh blood. Blank slates. Human clay to be molded in the image of the firm.

In return for their selfless devotion to the institution, there would be a dazzling pay package that permitted summers in the Hamptons, a sports car in the city and, eventually, private school for the kids, if it came to that. Implicitly, down the road, there was the potential of "making MD."

As those in the finance business knew, MD was not a medical doctor. It stood for Managing Director, of course, though some wags would tell you it stood for "million dollars." The managing director title symbolized true Wall Street royalty, roughly analogous to making partner in a law or accounting firm, but then again, something completely different. It conferred absolute power on its recipient in the ultimate world of absolute power. Unlimited expense accounts, special tropical-weather junkets, eye-popping stock options—these were the minimal perks for MDs.

The greatest perk of all, Gil McGeary told a few of the prospective recruits gathered around him, *is that once you make managing director, your ass becomes stainless steel and everyone else grows magnetic lips.*

What was that? Several young prospects who'd overheard this bon mot snickered. *Hey, who was this guy, anyway?* A horseshoe of transfixed students quickly gathered around this charismatic managing director named McGeary.

"I hope you guys realize that you're like baseball players," the managing director was saying. "You understand that, don't you?"

"How do you mean?" The prospect's name tag said he was GREGG SMITH. He resembled a California lifeguard more than he did a grad student concentrating in emerging markets finance.

"Well, Gregg, think about it. Think of the Wall Street community as kind of like the Major Leagues. The big four firms have great franchises. Goldman is like the New York Yankees, Merrill Lynch is the Los Angeles Dodgers, Morgan Stanley, the Boston Red Sox. I think of Salomon as the Oakland A's, always a threat for a World Series ring. You get an offer from any of these guys, pounce on it."

The baseball analogy intrigued the slightly intoxicated youngsters. "What about Lehman?" someone asked.

"I'm getting there. The next group's always in the hunt for a pennant. Lehman would be the Philadelphia Phillies, First Boston, the New York Mets. JP Morgan, now they're like the Atlanta Braves, the Cinderella wannabe—at the end of the day, JP's still a bank, after all. Still, with Glass-Steagall coming apart, JP's the team to watch. They make the playoffs season after season.

"Then there's the other top-tier Wall Street firms that comprise the possible champs. Bear Stearns is the Toronto Blue Jays; PaineWebber is the Seattle Mariners; Smith Barney is the Minnesota Twins; DLJ is the Baltimore Orioles. You get the idea."

"What about Wolcott Fulbright?" a bespectacled woman with wiry black hair asked.

"We're the Colorado Rockies," McGeary stated, swilling his Tanqueray and tonic. "We're the scrappy up-and-comers, the ones to watch.

Add a few of you big hitters to the roster, and we could come out on top of the league tables."

"So, like, we're the rookies?" Gregg Smith asked.

"That's right. You're the rookies. Columbia is just one of the farm clubs. You guys are the players and what we're all doing here with the raw fish and cocktails in hand? This is the draft. You guys are potential first-round draft picks.

"Now, just like in baseball, the star system prevails. You receive a tremendous amount of money simply for doing something you enjoy. If you're mediocre, however, you won't last long. First you'll be benched—meaning, you have your accounts pulled away from you and reassigned to a better hitter. Then you might be put on waivers."

"Meaning, fired?" Gregg Smith asked.

"Exactly right there, Gregg, A-plus for you. But just like in baseball, even mediocre utility infielders can jump around from team to team until finally they're either shipped to the Minor Leagues—Section 20 subs of regional banks—or go to Japan to play ball. Nomura, Yamaichi, Daiwa."

The recruits laughed at the analogies.

"Hopefully, in a few years," McGeary continued, "you'll prove yourself worthy once again to play with the Major Leaguers at Merrill and Salomon. But no matter what, a typical career in Major League baseball or on Wall Street is brief. Injuries shorten careers in baseball; stress and boardroom politics could render you damaged goods on the Street by your mid-thirties. How many thirty-, forty-year-old recruits do you think Wolcott's gonna hire for this year's training program?"

This question was met with silence and shrugs.

"*Zero.*" McGeary said. "Zero. Because on the Street, youth is king, people." McGeary lowered his voice to a conspiratorial whisper. "I hear Max Schomburg's willing to pay up this year, so make the best deal you can." McGeary's eyes dropped to his watch. "Got to run, everyone. Thanks for coming."

"Do you have a business card, Gil?" Gregg Smith asked.

"Yes, Gregg, I do, and I'd give it to you, but I don't want a chucklehead like you calling me on the desk while I'm risking the firm's money."

The group laughed in delight at the put-down of their hyperobnoxious classmate.

"Hope to see you in the training program next August," McGeary said, shuffling through the throng toward the exits. He suddenly felt a hand hook lightly around his arm. He turned and saw it was Alan Milgrim.

"Where are you going, Gil?" Alan Milgrim asked. "Max hasn't even gotten here yet."

"I've got a client meeting in the Jakarta Room."

"Jesus, Gil. Max wanted all the sales and trading MDs here for this recruitment function. I know it's as dull as watching paint dry, but your absence will stand out."

"Alan, do I need to repeat myself? It's a client meeting, a big client. Max of all people will understand that."

"Which client?"

"Money manager named GoldBridge."

Milgrim frowned, nodding in approval. "Charles Stone, that guy with the Middle East money, right?"

"Yes."

"Bobby, Irv and I think that's a good piece of business for us to be chasing. Within reason, that is."

"Glad to hear it," McGeary said. "We may need you to endorse the customer with some of the middle office guys. Let me hop, Alan, I don't want to keep him waiting."

Alan Milgrim stared at the back of Magilla McGeary as the Derivatives head disappeared into a waiting elevator. Finishing the remainder of his straight Absolut, Milgrim found himself wishing he could be a fly on the wall at that client meeting.

———————•———————

Charles Stone was what Julian Stainsby called a cheap date. Stone didn't want to be fruited up with courtside seats for the Knicks, or a dinner at the Four Seasons, or tickets to *Rent*. "No, thank you," Stone had said dryly, declining all offers. "I prefer just that we discuss the business at hand. I have two more meetings scheduled with your competitors on the same night, so we'll need to keep it brief and productive."

"Certainly," Stainsby had replied. "My kind of meeting."

The two sides gathered in the Jakarta Room to see if they could do some derivatives business together. The sodas, seltzers and sandwiches provided by Beverage Services sat untouched on the serving table as the meeting got under way promptly at 7:00 P.M. On the Wolcott side of the marble table sat McGeary, Stainsby and Monetti. Stone came without entourage. Stainsby came armed with a thick stack of four-color promotional materials on the vast derivatives capabilities of the firm, which he laid in front of Charles Stone.

Stone immediately shoved the literature to the side and smiled sardonically. "There is no need for putting on the Ritz, gentlemen. That we are sitting here indicates our belief that your firm could be one of the two or three we will rely upon for structuring the derivatives for our clients' funds."

"What exactly are your people looking for?" McGeary asked.

"We are looking for what our quants call SELF. Size, executions, liquidity and flexibility. The size we intend to deal in is nothing short of market-moving. You need to be prepared for that going in. Also, confidentiality is paramount. If we find that our activity is being leaked in the whisper circuit, we'll pull our business immediately. That provision must be written into any agreement between us."

"Confidentiality is not a problem," Monetti said. "We'll activate your account under a coded number so only three people at the firm will be in the loop on your identity."

"Good. I should also inform you that as important as what we're looking for is what we're not looking for."

"Okay."

"We will not look very favorably on those firms that are not nimble enough to provide us with prompt turnaround. We're not irrational; we recognize that there is a certain . . . *ritual* necessary to accept first-time transactions from customers. A due diligence, so to speak. However, it is exceptionally competitive out there. If you are not willing to do a certain transaction, of a certain size, then we will not hesitate to move our business to a more amenable derivatives dealer, of which at last count there were at least two hundred and fifty."

"You have nothing to worry about on that front, Charles," Stainsby reassured him. "Wolcott Fulbright has the capacity to do tremendous size."

"Good. Now what can I tell you about GoldBridge Capital Advisors?"

"How much do you currently have under management?" McGeary asked.

"Fifty billion U.S. dollars."

McGeary cocked his head sideways. "Fifty billion? How come we haven't heard of you before?"

"You have heard of the Dartmouth Funds Group, I presume."

"I have, but how are you related to—"

Stone said, "That's one of our subsidiaries. We control the mutual funds under the Dartmouth name."

Joe Monetti asked, "Aren't those funds still run by David Rosenberg and Kendra what's-her-name?"

"Kendra Price. Actually, yes. They still manage the funds pursuant to a six-month consulting arrangement. But our holding company controls the funds." Stone abruptly changed course. "Now, then. Our U.S. equity positions need to be hedged immediately. How quickly can we begin structuring products with Wolcott?"

Stainsby looked at his boss, McGeary, slightly stunned by the aggressiveness of this prospective customer. "Well, in part, that's up to you."

"Which part would that be?"

"For one thing, there's a standard master agreement you would have to sign."

"I presume you're referring to an ISDA master?" The International Swap and Derivatives Association master agreement was a forty-page standardized agreement used by most financial products dealers to govern derivatives activity with customers.

"Yes. Unfortunately, negotiations of the terms often drag on for several months—"

Stone interrupted. "Do you have one with you?"

"Yes. It's in your package of materials."

Stone flipped open the glossy two-pocket presentation folder. He located the thick staple-stitched document and yanked it from the pocket. Stone immediately withdrew his fountain pen and signed the agreement. Sliding it across the table to a stunned Julian Stainsby, he asked curtly, "What else?"

"The usual due diligence," McGeary said. "Credit's going to want your latest audited financials."

"We have $50 billion under management. I don't think your Credit Department will raise any objections to doing business with us, despite the potential magnitude of the notional amounts of our obligations with you."

"That's probably true," McGeary said. "Still, they'll want your financials."

"Including letters of credit from Hemisphere International, our primary bank in London, I suppose?"

"That would be helpful, yes."

"Perhaps this will help move things along." Stone opened his briefcase and produced a massive slab of printed pages. "This is the latest account statement from our prime broker, Infinity Technology Securities," he said, handing it over to Stainsby and Monetti.

Stainsby thumbed through it and suppressed a gasp. The statement was over three hundred pages, and it was only for the month of January!

"Infinity, huh?" McGeary said. "Never heard of them."

"They're a start-up broker-dealer. They have cutting-edge Internet trading capabilities. Our account representative there is Edward Slamkowski, a former trader at the Merc—"

McGeary brightened. "I know Eddie."

"You do?" Stone appeared surprised.

"Sure. The Slammer used to do executions for us as a trader in the S&P pits."

Stone said, "Yes, well, then you know as well as I do, he is a very capable executions professional. That's why we use Infinity."

Stainsby interjected, "Granted, Slamkowski's a good guy, but Infinity could never equal the capabilities of a Wolcott Fulbright. If you ever want to talk to us about our prime brokerage services, let me—"

"That won't be necessary, thank you. Back to the subject at hand. What else will your back-office people demand in order for us to commence doing business?"

"A certain amount of margin will be necessary for sizable short positions," Joe Money said.

"Actually, no margin at all is required by the regulators," Stone said. "Any swap, option or other derivative we'd structure with you would be subject to the Section 4(2) private placement exemption. I presume the trades will be booked out of your offshore affiliate, so Reg T doesn't apply. Technically, Wolcott would not need to collect any collateral at all—"

"I misspoke when I called it margin," Joe Money said, his ears burning. "It's actually referred to as 'performance assurance' and it would be demanded by our Margin Reconciliation group, not the regulators."

"A small amount of performance assurance will be acceptable," Stone said. "But we'd like to leverage our transactions by a factor of thirty, if possible."

"Well," McGeary said. "I think we've got the preliminary ducks in a row. Let's talk about your specific transaction."

"Music to my ears," Stone smiled.

———•———

"So what did you think?" Gil McGeary asked, once Charles Stone left the Jakarta Room to attend another Friday night meeting with a Wolcott Fulbright competitor.

"Real piece of work," Stainsby offered. "I've never seen anyone quite so aggressive before."

"Charm school dropout," Joe Money said.

McGeary winked conspiratorily at Stainsby. "The same charm school you dropped out of, Money?"

Joe Money scowled, but in a good-natured way. He never pretended he'd been hired at WF for his sparkling charisma.

McGeary rubbed his jaw contemplatively. "One thing that bothers me?"

They turned toward their boss.

Gil McGeary tapped his chin with a forefinger. "This guy claims to have $50 billion under management, yet I've never seen him in the market before. Have you guys?"

"No," Stainsby said.

"Me neither," Monetti asked.

McGeary swigged his seltzer. "Why are these guys doing prime brokerage business with a nobody like Infinity? If GoldBridge's such a big hitter, why don't they already have derivatives relationships with the majors?"

"You read the article," Stainsby said. "It's a new pool of oil money."

"In my humble experience, $50 billion doesn't just walk off the street looking for a home. It must've come from *somewhere*. Then again, why ask why, it's a stellar piece of business." The Derivatives desk head stretched and yawned as he spoke the words: "Chuck Stone, where have you been all my life?"

Thirty-one

RICK HANSEN AND ANTONIO VASQUEZ, the doorman, were leaning over Antonio's vestibule in the lobby. They were comparing two one-hundred-dollar bills, laid flat on facing pages of the logbook on Antonio's desk.

"I don't know," Hansen mused. "I think the new Ben Franklin bill is too cartoonish. See Ben's picture on the new bill versus his picture on the older bill?"

Antonio tipped his dark brown cap with the address of the building embroidered on its front and massaged his scalp in concentration. "Yeh. The newer bill doesn't even look real. Looks like play money."

"You're right, it does," Hansen agreed.

"And who was Ben Franklin, anyway? He wasn't even a *president*."

"Right." Hansen gave him a sideways glance. "I take it you prefer the older bill?"

"You mean, I can't have both?" Antonio flashed tobacco-stained teeth to show his remark was in half jest.

Hansen forced out a humorless laugh. "No. You can't—"

"Gimme the newer bill then."

Hansen slid it over to him. "Twenty minutes, that's all I ask."

"That's all you're gonna get." Antonio made the bill disappear in his front pocket. The doorman put on a forced air of uniformed pseudo-authority, as he muttered under his breath. "But twenty minutes only. I don't wanna lose my job over no lousy hunnerd bucks."

"Don't worry." Rick figured twenty minutes would be more than enough. In fact, in thirty-five minutes he had to meet Stephanie at New York Hospital for their Sunday night Lamaze class, so he was motivated to make it quick.

"All right." Without looking at Hansen's face, the Puerto Rican doorman waved the lawyer through to the elevator.

Key money, Hansen thought as the elevator doors closed. To gain access to the apartment building, he had just slipped Vasquez "key money," the term New Yorkers used to describe a bribe given to a doorman. To a guy like Vasquez, a hundred dollars was a lot of money. The night-shift doorman had family in Queens, kids demanding sneakers, Power Rangers toys. Family back in San Juan he was sending funds to. Key money was just another way things got done in New York City. There was an entire underground economy of people in this city with their hands out, waiting to get their palms greased.

On the tenth floor, Hansen stepped out of the elevator and walked down the corridor. Bingham's rent-stabilized unit was 10H. Not surprisingly, there were several notices staple-gunned to the door, curling up at the corners from the dry heat in the corridor. NOTICE OF PETITION FOR NONPAYMENT OF RENT. WARRANT OF EVICTION. *Wouldn't the landlord love to get his claws back on this apartment,* Hansen thought to himself, as he produced the key Elena Bingham had given him that morning and slid it into the keyhole. Pity the poor landlord—the city's landlord-tenant law was skewed in favor of the tenant, and it took as long as a year to evict a deadbeat from a Manhattan apartment. Could be even longer to evict a dead man.

Hansen jiggled the key and twisted it. Didn't work.

Just as Elena had predicted. Bingham had changed the lock to his precious rent-controlled apartment when they'd gone splitsville.

Plan B. The spare key he had found rummaging around in the desk of Kathleen Oberlin. He inserted this key, jerked it to the left. This time, the door opened with a satisfying *click.*

Hansen tentatively opened the door a crack, took a step inside. He placed his fingertips on the cool of the wall, sweeping along its surface in search of a light switch. Found it, flipped it.

As expected, nothing happened.

Dead men don't pay bills, he thought. As a result, the electricity had been shut off long ago.

Rick reached into the duffel bag with the Wolcott Fulbright logo and drew out a fifty-foot-long orange extension cord and a six-outlet power strip he'd borrowed from the office. He stepped back out into the hallway, found an outlet in the common area, plugged in the extension cord and unreeled it as he returned inside Bingham's apartment. Fumbling in the darkness, he unplugged the track lighting from the dead outlet in the apartment, and plugged it into the power strip. Instantly, the 120-

watt floodlights from the track lighting above flared on, throwing light over the living area of the apartment.

Hansen blinked in the sudden brilliance. An uneasy feeling washed over him. How strange it was to be standing in someone else's home after he was dead. *Maybe this is what it's like to be a cop*, he thought. A cop steps into the unvarnished living space of someone who was unprepared for his sudden death. From that perspective, the victim's home was like a snapshot of his station in life, the creature comforts he surrounded himself with. In the privacy of his home, he is his true self, not the role-player he is forced to be in the white-shirt/sensible-tie corporate world.

So it was with a cop's clinical detachment that Hansen stood in the center of the living area and scanned the attributes of Bingham's abode, regarding everything as a possible clue.

Twenty minutes. Maybe it wasn't much time to work with. He got busy.

Rick scanned the surroundings. Like many male-oriented living spaces, Bingham's main living area was subdivided into four functional quadrants. There was the audiovideo entertainment area, the exercise area, the library area and the work space area. In the work space area, as expected, a PC was situated atop a Danish blond wood workstation. Hansen walked over to it, crouched down on his hands and knees, disconnected the plug from the dead outlet. He then stretched the computer's electric cord to its full length, which was just long enough to reach the power strip. He plugged it into one of the outlets. He returned to the computer, snapped on the switch and watched the monitor flicker to life. As it booted up, he prayed that the power outage hadn't corrupted the integrity of the data stored on its hard drive.

The operating software loaded the batch files in less than a minute. Hansen dipped into the canvas duffel and came up with an Iomega Zip Drive device lent to him by Monica Chi from Systems. Moving rapidly, he hooked up the Iomega portable hard drive to the RS-232 serial port on the back panel of Bingham's 166 MHz Pentium PC. On the keyboard of the PC, he brought up the DOS prompt and typed C>COPY *.* D:\. With that, a copy of the entire contents of Bingham's hard drive began filling the one-gigabyte magnetic storage cartridge of the Iomega drive. Activating the backup Zip drive enabled him to make a mirror image of the hard drive of Bingham's home computer on backup tapes, which could be hooked up to another computer at a later time for off-site access. The question was whether he could complete the data transfer within the $100 worth of access time allotted him by Antonio the doorman.

Fifteen minutes remained.

As the PC buzzed, whirred and clicked industriously in the background, Rick made a quick circuit of the remaining areas.

First impressions . . . Contrary to the implications of his god awful handwriting, Bingham was definitely a neat freak. To be sure, there were spidery dustballs forming on the hardwood floors, a film of soot on the windowsills—filth inevitably collected in New York domiciles, particularly after going unchecked for months. More to the point, everything about the apartment was orderly and well kept—just like Bingham's office. Something Elena Bingham had mentioned during their first meeting struck Hansen just then: there was a noticeable absence of the color red in Bingham's home, consistent with her claim that her ex-husband had a bizarre superstition related to that color.

The place reflected solitude, yes, but not a life of loneliness. There were pictures of his also-dead paralegal, Kathleen. (Elena Bingham had been right to pass on his offer to accompany him to the apartment, predicting it would be "just a stroll down bad-memory lane.") The furnishings were strictly those of a young Manhattan divorcé: IKEA wall unit, Jennifer Convertible couch and chair, Ethan Allen coffee tables, Door Store kitchen table. Dead fish floating on the surface of the fetid water in a fish tank, starved to death. Low-maintenance plastic green plant in the corner. The big money in the apartment had gone into the Yamaha THX sound system. Little wonder: Tom Bingham appeared to be addicted to jazz. Bill Gottlieb black-and-white photographs of jazz greats adorned the walls, along with posters commemorating the Newport Jazz Festivals for the last five years. Five hundred jazz CDs were arranged in alphabetical order along the wall. Lee Morgan's *Live at the Lighthouse* loaded up on the disc player. It was somehow comforting to see a picture of the human side of Tom Bingham developing gradually, to see him fleshed out as a jazz aficionado, not just another faceless lawyer leading a juiceless existence in the black-and-white world of paper pushing.

Still, none of this was helpful to Hansen's cause. Eleven minutes to go.

He stepped over to Bingham's workstation, the hot spot. There was a fax machine stationed atop a German-manufactured shredding machine. In the wastebasket beneath the shredder was a fine residue of powder. The machine wasn't a shredder as much as it was an *atomizer*. Its presence added yet another layer of mystery to the affair. *Why would Bingham need such a powerful shredder in the privacy of his own apartment?* Hansen wondered. *Unless there were things he was hiding even from his lover.* Rick located the fax machine, plugged its cord into the power strip, and clicked the power on. He pressed the log button that would give him the phone numbers of the last fifty transmissions outgoing from the machine. *No luck.* The power outage had decimated the data in the fax machine's resident buffer memory.

Rick resorted to old-fashioned detective work: rooting through the drawers of Bingham's desk and file cabinet.

In the top drawer of the desk, he found a small device the size of an appointment book. He recognized it as a personal digital assistant, a miniature computer used for storing addresses, phone numbers and other data. Hansen opened the Sharp Zaurus PDA. Flipping on the switch, the tiny back-lit screen came to life.

ENTER PASSWORD NOW

That would have to wait. Hansen clapped the PDA shut and secreted it in the back pocket of his chinos.

In the file cabinet, he found a Redweld of files with curious names. The BEACON Project. Corporate Shells. Tax-Exempt Organizations. The manila file named The BEACON Project contained a single, un-sealed envelope. In that envelope was nothing but an unmarked white electronic passkey with a magnetic stripe. *But to what?* More mysteries. Hansen took the entire Redweld and stuffed it in the duffel. There were no other files that caught his eye.

In the bottom drawer of the filing cabinet, there was a finding that caused his heart to swell with elation. A videocassette. The label on the cassette said, PROF. GAMMAGE GOES TO WASHINGTON.

"Bingo." He actually said it aloud and clapped his hands in delight. *Gammage!* The name in the agenda, the guy Bingham was supposed to call the day after the market scare. The label called him PROF. Awesome. Maybe the guy could be located in *Who's Who of American Colleges and Universities.* Excitedly, Rick stowed the cassette in the duffel bag.

Less than six minutes left, and his work was almost complete. He stepped over to the computer to check on the progress of the transfer. On the screen: TRANSFER COMPLETE. 1,231 FILES OF 1,231 TRANSFERRED.

Beautiful. His work finished here, Hansen's mind turned to the La-maze class he had across town in another fifteen minutes. He had to meet Stephanie at the hospital across town for her breathing exercise class, and he was going to be cutting it close. Hansen reached around behind Bingham's PC to disengage the cord of the Zip drive. As he concentrated on the task, he was peripherally aware of Vasquez standing in the doorframe of the apartment. Without looking up, Hansen smiled and quipped, "You're five minutes early. I'm going to have to ask for a rebate of twenty-five dollars."

"What are you doing?" The querulous voice startled Hansen, for it was not the voice of Vasquez. This voice had a more sonorous bass, and a different accent from the doorman's.

Hansen pulled his head from behind the computer, whirled around. He saw a stranger dressed in bland street clothes—a dark leather jacket over a heavy, charcoal-colored woolen sweater and blue jeans. The man drew closer.

Pointlessly, Rick Hansen blurted, "Hey."

The swarthy stranger approached, seemingly more interested in what Hansen was doing than in Hansen himself. The lawyer was immediately struck by the stranger's Neanderthal ugliness. The flat, high-cheekboned canvas of his wide face was dominated by a priapic nose and rodent's teeth. The auricle of his ear was elfin in its shape, with cruel effect. His dark, filmy eyes were set far apart beneath a single, jagged eyebrow, lending the man an almost cross-eyed menace.

The flash of recognition hit Hansen in the next instant—this was the man captured in the elevator on the firm's time-lapse security video.

The intruder's gaze was fixed on the computer terminal. "Ah, you've made copies of the computer files." It was spoken like a revelation.

"Yes, he used to work at my firm," Hansen heard himself responding, as he stuffed the Zip drive into the bag. "Has some files we need."

The man's lips parted, but he made no sound. He just looked at the computer.

Hansen said, "You were the one who wiped the files in my office." It was meant as a question; it came out as an accusation.

The man turned his leaden gaze on Hansen. "I want that from you." His eyes dropped to the bag. "What else have you taken?"

With that, all that followed happened quickly; so quickly, Hansen would have difficulty recalling the sequence of events with clarity when he forced himself to do so later that evening.

Surreptitiously, Rick edged his left foot on top of the power strip. With the toe of his right sneaker, he kicked off the orangish-red power switch, cutting the power in the apartment. Both the computer and the lights went black. The man cried out, surprised by the unexpected darkness. Hansen instinctively dipped his shoulder and barreled into the meat of the man's chest, knocking him roughly against the wall. Rick could hear the man's breath rushing out of his lungs. The lawyer rebounded off the direct hit and sprinted out of the apartment, slamming the door shut behind him.

Go go go go go go. The voice that urged him toward the stairs was primal, born of self-preservation instinct. Everything began speeding up, moving in superfast action, and Rick Hansen's movements were driven not by a conscious thought process, but by the survival adrenaline rushing into his bloodstream. His sneakers slap-squeaked against the waxed-tile floor of the hallway. He gripped the canvas bag slung over his shoulder with a white-knuckled vise-grip. Rick blasted through the fire doors to the stairwell. The doors whip-cracked against the wall, and the report that echoed in the stairwell was thunderous, ringing in his ears like a sonic boom. He leapt down the stairs two, three at a time, experiencing the bizarre euphoria that accompanied the flight of the hunted. As he wheeled around the elbow bend of the first flight of stairs to the ninth floor, he was aware of a second thunderclap booming above him in the stairwell, this one deafening. In the same instant, a stinging spray of plaster struck him in the side of the face. *God!* the primitive voice screamed in his head, *He's shooting at me!*

Continuing down the stairwell, he realized, he'd be like a target in a shooting gallery. He hit the landing, burst through the fire doors, and veered into the hallway of the ninth floor. His heart was sledgehammering against his rib cage as he bounded like a pinball from one side of the hallway to the other, stabbing at three, four, five, six doorbells. Time stood still while he waited in agony for someone to respond, jouncing back and forth on the balls of his sneakered feet. In that instant, he believed he was going to die, as he imagined his pursuer coming through the doors, zeroing in on him in the sights of his gun barrel, squeezing the trigger. . . . Rick Hansen turned toward the fire doors, waiting for them to open, to accept his fate eyes-open—

—the doors parted with a bang and Hansen snapped off a retinal image of his pursuer's horrifying face . . .

"Yes?"

—as the woman in 9F tentatively cracked open the door to the apartment.

Hansen seized the moment. The lawyer barreled his way into the apartment, bumping the woman to the side. She squealed in fear, while Hansen slammed the door shut and snapped the chain lock into its slot with a tremulous hand. The lawyer stepped back from the door as if he half-expected it to be kicked down. There were audible footfalls in the hallway outside. "Don't open the door," Rick commanded. "There's a man, he's got a gun—"

"Please take what you want. Just don't hurt us."

The woman's quivering voice brought Rick Hansen back to earth. The lawyer summoned his senses and took stock of the situation. The heavy-set black woman in her fifties was cowering in a corner of the kitchen alcove, her hands palms up against her bosom in a show of compliance. Pasta and tomato sauce bubbled musically on the white gas-powered stove. A curtain of steam filled the kitchen. She was cooking dinner for herself. (*She'd said "us"—her family too?*) "I won't hurt you," he said in a small voice, holding his hands above his head. "I'm going to leave you alone now."

He crossed the living space, a cookie-cutter replica of Bingham's apartment. This unit, however, was cluttered with memorabilia from Broadway musicals. At the grand piano near the window, an octogenarian gentleman with Coke-bottle spectacles gawked in consternation at the intruder in his home. Hansen would later learn that the gentleman was once a very prominent Broadway composer, and the woman was his part-time nursemaid. But now was no time for get-acquainted conversation. "My name is Rick," was all he said, "and I really really appreciate this."

Hansen stepped over to the window, looked down. *Thank God!* The building-code-mandated fire escape provided an exit. The lawyer hooked his palms beneath the edge of the window frame and shoved it upward. The ancient window fixture gave with a wood-against-metal squeak, creating enough crawl space for Rick and his cargo to pass through. Outside, the cold air that blasted his face was invigorating. He sucked in fierce, desperate gulps of it. During his nine-flight descent to the sidewalk, the metal stairs creaked and clattered and swayed beneath his weight. Hansen rolled off the escape and fell to ground level, hitting the sidewalk with a painful jolt and losing a sneaker in the process. Without looking back, he sprinted south toward Columbus Circle.

He managed to flag down a cab half a block down Central Park West. He threw open the back door, tossed his bag onto the backseat and tumbled inside, giving the cabbie the address of New York Hospital. To his agony, the cab immediately hit a red light at the very next intersection. The lawyer slouched down in the backseat and squinched his eyes shut, praying to turn invisible. The light changed, and the cab trundled down to Columbus Circle. Once the cab turned onto Fifty-ninth Street, heading securely to the East Side, Hansen found himself unable to regain his breath. *Hyperventilating.* He tucked his head between his knees and tried desperately to regain control. *He shot at me. He shot at me. Why did he shoot at me?*

And just who was that sonuvabitch who squeezed off a shot at him? What exactly had Bingham gotten himself into? What game had he been playing? Was this all from a single incident of apparent insider trading, or was it the root of something bigger?

Was this goddamned Pandora's box worth chancing his life? The answer to that one was easy: *no fucking way*. It was over, his days of playing Macguffin had ended that night. He swore to himself and to any God who was listening, he couldn't give two shits about Tom's apparent prediction, not now, not anymore, not after all this. *Leave it alone, Hansen. Let it go.*

All eyes were on him when he burst into the classroom on the fifth floor of New York Hospital–Cornell Medical Center ten minutes late, still badly winded. "Sorry," he gasped in apology. Fourteen pregnant women and thirteen husbands watched him as he fell into the empty seat next to his wife and tried to catch his breath.

The Lamaze coach drew a good laugh when she quipped, "Well, Mr. Hansen might be a bit late tonight, but at least he's been practicing his breathing exercises on the way."

With the laughter ringing all around them, Stephanie studied Hansen's sneakerless foot with a cocked eyebrow.

"Don't ask," he pleaded.

And she didn't.

Thirty-two

Upper East Side, Manhattan

Monday, March 1

AT FIRST, RICK HANSEN DID NOT TELL his wife the true story behind the missing sneaker. To himself, he justified his decision with a variety of reasons. First, he didn't want to terrify his pregnant wife with a story of how some freakazoid fired a gun at him, what with her advanced stage. Second, he was beginning to convince himself that the part about the pistol could have been his imagination. The acoustics in that stairwell distorted all noises, amplified everything. It could have been the door banging against the wall. After all, he didn't actually see a gun in the man's hand, *did he?*

As he lay awake next to his dozing wife, Hansen wasn't certain what to believe. But the truth was, he didn't know how to tell her about any of it, so he said nothing at all.

Well past midnight, Hansen crept out of bed and walked into the living room. Tomorrow was going to be a five-alarm crazy-busy day, because McGeary wanted Hansen to work with Joe Money and The Stain to iron out the legal details on a new derivative instrument the desk was devising for a new money-management customer. But he was so jazzed up about his encounter on the West Side, sleep would elude him for at least another couple of hours. Might as well make productive use of the time.

He strolled into the living area of the apartment and turned on the tube.

He reached into his amorphous duffle and brought out the videocassette. PROF. GAMMAGE GOES TO WASHINGTON.

Hansen turned down the sound so as not to wake Stephanie, and plugged in the headphone. Then he sat cross-legged in front of the set, as if meditating.

It took a few moments for the VCR to load the cassette; then an image flickered on the television screen. A long table with a bank of microphones. A federal-looking room, something to do with government. Spectators in the gallery. Some sort of Senate hearings, Hansen realized, but judging from the sparse population of reporters and spectators, this was nothing on the order of Iran-Contra or the Clarence Thomas nomination. The camera was static, the picture was washed out and there was a faint feedback buzz to the sound. This was strictly limited-interest congressional activity, fodder for the dead-zone slot on C-SPAN.

In another moment, a thickset, scholarly-looking type with pince-nez glasses shuffled into the frame and took a seat in front of the microphone. Unbeknownst to this testifier, a cowlick of coarse hair spiked out from the side of his head with comic effect. Presumably, this was Gammage. The professor spread the pages of his prepared statement before him, then cleared his throat. The microphone amplified the rustle of the papers annoyingly.

"Mr. Chairman and Members of the Subcommittee on Telecommunications and Finance, I am pleased to appear before you today to discuss the dangers of financial derivatives."

Oh no, Hansen thought. Not another Chicken Little speech about the "potential dangers" derivatives posed to the financial security of the nation. In recent years, derivative investments have been widely misunderstood by the public and the media. Derivatives, according to one wag, became the eleven-letter four-letter word for a while, blamed for the spectacular collapses of Barings, Kidder Peabody and Sumitomo.

However, there's not as much mystery to derivatives as the public imagined. The concept of financial instruments that derive value from another, unrelated asset has been around for centuries. The original derivatives sold in this country were developed in the Chicago futures markets—for hogs and wheat. Risk-averse farmers were willing to sell their agricultural commodities to speculators to ascertain a fixed price for their goods. The speculators were willing to take the risk that the contracts would be worth far more at a future time—hence the concept of "futures."

A derivative is simply a structure by which financial engineers can "monetize" an asset. The coolest derivatives are built around an esoteric or static or nonsexy underlying asset. Like the right to pollute, or a pool of life insurance policies on AIDS victims. An investor can seek out derivatives based on catastrophe insurance, credit card receivables, lard, Third World debt, anhydrous ammonia, mortgages, bismuth, potato starch, Japanese raw silk, black-tiger shrimp, New Zealand wool, electricity, dried cocoons, lumber and, of course, frozen pork bellies.

If there is a right of transferability to an asset or a right, a derivative instrument can be structured out of it. In reality, Hansen thought, *derivatives are the most thrilling innovation to the financial markets since the turn of the century.*

But any innovation can get ahead of itself. With Barings and its ilk in recent years, it had been done to death in the media, the inevitable comparisons of derivatives to nuclear power, *beneficial overall, but there's a need for judiciousness and restraint, yada yada yada.*

So Gammage is expert enough to appear before a subcommittee on the subject. Wonderful, another academician making a name for himself by trash-talking the innovations of the financial community.

"According to the latest GAO report," Gammage read in a professorially dull monotone, "the derivatives market has experienced explosive growth, with its overall value having grown over a hundred and fifty percent in just the last three years alone. The trillions involved in the parallel universe of the derivatives world is four times the value of all the stocks traded on the New York Stock Exchange, and almost three times the size of the gross national product. There is no precedent to this growth in all of history. The derivatives market, in which there are $16 trillion in derivatives held by commercial banks and financial institutions in the United States, $25 trillion worldwide and an annual turnover trading volume of $300 trillion, could become the greatest bubble in history. Recently, severe losses by end users of OTC derivatives have also brought increased attention to the need to reduce potential sources of instability and risk wherever possible. The consensus is that some form of action be taken to ensure the stability of the U.S. financial system. That, of course, is why I have been invited to speak to you today.

"The highly leveraged nature of these instruments is what has led to their spectacular growth to over $1 trillion in notional amount. At the same time, the risk of a widespread default in these instruments has grown alarmingly. The concept of 'systemic risk' is very real—that is, a derivatives-engineered meltdown that spills over into the equity markets. The domino effect could easily cause a worldwide stock market crash."

Hansen's sleepy eyes widened at this offhand comment. *Worldwide stock market crash?*

On screen, Gammage took a long pull of ice water, pausing for dramatic effect. "This is not to say that derivatives are not extraordinarily useful financial innovations. They absolutely are, of course. The institutional users of these products can zero out the financial risks they don't want, and buy the speculative risks they *do* want. But therein lies the true paradox of derivatives. They were devised to reduce risk, but because of their enormous popularity, flexibility and leverage, they may introduce *more risk* to the financial system as a whole. Derivatives are like nuclear power—extraordinarily useful, but with attendant risks."

Aggh. The old nuclear power analogy again.

"Frankly, I believe the more established dealers are adequately incentivized to police their own activities. Collectively, tens of millions of dollars per year are spent on risk management techniques and systems by these blue-chip trading houses. It's the irresponsible dealers who are just coming into the business who may not apply the same prudent standards of risk management as do the majors.

"Derivatives have single-handedly changed the rules of the game— transactions are no longer confined to the trading posts of the stock exchanges and the cluster of buildings in a small quadrant of space in Lower Manhattan. No, the trading floor where billion-dollar trades occur these days is in an electronic cyberspace whose participants are linked anonymously by a seamless circuit of computers around the globe. Complex trades that used to take days or weeks to settle can now be fully executed over the Internet instantaneously. That technological breakthrough is both wonderful and terrifying at the same time.

"Therefore, if Congress decides to enact legislation that will require the federal government to monitor these potentially volatile, off-balance-sheet financial instruments, it should seek out the expertise resident at the academic communities at urban campuses throughout the nation—"

Here comes the sales pitch, Hansen said to himself.

"For example, as a tenured professor and assistant chair at Carnegie-Mellon University in Pittsburgh, I am privileged to have access to significant supercomputer resources that may be deployed by the federal government in creating forecasting models. Carnegie-Mellon could create these models and a monitoring program, which the Congress and Executive Branch might well consider utilizing to track the ongoing systemic risk financial derivatives pose to the global economy—"

At the mention of Pittsburgh, Hansen jumped up and raced to his briefcase in the kitchen. He retrieved the appointment book, and thumbed furiously through it. As he did, he picked up the phone and punched in 411, the number for information. When the operator came on line, Hansen asked, "What's the area code for Pittsburgh?"

"Four-one-two," she replied.

"Thanks," he said, disconnecting.

He turned to the January 30 page of Bingham's diary. Found the part in the notation he was seeking:

Call Gammage / 361-5212

Gammage was a professor at Carnegie-Mellon. *Which was in Pittsburgh, stupid, not New York.*

Quickly, Hansen dialed the number with the Pittsburgh area code as a prefix. In his haste, he misdialed and had to start over. Cursing, he managed to punch it in correctly and waited. After an eternity of clicks, the other end began ringing. Hansen shut his eyes, waiting for Gammage to pick up. *Pick up, pick up, pick up.*

Three rings.

It was after midnight, the guy had to be sleeping. *Well, this is your wake-up call, Professor.*

Then, an odd clicking noise and another ring, this one of a distinctly different tone. Call forwarding, or voice mail, Hansen guessed.

A recording answered, "This is, uh, Three, Three Rivers Algorithmics." The voice was not the professorial one of Gammage, but sounded more like a kid in his twenties. A student, perhaps? "We're not able to come to the phone right now, but your message is very important to us. Please leave a message and we'll get right back to you." Then, a sound bite culled from *Star Trek.* Mr. Spock saying, "Live long and prosper."

Beep.

Hansen cupped the mouthpiece and half-whispered into it. "Hello, my name is Richard Hansen. I'm an attorney with Wolcott, Fulbright and Company in New York. I really need to speak to Professor Gammage. I've been trying to contact him for weeks, but I just now managed to get his number. Professor, please contact me as soon as you get this message." Hansen recited his work number and disconnected.

"Who was that?"

Rick replaced the phone on the cradle and turned to his wife, who was glaring at him from the other side of the room.

"Who was that?" she asked again, this time more softly. "Was that your girlfriend, Richard?"

Rick closed his eyes. *In a way, you could say that,* he thought to himself.

"Stephanie," he began. "We really need to talk."

Thirty-three

TO UNDERSTAND WHAT A "DERIVATIVE PRODUCT" IS, it must first be understood what it isn't.

A derivative is not a tangible asset. It is not like a share of stock, which indicates ownership rights in a company. It is not like a bond, which reflects debt interest in the issuer. A derivative, for legal and practical purposes, does not confer a security interest upon its holder.

Instead, a derivative is a contractual right or obligation. If you are "long" the derivative, you have the right but not the obligation to do something. If you are "short" the derivative, you may have an obligation to the long holder.

It would not be inappropriate to consider a derivative a "bet." In fact, the commonplace act of purchasing a share of stock is also a wager— you wouldn't buy that company's stock in the first place if you weren't betting that it would increase in value. In this sense, derivatives are like stocks: there must be a buyer and a seller for a transaction to occur. A derivative instrument requires two consenting parties with different views of the market, two parties willing to place a wager with one another. *I'll pay you this if the market closes here. You pay me this if it goes there.* It's not much different from someone at the roulette wheel placing a bet on the red, and someone else placing a bet on the black. It's a zero-sum game, in that someone is going to win, and someone is going to lose.

Some critics would say you'd get the same result betting on a cockroach race.

But well-informed market participants don't see it that way. For hedging against the risk of stock or bond portfolio losses, there is simply no more efficient tool than customized derivatives.

Like snowflakes, there are no two customized derivatives that are exactly alike. Because of this, each derivative chews up a large amount of human resources to create, process and book. The GoldBridge trade was a textbook example of that.

On Monday, the trade was pitched to Legal.

Stainsby, Monetti and Hansen gathered in the cafeteria for a working lunch. Over a meal of sushi eaten from plasticware, the Wolcott team unbuttoned the second button of their starched white shirts and tucked their ties inside to protect them from the splatter of soy sauce. Then they got down to brass tacks.

Structuring derivative instruments is as good as it gets for an attorney on Wall Street. Ordinarily, the security lawyer's day-to-day experience is often agonizingly mundane—largely sweating over indemnification language or remedies for termination events in labyrinthine customer agreements. Assisting in the creation of a cutting-edge derivative instrument was far and away the most rewarding work a lawyer could perform.

As The Stain and Joe Money threw out ideas contemporaneously, Hansen scribbled each component down on a series of soy-sauce–blotched napkins, trying to build it into a workable term structure for GoldBridge. The derivatives marketers used the arcane jargon of the derivatives world: *zero-cost one-by-two straddle, manditorily convertible knock-in/knock-out feature, step-up strike trigger, digital barrier option* . . .

Just past two o'clock, the three men finished devising the product. They huddled around on the same side of the table, looking at the creation they had stitched together. To the uninitiated, the instrument looked as indecipherable as a chalkboard full of Einstein's stream-of-consciousness scrawl.

"What the hell do you call this?" Stainsby wondered.

"Beats the hell out of me," Hansen replied.

"It's a 'flip-floption,' " Monetti blurted out.

Stainsby and Hansen turned toward him. "A *what?*" Stainsby said, frowning.

"A flip-floption. Don't you see? It's a bet going in a bullish direction, but once it hits the trigger point, it automatically turns into a triple-up bet going in the opposite direction. It's a flip-floption."

"Did you just make that up?"

"Just now, yes."

Julian Stainsby whirled on Hansen. "Can we get that registered as a service mark immediately?"

Hansen nodded. "Let me talk to Kilmartin, see how we get that done."

① ON TRADE DATE:

ZERO-COST KNOCK-OUT/KNOCK-IN COMBO

Goldbridge (customer)
* BUYS at-the-money S+P calls
* SELLS at-the-money S+P puts

Wolcott Fulbright
(U.S.)
(Agent — gets edge)

Back-to-back trades

U.S. $ Premium on calls

U.S. $ Premium on puts

Wolcott Fulbright (Hong Kong)
short S+P calls
(takes in premium)

Wolcott Fulbright (U.K.)
long S+P calls
(pays premium)

② AT CLOSE-OF-BUSINESS on Friday, March 12

1. Goldbridge unwinds bullish position → goes flat
2. Goldbridge instantly initiates REVERSE
   (e.g., sells calls / buys puts)
3. Levers up bearish position by factor of 3

Stainsby studied the schematic they had documented on the napkin. "So this trade is perfectly legal, in your mind?"

"Yes. It's a private placement under the Section 4(2) exemption, so it doesn't have to be registered as an offering of securities to the public. It's a non-U.S. counterparty, so you don't have 15a-6 concerns. It's not an illegal off-exchange futures contract, because it's structured as a swap, meaning it fits neatly under the swap exemption to the Commodity Exchange Act."

"Yeah, yeah, whatever," Stainsby waved away the legalese impatiently. "You're the lawyer. As long as you're happy, it's on to Credit."

———•———

On Tuesday, they met with the Credit Department in the Barcelona Room.

Focus, Scott Mendelsohn willed himself. *Let's get through this.* "It's your meeting, Gil. What've we got in the pipeline?"

"GoldBridge Capital Advisors, LLC," Gil McGeary pronounced in his bullhorn voice.

Scott Mendelsohn frowned. "Never heard of 'em."

"Neither had I, but I think we'll be hearing a lot more about them in the future. I'm going to turn it over to Julian and Joe, who have been structuring the deal with the Legal Department." He turned over a flat palm indicating Stainsby. "Stainsby?"

Mendelsohn politely turned toward the Brit, who was fifteen years his junior yet took home an all-in annual comp that easily quadrupled the credit officer's own salary. Stainsby cleared his throat theatrically. "Right, then. GoldBridge is a hedge fund based out of London that represents scads of Middle Eastern oil wealth. It's the pooled assets of the families of top-tier oil barons. The fund is huge, possibly as big as 50 billion U.S. dollars, if you include its interest in the Dartmouth Funds Group."

"Dartmouth, the mutual fund family?"

"The same. They're one hundred percent owners of those assets."

Mendelsohn scratched his head. "I hadn't heard that. Anyway, go on."

"The investment adviser is looking to structure a synthetic product, giving the fund short-term exposure to the U.S. equity markets. I should mention that GoldBridge was profiled on the front page of *Derivatives Letter* last Monday." Julian confidently slid a photocopy of the article across the conference room table to Scott, as if this document ended all further debate. MIDEAST PETRODOLLARS HUNT OUT MEGA U.S. EQUITY DERIVATIVES PLAYS, the headline trumpeted. *Big deal*, Mendelsohn thought. *Derivatives Letter* was a $1,795-a-year gossip sheet that, at best, provided a modicum of insight into what was going on in the shadowy, underpublicized world of the off-exchange markets. Each item was written in a breathless, two or three-paragraph, barely-got-time-to-read-it format, easily digestible by the superstressed market professional. All the news that fits, they print. Hardly a paragon of hard-news reporting. One mention of GoldBridge in *DL* didn't legitimize the fund in Mendelsohn's world. "This doesn't tell me anything," Scott complained. "For all I know, GoldBridge is laundering drug profits behind the facade of investing a windfall from oil wealth. Where's Legal on this?"

"Hansen helped us structure the deal," Joe Monetti said. He produced the complicated schematic for Scott's review. "It's a pair of six-month relative-value mandatorily exercisable zero-cost collar, knock-in, knockout digital-basket option with a look-back feature."

Mendelsohn gazed at the eye-boggling schematic. *Damned derivatives!* For all his years of experience with exotic securities transactions, this trade looked to him like a game of hide-the-salami, smoke-and-mirrors. What was GoldBridge's interest in doing such a complicated trade? "What are you calling this structure?"

"A flip-floption."

"A *what?*"

"A flip-floption. Once it hits a trigger level, it instantly converts to the complete opposite of the original transaction, times three."

"Do they have any previous experience in this type of transaction?"

"No one does, Scott," Stainsby said. "I don't mean to be facetious, really. We just invented this thing yesterday."

McGeary jumped in. "Scott, these people are very sophisticated. The structure was essentially presented to us by Charles Stone, the investment manager. We just ginned it up with some bells and whistles, to reduce the premium payout."

"Do they have independently audited financials for the most recent quarter?"

"GoldBridge is perfectly willing to provide you with all the *papers* you need, Scott," McGeary said crisply, putting a patronizing "quote-unquote" spin on the word "papers." The implication was that the Credit Department was a paper-ravenous bureaucracy.

Mendelsohn resented the implication, but pushed on. "Why did they come to Wolcott? Have they been turned away elsewhere?"

"To the contrary—they've shopped the bid with a number of our best competitors. And the beauty contest goes to only two or three dealers."

"And what did you say was the notional amount on this transaction?"

"We didn't," Stainsby said, looking at his cohorts. "It's 725 million U.S. dollars."

Mendelsohn gasped. It was astounding! Mendelsohn said nothing, but began punching numbers into his Sharp calculator. The firm would be on the hook for 94 percent of the notional value of the trade—$681.5 million! A hickey on a trade like this could be poison in the months before the IPO.

More and more in recent months, Mendelsohn had felt the subtle pressure from the business people to lower the bar little by little, at least for the time being, to pump up the balance sheet in anticipation of Wolcott's upcoming initial public offering of stock. *You got to play ball with the business people for the short term. Nobody gets paid if the business people can't do the trade.* Other top-tier firms on Wall Street wouldn't touch the toxic waste Wolcott considered these days. The other firms had *controls. Governors. Risk-management matrices.* Here the culture demanded—*DO THE TRADE*—and those who didn't climb aboard the train with similar enthusiasm were committing interface political hara-kiri. Still, in his heart of hearts, Mendelsohn's mandate (to protect the firm from unreasonable credit risks from unproven counterparties who could either default or refuse to pay on a multimillion-dollar obligation) was one he profoundly believed in. If he didn't step up to the plate as a dissenting voice among the choruses of "*DO THE TRADE*," who would? Who else would walk the tightrope, make the tough call, determine whether the potential reward outstripped the actual risks? Certainly not his boss, Penny Brassil, the head of Credit, who was off racking up the frequent flier miles on some three-week junket to the European region, ostensibly to verify the "credit worthiness" of possible customers in Britain, France and Germany. Bullshit, Mendelsohn thought. Penny was an admitted travel junkie; in a weak moment, she confided to Scott that her dream job would be a travel writer. She saw herself in the organization as strictly "big picture," and never got her hands dirty. Her desk was spotless.

Nope. Mendelsohn was the first-and-last line of defense for the organization. The cop of final resort. Judge and jury. If he was a soft touch and a trade he approved blew up, the business guys would rightfully point a finger at him and say: *Hey, Credit signed off on it. What do you want from us?* Not on his watch . . .

McGeary knew it from Scott Mendelsohn's prolonged silence. The smile spread across his face. "Scott, you're gonna nix this trade, aren't you?"

Scott Mendelsohn paused, then expelled a breath. "It's too soon to draw any conclusions, Gil, but I've got to tell you, something here doesn't pass the smell test . . ." Mendelsohn closed his notepad and shuffled his papers into a neat stack. "Right now I'd have to say no, but I'm willing to keep the door open. Have GoldBridge send me the audited financials and we'll see where it goes from there."

McGeary nodded solemnly, as if accepting defeat graciously. "We'll abide by Credit's decision, whichever way you come out. But I've got to believe that the big-picture guys upstairs would get behind this kind of trade, what with our initial public offering coming up."

"Gil, you may be right," Mendelsohn shrugged. "But on the face of it, it's not the kind of trade *I* can get behind." Mendelsohn left the Barcelona Room.

———•———

On Wednesday morning, Mendelsohn's Merlin phone rang at 8:17. The LED display indicated the caller was Alan Milgrim from the executive suite. The number-four most powerful executive in the firm was calling. Mendelsohn felt a foreboding chill spread over his already sour stomach. "Mendelsohn here."

"Scott? Alan Milgrim here. Bob Wolcott and I have taken a look at the GoldBridge trade upstairs and wonder what exactly your reservations are."

Fucking McGeary. Mendelsohn recalled the desk head's parting words . . . *the big-picture guys upstairs would get behind this kind of trade.* There was a game going on here, and Mendelsohn wasn't a player in it. In fact, he began to wonder whether he even had tickets in the cheap seats. The credit officer pinched his eyes closed and attempted to will away the cluster headache that was rapidly forming in his cranium like an angry storm cloud. As he did so, he went through the charade of ticking off the blemishes on this trade. The risks of doing business with an unknown entity in the Middle East. The daunting size of the notional amount. The complexity of the instrument.

Milgrim punctuated each concern with an impatient "uh-huh." Then he said, "I can't disagree with you on virtually all points, but it's a short-dated trade, isn't it?"

"Yes. Six months."

Milgrim said, "Anyway, we think it's a good trade for the firm. Profitable and innovative. A 'flip-floption.' Christ, that's *clever.* Look, let's just charge the sheiks a double haircut and pull the trigger on this one."

"Consider it done, Alan," Mendelsohn said cheerfully. He replaced the phone on the cradle and began writing the requisite cover-your-ass memo for the files. In the months to come, he would be very glad he did that.

———•———

On Thursday, the GoldBridge derivatives trade was handed off to the Operations group to get booked.

Get booked. That is to say, getting the terms of the derivative instrument keypunched into Wolcott Fulbright's mammoth computer systems by the mustachioed, young, $32,000-a-year reconciliation clerks in Parsippany, New Jersey. Once this was accomplished, the trade would be "live," existing in the vast universe of transactions already residing on Wolcott Fulbright's books and records.

To book a derivative is not nearly as simple a process as it might sound. Unlike a commercial banking transaction in which money is simply taken in from a customer and credited dollar for dollar to a savings account, a securities trade has innumerable complications—"it has a lot of hair," in Wall Street parlance. Margin, valuation of securities, restrictions, settlement, credit risk, legality, suitability . . . any one of these considerations could cause a trade to blow up and send a team of Ops personnel into a weeklong black hole trying to repair it. But there was no animal so intimidating to the back office crew as a one-of-a-kind type of cross-border hybrid derivative product like the GoldBridge trade.

"A *flip-floption?*" At 7:40 A.M., Ed Pascarella sat down at a round table in a windowless conference room in Parsippany, peeled back the plastic top of his machine-brewed coffee. "What kind of propeller head at 44 Wall dreamed up this Frankenstein's monster?"

"It's a nightmare, all right," moaned Johnnie.

"Damn straight," Auggie said. "We got seventeen manhours into it already and nothin' to show for it."

Ed Pascarella was the Director of Operations at Wolcott Fulbright's Parsippany, New Jersey, outpost. A sixteen-year veteran of the firm, Pascarella led by example, outworking, outlasting, outthinking the people who reported in to him. In return, he was blessed with 147 people who responded with the work ethic of a sled dog and tireless devotion to the franchise that clothed and fed their families.

The people in the back office schooled themselves in complex UNIX-based computer systems technology and became experts in the nuts and bolts of securities of every stripe and variation—mortgages, corporate bonds, equities, converts, asset-backeds, governments, Treasuries, swaps and derivatives. As an organization, the back-office team had to be nimble; the nature of their industry was such that Wolcott could suddenly announce it was exiting the marginally profitable municipal bond business and just as suddenly announce a ramp-up in the asset-backed securities business based on pools of JCPenney's credit card debt. Some of Ed's people were taking Berlitz crash courses in French and German to better interface with their counterparts in Paris and Frankfurt Ops.

Ed's people were a distinctly different species from the flashy producers on the trading floors and the big-picture guys in the executive suites.

Their first names were often Vinnie or Johnnie or Frankie or Sal and their surnames predominantly ended in vowels. The Ops guys often reveled in the ethnicity that their counterparts on the business side worked so hard to suppress. They were often born, raised and currently residing in some New Jersey suburb. They were truly family men whose windowless offices were shrines to the American nuclear family, adorned with numerous enlargements of the little lady and the kids. Like Ed himself, the back-office guys were loyal to a fault, rarely divorcing their high school sweethearts and even more rarely leaving the securities firms that first employed them. Ed's people wore their beepers with pride, and were hopelessly addicted to tobacco and coffee, but seldom consumed anything stronger than Budweiser. They alternated among one another's homes for weekend barbecues. Their hours were atrocious, but never so much so that they couldn't scratch out the time to coach their daughters' Baby Ruth softball team. They put in an honest day's work—wiring funds, creating sweep accounts, making margin calls, issuing confirms and statements, soothing irate customers who had been made some unrealistic promises by an overreaching salesman.

When the system was running at its best, it was like chopping meat, Ed would say. Processing trades were best when done in bulk. "Speed, economy and control" were the three buzzwords that best summed up his team's mission. Pascarella's employees handled 11,000 transactions every day, representing $17 billion in value, so he saw some of the best bulk trading activity on the Street. But too many new cross-border, cutting-edge derivatives trades were mucking up the gears of his machinery. This GoldBridge trade was the mother of all derivatives, at least from a back-office perspective.

"Okay, ladies, what are we gonna do about this GoldBridge mess?"

Auggie shook his head. "I haven't a freaking clue. I've never seen a two-headed animal like this before."

Johnnie tapped a Bic against his spiral notebook, "Yeah, this is gonna be a systemic nightmare."

Ed smiled. "Hey, you want peaches-and-cream served on a Sunday platter, go work for First Jersey Savings and Loan. Just so we're on the same sheet of music, anyone speak to Legal, break it down into its component parts?"

"Auggie did."

Auggie sighed. "Yeah, I parsed through it with that new lawyer, that guy Hansen. The problem is that it doesn't fit any one type. It's a hybrid, which means if you code it one way, it's not gonna get marked-to-market properly."

"I can deal with that," Ed said. "We'll just have to do the weekly marks by hand. It's a pain in the ass, but we gotta step up to the plate for the business people."

Johnnie shook his head. "Goddamned business guys. God forbid they should give us a call before pushing this product through the pipeline."

"Never mind about that," Ed Pascarella growled with a dismissive wave. Ed's philosophy was that his team was in a partnership with the business people to get the trade done, and he didn't care for any of his guys bad-mouthing the business side. The way Ed saw it, on Wall Street, the symbiotic relationship between the back-office guys and the revenue producers was not unlike the star system in Hollywood. The producers (salesmen and traders) were the movie stars, awash in prestige and stratospheric compensation. His people, on the other hand, were the salaried film crew, performing various functions like key grip, best boy, Foley editors, boom mike. True, movie stars were irreplaceable, but there would most certainly be no movie if there weren't a film crew to create it. The upshot of it was that the Operations personnel in the financial powerhouses were truly the unsung heroes of Wall Street. If they all stayed home one day en masse, the Street would come to a grinding, screeching halt. But this was no time to gripe about the movie stars; it was time to get the film in the can. "What's done is done. Can't put the genie back in the bottle. What I want to know is how we can get the system to accept a derivatives trade with all these bells and whistles."

"Can't do it." Johnnie shook his head. "STEPS wasn't created with derivatives in mind, especially hybrids." STEPS was Wolcott's proprietary UNIX platform created by the Trading Technology wonks. It was an acronym for Securities Trade Entry and Processing System. "It's a chocolate mess."

"You think I'm going back to McGeary and tell him we can't do it? He'll go right to Milgrim and Bobby W. and tell them Parsippany's just not getting it done. Auggie, what's your read on it? We SOL?" (SOL, being Wall Street shorthand for "shit outta luck.")

Auggie massaged his jaw. "I suppose we could book it as a swap, then trigger it off the reset feature. Treat each piece as if it's a new trade every time it hits the new benchmark. That way STEPS would automatically close out the existing trade, establish a new one with a new strike price. It'll definitely take some micro-massaging, but that might get it done."

"Would it be totally transparent to the customer?"

"It would be if we suppressed the system-generated confirms each time, just have them automatically routed to an in-house address."

"Attaboy, Augs," Ed nodded. "That's what we need more of around here—a can-do attitude."

"This could be a Krakatoa trade," Johnnie groused. "If it blows up, it could be hot oil."

"Credit and Legal are okay with it," Pascarella said. "Ours is not to reason why. Let's just do it."

———•———

On Friday, Julian Stainsby rang up Stone's international voice mail system and barked, "You're done, Charles. Trade confirm to follow by fax and modem." Later that afternoon, an electronic confirmation of the terms and conditions was simultaneously faxed and modemed to Mr. Charles Stone, the contact person for GoldBridge. A fourth confirmation would be sent by first-class mail.

The data sent via high-speed ISDN modem were downloaded into the CPU of a system at the other end of a Pittsburgh phone number. The artificial intelligence software program named LINDA crunched this information, linked it up with other information stored in its database and spat out the following message:

TRANSMISSION RECEIVED.
STATUS—107% AHEAD OF SCHEDULE.
014 DAYS TO TARGET DATE

Thirty-four

CAPTIVA ISLAND, FLORIDA

Sunday, March 7

AS COLBERT'S LIMOUSINE THREADED along the palm-lined drive, the mansion came into full view. Even the driver cursed in astonishment at its opulence.

Château-sur-l'Océan. A three-level Mediterranean structure consuming two parcels of oceanfront real estate.

It was the finest home $17 million could buy.

Colbert guided the driver past the handpainted fresco belltower, around the gentle elbow of the drive to the tiled loggia entranceway. The car idled there for only moments before she emerged from within the glass-housed courtyard with the trickling wall fountain and the DeWain Valentine glass sculpture.

Colbert lowered his electric window as she approached. For a moment, she just stood there studying him—or more likely, providing him with the opportunity to study *her*. Then she bent over gracefully, leaning into his window.

"You arrogant bastard," Zoe Pierpont-Colbert purred. "What gives you the right to set foot on my property?"

Colbert regarded her with a smirk of amusement. Zoe. Beautiful, beautiful Zoe. Of all his ex-wives, Zoe was his favorite. Always resplendent, positively electric with self-confidence and natural beauty. Even now, she was put together like a work of art, in the Jil Sander tropical white sundress and the Harry Winston jewelry that literally dripped from her limbs. She flashed him a dazzling smile—not so much a smile as an explosion of pearly movie-star teeth. Looking at her now, one couldn't have imagined Zoe Pierpont-Colbert as a ruthless status climber whose lower-class beginnings in Abilene, Texas, had sharpened her killer's instinct to attain the good life. Hungry, ambitious, *real*—not like the jaded old-money debutantes Margaret and Julianne—Colbert's other ex-wives. Those blue-blooded bitches were flesh-covered mannequins, do-nothing princesses, high-maintenance trophies, unsparingly pampered by their daddies.

Not so with Zoe. True, material wealth was her religion and she prayed at the altar of her false god each day. She might have her quirks—a fondness for those damned ugly hairless cats and insistence on charting her daily activities only after a morning consultation with her personal astrologer in Palm Beach—but at the same time, Zoe was also a very sensual woman, one who undertook Colbert's every orgasm as an op-portunity to prove her appreciation for his largess. Zoe was Colbert's soulmate, to the extent it was possible that Colbert could have one.

In the eyes of the law, of course, they were divorced. But it was in reality a legal ploy arranged by Colbert's lawyers to place assets in her name and out of the reach of the armies of frustrated creditors. Even if some sharpster proved the divorce a sham, Colbert had long ago declared personal bankruptcy; Florida's so-called "homestead" laws made Châ-teau-sur-l'Océan untouchable by creditors. America was truly the land of opportunity.

"Why am I here, you ask?" Colbert asked playfully. "To see how you've squandered my personal fortune."

He said it only in half-jest.

She cocked an eyebrow and beamed at him once more. "Come inside and see for yourself."

He disembarked from the limousine. She led him by the hand into a home that was all but unimaginable to the common man—but then again, they were not common.

She took him past the trickling wall fountain and into the house itself, where they stood in the grand, circular living area with its thirty-foot dodecagon roof of cypress wood, Italian marble and Lavor Kerman ori-ental carpeting. Then she brought him through the vast hallways with their textured ebony-teak-pearwood-and-stone-coral motifs, Savonnerie carpets, and into the shimmering kitchen with its Almilmo cabinetry and Corian granite countertops. She skipped the elevator and made him as-cend the travertine marble staircase leading to the magnificent master bedroom, the largest of the enclave's seventeen bedrooms, with a wall composed entirely of a seawater aquarium. She demonstrated the mo-torized crystal skylights and the mechanized doors that opened out into a lanai, with soaring cantilevered, waffle-gridded ceilings. The sweeping view looked out over the compound's free-form pool, concrete-and-glass fishpond and the seascape vista that was afforded by the property's five-hundred-foot seaside frontage.

Even Colbert, who was accustomed to the most flagrant demonstrations of conspicuous consumption, was amazed by the sheer opulence of the estate. "It's really come along since I was last here," he said. "Very impressive, darling."

"Oh, do you really think so?"

"Of course I do."

"I'm so thrilled to hear you say that. I've worked hard to make you happy."

"I know you have. It shows."

"Do you have time to sit for a while?" she asked.

"Just a short time, I'm afraid. Business calls."

For twenty minutes, they sat around the pool as the servants brought them Gulf shrimp and cocktails. Zoe animatedly relayed anecdotes about browbeating the construction crew to stay on track with their deadlines. Colbert was content to let her talk, nearly lulled to sleep by the soothing crash of the surf on the beach.

"Oh yes, I nearly forgot," she said abruptly. "There's someone here to see you."

Colbert snapped awake. "There is? Who?"

"Oh, you know, that fellow I met when you took me to Zurich last year? The Russian security consultant."

"Alexeyev's here?" Colbert made a show of his irritation. "Why didn't you tell me?"

Zoe playacted, feigning hurt feelings. "Why, darling, I just did."

"Meaning, *as soon as I arrived.*"

"What?" She acted startled. "And spoil your first impressions of Château-sur-l'Océan?"

———◆———

Viktor Alexeyev had been deposited in a mahogany-paneled study secluded in the west wing of the mansion. Colbert found him there, intently peering at an illuminated globe, as if still stunned at what history had done to his mother country, the former Soviet Union. One of those goddamned hairless cats was cutting figure-eights about his ankles. Colbert closed the door to the study, sealing their conversation off from the servants. "Have you been waiting long?"

Alexeyev straightened, then shrugged. "Forty minutes."

As a rule, Colbert never apologized for any of his conduct; this time was no exception. "You're early."

"I had nothing more important to do than this."

"Good answer, Viktor." Colbert smiled. "What have you got for me?"

"An update. Some news. Nothing terrible."

"I see." Colbert made a head motion toward the manila envelope in the Russian's hand. "You have some candid camera to show me?"

Alexeyev nodded.

"All right. Follow me."

Two rooms down the hall was Colbert's office. As they made their way down the hallway, Colbert was gratified to note that Alexeyev's eyes darted around, drinking in the details—the Imari vases, the kentia palms, the René Lalique crystal nudes. Like many men of his stature, Colbert craved the envy of other men. After all, his accomplishments were largely meaningless without it.

"In here." Colbert held the door open for his chief of security, then followed him inside. This was Colbert's office, designed to his precise specifications. It was a temple to the advent of the information age, a wet dream of a media and trading facility that exceeded the imaginings of the most avid technophile. With the flip of a single switch on the console of the $200,000 hand-carved desk, a dozen television screens flashed to glowing life in a honeycomb comprising an entire wall. Each monitor carried a different picture. There was either the data feed of real-time market information—Reuters, Dow Jones, Telerate, ADP, Bloomberg, Bridge, ICV, PTI Scan, Quick, Telekurs, SEAQ International—or international news channels—CNBC, CNN, BBC, ASkyB. Another switch turned the screens into a sea of blue, waiting to be fed some software.

"Okay," Colbert said, assuming a chair behind the desk. "Update me."

The Russian shifted uncomfortably from one foot to another. "The Pethers situation has turned critical."

"Is that so?" Colbert opened the drawer to his desk and withdrew a humidor containing Cuban cigars.

"Yes. Our surveillance indicates that he is preparing a letter to the Securities and Exchange Commission."

"*What?*" Colbert exploded. "Are you certain?"

"Yes. We've intercepted a number of faxes between him and his personal attorney. He's going back and forth on the language. His only hesitation is that he wants to bargain with the authorities for personal immunity."

Colbert's face contorted with rage. He leaned forward and hissed, "Remember what you told me in London? Your suggestion that I 'eliminate the threat'?"

"Yes. By that do you mean—"

"I mean, *eliminate the threat.* I think you know what that means. And have it done quickly, before he decides to ring up the goddamned SEC. And I want you to report back to me the instant it is done." Colbert fired up the cigar, and inhaled deeply. "What about the lawyers?"

"The Wolcott lawyers?"

Colbert exhaled a plume of smoke. "Yes, Kilmartin and the new attorney. There's two weeks left. Are we comfortable that these two will not be an obstruction to the initiative?"

"Kilmartin is not a problem. Our surveillance shows he is distracted by problems at home. His wife's mother has fallen ill and has moved into his house. It's caused a tense situation between him and his wife."

"Uh-huh."

"Kilmartin is going on a two-week fishing vacation to Florida beginning tomorrow afternoon. Without his wife."

Colbert smiled. On Kilmartin's first day back at the office, the world would be very different from the one he'd inhabited just two weeks before. "What about the junior attorney?"

"Hansen. We could have problems there."

Colbert's eyebrows climbed his forehead in surprise. "How so?"

Alexeyev met Colbert's level gaze. He described Gagarov's encounter with Hansen at Bingham's rent-stabilized apartment, noted that the Wolcott attorney left the premises with copies of computer files and manila folders possibly related to the initiative. Alexeyev confessed that in the heat of the moment, the Gargoyle impulsively fired a wild shot at Hansen. "The lawyer has a persistent interest in the affairs of his predecessor," Alexeyev said, by way of summary.

"Let me see the surveillance tape," Colbert said bluntly.

Alexeyev handed it over and Colbert inserted the cassette into one of the videocassette machines in the room. He pressed Play. The stacks of television screens remained blank. Colbert cursed, then pushed a switch called Monitor Master on the remote control mechanism. The room brightened immediately with the eerie artificial light thrown off from more than a dozen twenty-seven-inch television screens. Colbert looked up at the bank of video images.

The tape revealed nothing of significance. It was composed of various shots of this Richard Hansen at work and home. An overhead shot of him on the phone in his office. Hansen leaving his office building. Hansen disappearing into Bingham's old apartment building. Hansen making love to his pregnant wife. Colbert began to suspect that the tape was edited in a manner intended to impress the one who was *paying* for it. *Big deal*, the Russians had pinhole cameras surveilling the lawyer's every move. Colbert sneered, "This tape tells me nothing except that he enjoys fucking his attractive wife." The financier snapped off the video. "What is this lawyer's interest in Bingham?"

"We don't know," Alexeyev mumbled. "Foolish curiosity."

"Viktor, can you guarantee me that the security risks are going to be contained over the next two weeks? Can you assure me that I'm simply overreacting here?"

Alexeyev hesitated. Then he said in a measured tone, "I believe I can."

"Good," Colbert thundered. "That's good. Still, I want you all over this Hansen. If you can't trust Gagarov to get it done, then do it yourself. Pethers and Hansen, those situations need to be brought under control immediately."

Minutes later, after Colbert finally calmed, he insisted that Viktor Alexeyev join him in a smoke. Alexeyev initially declined; but Colbert overcame his resistance by informing the Russian that his private stock contained not just *any* cigar. This particular one was a special blend made especially for Castro himself. Very rare.

Although Alexeyev was not a connoisseur, he had to concede it was a goddamn enjoyable smoke, this Liguito Number Two.

Thirty-five

THE CONFERENCE ADMINISTRATOR RANG HANSEN in his office and said, "Your two o'clock teleconference call will be connected in five minutes, Mr. Hansen."

Rick thanked the woman and replaced the phone on the hook. He grabbed the floppy disk created for him earlier that morning by Presentation Technologies and headed to the "Star Wars" Room.

Star Wars Room was the informal name for the New Delhi Room, which was loaded with high-tech gadgetry for conducting global teleconference calls. Participants could be connected simultaneously by facsimile, computer, telephone and video-conference. It was *de rigueur* for global investment firms to maintain at least one Star Wars facility in its corporate headquarters. Some had several.

Hansen arrived in the room for the 2 P.M. call with two minutes to spare. In the time before the call was connected, the two projection screens in the corners of the Star Wars Room showed the image of Hansen walking in. Fortunately, the previous occupants had ordered in lunch, and Hansen scored a bottle of untouched Evian. He inserted the floppy disk into the laptop computer next to the control console and mouse-clicked his way through the PowerPoint software.

Then he waited, sipping at the bottled water.

At precisely two, the call was put through.

After a single ring, the other party's image appeared on both projection screens. "Hello?" Kenneth Bellchambers spoke in a tentative voice. He was a thin man, with a thin florid face and dimples. He wore a yellow tie with a pink shirt, which wreaked havoc on the picture quality.

"Hello, this is Rick Hansen. Can you hear me all right?"

"Not only can I hear you, but I can see you quite clearly as well,"

Bellchambers said with a grin. The thing immediately noticeable about Bellchambers was the speed at which he spoke. The words tumbled out of the Canadian stockbroker at a remarkable velocity. "We don't get to use the teleconference facility all that often, but I suppose this is as good a use of it as any. You said this morning you'd have some pictures to show me?"

"I do," Rick said. "Hopefully, I can get this device to work."

"A bit mind-boggling, isn't it?"

"Yes, bear with me a moment." Rick navigated through the software program until the first picture came up on the laptop screen. It was the official Wolcott Fulbright identification photo of Tom Bingham. The firm's Presentation Technologies group had scanned several photographs into an Adobe PhotoShop environment, which converted the images into a digital computer file known as a "bitmap." The lawyer was now bringing the images up for Bellchambers' inspection over the video-conference line. "I think this gets it done," he said, toggling a switch on the console. The camera beaming Hansen's image to Bellchambers winked off and the image on the computer laptop was fed to Toronto at the other end of the line.

"That did it," Bellchambers said. "I now see the photo."

"This is a picture of Tom Bingham," Hansen said over the image. "Do you recognize him?"

"No. This is not the gentleman I opened the account for."

"It's not? You're positive of that?"

"Positive. This gentleman that you're showing now is fair-haired and fair-skinned. Quite the opposite of the individual I dealt with."

The lawyer felt a jolt of excitement, but remained calm. "Maybe this is not a good picture. I'm going to show you a few shots in a row and you tell me if this is the individual who claimed to be Tom Bingham."

Hansen clicked the mouse, and a short procession of images of Bingham flickered up on the computer screen. The photos provided by Elena Bingham were a few years old—shots of them together on vacation in Nantucket, at a wedding together, at home in the Central Park West rent-stabilized apartment. . . .

"No," Bellchambers said. "Most definitely not."

"That's not the guy?"

"No, it's not. I've never seen him before."

"What about the person in this next photo?" Hansen asked, as he tapped the mouse. A grainy black-and-white image flared on the screen.

"That's him!" Bellchambers said. "There's the fellow who set up the account under the name of Tom Bingham."

Hansen felt dizzy. Bellchambers was responding to the image of the intruder who had broken into his office and wiped out his computer files, the man who had fired a shot at Hansen in Bingham's apartment building. Bancroft had used a Mitsubishi video-capture printer to make a copy of a frame from the time-lapse surveillance video. Presentation Technologies had bitmapped it and loaded it onto the disk. Now Bellchambers was making a connection. The lawyer's head was swimming. "Are you certain this is him?"

"Mr. Hansen, I have never been so certain of anything in all my life. This fellow that's now up on the screen is—well, how to put it? As you politically correct Americans might say, the fellow is rather facially challenged, eh?"

———•———

So, Tom Bingham had been set up. The insider trading account was not his.

But who had set him up and why?

The plot thickens, Hansen sighed to himself en route to Mike Kilmartin's office.

Hansen rapped on Kilmartin's partially opened door.

"He's not in," Mike's secretary, Felicity, said, not looking up from her typing.

"He left already?"

Felicity nodded. "Gone fishin'. You may be able to catch him at the elevator."

Now it seemed important to find his boss, convey this revelation to him. Hansen raced down the corridor to the elevators. No sign of Kilmartin there. Hansen rode down to the lobby, made his way to the curb outside 44 Wall. His eyes swept up and down the turgid traffic moving on Wall Street. There was no sign of Kilmartin's radio car. The lawyer's boss had already gone fishin', and he was out of pocket for the next two weeks.

Thirty-six

FIFTH AVENUE, MANHATTAN
Wednesday, March 3

GRAHAM PETHERS TOOK ANOTHER SWALLOW of brandy and peered critically at the words glowing on the screen of his Apple PowerBook.

Dear Mr. Chairman:

The purpose of this letter is to inform you of a multibillion-dollar market manipulation scheme designed to trigger a 40% to 50% stock market decline within the next three weeks. The 7% decline on a single day last January was engineered by the same individuals as a precursor to an even more devastating market decline planned some time in March.

The artificial warmth of the alcohol did little to soothe the anxiety that had crushed his stomach into a knot. Contacting the Chairman of the U.S. SEC would be opening Pandora's box, he knew. Graham Pethers had amassed his fortune by diverting millions from its rightful owners. If he contacted the U.S. government about The Contrarians' scheme, he was inviting scrutiny into his own activities.

Rock and a hard place.

The forty-one-year-old Australian-American lawyer printed out a copy of the letter in draft form. He rose from his Biedermeyer chair, carrying the printout in one hand and the goblet of brandy in the other, drifting over to the southern exposure of his eleven-room, 7,500-square-foot prewar co-op on the sixteenth floor of 834 Fifth Avenue. Outside the floor-to-ceiling Palladian windows, the city lights of the wintertime Manhattan skyline glittered like a galaxy of luminescent jewels. The commanding view was magnificent as always, and relaxing to Pethers' troubled psyche. The tuner on the Bang & Olufsen stereo system was tuned to a classical music station broadcasting in FM stereo. The tranquil elegance of Glenn Gould's "Goldberg Variations" poured forth from the speakers—Variations 26 through 29, followed by the boisterous *Deutsche Freundlichkeit* and the *Aria da capo* of the *Sarabande*.

Pethers' eyes dropped from the view of the skyline to the draft letter in his trembling hand. Reading his own words once more, the enormity of his fate struck him. His entanglement with Colbert and The Contrarians had immutably altered the course of his life. He had stressed to Feldhof, his personal attorney, that the government had to grant him immunity for testifying against the others. No charges could be filed against him. Also, a return of his capital was a condition precedent.

Feldhof dryly noted the chances of that were slightly beneath those of the proverbial snowball in hell.

So Pethers sought to strike a bargain with the devil himself.

But how could he, if he couldn't get the devil to the bargaining table? Pethers had made his discontent perfectly clear to Colbert on three occasions over the last fortnight, ever since he became convinced that people were being murdered in the name of the initiative. Three times he had left messages with Colbert's voice mail system—by design, the only way to contact him—yet, frustratingly, Colbert remained incommunicado.

But by hook or crook, Graham Pethers was bailing out of the Contrarians. *No hard feelings, mates, just cash me out.* Liquidate his stake, return his $27 million in original seed money and off they went, a parting of the ways. Happened to partnerships all the time. One partner left, the other partners remained to carry out their appointed mission. And though Colbert had every reason to doubt it, Pethers was perfectly willing to keep quiet and let the scheme play itself out; but he could not profit from a scenario in which people were quietly being murdered.

—the phone jangled—

Pethers looked up, startled. Only a handful knew his unpublished telephone number, Colbert among them. Or it could be Feldhof, finally out of his meeting.

He crossed the antique French carpet to the other side of the study. He picked up on the second ring: "Yes?"

"You misspelled 'manipulation.'" The chilling voice on the other end was electronically altered with some sort of masking device, leaving it devoid of all characteristics and emotion. The artificial voice was low, sonorous. "In the first sentence of your letter. It's missing an '*i*.'"

Pethers was shocked. How did they know—? Then he exploded into a sputtering, choking rage. "You bastards! Why hasn't Colbert returned my calls?"

"He has nothing to say to you." The voice sounded like a recording that had been slowed.

Pethers stormed to the other side of the room and screamed fiercely into the phone. "Tell Colbert I want out! Cash me out *right now* or I'll bring the whole bloody thing crashing down." With that, he slammed the phone down on its cradle.

Seconds later, the phone rang.

Pethers stared at it for a moment. Then picked it up, put it to his ear. Said nothing.

On the other end, his own petulant voice. *Tell Colbert I want out! Cash me out right now or I'll bring the whole bloody thing crashing down!* Mocking him.

The phone then went dead.

Pethers returned the phone to the hook, suppressed his rage. Waited.

Within fifteen seconds, it rang again.

"I have a letter for Colbert," Pethers said by way of answering. "I want to meet."

The mechanical voice replied, "When?"

"Right now."

"Where?"

Pethers' mind raced to identify an advantageous meeting site, one with the largest crowd of people imaginable. "Rockefeller Center. The passageways beneath Radio City. There's a McDonald's down there. Do you know where that is?"

"Yes. When?"

"In thirty-five minutes, it will be seven-thirty exactly. If you're not there by seven-thirty-five, I'm gone. And my lawyer knows everything, so don't make a stupid move."

The other line disconnected once more.

Pethers found himself trembling. Events had been set into motion and, now more than ever, he was clearly not in control. He immediately wrote a brief note on his personal stationery to Laurence Feldhof, his personal attorney: *Larry, I have reason to fear for my life. This is the letter I mentioned to you over the weekend. Should anything happen to me, see that it reaches its destination immediately. Will contact you shortly to explain all.*

Then he faxed the latest draft both to Feldhof's home and office facsimile machines. In doing so, he'd hoped that he had effectively taken out a life insurance policy for himself. But instead of reaching its intended recipient, the fax transmissions were diverted by a black box device to a machine in a locked office at TCI Security.

———•———

Six minutes before the rendezvous, Graham Pethers arrived at the agreed-upon location. He paid the driver, closed the door and watched the cab motor off into the flow of traffic. Pethers walked around the expanse of the gleaming Art Deco edifice that was Radio City Music Hall, feeling secure among the hordes of people filtering out of office buildings. At precisely 7:27 P.M., he descended the staircase leading to the subterranean world beneath Rockefeller Center.

The strategy unspooled in his mind. It was this: hand over the envelope marked COLBERT—EYES ONLY, look the messenger in the eye and say, "Tell Colbert he's got twenty-four hours to reply, or my attorney goes to Washington to make a hand delivery."

That was it. Short and sweet.

It occurred to Pethers, of course, that he was possibly putting himself at risk simply by arranging this brief meeting with Colbert's thugs. He came prepared for violence, with a Kevlar bulletproof vest beneath his raincoat and his newly acquired Glock TacStar pistol in a holster against his hip. At the same time, he did not believe they would make a move to abduct him or kill him in the midst of thousands of rush-hour commuters. *Safety in numbers*, he thought, fingering the letter in his breast pocket like a talisman.

At this time of day, the vast underground network of interconnecting passageways linking several of New York City's most famous skyscrapers—Time-Life, Equitable, McGraw-Hill—was literally teeming with human life. Their meeting place was surprising well lit by banks of halogen lights that gleamed off the cream-toned Italian marble walls. Not a scrap of paper or blotch of chewing gum was to be spotted on the tiled floors. The ceiling was only nine feet above the ground, which wreaked havoc on the acoustics. Even ordinary sounds were amplified to monstrous volume: the swish of winter coats, the scuff of shoes, the squeak of sneakers, the ringing of cash registers, the jangle of loose pocket change. A cart of empty milk crates rumbled by with the racket of a subway train.

Pethers traversed the first fifty yards of the tunnel, turned left and positioned himself in front of the McDonald's. His back was flattened against the wall, permitting him to maintain a 180-degree perspective of the goings-on.

He casually scanned the orderly rivers of commuters streaming past in each direction. Armies of the Manhattan workforce outfitted in Burberry trenches, all bearing sullen, humorless expressions. Pethers was an alien among the refugees of the workaday life—he never would know this life, and thank God for that. A gaggle of unruly schoolchildren with backpacks floated by, a controlled riot, shepherded by an attractive no-nonsense teacher, a redhead in her early twenties. A teenager with a pompadour and a Stuyvesant High T-shirt kicking a soccer ball weaved in and out among the obstacle course of shuffling commuters. A blind man with a cane moved adeptly through the tunnels.

Twelve minutes passed. Pethers' anger rose within him like an iceberg. Screw Colbert! *Time's up.* He owed him *nothing.*

Pethers pivoted slightly to his left to wedge the envelope beneath the glowing McDonald's sign.

A sharp sting in the meat of his thigh caused him to cry out in pain.

Instinctively, his hand slapped down on the tender area—at the same time he whirled around to look for the prankster.

Nothing struck him as peculiar among the faceless masses streaming past.

Pethers cursed and continued massaging the back of his thigh vigorously.

Despite this, the wound began to swell alarmingly.

Graham Pethers would never fully understand that he had been injected with a tiny metal cone, roughly the size of a pencil point. Once the payload had been lodged securely into his flesh by the umbrella-gun, the Russian-engineered "viral bullet" immediately began releasing its compound toxins—succinic acid and choline, muscle relaxant, synthetic curare, cumadin. In concert, these chemicals set about systematically shutting down Pethers' vital body functions and leading to a swift but cruel death that doctors would misdiagnose as advanced viral leukemia.

The initial effects of the poisons were small in scale, but in their sum significant. A persistent ringing began in his ears, a dull ache gathered intensity behind his eyes. Blood kept seeping from the puncture in the skin of his thigh, despite his pressure on the area. His breathing became labored. *What's happening to me?* a voice screamed inside his head.

In the next moment, Pethers felt a painful sensation within his chest, as if his heart had exploded. Then he was aware that his heart rate was accelerating for no apparent reason. At the same time, he found it increasingly difficult to draw a breath. It was as if the muscles that powered his lungs were freezing up. He began to panic. *Find help.*

He struggled to work his legs, but found they had weakened alarmingly, impairing his locomotion. With each step a burning, prickly sensation erupted beneath the skin—ten thousand pinpricks.

"Help me," Pethers called out, in a cracking voice. "Please, I need help." With superhuman effort, he began wobbling uncertainly toward the staircase leading to the surface of the city.

His vision began to fail. Fireworks exploded randomly in his skull; his world became a sea of fire. Pethers' eyes began to water uncontrollably, obscuring his vision. The pressure behind his eyes had become virtually unbearable; amid the panic erupting in his brain, he feared the force would cause his eyeballs to burst from their sockets. He began to understand that Colbert was responsible for this and that he was dying.

He lurched toward the staircase with all the effort he could muster. *Why wasn't anyone helping him?* Each breath was like inhaling liquid flame. He tried to cry out, but the toxins had corrupted his vocal cords and all he could manage was a pathetic whimper. *Please, God. Not like this. Not this way.* His legs had become useless, no longer able to support him. But a flicker of hope flared when Graham Pethers became aware of someone dropping to his side. Leaning in close.

The blind man.

"Help me, please," Pethers begged in a phlegmy whisper.

"Good news from Colbert," the blind man rasped in a low voice.

Colbert?

The blind man waved the EYES ONLY letter in front of Pethers' face. "Your request to withdraw from The Contrarians," the blind man said, "has been approved."

The blind man punched Pethers in the stomach. Pethers collapsed to the cool of the marble floor, unable to draw another breath. Blackness closed in on him. By now, he had no fight left, and he welcomed the end.

"A doctor!" the Gargoyle cried out, affecting a false Hispanic accent. "Please! This man needs a doctor!" And as a crowd began to thicken around the stricken form of Graham Pethers, the Gargoyle stepped back and slipped away from the chaotic scene, climbing the staircase to the surface and disappearing into the chill of the early March night.

Thirty-seven

UPPER EAST SIDE, MANHATTAN
Thursday, March 4

"THANKS FOR AGREEING to meet with me."

Detective First Grade Daniel F. X. O'Bannon shrugged. "It's not such a favor. I come by here most every night anyway."

Here was a lively uptown law enforcement hangout named Churchill's. Located on Third Avenue at Seventy-third Street, it was something of a wood-paneled clubhouse for those whose livelihood stemmed from the law enforcement business. NYPD cops bellied up to the bar with fibbies, defense attorneys bought a round of drinks for a group of district attorneys. It was an interesting amalgam of people, and some of those drinking and laughing together were often on opposite sides of the fence in their daily work.

It was just after six o'clock, and the back room at Churchill's was packed with raucous off-duty police officers. The conversation between Hansen and O'Bannon was nearly rendered inaudible by a boisterous bevy of uniformed police officers two tables away bellowing with cruel laughter over the tale of the rookie cop who'd been ordered by his superior to perform his first body cavity search of a crack suspect. "So, halfway through the prodding and probing," the storyteller says, "Roscoe here holds up some rubber gloves and says, 'Gee, guy, wouldn't you prefer to use these?' " The table exploded in guffaws.

O'Bannon swilled the mug of draft beer Hansen had bought. "You said you wanted to discuss the Berger suicide?"

"Bingham."

"Yeah, okay, right, Bingham. I remember, the jumper who went around Christmastime. Went through the roof of a cab."

"That's right. But I have reason to believe it wasn't suicide."

O'Bannon squinted at his drinking companion. "You're not a family member, are you?"

"No. I'm just the guy who got his job."

The detective's eyebrow shot up. "Okay, tell me what you've got."

Hansen told O'Bannon about the evidence he'd gathered to date. How someone had wiped out the files on his computer. How the insider trading scheme was a setup. How someone had fired a gun at him in the stairwell of Bingham's apartment building. Throughout, the detective doodled on the beer coaster and nodded mechanically. *Uh-huh, yeah, right, gotcha. Izzatso?*

"And I think I've got a picture of the guy." Hansen passed the video-capture still to O'Bannon. The off-duty detective peered at the image with an unimpressed expression on his face.

Hansen asked, "So what do you think?"

The detective gave a fractional shrug. "I'll look into it."

The lawyer tilted his head in dismay. "You don't seem all that motivated to solve this case."

Detective Dan O'Bannon bristled at this. "*Solve* this case? *Solve*, did you say? As far as the New York City Police Department is concerned, this case is closed. You're asking me to *reopen* it."

"Okay, reopen then, whatever. Point is, there's enough circumstantial evidence that—"

O'Bannon cut him off with two pointed fingers. "Let me make sure I understand this. You're hypothesizing that Bingham was killed off because of his involvement in an insider trading ring—"

"No. The insider trading thing was a sham, a setup to make Bingham's suicide look legitimate."

"Uh-huh. Okay, and you're presupposing that the bad guy who offed Bingham was the same guy who popped off a shot at you?"

"I don't know that he killed Bingham, it's possible. But this guy is intimately involved because *he* was identified by the stockbroker in Toronto as the one passing himself off as Tom Bingham when the insider trading account was set up."

"I need another beer." O'Bannon held up two fingers to the waitress and pointed to his glass, empty except for a foam residue. "Let me give you a crash course in real-world reality, Rick. My world, out on the streets? It's a shitstorm out there and they don't hand us umbrellas. The stuff we see every day? It'd make you puke. Much as you develop a tolerance for all the genetic garbage out there, you never fully become immune to it. Look around. You see how this place is packed with hard-drinking cops doing shots of whiskey? What they're doing is, they're taking their booster shots for tomorrow's shitstorm."

Hansen knew this, and had enormous respect for the thin blue line. But to articulate it at this point would have sounded gratuitous. He kept his mouth shut and let O'Bannon talk.

"A Wall Street lawyer buys the farm? Hey, there's a lotta pressure where you guys work. It doesn't take any fantastic leap in logic to believe your guy took his own life. And if at the end of the day, he didn't? Yeah, well, like I said, I'll reopen the file. Otherwise, I've got about five other dead bodies in my in-box to contend with. In May, when I graduate from Fordham Law, I'm out of this business, Rick. I'm going to do what you do—be a Wall Street lawyer. What I don't understand is why a Wall Street lawyer would want to be doing a *detective's job*."

Hansen stared at his beer. "I don't know either."

———•———

The meeting with O'Bannon was a complete bust, leaving Hansen bummed out. The truth was, whether Bingham's death was murder or suicide—whatever, life went on. Which was precisely what his murderers were banking on.

O'Bannon's words rang in his mind. *Why would a Wall Street lawyer want to be doing a detective's job?*

He was after a faceless criminal, or group of criminals, who had committed no crime against him. His sole motivation for pursuit was that it struck him as the right thing to do.

To solve a murder. Two murders. Maybe even three murders.

Murders that had something to do with predicting the direction of the stock market.

He reflected back to his speculation that they had also killed Gammage, *eliminated* him.

Was it simply *greed*?

The impulse to take the life of someone else probably resided in almost every human being capable of forming the thought. It was a component of human nature. The urge to kill was the by-product of some primordial fight-or-flight genetic coding, hardwired into the human animal. But impulse was one thing; to act upon the impulse was another. The rational human being was expected to suppress the urge, not to act upon it. Committing homicide was impossible to imagine for Hansen, unless of course, he was forced to kill in order to spare the lives of loved ones. Stephanie. His parents and twin sisters. His soon-to-be-born child.

Under those circumstances, absolutely, he could be compelled to kill.

But in the name of *money*?

Greed as a motivating factor for committing homicide was certainly nothing revolutionary. But it was the most repugnant reason of all for taking a life. Blood money. It was a disservice to his own existence if he didn't pursue the bastards responsible, particularly if there was a connection to his livelihood.

At the same time, he worried for the first time that if they had killed before, they would most certainly kill again. And the man he encountered at Bingham's apartment demonstrated no hesitation to shoot at him—if circumstances so required. O'Bannon was not going to be an ally, he realized. He was going to be a lone wolf on this. Not for the first time, he told himself that his quest could be putting his life in jeopardy from some faceless, malevolent force. It was very possibly a death wish, but he could not resist its siren song.

———•———

Before going home to Stephanie, Hansen traveled downtown to pick up some papers to work on that night. The flashing light on his phone told him he had a message on voice mail.

Without much enthusiasm, he connected with the Wolcott voice-mail system. "You have one new message," the recording informed him. "Press one-one to hear your messages now."

Rick Hansen punched in the numbers as he deposited a stack of papers into his briefcase.

The recorded message came on with some background hiss. "Hello, er, uh, my name is Freddie Zaraghi, and I'm responding to your message, the one you left last Sunday? Professor Gammage is, uh, no longer with Three, Three Rivers Algorithmics. Please contact me and I'll see if I can help you, especially if you have a billing question." Freddie Zaraghi left a number with a Pittsburgh area code.

Hansen promptly dialed it.

One ring, an answer. "Hello?"

"Is this Freddie Zaraghi?"

"It is. Who's this?"

"Rick Hansen. You left a message on my voice mail."

"Oh, yeah, Mr. Hansen, right." He sounded like a kid, a pimply-faced kid trying to come off as mature and confident. "Sorry I didn't get to you sooner, but I've been traveling and I just now got back—"

"I understand Professor Gammage no longer works for Three Rivers Algorithmics, but do you have another number for him? It's imperative that I speak to him right away."

"Well, this is his business partner. You can speak to me."

"I really need to speak directly with Professor Gammage," Hansen insisted.

The voice on the other end cut him off. "Professor Gammage died recently."

Hansen's blood ran cold. He stood there, gripping the phone tightly, unable to speak. When he regained his ability to talk, he whispered hoarsely, "He did?"

"Yes, died last month in an accident in his home." Freddie Zaraghi changed course. "You say you're from Wolcott Fulbright?"

"Yes, I am."

"Do you work with Tom Bingham?"

"Tom . . . Tom is also dead."

"Fuck," Zaraghi muttered. "That's weird."

There was a silence as each contemplated the import of the information they had just swapped. Gammage was dead too? Zaraghi knew Bingham? At once, Hansen said, "You say you were Professor Gammage's business partner?"

"Yes," the kid said. "I was. Unfortunately."

Rick Hansen sat down and positioned his pen over a fresh sheet of paper on his legal pad. "Precisely what sort of business were you and Gammage in?"

Thirty-eight

PITTSBURGH, PENNSYLVANIA
Saturday, March 6

MIDWAY THROUGH THE 9:10 A.M. flight from JFK to Pittsburgh International, Rick Hansen experienced an irrational feeling that he was going to die in a fiery plane crash.

There was no basis for this. The relentless rasp of the twin props that propelled the SAAB 340B commuter plane hadn't stuttered in midair. There was no precipitous drop in cabin pressure. It was, admittedly, all in his head. Still, the paranoia that accompanied impending parenthood dogged him, especially twenty-seven thousand feet above the earth. *Will I die before seeing my child?* Bingham was dead. Hansen could be next.

Ridiculous. But still, he couldn't lose the feeling. To soothe his dread, Rick resorted to a game he from his childhood, glancing out the window and playing a free association with the shapes of the fluffy clouds. Whipped cream. Bunny rabbits. Cotton puffs.

Nuclear mushroom clouds. Slow motion explosions. Billowing smoke. *Arrrgh.*

Finally, the constant drone of the twin props permitted Hansen to drift off into a troubled snooze.

He awoke slightly before the scheduled arrival time, as the plane dipped out of the dishwater-gray skies of Pittsburgh in its approach to the runway. Peering out the window, Rick Hansen found himself suitably impressed by the footprint of the city's skyline below, which he'd never seen before. Contrary to his premonition, touchdown onto the snow-dusted tarmac was perfect.

Within minutes, Hansen was making his way through the sleek, pristine and impersonal confines of Greater Pittsburgh International Airport with his single carry-on bag slung over his shoulder, humming to the Muzak of a Michael Jackson tune. By 9:50 A.M., he pushed the keys into the ignition of a white, fifty-dollar-a-day Chevy Lumina rental, tuned the radio to a heavy-metal station named X-ROCK, and headed at a brisk sixty-five-miles-per-hour clip toward the city of Pittsburgh, some twelve miles to the east on Interstate 279.

Forty minutes of driving passed. As it turned out, Freddie Zaraghi's directions left much to be desired in the way of precise details, but despite a misstep off the Penn-Lincoln Parkway that sent Hansen circling uselessly around Three Rivers Stadium—

(*Aha! That's why it's called Three Rivers Algorithmics!*)

—the lawyer somehow stumbled onto Forbes Avenue anyway, and headed east to the Oakland section of town.

In minutes, the campus of Carnegie-Mellon University loomed on the right. A quick left on Moorwood Avenue to Fifth, another right-hand turn, up a block to Wilkins, and Hansen found himself in the Shadyside section of town. Moments later, he drew up to the tired-gray brick residence where Zaraghi lived and killed the engine.

From the outside, the residence reflected the strictly low-rent existence of a part-time employed college dropout without parental financial support. The tired gray brick exterior bore jagged cracks running diagonally across its face. The roof tiles were peeling free. Cracks in the attic windows had been repaired with mud-colored duct tape. Rent probably cost Zaraghi between $250 and $300 a month, including all utilities, Hansen figured.

Rick's footfalls crunched on the gravel as he stepped around the two autos out front—a garish orange VW minibus circa 1971 and a white Datsun 310EX compact with two flats. He descended a short set of stairs and approached the front door. Knocked.

The muffled reply floated through the door: "Hold on! Coming!" In the next moment, the door opened and before him stood Freddie Zaraghi.

"You the lawyer from New York?" he asked.

"That's right. You Zaraghi?"

"That's me."

Freddie Zaraghi and Rick Hansen gave each other a brief inspection. They came from decidedly different worlds—the yuppie vs. the techno-wonk—the gulf between them being largely monetary in origin. Zaraghi was dressed all in black, with a turtleneck completing the too-cool-for-color look.

"You're early, aren't you?" Zaraghi asked.

"My flight made good time. Should I come back later?"

Zaraghi shook his head. "No. It's all right. I've got something to show off anyway."

Zaraghi opened the door wider and Hansen entered.

It was coal-mine dark in the one-room basement apartment. Zaraghi had installed blackout shades in all the windows and the only light in the room flickered from the television set. Captain Kirk and Mr. Spock dubbed in Japanese—a most peculiar sight. The furnishings were IKEA Spartan—basic, functional, college-student stuff. Iron City Light beer cans, Jolt cola bottles, Little Debbie snack cake wrappings and cartons of half-eaten Szechwan Chinese food were strewn about the room.

A bookshelf overflowed with books on computer programming and a collection of every *Star Trek* television episode ever produced. As Rick's eyes adjusted to the pitch darkness, he was aware that a thin, beautiful Japanese woman dressed all in black was on the other end of the sofa, oblivious to Hansen and Zaraghi. The top part of her head was obscured by a scuba-diving-mask-like set of dark goggles. The contraption included headphones that completely sealed her off from any external stimuli.

Zaraghi smiled. "That's my sort-of fiancée, Suki. With that thing on, she'll never even know you came or went."

"What is that thing?"

"It's called a facesucker."

"A what?"

"A facesucker."

"What is it, some sort of sensory deprivation thing?"

"Kind of just the opposite of that." Zaraghi reached over and retrieved his own facesucker from the couch. "Try it, tell me what you think."

Hansen accepted the headset from Zaraghi, strapped it on over his face. It was composed of wraparound goggles and Sony digital headphones. He adjusted the strap and wriggled it into position over his eyes and ears. Zaraghi snapped on a switch at a black-box unit next to the couch. Instantly, the crystal-clear image of Captain Kirk and Mr. Spock leapt to life, seemingly before his face. Hansen was not especially a die-hard Trekkie, but he recognized the episode from its endless repetition in the cyberspace of syndication. It was the one where Captain Kirk falls in love with Joan Collins after traveling back in time to the American Depression. "City on the Edge of Forever."

But it was unlike any he'd ever seen or heard before—the picture was 180-degree wraparound, virtually 3-D like a ViewMaster. The audio was Dolby-enhanced digital-surround sound. Hansen was blown away by the experience.

"This is an incredible device," he exclaimed to his host, returning the facesucker. "What's the story with this?"

"It's an invention I've been working on, called the JackMan. Takes ordinary analog audio and video source material and feeds it through this black box, which is wired to trick the viewer into perceiving it as three-dimensional and stereoscopic. It's all illusion."

"It's cool."

"Yeah. I had a lot of time on my hands since I dropped out of school and declared personal bankruptcy." Zaraghi gave him a look devoid of irony or humor. "Look, this is your call. I thought we could go over to the cafeteria for some lunch, talk more about this thing."

"Sounds good."

"Thing is, you're gonna have to pick up the check, because thanks to Gammage, I don't have a dime to my name, all right?"

———◆———

The four-block walk along the perimeter of the Carnegie-Mellon campus took ten minutes. Hansen and Zaraghi took a table in a corner of the half-empty student cafeteria, and began tearing into their high-carbohydrate lunches of sun-lamped cheeseburgers and fries.

The lawyer was the one to end the companionable silence. "That JackMan was an amazing device."

"I know, thanks."

" 'City on the Edge of Forever.' Best *Star Trek* ever."

"One of the best five," the kid countered.

"You a big fan?"

"*Major*. I have every episode on tape. Some episodes I have in five different languages."

"Now that's an interesting paradox," Hansen mused.

"What's that?"

"A Trekkie who follows the stock market. What caused you to take an interest in finance?"

Zaraghi gave a fractional shrug and tore off a greedy bite of his cheeseburger. "The obsession started 'cause of my dad, but not the way you'd think. You know, it's not like my dad bought a single share of Disney and hung the certificate up on my bedroom wall, or put my allowance into mutual funds or some shit like that. Actually, it's not a real pretty story."

The kid then relayed the tale of his parents' emigration to the United States before Freddie was born. His family settled in a Turkish-American community in Hamtramck, Michigan, where the mother had cousins and the Detroit auto industry promised decent wages. In short order, Zemach Zaraghi became employed on the assembly line at General Motors'

Cadillac plant in Hamtramck, affixing windshield wipers to factory-new DeVilles. The senior Zaraghi worked on that line for twenty-three years, ultimately rising through the ranks to become a shift supervisor.

"Each and every payday, my dad drove his AMC Pacer to the Campau Avenue branch of People's State Bank and deposited a little money in a college fund for me and my three sisters. My mom's family used to bust his balls for being so timid with his investments, but Dad was intimidated by the American stock market. There was no such thing back in the old country."

"Then came the go-go 1980s. Junk bonds. Hostile takeovers. Easy money. Every no-luck sucker in Hamtramck tried his luck in the stock market. Everyone kept winning. The neighbors used to drive my dad nuts—'Zem, you simply buy a company's stock and watch it go up up up.' They would tell him how this was the *real* American Dream, this was how the rich got richer. And it finally got under my dad's skin. His thinking was, suddenly, if he took a little risk, maybe he could afford to send us all to MIT and Harvard.

"So my mom's cousin set him up with his stockbroker from Grosse Point. That was, I think, August 1986."

At this point, Zaraghi peered at the spearmint green wall of the cafeteria, as if staring distantly at the events of a decade ago. "I remember every single detail of the day the stock market crashed on October 19, 1987. I remember coming home from school and seeing my dad at the kitchen table, with an ashtray full of crushed-out cigarette butts and a half-empty bottle of vodka. You could immediately tell he was wasted. His hands were shaking like this." By way of demonstration, Zaraghi vigorously fluttered his fingers. "Soon as he saw me coming into the kitchen, he started bawling. All he could say, over and over, was that he was sorry, he was so sorry. Over and over, he said it. He was sorry. Six months later, of course, the backlash from Black Monday hit and GM laid Dad off for ten months."

Rick self-consciously rubbed his jaw and murmured sympathetically.

Zaraghi continued, "I was ashamed. You know why?"

Hansen shook his head.

"Because my first thought was: *Hey, where did the money go?* I mean, it was there yesterday, and now it's gone. How is that possible? And at that moment, I realized: for Dad to have lost all that money, someone else must have *taken it out of his pocket.* It's a zero-sum game—for someone to win, someone has to lose.

"So, for the rest of my high school days, I studied the history of the stock market, the price trends, the crashes. I created computer models to analyze the market. And I won a Westinghouse National Science Talent Search scholarship for a program I designed that proved money could be made in the stock market regardless of its direction, as long as the market *moves*. The program proved that if you can somehow figure out with a degree of confidence which direction it's going to move and how dramatically it's going to move, you could become very very very rich."

"So you used the Westinghouse scholarship to go to Carnegie-Mellon?"

"Yeah. That and some matching aid. When my dad lost all that money and then got laid off, the fund was pretty much tapped out by the time I was ready for college." Zaraghi paused. "From that day on, my obsession was to come up with a system that would allow me to win back from the stock market all the money my dad lost. Then I'd go up to him with it in a shopping bag and hand it to him. 'Hey, Dad, remember all that money you worked your ass off to make? Well, here you go, you're even. Now go have a great retirement.' " Zaraghi smiled. "Nice fantasy, huh? Of course, it hasn't worked out that way, not yet anyhow."

The lawyer shifted gears. "Let's talk about Gammage."

"Ugh, I hated that bearded fuck." Zaraghi words were nearly choked off by his bilious anger. "I got screwed by him more ways than Madonna. Look, I don't mean to come off like some bitter young asshole, but, well, it so happens I am. Gammage made me that way. No apologies."

"I'm not looking for apologies."

Zaraghi peered at the lawyer. "Exactly *what* are you looking for, Mr. Hansen?"

"Just what I told you on the phone." Hansen set his cheeseburger down on the brown plastic tray and leaned forward. "I've got this very weird puzzle on my hands. The more I work the puzzle, the more illogical it becomes. Freddie, you have a connection to two dead people—Gammage and Bingham—and you may be the missing piece that solves it."

The kid fingered his Fu Manchu and stared into space thoughtfully. "Let me start from the beginning. Going back before Howard Gammage caused me to drop out of CMU, lose my full scholarship and end up in personal bankruptcy."

"Okay."

"First semester, junior year, around December, two years ago. First, I was an advanced computer science major at Carnegie-Mellon, which as you know, has one of the two or three most advanced computer science curricula in the country. My adviser at the time had gotten me into Howard Gammage's Advanced Neural Supercomputing course, which was open to graduate school students only." Zaraghi placed the remnants of his third cheeseburger on his tray. "Something you need to understand, Mr. Hansen—and this is not in any way an attempt to impress you, because personally, I have nothing whatsoever to gain from saying this—but you need to realize that I was considered the most promising computer science student this institution has accepted in roughly a decade."

"I have no doubt," Hansen replied, not knowing how else to respond to the boast. "And so you enrolled in Gammage's graduate-level class."

"Yes. Best student he ever had."

"Uh-huh."

"So good, in fact, he wanted to start a business with me. Based on this." Freddie reached below the table and pulled his knapsack up onto his lap. His hand fished about its contents. Then he came up with a thick rust-colored accordion folder of printed materials labeled LINDA LITI-GATION DOCUMENTATION. Freddie thumbed through the sheaf of documents until he retrieved a thick, dog-eared term paper. He handed it to the lawyer.

Rick peered at the cover page:

HACKING GLOBAL FINANCE AND BEYOND: APPLICATION OF MPP SUPERCOMPUTING TECHNOLOGY TO PREDICT THE DIRECTION OF STOCK MARKET PRICES

At the bottom of the front page, there was a handwritten notation in crisp blue-black fountain-pen ink.

A+

Excellent work. One of the most stimulating student theses I have ever had the pleasure of reading. Pls. drop by my office next week to discuss your thesis in greater detail. (Coffee is on me.)

-Dr. Gammage

"So we had coffee," Zaraghi said, picking up the story. "And over coffee, we agreed to start a business in which we developed systems intended to predict stock market trends. We called it Three Rivers Algorithmics. At the time, I was flattered; my professor thought I was enough of a whiz kid to go into business with—that's heady stuff for a twenty-year-old. I know now, of course, that Gammage was a greedy fuck who wanted to exploit me. Once I developed the technology and made a few client presentations, he cut me out completely."

"Who were the clients?"

"A couple of major Wall Street firms. I'm not certain how many because Gammage controlled that part of the business, the marketing. But I know the one that expressed the most interest." Zaraghi pointed at Hansen. "*Your* firm."

"Wolcott Fulbright?"

"Yes. That's how I met your man Tommy Bingham. He came to Pittsburgh one day and grilled me on my research. I think I sold him on it."

"Tom purchased a system from you?"

Zaraghi's expression went dark. "To this day, I don't know if he did or not. See, basically, Gammage suddenly cut me out of Three Rivers. He purposely drove the venture into the ground. Some crap about our financial angel was pulling the plug. The scumbag then filed for bankruptcy without first telling me. Just came to me out of the blue one day and said 'It's a bust, guy.' Those were his words—*it's a bust, guy.* Since it was a partnership, he said, the law said I was in hock for fifty percent of the debts. That meant my share was more than $100,000. Gammage told me that he was jointly responsible and that he would mortgage his house to pay my share if I agreed to file for personal bankruptcy and sign a promissory note. What choice did I have? I signed the freaking thing. Way after I signed it, I learned it said I could never take him to court over anything having to do with the business.

"Almost immediately after that, I learned through the grapevine that Gammage announced he's leaving CMU at the end of the school year. Turns out he's starting a new firm, Gammage Financial Algorithmics!

"I went postal. I confronted him in his office, started screaming in front of some other students. Threatened to sue, that sort of shit. Next thing that happens, I'm talking to some shiny-shoed lawyers about a lawsuit."

"Sounds like you had a strong case for fraud."

"If only *you* were my lawyer. They said the documentation made it clear my program was a 'work for hire.' In other words, our partnership was based on a handshake, but the legal documents Gammage put together said I was just an independent contractor. *Working for him!* To take on such a long-shot intellectual property case, the lawyers wanted an up-front retainer of $25,000.

"So I've been busting hump, working two jobs to raise enough money to sue the son-of-a-bitch. Then he up and *kills himself.*"

Hansen's antenna went up. "How did Gammage die?"

"Lots of bizarre rumors going around the campus. You ever hear of a thing called 'auto-erotic asphyxiation'?"

"I've heard of it," Hansen said. "Isn't it some freaky sexual thing?"

"Right. Also known as a choke-and-stroke. Well, the cops said the good professor killed himself by cutting off his oxygen intake as he was, uh, jerking himself. Gives a whole new meaning to 'choking the chicken,' don't you think?" Zaraghi lit a clove cigarette, shaking his head at the thought.

Hansen grimaced. "Gammage didn't kill himself, you know. Someone made it look that way."

"Come on." Freddie's features screwed into a mask of gimme-a-break disdain. "You think some killer *set that up* to cover up a murder? Pardon me for saying so, Mr. Hansen, but that's a pretty far-fetched theory, even for Columbo." Freddie took a long drag from the clove cigarette and exhaled it all at once. "Granted, LINDA's awesome, but not worth killing over."

Hansen blinked in mute confusion. "Linda? Who's Linda?"

Zaraghi laughed. "Not who. It's a *what*. LINDA is the neurogenetic, algorithmic data-mining application I created."

"What's LINDA stand for?"

"Uh, actually, it's not an acronym. It's just the name of the first girl who ever dumped me."

Hansen suppressed a smile. The ultimate geek-punk revenge was to name a killer system after someone who spurned you, an anti-tribute. "So LINDA is the system you and Gammage created to predict the direction of the stock market?"

Freddie bristled. "No, LINDA is the technology *I* created to predict the stock market. All Gammage did was rip me off."

"Right, right. Sorry."

Freddie's face softened to reflect the pride of his creation. "Trust me when I tell you that this is Wall Street's ultimate cream-your-Calvins wet-dream killer app. We've done turnkey applications that prove it to be fifty times more effective than anything else out there."

"What makes it tick?"

"Are you familiar with the concept of neurogenetic expert systems?"

"Can't say I am."

"Scalable massively parallel processing?"

"No."

"How about back-propagation paradigms? Feed forward architectures?"

"Look." Hansen felt his frustration well up in the face of the relentless technobabble. "Go easy on me. I can get my PC to spit out an interoffice memo, but that's about the sum total of my computer expertise. I'm afraid you're gonna have to put it in English."

"All right. It's technically complicated, of course, but the basics are fairly plain vanilla." Freddie had assumed a haughty attitude, a maddening sort of the-geeks-shall-inherit-the-earth superiority Hansen had often encountered among quant jocks. "We'll take it from the beginning. Let me have that back."

Hansen returned the term paper to its author. Zaraghi whipped through it, flipping to appendixes in the back. He folded the pages back, displaying Appendix FF. "This should clarify things."

Hansen squinted at the complex flowchart. It didn't clarify things at all.

Overview of LINDA

Software	Systemic Theory	Hardware
ARTIFICIAL INTELLIGENCE	CHAOS THEORY	ADVANCES IN SUPER-COMPUTING TECHNOLOGY
Expert Systems	Nonlinear, Complex "Chaotic" Systems May Be Predictable	136,000 MFLOPS Clock Speed and Gallium Arsenide Logic Circuitry
Fuzzy Logic/ Neural Nets	Global Financial Markets	Asynchronous Transfer Mode (ATM)
Back Propagation Paradigms	Twin Myths of the Random Walk and Efficient Markets	Scalable Massively Parallel Processing (MPP)
Feed Forward Architectures	Irrational Investor Behavior: Greed and Euphoria; Fear and Panic	BACKBONE ATM Network and GigaRouter
Neurogenetic Algorithms	"Pockets of Predictability" in the Digital Flow of Wealth	DataKnife
Data-Mining/ Data-Filtering	Real-time Data Feeds and Historical Pricing Database	
Spatio-Temporal Pattern Recognition	LINDA and Direct Electronic Uplink to World Stock Exchanges	
CONCLUSION: Broad-Based Stock Market Movements Are Inherently Predictable in the Short Term (15 to 60 Calendar Days)		

As he peered at the schematic, he heard Freddie saying, "Being in the financial industry, you happen to be witnessing the revolution from the front lines."

Hansen looked up. "Which revolution would that be?"

"The technological revolution. How it's changing the game of finance."

"Absolutely. Wolcott's got almost a thousand tech people on payroll, creating front-end trade entry systems—"

Freddie shook his head. "That's not what I'm talking about. I'm talking about what technology has done to the concept of *wealth* itself."

Hansen frowned. "I'm not following you."

"Money has been *digitized*, you see. It has been converted into just another stream of electronic information blipping around the globe at the speed of light, twenty-four hours a day. Because of that, there are games you can play with digital money."

"You mean, it can be stolen electronically?"

"No, no. I mean, yes, of course it can, but that's strictly low-tech at this stage of the game. Do you know what's meant by the velocity of money?"

"No."

"It's a term from economics, a measure of how quickly money is being spent once it's obtained. The speed at which an average dollar changes hands in a year's time."

"Okay-y-y-y." Hansen wasn't following him.

"To illustrate the significance of money's velocity, let me quote cybersage Kevin Kelly." The kid closed his eyes tightly, recalling the passage from rote memory. " 'When money is disembodied—that is, removed from any material basis such as paper or metal—it speeds up. It travels farther, faster. Circulating money faster has an effect similar to circulating more money. Satellite technology now enables near-the-speed-of-light, round-the-clock world stock trading, expanding the amount of global money by five percent. Once digital cash goes global, it will further accelerate the velocity of money. Electronic money is as malleable as digitized information.' " He opened his eyes and grinned. "Therefore, as Kelly points out, you can now 'hack' finance. That was the subject of my term paper."

"Hack finance? With computers?"

Zaraghi nodded.

Hansen frowned. "How?"

"What I'm saying is that if you apply modern economic theory and enormous computational power to the mountains of data related to the financial markets, you can extract obscure but *meaningful* patterns in the flow of digitized wealth."

"Okay." Hansen thought he now understood. "Go on."

"If you can discern those certain patterns among the turbulent flows—called 'fractals'—and you can anticipate when those patterns will reoccur in the near-term future, you can become very very wealthy in short order. Let me throw another buzzword at you. Ever hear of chaos theory?"

Hansen recalled his conversation with Joe Money on the subject just weeks before. "Yes. Some of our derivatives guys at Wolcott have studied the concept and believe it works."

"It does, oh yes, it most certainly does. The chaos theory engine in my software absolutely works. Not every time, but almost every time. To a certain extent, therefore, it is possible to predict the stock market. It is even possible to *influence* it."

The lawyer tipped back in his chair, crossed his arms and bit his lower lip. *Did LINDA enable Bingham to predict Freefall Friday?* The lawyer decided to toss down the gauntlet to the geek-punk. With an unimpressed shrug, Hansen said, "Yeah, I've heard a lot about market timing and forecasting models. Elliot Wave, Gann lines. Pardon my skepticism, but the truth is, LINDA sounds like just another 'black box' technique to me, albeit with cool bells and whistles."

"You Wall Street types." Freddie cackled in self-amusement. "Seeing is believing, right? Where's the beef, show me de money, and all that. All right, then. I suppose it's time you saw LINDA for yourself."

Thirty-nine

THE DRIVE TO THE FACILITY took roughly twenty-five minutes.

Feigenbaum Technology Park was located in a suburban enclave thirteen miles off I-279 northwest of the Allegheny River. After a short distance on a two-lane thoroughfare choked with strip malls and fast-food franchises, Zaraghi said, "Make a quick right here or you'll miss it."

Hansen complied, turning on a road marked only by an innocuous sign identifying the area as NORTH AMERICAN SUPERCOMPUTING CONSORTIUM OF INDUSTRY AND ACADEMIA. The Chevy Lumina wended its way up the drive that sliced through the park's well-manicured campus.

"Let's see if James C. is in the box today," Zaraghi mused more to himself than to his companion.

The Chevy reached the crest of the hill where the guardhouse was located. Hansen brought the car to a halt at the black-and-yellow-striped security gate and lowered the window. An imposing linebacker of a uniformed security guard materialized from the mirrored guardhouse, his arms thick as some men's thighs. The guard strode purposefully over to them and peered into the opening with an unfriendly expression. "How can I help you?"

Zaraghi leaned over and fired off a salutary greeting at the guard. "It's okay, James C. This guy's with me."

The guard beamed when he saw Freddie in the passenger seat. "Hey, how you doin', Freddie?"

"Seen better days, if you wanna know the truth. Enough about me. How's the rotisserie hockey standings? You still in the hunt for first place?"

"Hell, no. The Pens can't win for losing, so neither can I." James folded his arms in an informal manner, resting his elbows on the bottom frame of the open window. "Who's your friend?"

"VIP from Wall Street." Freddie winked. "Don't tell him, but I'm hoping that if we roll the out red carpet, and dazzle him with brain candy, his company will sink a few bajillion dollars into LINDA."

The guard nodded amiably. "We like those big money Wall Street types here at NASCIA." He reached through the open window and inserted a green one-day parking permit at the bottom of the dashboard. "You're good to go."

"Have a good 'un, Jamester."

"Likewise." James thumbed the button at his console. The striped arm jerked and lifted skyward. Hansen drove through into the complex.

"This is where you work?" Hansen asked.

"Twenty-five hours a week at six seventy-five an hour. Writing UNIX code. Not much of a living, but the work makes up for the lousy wages."

The facility floated into sight. It was a cluster of four impersonal Bauhaus cubes with mirrored exteriors that revealed nothing of the activities within. A half-dozen crescent-shaped satellite dishes were scattered around the buildings. The sterility of the complex struck Hansen as that of a secretive enclave. *A suitable headquarters for an outfit like the CIA*, he thought to himself.

Only then did he notice the smirk on his companion's face.

"Prepare yourself for the revolution," Freddie said, cryptically.

———————•———————

Inside the largest of the cubes, the main reception area possessed a distinctly corporate feel. The plush crimson carpeting, the glass-and-steel sculptures, the neo-modern artwork on the walls—the effect suggested the facility was awash in an ocean of Fortune 500 riches.

Hansen mentioned this observation as Zaraghi used his magnetic picture pass card to gain entry through the turnstile at the security checkpoint. "Feigenbaum used to be a DARPA site," Zaraghi replied.

"DARPA. That has something to do with national defense, doesn't it?"

"We're going this way." Zaraghi led them down a corridor with muted lighting that seemed to snake its way belowground. "Right. DARPA is a highly secretive arm of the Pentagon. Stands for 'Defense Advanced Research Projects Agency.' This facility was a DARPA hot site for six years during the Cold War. They used artificial intelligence to defeat the Russians, SAM AND IVAN, the machines designed to play mutually assured destruction war-gaming scenarios, code breaking, that sort of thing."

"'Artificial intelligence'?"

"It's a term for the next generation of computing technology. Artificial intelligence allows computers to mimic the reasoning process of human intelligence. Well, guess what? Turns out that computers these days are far superior to their human counterparts. Perhaps the ultimate example of the student surpassing its teachers." Zaraghi allowed himself an ironic snort of amusement. "Anyway, once the Cold War faded away and there was no more spy versus spy to occupy the machines, DARPA turned the facility over to the academics. Feigenbaum gets some taxpayers' money from the NSF—that's the National Science Foundation—but what with the federal budget crisis, nine out of every ten dollars needed to fund this place has to come from private industry. Westinghouse, General Electric and Hughes have kind of stepped up to the plate. Of course, they're not in it for charity; they get dibs on the precious access time. It's been getting a lot more precious lately. NASCIA has about three hundred projects ongoing, with about eight hundred users logging on every month. How the universe was formed. Modeling ocean currents in the Gulf of Mexico. Mapping the sun's turbulence. Molten steel disbursement."

A young Asian-American programmer passed them in the hall, nodding in greeting to Freddie. He wore a T-shirt that said:

~~JIM MORRISON~~
~~JERRY GARCIA~~
SEYMOUR CRAY IS GOD.

"Geek humor," Freddie Zaraghi muttered by way of explanation.

As they proceeded, the illumination in the passageway grew dimmer, lending a creepy, Big Brother feel to the journey. At the end of the passageway was an unmanned vestibule with a DB Hertz electronic surveillance mechanism. Zaraghi stepped up to the vestibule. A greenish light was projected from a lens recessed into the wall. Hansen watched in amazement as the image of Freddie Zaraghi's scanned face was reconstructed on a small color monitor built into the vestibule. A series of chirps, clicks and beeps was emitted from some unseen computing device. Moments later, there was an electronic birdsong of approval and a heavy mechanical click sounded from within the twin steel-reinforced doors.

On the monitor, the words glowed in green letters: FREDDIE ZARAGHI FTP/ID#06810—PLEASE PROCEED.

Zaraghi stepped forward, opened the door and entered. Rick followed.

Once inside, Freddie turned to him. "This," he said in a voice of hushed reverence, "is the NASCIA Machine Room."

It took several seconds for Hansen's eyes to adjust to the luminescent white brilliance of the machine room.

First impressions: the room was huge, brightly lit and, above all, noisy. The area was unexpectedly expansive, perhaps the length and width of two thirds of a football field. The ceiling had been elevated to permit dissipation of the heat thrown off by the three dozen or so constantly thrumming machines that never saw any downtime except for some periodic maintenance. For some reason, the floors, walls and ceiling had all been painted in a gleaming antiseptic white. And the racket of the machines—constant and unsettling—would take some getting used to.

"Consider yourself exceptionally privileged, my friend," Zaraghi said. "You happen to be gazing at one of the most highly concentrated force of computing power in private hands on the face of the earth."

"What *is* this place?"

"This is the North American Supercomputing Consortium of Industry and Academia, or, as we call it, NASCIA. Let me give you the nickel tour." Zaraghi gestured in the direction of the far corner of the room. "Right this way."

Hansen followed his host around the room, peering with interest at the exotic machinery. "As you can imagine," Freddie said, "this place takes truckloads of money just to keep the machines running. Out back, we've got six diesel-powered generators that kick on instantly in the event of a power outage, courtesy of our benefactors at General Electric.

"But although a power outage is the ultimate doomsday scenario, the constant problem is heat management. On either side of the machine room, we've got two eighty-five-ton liquid-Freon-cooled air conditioners keeping the machines chilled. And underneath the perforated tiles under our feet? There's an eighteen-inch false bottom, where six-inch pipes with chilled water crisscross the entire length of the machine room, with reverse-direction fans that suck out some of the residual heat."

"That's why everything in the room is painted in white?"

"Correct. The reflective white motif requires less light."

"Less light, less heat."

"You got it. These machines are higher maintenance than my fiancée. Costs roughly $40,000 per month to maintain 'em. And the machines themselves ain't a bargain either. Each processor costs roughly $35,000 and these top-of-the-line machines contain as many as 512 processors. Do the math and you'll see why they pay UNIX programmers like me palm reader's wages. There's nothing left in the budget."

Freddie came up to a ten-foot-high oblong box that reminded Hansen of an oversized industrial refrigerator. It was an unassuming cabinet with an exterior of dull charcoal gray with red trim, remarkable only for its ordinary appearance. There was no monitor, no keyboard, no displays of any sort to suggest it was a computational device. It was hard to believe that the electronic impulses coursing through the chips, wires and processors of this machine were performing tasks utterly incomprehensible to the human mind. "You ever see one of these bad boys before?"

"This is a supercomputer?" Hansen frowned. "Doesn't look especially super."

"This is not just a supercomputer. This is a Cray T3E. This is the bleeding edge, dude."

"It's much . . . smaller than I would've expected a supercomputer to be."

Zaraghi laughed. "That's precisely why it's so bleeding edge. Keep in mind that the first computer invented in the fifties—the ENIAC at the University of Pennsylvania—was the size of a mobile home. This nine-ton bad boy is built for clock-speed. I mean mind-blowing speed. If you tried to export this machine to a Third World country without the express permission of the U.S. Customs Department, you could be executed for treason. It would take this machine all of two days to put a Banana Republic in the nuclear weapons business."

Zaraghi cracked open the door of the machine. Hansen leaned in, looking at the guts of the thrumming system. It was an orderly jumble of color-coded cables, gold-plated connectors and a small monochrome monitor. The monitor said:

FAULT	READY	*BUSY*
SLOT 01 A/B - 71.3		SLOT 02 A/B - 70.7
SLOT 01 C/D - 70.4		SLOT 02 C/D - 71.4
SLOT 01 E/F - 69.7		SLOT 02 E/F - 71.3
SLOT 01 G/H - 70.6		SLOT 02 G/H - 70.4
SLOT 01 I/J - 70.7		SLOT 02 I/J - 69.7
SLOT 01 K/L - 71.4		SLOT 02 K/L - 71.3
SLOT 01 M/N - 71.3		SLOT 02 M/N - 70.4
SLOT 01 O/P - 70.4		SLOT 02 O/P - 69.7
SLOT 01 Q/R - 69.7		SLOT 02 Q/R - 70.6
SLOT 01 S/T - 71.3		SLOT 02 S/T - 70.7
SLOT 01 U/V - 70.4		SLOT 02 U/V - 71.4
SLOT 01 W/X - 69.7		SLOT 02 W/X - 71.3
SLOT 01 Y/Z - 70.6		SLOT 02 Y/Z - 69.7

PRESSURE—OK   TEMP—OK
MOTOR GENERATOR VOLTAGES—OK
MEMORY—OK   CLOCK—OK   CPU—OK

Freddie Zaraghi disengaged a memory module from the I/O channel and held it up for Hansen's inspection. "This is what's known as a zero-insertion force module. Weighs about seventy-five pounds. You have the memory chips embedded on a cold plate to reduce the number of component parts and to significantly reduce the distance the signals have to travel from one part of the machine to another. See, information moving at the speed of light takes a billionth of a second to travel 11.8 inches in a vacuum."

Hansen raised an eyebrow. "That's amazingly fast."

"Actually, in supercomputer terms, it's not. What you have to understand is that the speed of light is agonizingly slow for the mountains of data these machines are crunching. Even worse, data drift can occur. Even an insignificant skew can become magnified *ad infinitum* and completely destroy the integrity of the simulation results.

"The idea, then, is to get the connectors down from 11.8 inches to the size of a grain of pepper. And to use some high-performance connectivity. Here they use yttrium and bismuth superconductors." He pointed into the cavity of the gleaming cold plate. "The designers have to compress all the hardware into as small a space as possible so the signals don't have as far to travel. This Cray is a perfect example of that design architecture. Only a third of the machine actually computes; the rest produces the two hundred and fifty kilowatts of juice necessary to feed this baby."

As Freddie proceeded to point out other attributes of the machinery—something called a Josephson Junction switcher; a GigaRouter; RAID Level 5; gallium arsenide logic circuitry versus silicon chips—Hansen hit overload with the technical minutiae. He cut in impatiently, "Okay, conceded, the machines are incredible, Freddie. What does this have to do with chaos theory and predicting the markets?"

"Everything," Freddie replied. "Do you understand what we're talking about here? A two-thousand-dollar computer can boost the IQ of its human user from a hundred and fifty to two thousand points. Do you realize the consequences of harnessing the human mind to a supercomputer?"

"Not really."

"To fully comprehend the magnitude of supercomputing technology, you first have to recognize the limitations of the human brain. Centuries ago, mankind conceded those limits, and devised tools to amplify human intelligence. First, they were simple tools—quill and paper, abacus. Then the slide rule. The calculator. Then, in this century, computers arrived. *Computers.* This was the single-most influential invention in history, because for the first time, mankind had developed a tool that had the ability to outthink its creator. Think of it! A device that not only amplifies human intelligence. *It multiplies it!* Our first real taste of it was when an IBM supercomputer named Big Blue kicked the ass of the planet's best human chess player." The kid realized he was getting carried away and he pulled back from his tour-guide enthusiasm. "Have you ever heard of a technology called 'massively parallel processing'?"

"That's what MPP stands for, right?"

"That's right. Now, suppose you wanted to get your house painted, okay? Well, you may be the greatest housepainter in the world, but you have to admit, your house will get painted faster if ten of your friends came over and helped out."

"Right. Of course."

"And if each of your friends brought ten of *their* friends, then the task would be accomplished even more efficiently."

"I think I get the picture. A lot of people sharing smaller parts of an overall task. That's 'massively parallel processing'?"

"Yes. MPP is the latest quantum leap in supercomputing, because it permits you to tie together hundreds of supercomputing processors, typically through ultra-high-speed telephone lines, and get them to work in concert, much like a hungry pack of piranhas. Working together, they'll pick the skeleton clean in no time.

"At NASCIA, we're blessed with an embarrassment of riches." Freddie pivoted around and pointed out the other supercomputers residing in the facility. "We also have on-site a DEC 3000 Alpha AXP Super-Cluster and an IBM SP2 Scalable Power Parallel System, neither of which are slouches. But with ATM technology, we can also uplink our supercomputers with the ones in Ithaca, Urbana and San Diego. Geographical dispersity is a nonevent. You still following me?"

"I think so."

"Good. This way." Freddie brought him over to a peculiar, glass-enclosed tape-robot that clasped data cartridges at an amazing speed, wheeled down a track and shoved the cartridge into the I/O slots. "This is a StorageTek 9310 Nearline Tape Robot. It frees the supercomputer memory up from having to maintain inactive data, an inefficient use of its computing powers. It contains about six thousand cartridges, with about ten gigabyte per cart. It can upload the data within seconds. The tape silo acts as a data warehouse with a sixty terabyte capacity—sixty trillion bits of information. The various models are stored in archives of this tape silo. For LINDA's purposes, the tape silo archives a trillion-byte relational database on the last fifty years of the world's stock markets."

"That's incredible."

"You see, Mr. Hansen," Freddie Zaraghi said with deep sincerity, "the human race has come a long way since the abacus. Taken as a whole, these fuckers scream at mind-smoking speeds. The minimum standard for a supercomputer is two thousand MFLOPS. MFLOPS is a measurement that refers to *millions* of floating rate operations *per second*. In other words, two billion operations *per second*. A mathematical operation that takes a supercomputer one second to perform would take *three thousand years* on a calculator. In 1996, Intel nailed down the Holy Grail—a teraflop. One trillion floating point operations—*in a single second*."

"Jesus." Hansen was blown away.

"How fast is that? Well, if you had every man, woman and child in this country working twenty-four hours a day on a calculator, it would take them a hundred and twenty-five years to do what the Intel computer does in *one second*."

"Jesus Christ," he cursed again.

"Now this T3E isn't quite as mind-smoking fast. It's capable of 167,000 MFLOPS—millions of floating point operations per second—meaning it solves a *mere* 167 billion applications per second. Still, that's a hundred times more powerful than its predecessor of just a decade ago. By utilizing MPP technology, well, Christ, you can multiply that benchmark ten-, twenty-, *fifty* fold. At that point you're capable of some very serious data-mining projects. Supercomputers will permit us to tap energy from the aurora borealis; create synthetic blood; resolve the ozone depletion problem; cure AIDS. But that's tomorrow's killer applications. Stock market prediction is the world of here and now. Let me show you how."

Freddie Zaraghi led Hansen to a tiny metal desk wedged into a partially enclosed honeycomb of cubicles centered in the middle of the machine room. He beckoned for Hansen to take the seat next to him. Hansen complied. Zaraghi booted up the Digital workstation atop his desk. Waiting for it to come up, he opened a drawer and pulled out two Little Debbie chocolate snack cakes. He offered one of the packages to Hansen. "Brain food?"

"No, thanks."

The screen of the monitor came to life. Zaraghi fired off a flurry of keystrokes and the screen changed. WELCOME TO LINDA. The words were superimposed over a provocative movie still of an orgasmic Linda Lovelace from the film *Deep Throat*. Zaraghi blushed in front of his guest. "Uh, geek humor."

A few more keystrokes and the screen flashed again.

```
REMOTE/LOCAL: LOCAL
SALESMAN: NONE
OWNERSHIP: USER
MAX LOT OVERRIDE: YES
MAX LOT: 150
GTC COMPULSORY? YES
GTC_DEFAULT TYPE: STANDARD
DEBUG: NO
ON_ID: 72
PORT: 8000
LOGFILE_NAME: fZaraghi
MODE_RECOMMEND/AUTO: recommend
```

As the program uploaded, Freddie Zaraghi explained, "See, LINDA is a Windows-based, front-end interface to the supercomputers. What I mean by that is that she acts as the MPP quarterback to the data-mining application. LINDA activates a neurogenetic expert system I've embedded onto the Cray, which mimics the reasoning of the human brain. It learns from trial and error and applies it to its analysis of the financial markets."

The Digital computer buzzed industriously and the screen reflected the uplink activity.

```
UPLINKING . . . UPLINKING . . . UPLINKING . . .
```

Isbister's Options	Optionmetrics	S&P Comstock
Knight Ridder	Quotron Advantage AE	Bloomberg
ADP	Candlestick 4caster	Dow Jones
DTNstant	CQG	Teletrack
Reuters	Telerate	DBC Signal

"Those are the real-time pricing feeds that are analyzed against the trillion-byte relational database in the tape silo," Zaraghi explained. "With LINDA leading the charge, the supercomputers will sift through millions of permutations, crunching out 200,000 what-if scenarios per second. Then it will act on either—"

Zaraghi abruptly fell silent.

Hansen followed his haunted stare to the computer screen.

The screen said: FATAL ERROR #072—APPLICATION ABORTED.

"Mother," Zaraghi said, not breathing.

"What's the fatal error?" Hansen asked.

Zaraghi held up a silencing hand.

He typed in some commands. Hit the Enter key.

FATAL ERROR #072—APPLICATION ABORTED.

Hansen waited in patient silence as Freddie Zaraghi tried furiously to reactivate the program—one, two, three more times.

Maddeningly, the same end result:

FATAL ERROR #072—APPLICATION ABORTED.

Freddie Zaraghi's eyes went wild. Without turning to his companion, he whispered:

"*Someone is hacking* LINDA."

Forty

"I CAN'T BELIEVE IT," Freddie Zaraghi muttered tonelessly to his half-gone glass of beer. "I didn't think it was possible."

"Yeah," Hansen said sympathetically. "Confirms the worst, doesn't it?"

"I still can't believe it. Someone is using LINDA *right now*."

"And you're not getting paid for it," Hansen said.

"*Don't* even remind me; it makes me sick to my stomach."

Zaraghi and Hansen were drinking away the minutes before the boarding call for Hansen's 6:20 P.M. flight back to New York. They patronized a marginally acceptable sports bar tucked in the ass-end of the USAirways terminal. The drafts on tap were fizzless and stale-tasting, as if the tubes of the keg-erator hadn't been cleaned since last year's Final Four. Not that the bottled beers were any better—they were barely lukewarm. Curiously, despite the place's sports theme, there were no hoops and hockey on the tube; just MTV, where an old shoestring-budget *Hootie and the Blowfish* video unspooled. Hootie and crew playing golf. The dull illumination of the place added to the depressing nature of Zaraghi's sulking funk; against the light thrown off by the neon beer signs behind the bar, the kid's face was a bluish-red Kabuki mask of victimization.

"Mr. Hansen?"

"Yes?"

"You mind if we run through it, what you know?"

"Sure." Hansen closed his eyes in concentration. "What we know . . . we know you invented a killer system that you claim can predict the stock market. Your professor-slash-business partner cut a deal with a party or parties—unknown to us—who are using the system without compensation to you. At least one of those parties may be my firm,

Wolcott Fulbright, since we know you once met a guy named Tom Bingham to discuss how the system works. Bingham made a super-fucking-accurate prediction of the mini-crash back in January, possibly—probably—using LINDA. Both Gammage and Bingham are dead. Bingham's paralegal is dead. On top of that, some asshole took a shot at me while I was in Bingham's old apartment. We know that someone has hacked into your system and whoever is using it may have connections to whoever killed Gammage, Bingham and Oberlin. Not to mention the guy who took a shot at me."

"*Why* would they kill Gammage?" Zaraghi asked.

"You yourself stated that LINDA was a turnkey program. Push the green button and watch it go, right? They didn't need him anymore, so they eliminated him." *Eliminated him! Christ, listen to how he was talking.*

"Jesus," Zaraghi breathed. "This really is big."

"Yes. Yes, it is." The lawyer peered at the college dropout. "How you doin'? You okay?"

"No, I'm not okay. I'm *pissed*."

"Can't say I blame you. Another beer?"

"Yeah, sure. I could kill a six-pack right about now."

Hansen captured the attention of the disinterested bartender and made a circling motion over the crowns of the beer glasses, indicating another round. With a put-out expression, she slapped her Judith Krantz paperback down on the bar and jerked the tap open. Hansen ignored her ill-temper. Nothing could spoil his private elation.

He sensed now was the time to close the deal. "I guess you're going to have to come to New York with me. Gather fresh evidence for the lawsuit."

"New York?" Zaraghi shook his head. "I can't afford to do that."

"You don't have to. I have a proposition for you."

Zaraghi looked at the lawyer.

Hansen said, "You come to New York. You give me forty-eight hours of your time and the trip won't cost you a penny. I'll pay for your flight with the bazillion frequent flier miles I have in my USAirways account. I'll arrange to have you put up for two nights in one of the firm's executive apartments in Battery Park City. If I can't swing that, then you crash in my apartment. In return for your time, I'll help you prepare a lawsuit against whoever it turns out misappropriated your program. If it turns out it was my firm, I'll see that our Accounts Payable Department makes the check out to you, and not to Gammage's estate. As a bonus, I'll help you get JackMan patented in Washington. That's the deal."

Zaraghi peered at him. "What would I do in New York?"

"For starters, the contents of Bingham's hard drive are all encrypted. I was hoping you might have some experience in decoding files."

"I might," Zaraghi said, cautiously. "But we need to get one thing straight before we proceed."

"Which is?"

"I'm no scumbag-phreak-hacker. I'm a UNIX computer programmer. Although I may have the same capabilities as your basic scumbag hacker, I'm not one of them."

"Okay," Hansen acknowledged. "Point taken. You're no hacker."

"What else would I do there?"

"Bingham left behind a mountain of files. I'd like you to look at some of the memos, see if he got that stuff from his talk with you."

"Sounds reasonable."

Hansen went for it. "So you'll come to New York?"

"Well, I have to admit—the price is right. Ah, what the hell. Sure, I'll come to New York."

"Awesome!" Elated, Hansen clinked beer tumblers with the kid. For the first time, he had an ally, a computer-savvy ally at that. "Can you come in first thing Monday morning?"

Zaraghi shook his head and wiped the foam from his lips. "Uh, no. Actually, tomorrow, I've got to work double shifts at NASCIA. Then, beginning Monday, I've got three days of consulting with some generals at the Pentagon on Information Warfare, so I'm completely out of pocket in Washington. Thursday through Sunday, I'm scheduled to conduct maintenance in the machine room. I guess that means I couldn't come to New York until the following week, at the earliest."

Hansen shook his head vigorously. "That doesn't work. I need you much sooner than that."

Zaraghi fingered his Fu Manchu. "I suppose I could see if I could switch Thursday and Friday with Kwan. If that's cool with him, I'm all yours on Thursday and Friday."

Hansen nodded at the compromise. If it was the best they could hammer out, he would have to make do. "Done."

"Double done."

The lawyer brought his wristwatch into view. 6:03 P.M. His flight home boarded in another seventeen minutes. Hansen filled his mouth with Killian's Red, held it for a thoughtful moment before swallowing. "There's some things you can do in the meantime."

"Such as?"

Hansen gathered his stubbled chin in the cone of his hand, thinking. "To activate LINDA, you have to access NASCIA's supercomputing network. You do that from dialing in from a remote line, correct?"

"Correct. You could be calling in from anywhere in the world and if you know the passwords, you can activate the system. Once activated, the thing runs on autopilot."

"Right. Is there any way to trace the calls into NASCIA?"

"You mean, to determine who's activated LINDA?"

"Yes."

Freddie Zaraghi looked skyward in contemplation. "I'm not certain if it could be done real-time. I could hack around, see if there's a caller-ID function built into the user interface."

"Good. Even if that doesn't work, there must be another way. In order for someone to access NASCIA's supercomputing resources, wouldn't they have to have an account of some sort?"

Freddie Zaraghi brightened a bit. "Sure. It costs two hundred twenty-five bucks an hour to tap in through the Backbone fast-packet net. At month's end, time allocations are calculated and they're sent out electronically as bills."

"Bingo! If Gammage was murdered in January, then conceivably, LINDA's been used for at least a month or two. Could you obtain, say, the last three months' billing records for NASCIA? If running LINDA takes as much computing power as you say, then the biggest user may be our leading suspect. Particularly if that user happens to have Wall Street connections."

Zaraghi turned to Hansen and looked at him for the first time in a while. "Yeah, that's doable. I can do that."

"What about files in Gammage's office on the Carnegie-Mellon campus? Any way you can get access to them?"

Zaraghi smiled conspiratorially. "Worth a shot."

"I mean, don't do it if it's going to put you in Dutch with Campus Security, but those files could be revealing."

"Oh, let me worry about Campus Security." Zaraghi said this with a measure of childish glee.

Over the public address system, they announced last call for Hansen's flight to La Guardia International Airport.

"That's me." Rick pointed to the Redweld folders of LINDA documents. "Mind if I keep hold of these files for the time being?"

Zaraghi shrugged. "Be my guest."

Hansen drained the rest of the foamless amber liquid, gathered up the folders of LINDA documentation and placed a twenty on the bar for the drinks. "Here's cab money for the ride home." He handed Zaraghi a twenty. "And I need you to look at this thing."

Hansen reached into his coat pocket and produced Tom Bingham's Sharp Zaurus.

"Whose PDA is this?" Zaraghi said, eyeing the device.

"Bingham's. Password-protected, of course. I need you to crack the code—even if you aren't some scumbag hacker." Hansen winked.

This elicited a rare smile from the college dropout. "I'll fool around with it, see what I can do," he said, accepting the handheld with a mix of curiosity and awe.

"And if I were you," Hansen said, "I'd be ecstatic rather than down in the dumps."

"Oh yeah? Why's that?"

"As long as they're hacking LINDA, we've got a prayer of catching the fuckers."

Zaraghi grinned. "Yeah, we do, don't we? It could be fun."

It could also be lethal, Hansen thought to himself.

Sprinting toward his gate, Rick Hansen encountered a woman selling discounted flowers at a kiosk. Impulsively, he purchased a dozen red, long-stemmed roses for his hopefully understanding wife. He tossed the fifteen bucks on the counter and raced to catch his flight. As he thundered down the jetway and into the aircraft, he realized it was going to take a lot more than cheap roses to make the Bingham affair up to his eight months pregnant wife.

Hang in there, Stephanie, he pleaded to his wife 388 miles away. *It shouldn't be much longer now.*

Part IV

DIGITAL CHERNOBYL

March 14–21

Financial crises are associated with peaks of business cycles. Speculative excess and revulsion from such excess in the form of a crisis, crash or panic [is] inevitable and historically common.

—KINDLEBERGER, 1978

Skyrocketing markets that depend on purely psychic support have invariably succumbed to the financial law of gravitation. Unsustainable prices eventually reverse themselves with the suddenness of an earthquake—the bigger the binge, the greater the resulting hangover.

—MALKIEL, 1990

Forty-one

Manhattan

Monday–Thursday, March 15–18

ALWAYS, ALWAYS—TIME MOVES with a fluid velocity on Wall Street. In times of exceptional market volatility—like this, the third week in March—one fourteen-hour workday segued into the next, distinguished from the other only by a six-hour band of sleep, a shower, the daily commute. Meals were hastily consumed between conference calls and meetings without the luxury of tasting the food—that is, if you remembered to eat a lunch.

Waiting for Zaraghi. Rick could do nothing but wait for the kid to arrive on Thursday afternoon. But it was simple enough to immerse himself in the thicket of documents stacked up in teetering piles on his desk, in his in-box, atop his credenza. There was no shortage of derivatives deals in the Wolcott Fulbright pipeline.

For the next four days, Hansen became so narrowly focused on the nuts and bolts of each deal, he was utterly oblivious to anything not covered in *The Wall Street Journal.* Over the weekend, Clapton, the guitar hero of his college days, rocked the Garden, yet he somehow missed the show. His beloved Knicks were playing superb basketball, yet he was unable to squeeze in a game. Paul Gelbaum rang him up to bust his chops about forgetting his birthday, but Rick was too busy to take the call. St. Patrick's Day came and went. A citywide garbage strike was threatened. A serial rapist prowled the subways. The promise of spring had been betrayed by predictions of a vicious nor'easter blowing in from northern New England later in the week.

In a time like this, the real world was an adversary, a hostile planet filled with white noise to be tuned out. Rick Hansen was hard-pressed to tell his wife what he had for breakfast the day before, but he knew precisely where the Dow Jones Industrial Average finished. (And it was, invariably, another record.)

From time to time, he thought briefly of Freddie Zaraghi working to crack Tom Bingham's PDA. But then he put the kid out of his mind and dug back into his work. It was out of his hands, at least for now.

———•———

Monday, 8:00 A.M.

Hansen was on the equity trading floor, working with Joe Money to set up a synthetic convertible trust structure for one of the desk's insurance company customers, when Max Schomburg brought Donald Trump to the floor for a tour of the facilities.

An audible buzz went up on the trading floor. For months, rumor had had it that Trump would seek a 10 percent stake in Wolcott Fulbright once it went public. The presence of the mediagenic mogul among the Wolcott equity troops all but confirmed the scuttlebutt.

Max Schomburg picked up a microphone to the hoot'n'holler, a sort of internal CB radio that was used to communicate with Wolcott's personnel throughout the world. Depressing the trigger key, the chief executive officer's voice reverberated instantly around the globe:

"Good morning, everyone, this is Max Schomburg. Despite the doom-and-gloom forecasts of some market pundits suggesting the stock market would shed half its value after Freefall Friday, the American equity markets have shown incredible resilience. Over the last six weeks, the stock market has completely recovered all of the losses incurred on Freefall Friday and is once again setting new records."

Sporadic applause arose from the sales and trading personnel.

Schomburg continued, "Yes, the stock market's a nail-biter, but the fainthearted who move prematurely from equities into Treasuries face the prospect of losing out on an additional seventeen to twenty percent run-up our chief economist Roslynn Blum has predicted by year's end.

"You, as a team, have pulled it together in an exceptionally volatile market and provided service to our customers that rivals that of any firm on The Street. With your continuing efforts, I'm confident that our public offering in May will be an overwhelming success. I personally thank each and every one of you for your contribution."

With that, Schomburg signed off and the inhabitants of the equity floor applauded politely. As the two titans of power walked off the floor, Trump leaned over and whispered something in Schomburg's ear and the two men shared a private chuckle.

Joe Money casually watched them leave. Once they were out of sight, he shook his head. "Looking for a biblical sign that the bull market has come to an end? You just got it."

———●———

Tuesday, 1:35 P.M.

Mike Kilmartin phoned in from Lake Okeechobee in Clewiston, Florida.

"Are the fish biting?" Hansen asked his boss.

"Yeah, but not for me," Kilmartin said. His voice was relaxed, happy. "My old college buddy is reeling in the bass like you wouldn't believe. Me, I couldn't catch a cold. But know what? Stick me in a boat, put a fishing pole in one hand and an Old Milwaukee in the other and I'm a happy camper. What's the weather like up there?"

"Bloomberg says it's about to turn lousy. Nor'easter coming in."

"Music to my ears," Kilmartin laughed. "Sorry, Rick, but a Florida vacation is pointless if you can't brag about the seventy-degree sunshine. How are things back at the shop?"

"You picked a good week to be out," Hansen informed him. "The market's setting records again. We're busy, but not a lot of five-alarm fires."

"There's a triple-witch expiration this Friday, isn't there?"

Triple-witch expiration. The fabled triple-witch occurs only four times a year, one Friday each quarter. On this day, index options, stock options and equity futures contracts all expire simultaneously. The stock market experiences unusually large volatility and unpredictable price movements on triple-witch Fridays, which keeps the sales and trading types busy—not to mention the lawyers.

"That's right, there is," Hansen replied. "Don't worry, the firm's not going to blow up while you're in Florida."

"Don't worry, he says. I *must* worry, Rick. It's what I do for a living. Anyway, I have my SkyPager on at all times, in case McGeary gives you a hard time—"

Cliff Weiner popped into Rick's office. "It's a Mr. Zaraghi for you on the other line. Says he's calling from the . . . *Pentagon?*"

Hansen felt an electric jolt. He told his boss, "Mike, I've got to take this."

"The natives are restless, eh? No prob, transfer me to Irv Siegel's line."

"Have a great vacation." Hansen dutifully transferred Kilmartin to Siegel, then he punched up the other line. "Freddie, how are you?" he said, anxiously.

"I'm here in Washington."

"I know."

"You know, as *cool* as the Pentagon is from the outside? It's a hundred eighty degrees as dull on the inside. Really shabby offices and stuff. I was majorly disappointed."

Hansen forced himself to stay cool. "Things going well in D.C.?"

"What can I say? This is a great gig. The generals can't get enough of this Information Warfare stuff. Gives 'em something to worry about with the end of the Cold War. Anyway, I've got good news for you, real good news. I cracked the dead guy's PDA." There was more than a small measure of pride evident in the college dropout's voice.

"You did?" Hansen felt his hand involuntarily tighten around the phone.

"Yeah. These PDAs . . . nifty little device for storing rudimentary information, but it's a creampuff security-wise. I hooked it up to my laptop and just pumped CodeCracker 2.1 into it till she popped open like a clam."

"CodeCracker is what, software?"

"Yeah, it's password-sniffer software used by Information Warfare terrorists. Just FYI, the password was 'Neelhtak.' "

"What does that mean?"

"It's 'Kathleen,' spelled backward."

Hansen bobbed his head. "Anything of use on his PDA?"

"Well, it turns out your buddy was one of those anal-compulsive types who transfers every boring detail of his yuppie life into his digital diary. His collection of jazz CDs, the restaurants he's eaten at, sex fantasies. In fact, the sex diary stuff would knock your socks off—"

Hansen cut in, "I don't need to know about that—in fact, I don't even *want to know* about that."

"Okay, okay. Lemme cut to the chase. The encryption key is loaded on here."

"It is? You mean the key to his PC files?"

"I think so. We'll have to try it when I get to New York. Incidentally, do the words 'BEACON Project' mean anything to you?"

BEACON Project! "Yes. Yes, they do."

"Whatever it is, it's all over this guy's PDA. Listen, my break is up, I've got to get back to the generals. I'll see you in a few days."

Rick replaced the phone on its cradle and yanked open the file drawer of his desk. Feverishly, he scanned the tabs for the hanging file folder marked *Bingham's Stuff.*

Found it.

Pulled out the manila envelope from Bingham's Central Park West apartment. The one named cryptically BEACON.

The lawyer shoved his hand inside and came out with the only item there.

An unmarked white rectangle of plastic the size of a bank card with a black magnetic stripe along its backside.

An electronic passkey.

But to what? the voice in his head demanded.

The answer would have to wait, but for the first time, he felt confident he would soon have one.

———•———

Wednesday, 7:45 A.M.

Hansen sat in on the morning derivatives strategy call. While he waited for the caffeine to wake him up, he struggled to keep up with the international back-and-forth about calls, puts, spreads, straddles, strangles, deltas, gammas and rolls.

A few minutes into it, he noted something curious about Gil McGeary. The guy was dead silent. The desk head remained uncharacteristically quiet throughout the entire fifteen-minute call.

And, God, he looks like hell, Hansen thought. McGeary appeared drawn and grizzled, as though he hadn't slept for several nights. It was no secret that this was "comp week"—the period in which the desk heads negotiated year-end bonuses with management. Word on the trading floor was that Magilla was engaged in a bloody battle with Milgrim and Schomburg for his group's piece of the pie and he was losing big time. At the morning call, McGeary seemed consumed by private demons. He hadn't shaved that morning, and it was entirely possible he hadn't shaved the day before either—perhaps using personal hygiene as a visible symbol of protest.

Toward the end of the call, the trader in London said, "Magilla, haven't heard a peep from you this morning. How do you see things on your side of the water?"

Gil McGeary stared out of the window and absently stroked his stubble. "All good things must come to an end," he pontificated, "and I personally think the end is near. I can't say why, exactly, but it's just a gut feeling. Things have been too good for too long. I've got an . . . intuition that triple-witch Friday is going to be bloody."

This provoked an international silence. No one could remember the last time Gil McGeary was so downbeat about stocks.

London said, "That sounds more like an astrological forecast than a view of the market."

Amid the uneasy laughter, Gil shrugged. "Sorry I couldn't be more upbeat, Nigel, but they don't pay me to sugarcoat a stock market downturn."

"Right, then," London said, resignedly, "where do I tell my customers to put their money?"

McGeary rubbed his tired eyes and stared at the floor. "In 1624, the Dutch bought Manhattan Island from the Indians for twenty-four dollars. Today, that investment is worth about three trillion. I don't know, guys. Screw the stock market. I like real estate."

The New York gang laughed, albeit uneasily.

"Over and out," McGeary mumbled and poked the disconnect button.

That afternoon, Julian Stainsby informed Hansen that Gil McGeary had holed himself up in his fishbowl office all day. Magilla didn't even emerge for lunch. The equity derivatives desk regarded this as an omen that bonuses were going to be piss-poor this year.

———●———

Thursday.

The threatened nor'easter finally blasted into Manhattan. For certain, the storm front that had closed down much of Vermont and Massachusetts had diminished in its fury by the time it rode into the lower Atlantic states, but it still had enough life left to make New Yorkers miserable. The sleet pelted down on the city like shards of broken glass. By daybreak, the streets were a godawful mess and the mercury had plummeted ever lower. The most powerful and vibrant city on the face of the earth was once again humbled by the force of nature.

Shielding his sleep-deprived eyes with an upraised forearm, Hansen goose-stepped through the treacherous slush along Broad Street. His subway ride to work had been twice its usual length that morning. He felt a twinge of sympathy for the poor bastards schlepping in from the suburbs on Metro North and the LIRR: they faced up to three-hour commutes that morning. Rick bunched up the collar around his exposed neck and dipped his chin protectively against the ice storm.

The gaunt, cadaverous man in the hooded ski jacket stepped out from beneath the entranceway, blocking Hansen's path. Rick collided with him. Startled, the lawyer squinted up into the man's face. His skin was alarmingly red, the arterial crimson of a frostbite victim. Chunks of ice crystals were cocooned in the man's orange-blond facial hair. His voice was that of the walking dead:

"Repent, my brother. A Samhain moon is upon us and the end is near."

"A what?" Hansen nearly shouted back.

The man slapped the document into Hansen's gloved hand as if he were delivering a subpoena. He then melted away into the platoons of workers.

Hansen waited until he was safely ensconced in the elevator at 44 Wall before unfolding the circular. It was printed in an almost psychedelic array of colored inks. The forty-eight-point headline screamed:

WALL STREET APOCALYPSE NOW!
The Countdown to the End of the Millennium Has Begun!
The Stock Market Will Crash SOON!

This is not a test! This is not a test! The Apocalypse is upon us! The Eschaton is near! The Great and Secret Show will reveal itself! The Signs can no longer be ignored:

1. **Earthquakes** (7.0 or above) in Loma Prieta; Sulawesi, Indonesia; Eilat, Israel; Tuxtla Gutiérrez, Mexico; Mt. Minami, Japan.
2. **Volcanic eruptions** in Kamchatka Peninsula, Russia; Cerro Negro, Nicaragua; Japan's Mt. Kujú, New Zealand's Mt. Ruapehu.
3. **Ultra-low-frequency humming** in Taos, N.M., and Monterey Peninsula.
4. **Hole in ozone layer** above Antarctica is now the size of Europe, twice its size last year.
5. **Global overpopulation** causes **extinction of three species per hour**.
6. **Viral outbreak** in Australia kills millions of rabbits; **bubonic plague** among squirrels in Angeles National Forests; Hanta virus, Ebola strain proliferate.
7. Twenty-year decline in the **sperm count of human males**.
8. Birth of **the white buffalo calf** in Madison, Wisconsin, fulfills 2,000-year-old Native American prophecy.
9. **Stock market** continues to reflect an irrational extreme of popular optimism.
10. *Pluto is squared at a ninety-degree angle by an alignment of Venus, Mars and Jupiter. Uranus entered the sign of Aquarius last week.*

In the face of this planetary alignment and the Samhain full moon, the ingredients have come together for an historic . . .

Elliott Wave Grand Supercycle Market Crash

The current Grand Supercycle Top is similar to what occurred just before World War II! After the decimation of the U.S. stock market, another social collapse will occur, this time involving financial panic, an international economic depression and—as prophesied—global thermonuclear war with the Soviet Union. . . .

Spooky, these end-of-the-world prophecies. Still, the corners of Rick's mouth turned up in amusement. *Of course! A Samhain moon. That explains McGeary's "intuition."*

Rick stuffed the fire-and-brimstone manifesto into an interoffice envelope and addressed it to Magilla on the equity derivatives desk.

Maybe it would cheer him up.

Then Rick worked the phone.

The day flew by.

When his alphanumeric beeper went off, Hansen was stunned to realize it was after five o'clock. He thumbed the button that called up the message display.

HELLO! I'M AT PENN STATION.
COME GET ME. FREDDIE Z.

Forty-two

THE WHITE-GLOVED CONCIERGE at the St. Regis drew himself erect as the familiar face approached his vestibule. "Ah, good to see you again, Mr. Colbert."

"Likewise, Matthias. Tell me, how's Irina?"

"Wonderful. And Mrs. Colbert?"

"Doing just fine, Matthias."

The concierge nodded. "How was your trip to New York?"

Colbert grimaced. "The ice storm was hell. We had to put into port in the Chesapeake until the storm passed."

The concierge's lips pursed into a sympathetic O.

Enough idle chitchat, Colbert thought, drumming his fingertips on the edge of the vestibule. "Now then, I suppose I should give you fair warning. I have brought with me a number of parcels on this trip."

"That is not a problem," Matthias said helpfully. "We'll have all your items brought up to your suite immediately."

Colbert placed a $100 bill on the vestibule. "By that, Matthias, I mean a *large* number of parcels."

In fact, there were thirty-two in all, *excluding* the financier's luggage. It took three bellmen and four carts to transfer the assemblage of boxes from the two limousines on Fifty-fifth Street up to Colbert's $4,500-a-night suite on the sixteenth floor. Many of the parcels were odd-shaped and cumbrous. One of the bellmen pulled a muscle in his back wrestling with an especially heavy carton.

Although Matthias permitted the three bellmen to split the $100 gratuity among themselves, they still cursed the vanity of this arrogant guest. *What sort of man travels with such an absurd pile of personal belongings?*

———— • ————

Within the next half-hour, Alexeyev dispatched two Russians to Colbert's three-bedroom suite to assemble the components. The Russians were clearly philistines, roughly pushing aside the Louis XV furnishings to accomplish their task. But they worked expertly, linking the electronic devices into a single console with yards of multicolored, banana-plug cords.

Colbert stayed on the phone the entire time they worked, providing eleventh-hour status reports to a few of The Contrarians.

After eighty minutes of work, the task was completed.

Colbert's portable trading floor was now fully operational.

He paid the men for their time. They thanked him in Russian.

When they were gone, the financier flipped a switch on the console and ten computer monitors flashed to life in a semicircle around the two desks. This drew a rare smile from Colbert. It was the eve of destruction, so to speak, and he was now ready.

———— • ————

This time, Stiletto was punctual. The Wall Streeter rapped on the hotel room door just before 5:30 P.M. Entering the Christian Dior–designed Presidential Suite, Stiletto gazed at the sculptured ceilings, twenty-two-karat gold leaf moldings and the Waterford crystal chandelier. He whistled in awe. "Very impressive, Philip. Better not let the Partners see you living in the lap of luxury with their money."

Colbert smirked. "You want to see impressive? I'll show you impressive. But first things first. What are you drinking?"

"Got Chivas in there?" Stiletto motioned toward the Servobar.

Once they had drinks in hand, Colbert brought the Wall Streeter to the center of the suite and demonstrated the features of the ad hoc trading facility. There were six different computers—NeXT, Sun, Compaq Pentium among them. Several analog Arvey Dynamics screens for viewing CNBC and CNN. Data feeds from Reuters, Bloomberg and the Internet. Historical information on every security ever traded in the United States provided by Chicago-based Prometheus. A twenty-three-inch Mitsubishi monitor displayed the faster-than-the-eye activity of the computer program Gammage had called LINDA. Of course, the suite did not come equipped with enough capacity for all the required phone-line connections, so Colbert had sidestepped that problem through cellular services and satellite uplinks.

"Stunning," Stiletto said in amazement.

"Yes, it is, isn't it?" Colbert cracked a half-smile. "All of this was unfathomable just a few years ago."

"Tell me about it," Stiletto said. "You can't imagine the millions Wolcott Fulbright has squandered over the last few years on technology that went obsolete in thirteen, fourteen months."

"Yes, I'll bet," Colbert said, staring intently at his visitor. "Did the third wire hit your offshore account yet?"

Stiletto blushed visibly at the crass reference to the payment. "Yes. You know it did."

"Just wanted to make certain. As you know, your participation in this has been invaluable."

Stiletto nodded, said nothing. He drew a long swallow of his drink.

Colbert refilled his glass. "You look tired, my friend."

Stiletto grimaced. "It's been a hard week. Internal politics at the firm. It's been brutal. I envy your independence." Before Colbert could continue along that avenue of conversation, Stiletto turned it around. "And you, you bastard. You look anything but tired. You look positively invigorated."

"Why shouldn't I be?" Colbert said. He held up a single finger, as if pointing to the gilded ceiling. "In just sixteen hours, this will be the most powerful finger on the planet. One simple motion . . ." Colbert demonstrated by bringing the finger down to the keyboard and pushing the Enter button. ". . . One single keystroke tomorrow morning will change the history of the world. Billions will be lost when I push this button tomorrow morning."

The color drained from Stiletto's face. He appeared queasy.

Relishing the game, Colbert pushed on. "You have vested this power in me. I hope you feel you have been rewarded commensurately for that."

Stiletto's voice was hoarse. "Yes, of course. The money . . . it's very generous."

"Still, you seem . . . apprehensive."

Stiletto waved the concerns away. "Butterflies. Opening-night jitters, that's all."

Colbert smiled. "If given the chance to do it all over again, would you have forged this alliance with me, knowing what will transpire tomorrow?"

Stiletto hesitated just an instant before saying, "Yes."

You're a bad liar, Colbert said silently. *You have always been, always will be.* Not that being a liar was a detriment, per se. On the contrary, it was an attribute and Colbert had long prided himself on being one. Colbert regarded himself as a practiced professional at it. There was a world of difference between the professional liar and an amateur liar.

Colbert flashed a grin at the Wall Streeter. "I never doubted your loyalty. You've always been a trusted business partner, and always will be. Thank you for coming by. We will speak tomorrow. Before the markets open, eh?"

Forty-three

ZARAGHI HAD BEEN to New York City only once before, so Hansen caught the subway uptown to Penn Station to hook up with him. The kid had brought along a lot of expensive hardware and God forbid he should get mugged on his way to Wall Street. Escorting Freddie to 44 Wall was the least Rick could do.

It was the height of the rush-hour crunch when Rick arrived at Penn Station a little past 6:15 P.M. Still, despite the blur of suit-and-ties, picking Freddie Zaraghi out of the crowd was not especially difficult. Zaraghi was at the agreed-upon location, waiting hands-in-pocket below the large golden clock in the center of the terminal. The kid sported a week's worth of beard stubble and wore dark glasses on a dark winter day. Predictably, he was dressed all in black.

Hansen zigzagged through the shuffling mass of commuters and approached his guest. "How was the trip from D.C.?" he asked.

Zaraghi pulled off the shades. "Wasn't exactly a piece of cake. All the flights out of Dulles were completely rejiggered. Thank God for Amtrak."

The lawyer gestured toward the large Rollaboard suitcase at the kid's feet. "This all you brought?"

"Trust me, that's all I need. I'm loaded for bear."

"You don't happen to have a suit and tie in there, do you?"

Zaraghi broke into a grin. "Dude, what on earth makes you think I own either one of those?"

"Just a shot in the dark, I guess."

"You don't dig my look, that's what you're saying?"

"It's just not very . . . corporate."

"Yeah, it's not, is it?" Zaraghi smiled. "I somehow doubt it ever will be."

Hansen genuinely liked the kid. He picked up the wheeled suitcase and steered Freddie across the terminal toward the entrance of the subway. "Just out of curiosity, Freddie, you ever wear anything other than black?"

"Rarely."

"Black socks?"

"Of course."

"You wear black underwear too?"

Freddie deadpanned, "If I ever wore underwear, it'd be black."

Hansen made a face of distaste. "Sorry I asked."

"Mr. Hansen, I'm just busting your hump," Zaraghi laughed. "*Of course* I wear underwear, and you know what, it happens to be *white*."

The lawyer laughed. Rick deposited two tokens into the subway turnstile. "I think it's about time you started calling me Rick."

———•———

The seats were all taken on the subway car. They stood, holding on to the metal pole as the express train rocketed southbound beneath the surface of the city. It was Freddie's first trip on a New York subway and he spent most of the fourteen-minute ride staring at the hypnotizing blur of signal lights blurring past outside the window. This afforded Hansen the opportunity to recede into his own private thoughts.

Near the end of the trip, Freddie asked, "Are there really alligators in the New York subways?"

"It's the sewers," Hansen corrected him. "There are alligators in the sewers. But the rats here are much bigger than the alligators." Hansen hesitated before speaking up again. "Freddie?"

"Yeah?"

"Something I need to know you're on board with?"

"Yeah?"

"People connected to this thing have been killed."

Freddie Zaraghi tore his eyes away from the window. "Yeah, I know that. What's your point?"

"My point? It's kind of obvious, isn't it? I mean, this could be dangerous."

Zaraghi shrugged and turned his attention back to the blur of lights outside the glass. "That's the fun of it."

———•———

6:47 P.M. They arrived at Wolcott Fulbright's office building on 44 Wall Street.

Zaraghi was stunned by the outwardly moneyed opulence of the structure. He examined the marbled interior with an openmouthed gawk. "Nice offices you guys have here."

"Forty-Four Wall's not bad as far as office buildings go." Hansen signed Zaraghi in at the Security desk's guest book as a "technology consultant."

The kid turned to the lawyer and said, "You must make a lot of money, huh?"

Hansen handed Freddie a building pass. "Believe it or not, it's a struggle to pay my New York City rent. Elevator's this way."

On the elevator up to the LR&C Department, Hansen said, "You want to get something to eat before we get into things?"

"You order a pizza, that's fine."

"Pizza? You're in the world's culinary capital and all you want is pizza? You ever hear of Smith and Wollensky? It's a famous steakhouse in Midtown and we can—"

"Thanks all the same, but I'd really just prefer pizza. And two cans of Mountain Dew. Let's not make a big production out of the food, so we can get right to work."

Hansen nodded, impressed by the kid's work ethic. "Pizza it is."

———◆———

6:53 P.M.

Once on the thirty-seventh floor, Hansen quickly moved the unshaved college dropout past the gauntlet of secretarial workstations. To his relief, the secretaries were mostly gone by that time, so he didn't have to explain the black-garbed cybernerd's presence. Down the hall, he spied Mike Kilmartin's secretary, Felicity, working late on something in her cubicle. *Damn.* Rick hustled Zaraghi into his office, hoping she hadn't caught a glimpse of them. Rick closed the door halfway.

Zaraghi had barely shrugged off his black bomber jacket before zeroing in on the computer. He touched the surface of the putty-toned box with a flat palm. "This the machine storing Tommy Boy's files?"

"Yes. All the files I copied from Bingham's home computer were transferred onto the hard drive of this one."

"And all the files you've found are encrypted, right?"

"That's right."

"Cool. Lemme do the voodoo that I doo-doo." Zaraghi rubbed his hands together and began the task. He unzipped the Rollaboard and produced a pair of bright orange connecting cables. From the interior pocket of his bomber jacket, he produced Bingham's Sharp Zaurus palm-top PDA. He switched the PDA on and connected it to Hansen's PC, using the orange cables and an adapter plug.

Freddie typed Bingham's password into the palmtop.

—NEELHTAK—

"Okay, now, on the PC, bring up one of the encrypted files," Zaraghi commanded.

Hansen did as he was told, picking a file at random. The screen filled with unintelligible gibberish.

"Mmm," Zaraghi said. Then, in a low-pitched singsong, Zaraghi said, "One for the money, two for the show, three to get ready and four to decode."

Freddie Zaraghi stabbed the Return key on the tiny keyboard of the Sharp Zaurus.

Instantly, the screen on the PC flickered and went black with an electronic sigh. In another instant, it flashed back to life. The document on Hansen's computer screen was now in plain English.

"Presto-change-o," Zaraghi said with a grin.

Hansen whooped. "You cracked the code."

"No biggie," Zaraghi shrugged. "The guy kept the encryption key stored in his personal digital assistant. It's shootin' fish in a barrel, as they say."

Hansen turned to the monitor to read the contents of the decoded document.

September 12

Dear Elena:
I received the latest letter from your divorce attorney. Please send him my warmest regards and my fondest hope that he dies slowly of rectal cancer. You're making a big mistake leaving me, Elena. I can't tell you exactly what's going on, but believe me, this time it's the Major Leagues for real.

Rick cringed. A groveling letter to the guy's ex-wife. What if all the encrypted files were just embarrassingly personal missives to his ex-wife? Hansen felt dirty for scoping out something as intensely personal as the aftermath of Bingham's divorce. Still, the note contained yet another hint that Bingham was wrapped up in something big. Something big and *secret*.

"Bring up another file," Zaraghi said.

Hansen did. Zaraghi decoded that one too. This time, it was a scathing letter to his father for not keeping up with his student loan from Harvard. Again, Hansen cringed at the tone. The next decoded document was a year-old list of "things to do." Document #4 was a list of new wines Bingham wanted to sample.

Document #5 was . . . intriguing.

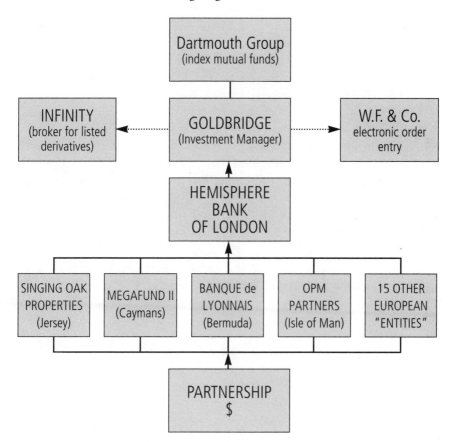

"What the hell is that?" Zaraghi asked.

Rick squinted at the complicated flowchart of boxes and arrows. "It looks like a series of shell corporations. Possibly for hiding assets. Could be a tax evasion scheme or something."

The cigarette-graveled voice of the woman caused them to jump. "Late-nighter, Rick?"

Hansen whirled around. The matronly form of Felicity Robbins filled the doorway. The secretary peered judgmentally at the two, her eyes narrowed into nickel-thin slits.

How long has she been standing there? "Oh, hey, Felicity. Yeah, it looks that way. I'm having computer problems."

Like twin laser beams, her suspicious glare turned on the unshaved college dropout with the tiny PDA in his palm. "Aren't you going to introduce me to your friend?"

"This is Frederic Zaraghi. He's a computer consultant."

"Oh?" She put a finger to her lips. "I don't recall seeing the requisition form for an outside consultant."

"And you won't be seeing one," Rick said. "Frederic's not charging the department for his time."

"Mike will appreciate hearing that," she said. After a leaden silence, she dislodged herself from the doorframe. "Well, good night."

"G'night," Hansen mumbled, turning back to the screen.

Felicity disappeared.

Freddie Zaraghi looked at Hansen and made a citrus-sour face. "*Frederic? Do I strike you as a *Frederic*?*"

Hansen could just imagine what sort of spin she'd put on it the moment Kilmartin returned from Florida. *And you wouldn't have believed your own eyes, Mike, Hansen had this unshaved scuzzball in his office late at night doing God-knows-what to the firm's computer systems.* Well, so be it. Nothing could be done about a chronically catty secretary. He dismissed the encounter from his mind.

Hansen said, "Let's just print this one out and keep going."

They spent the next several hours doing just that.

Forty-four

"DORITOS," HANSEN MURMURED as he headed purposefully down the junk-food aisle of the all-night deli. "Where are the nacho cheese Doritos?"

It was now coming up on ten o'clock Thursday night. It was becoming evident that what had first been conceived as a late-nighter was irreversibly turning into an all-nighter. Hundreds of pages of documents had been produced through the two-pages-per-minute laser printer, and hundreds more had yet to be decoded and printed. Hansen and Zaraghi seemed destined to cross the invisible borderline to that realm where it made more sense to remain awake than it did to go home and cop a few hours of sleep. In Rick's college days at Cornell and his subsequent law school years at Fordham, "pulling the all-nighter" had had vaguely heroic connotations: an intense, all-out effort to cram the brain with precious knowledge in preparation for a make-or-break, do-or-die final examination. The sacrifice of a night's sleep could never be fully recouped; that in and of itself was a testament to the importance of the mission at hand. But the law firm life deconstructed the romantic implications of the all-night quest. In its insatiable starvation for billable hours, his old firm had routinely expected him to sacrifice sleep for the cause of baby-sitting the production of IPO prospectuses at the midtown photoprint shops. Invariably, Rick Hansen would kill the night largely by stewing for hours on end, palming Styrofoam cups of acidic and lukewarm black coffee, wondering why the hell he was squandering his life on such crap. The demands of law firm life and the concept of billable hours had drastically cheapened the esteem of the all-nighter, converting the thrill of a quest into a despisable method of lining the senior partners' pockets at year's end.

Tonight was different. Tonight, the nobility of the quest was back. Hansen felt wired, a bright buzz of elation that he could fall back into all-nighter mode so effortlessly. They were on the verge of a breakthrough, Hansen could feel it, and to keep the momentum going until daybreak, they needed provisions. *Brain food*—that's what Zaraghi had dubbed the junk food he required. Sugars, salts, caffeine—all were called for in massive quantities.

Hansen had offered to make the late-night run to a favorite all-night deli, which was mercifully close to the office. It was like all New York delis, distinct in its own way, but undeniably a New York delicatessen. It was operated by hardworking Korean-Americans, who staffed it with family members around the clock.

Zaraghi's list was undeniably indulgent—a dozen Ho-Hos, a package of Little Debbie devil's food snack cakes; two cans of Jolt Cola; a six-pack of Freddie's beloved Mountain Dew; peanut-butter Snickers bars; microwavable burritos; two large coffees with twelve packs of sugar and, finally, the economy size package of Jack Cheese Doritos. Rick Hansen was cheered by the progress they were making and happily attended to the needs of his computer genius. Whatever it took to keep all pistons firing until daybreak, Hansen was ready, willing and able to do.

"This is not all for me," Hansen offered to the stone-faced Korean-American clerk manning the checkout counter. For good measure, Rick impulse-purchased a box of artificially flavored grape frosted Pop-Tarts. The clerk rang up the items, which totaled $17.48. The price reflected the premium paid at the twenty-four-hour New York delis. Hansen grabbed the bag, thanked the clerk and stepped out onto Pine Street.

———•———

Outside, the buildings of the financial district glistened in the lamplight as if glazed in rock candy. On the walkways, treacherous craters had formed, and it was like walking on the icy frosting of a cake. The sidewalks had frozen up into a polar icescape. The weather report for Friday promised a break in the freak cold snap. Hansen hunched up his shoulders for warmth against the biting chill.

Turning left on William Street, his mind whirled back to the current state of his investigation, the significance of the details he had gleaned so far.

The papers they had decoded that evening clearly evinced some sort of secretive arrangement that was obviously designed as a subterfuge of some sort. Hansen had found tangible evidence that Tom Bingham had assisted a group of unnamed people in moving money in a manner that was intended to avoid detection. At first, Hansen's initial premise seemed to hold water: that Bingham had been brought in as an external consultant to assist a hedge fund in creating a web of companies. The schematic they had found early on showed a tangled web of companies intended to obscure the flow of money. But just who was the network supposed to deceive? The first guess would be the IRS. A more unsettling answer would have been Wolcott, or the SEC. But the true question was why was it necessary to set up such a network of shell companies if Bingham had been involved in a legitimate hedge fund. Maybe it was a tax evasion mechanism.

One thing was clear—Bingham had been up to some shady business.

Now the question was whether his involvement in the enterprise had gotten him killed.

Again, Hansen's instincts told him this was so. With Zaraghi on the case, they might gather enough evidence that O'Bannon could no longer deny the Bingham case needed to be reopened.

———•———

"Good eatin's!" Zaraghi said excitedly when Hansen returned to his office with the booty. Hansen set the bags down on the surface of his desk, tore them open and spread out the bounty of junk foods.

"Find anything else of importance?" Hansen inquired, dissecting the bag of Doritos down the middle with a letter opener.

"I printed out about two tons of pages for you to sort through. Nothing as dramatic as the flowchart. A lot of personal stuff. Some lovey-dovey e-mails to the namesake of his password, that woman Kathleen? You wouldn't believe the juicy stuff he'd write to her—"

Hansen held his Dorito-tinted stained hands up defensively. "I don't want to know."

"Yeah, yeah." Zaraghi smiled as he tore into a two-pack of Hostess Ho-Hos. "Listen, before I forget, your wife's named Stephanie?"

"Yes?"

"She called about ten minutes ago. Said it was very important."

The lawyer's stomach crushed into a knot . . . *The baby!* "Did she say what it was about?"

"No. Just said to call her back soon as possible." Zaraghi stuffed an entire chocolate-covered Ho-Ho into his mouth in one bite. "Better food through chemicals."

———•———

For privacy's sake, he called Stephanie from Kilmartin's office with the door closed. Two rings passed. Time crawled unmercifully as he waited for her to pick up.

Her water's broken, Rick predicted. *And I was out buying fucking Ho-Hos! Christ, she's probably already at the hospital, legs up on the birthing table, doing the goddamned Lamaze without me—*

Stephanie answered in a susurrous voice: "Hello?"

"Steph, it's me. I just got back. Everything all right?"

"I need you to come home right now." Her tone became desperate, causing gooseflesh to prickle up on Hansen's skin.

"Is it the baby? Is the baby okay?"

"It's not the baby," she whispered.

"What is it then?"

"Not over the phone. Come home now. Please, Rick. I'm really scared."

———◆———

God! God! How he wished he was driving the taxicab himself!

The driver expertly serpentined around the slower-moving traffic on the northbound side of the FDR, but it was impossible for him to move quickly enough to satisfy his anxious passenger from Wall Street. Rick Hansen continued to verbally flog the driver from the backseat, like a jockey with a crop, urging him to go faster, faster, faster.

"Sir, the only faster way is by plane," the driver complained loudly.

"As fast as you can, please. My wife may be having a baby."

The driver muttered something inaudible to Rick, but Hansen wasn't about to challenge the cabbie to a verbal sparring match. "Just get me there," he pleaded.

At the apartment building, Hansen threw a twenty down on the front seat. He sprinted inside the lobby, up the elevator. A quick rap on the door to the apartment. He shoved the key inside and turned it with an urgent jerk, shouldering it open.

"Stephanie?" he called out. "Stephanie, everything all right?"

First thing he noticed was the radio playing softly in the living area; it was a classical music station on the FM dial that Stephanie had grown accustomed to over the last six months.

Then his eight-months pregnant wife appeared from the kitchen. Her face was expressionless, but it was evident that she had been crying recently. Stephanie had a blue spiral notebook in her hand, the one she used to take notes for their Lamaze class. She locked his eyes up with hers. Hansen waited, expectantly.

She tapped the open page of the spiral notebook with a ballpoint pen.

Rick peered at the spot the pen pointed to. A brief note in her elegant penmanship in the center of the page:

BE CAREFUL WHAT YOU SAY.
I THINK THE APARTMENT IS BUGGED.

"What?" he whispered. "What makes you think—"

She put a silencing finger to his lips. Turned the page of the notebook to another note she'd written out in advance.

IT MAY SOUND PARANOID, BUT MY PHONE
CONVERSATIONS ARE COMING OUT OVER THE
RADIO.

Hansen shook his head in disbelief.

Stephanie beckoned for him to come with her. She took him by the hand, led him to the living area.

The radio on their Yamaha stereo system was tuned to an FM station. A fizzy interference faded in and out over Haydn's Symphony No. 101, *The Clock Menuetto*. Stephanie hiked up the volume, then crossed the room to where her husband was standing.

"Listen closely," Stephanie whispered in his ear.

Then with a quivering hand, Stephanie took the handset of the phone off the receiver.

The dial tone from the phone throbbed in a faint echo over the Bose speakers, fizzy with distortion. Yes. Barely audible beneath the symphony. *But it was there.* Unmistakably. Transfixed, Hansen moved toward the stereo receiver. He adjusted the AM/FM antenna slightly, moving it in the direction of the phone. Then he eased the tuner dial to the right, increasing the kilohertz of the frequency. As he did, the dial tone deteriorated in quality. The lawyer turned the knob in the opposite direction. Instantly, the dial tone from the phone came out of the Bose speakers with more clarity than the signal of the radio station itself.

Hansen looked at his wife and nodded.

Stephanie pushed the fifth speed-dial button on the phone, which was marked MOVIE-FONE.

Over the speakers, the ringing was picked up in a crystal-clear reproduction. Hansen went numb.

After a single ring, the familiar hyper-enthusiastic male voice they had heard dozens of times rang out over the speakers. "Hello and welcome to Movie-Fone! If you know the name of the movie you wish to see, press one now!"

Hansen stood in the center of the living area, dumbstruck, disoriented. Their phone was not the wireless type that operated on radio waves. It operated on land lines—which meant there was a device inside the apartment transmitting the call in the form of radio waves, *a listening device someone had planted for the express purpose of eavesdropping on their conversations.* His skin crawled with anger and humiliation. *How long had this been going on?* Their every conversation, their every intimacy . . .

Rick Hansen disconnected the call. He embraced his wife in a tight hug, sandwiching their unborn child protectively between their entwined bodies. In his wife's ear he whispered, "Pack an overnight bag."

———•———

In the semidarkness of a well-appointed room on the fifth floor of the Millenium Hotel, husband and wife lay on the bed in a desperate clinch. The silence between them articulated their anxiety, a silence filled by the comforting noise of midnight traffic on Church Street below. Rick Hansen stared up at the lights and shadows playing on the ceiling, stroking Stephanie's hair.

She moaned, "Oh, Rick. What have you gotten yourself into?"

The query was an icy dagger to the heart. What malevolent force had he unleashed by pursuing this mystery? "Stephanie, let's not rush to conclusions. We can't be certain the apartment was bugged. It could be some . . . I don't know, a quirk in the wiring . . ."

"No," she said firmly. "Not according to your own theory. Remember? They killed Tom Bingham, they killed the professor in Pittsburgh. Now they're going after you."

Hansen didn't say a word to this; he kept running his fingers through his wife's silken hair.

Stephanie's voice was mournful. "When I think about it, being *bugged,* I just want to run far, far away. Things we've said to one another, all overheard by *strangers.* Our intimacies, our fights. Our lovemaking. Who knows how long it's gone on?"

Hansen regarded his neglected wife with remorse. It had been his protective instincts that had led him to shield her from undue worry. But in the end it had let her be completely blindsided by this unexpected invasion into their personal lives. He fumbled for the appropriate words, but they came to him without thinking. "I love you."

"It's been two weeks since you've said that to me," she noted softly. "It's nice to hear." Her voice trailed off. Then she said, "For all we know, they could have followed us here."

They. Who were they? Solving that maddening riddle was now imperative—they had killed before, they would certainly kill again.

The revelation came to him then: *Bingham cannot be the only Wolcott Fulbright insider to this scheme.* A hypothesis instantly crystallized. Tom Bingham was nothing more than a small wheel in the plot, an errand boy. In the big picture, Tom was just the corruptible lawyer who wormed his way into the scheme by providing a credible analysis of Professor Gammage's theories on stock market crashes. Once he was in the circle of thieves, Bingham proved to be useful, at least in the beginning. It must have been Bingham who instructed Gammage to create the bogus documents purporting to prove that Zaraghi was not the creator of LINDA, but just a work-for-hire freelancer. Tom Bingham developed the schematic of shell companies for the purpose of concealing the flow of money from the authorities.

Then there was a falling-out of some sort. Perhaps over money—no, *definitely* over money. Maybe Tom wanted more for his contribution, or maybe he wanted hush money. As a consequence of making such a demand, Tom Bingham was tossed over the side of his balcony and turned into a strawberry sundae.

The other Wolcott executive had to be someone higher up the food chain than Tom himself. Someone with top-level access to Wolcott's personnel files, fingerprints, personal data. Someone who could give access to outsiders to delete files on Hansen's computer. Someone with the capability and expertise to frame the dead lawyer by putting him at the center of a bogus insider trading scheme out of Toronto, a ruse that was *meant* to be detected.

Hansen thought of Freddie Zaraghi alone in his office, wired on several pounds of chemically enhanced junk food, burrowing through Bingham's computer files for clues at this very moment. The digital alarm clock said it was just past midnight. Rick Hansen needed to get back to 44 Wall.

"Stephanie—" he began gently.

"I know, I know," she said. "You have to go back to the office to get evidence for the police."

"The nightmare's never going to end if I don't. With this kid Zaraghi, I think we're on the verge of a breakthrough. No matter what, I'm telling Mike Kilmartin everything I know tomorrow afternoon, and the cops if they'll listen."

She was quiet for a moment. "Please be careful."

He kissed her. "The office is just five minutes away, Steph, so call if you need me. Keep the door double-locked."

"No shit, Dick Tracy," she said.

Then the only sound in the room was the whisper of garments as

Hansen shrugged on his overcoat. Absently, Stephanie Hansen cradled the baby in her midsection and massaged it lightly. "I've decided to name Baby X either Julianne if it's a girl or Grant if it's a boy."

Hansen's smile was wan. "I like both of those names," he said agreeably. "I love both of you."

Forty-five

COLBERT MET TWO of The Contrarians, Zull and Jermyn, for a late dinner at Lespinasse, the Asian-accented gourmet French restaurant on Fifty-fifth Street.

Colbert ordered both the Bay of Fundy salmon pavé with summer truffles and turbotin with herb broth, pea shoots and apio root. As was his custom, he sampled both entrées and sent one entrée back. For no particular reason, he rejected the salmon in favor of the turbotin.

Over the course of the evening, the three partners compared recent business ventures. Several bottles of '82 Château Haut-Brion Bordeaux were consumed. Talk of the initiative was conspicuously avoided, at least until Colbert was willing to give a sign that he cared to share details. Finally, as the plates were cleared, an inebriated Jermyn could stand the suspense no longer. He banged the table with an open palm and implored Colbert, "Please, Philip, no more suspense. Tell us about this miracle black-box system that will turn us all into billionaires tomorrow."

Zull fired an admonitory look at Jermyn, but Colbert held up a hand. Plied by ego and alcohol, Colbert found himself *wanting* to talk about it, to share his excitement with business partners. Anyhow, only twelve hours remained until the first domino tumbled. What harm could come to the initiative by mere table talk among partners? "Very well, Dirk," Colbert grinned, "if you must know . . ."

The system was named LINDA. It was a computerized stock trading program that was created to make its own trading decisions. It operated on an *if-then* logic, meaning *if* the stock market moved in a particular direction, *then* LINDA would respond accordingly with a buy, sell or hold of a particular stock or multiple of stocks.

The professor from Pittsburgh, the one who had brought the system to Colbert's attention, had completely rewritten the original source code of LINDA. LINDA was now reprogrammed to cause a massive stock market decline. And because it was a machine, it would refuse to stop until that objective was fully accomplished.

Colbert's dinner companions stared at him blankly. How was that possible? "Is it all done through the program trading wires of the stock exchanges?" Zull asked.

"God, no," Colbert said dismissively. "The stock exchange has some very smart people guarding the electronic trading mechanisms. If LINDA tried to crash the market using program trading wires alone, the initiative would be shut down by the regulators in five minutes. The solution is the Internet."

His partners waited for him to continue.

Colbert smiled. "Let me paint you a picture.

"Tomorrow at ten A.M., London time, five A.M. New York time, the Dartmouth Funds Group will execute a sale of twelve billion dollars' worth of U.S. blue-chip stocks on the London Stock Exchange. These stocks comprise the two major indexes of the American Stock market— particularly the Dow Jones Industrial Average. The sale will be highly publicized on financial news wires around the world. The fire sale will send a signal to the managers of pension plans, hedge pools and mutual funds that a prominent American mutual fund company no longer has confidence in the stock market. They will experience a seizure of paranoia and ask themselves, *What does Dartmouth know about the market that we don't?* Of course, the sale doesn't actually exist—the counterparty is a Swiss-based shell company the partnership controls, so the trade is a wash."

Zull and Jermyn snickered at this.

"At exactly nine A.M., I push a button. LINDA takes control. It starts with a 10-billion-dollar sell order sent to the floor of the New York Stock Exchange through the electronic trading system of a New York securities firm." Colbert saw no reason to identify Wolcott Fulbright to his partners. "Once that sale is confirmed, then LINDA begins routing more sell orders over the Internet to forty-seven other securities firms around the globe. Each of these brokers thinks it is acting on behalf of the Dartmouth Funds. Each has been instructed to used a numbered code name for the account to protect the identity of Dartmouth. Dartmouth, of course, will be selling stock it doesn't own, stock it will fail to deliver on settlement date three days forward . . ."

Colbert tone became impassioned as he described the chain of events that would inevitably follow. One hundred billion dollars' worth of stock sell orders in the first few hours of trading on a triple-witch expiration Friday . . . no one would know where it was coming from . . . institutional investors would simply think the market was crapping out . . . trillions of dollars—trillions!—would race for the exit all at once, the exit being a rapidly shrinking pinhole. The foreign moneys that had artificially propped up the overinflated U.S. equity markets—from England, France, Japan, Germany, Israel, the Mideast—all of that would be yanked.

Mutual fund companies—which by federal law had to have enough liquid assets on hand to meet redemption requests—would have no choice but to follow Dartmouth's lead and liquidate significant portions of their portfolios in the marketplace.

The institutional investment managers—charged with responsibility for protecting hundreds of billions of other people's assets—would have to move decisively in the face of the massive selling pressure. They too would have to sell.

The equity market's symbiotic relationship with the equity derivatives market would go haywire as well. As institutional investors rushed in to buy "portfolio insurance" to shield against massive losses in their rapidly devaluing stock portfolios—selling calls, buying puts, selling index futures—all that bearish activity would continue to exert downward pressure on the value of stocks.

Then the lagging institutional investors would come rushing into the downdraft, punished for sitting on the sidelines hoping for an equity bounce-back.

The small investor, the little guy, John Q. Public, would once again be a loser in the cosmic game of musical chairs. By the time his phone call got through to his broker, the holdings in his pension plan would be worth *half* what they were a few days before.

The blood would gush through the urban canyons of Wall Street and spread through Main Street America—and the ripple effect would reverberate around the world.

In the course of two business days, the American stock market would suffer its biggest nuclear meltdown ever—far worse than October '87, or 1929. According to LINDA's models, three thousand to four thousand points would be whacked off the value of the Dow Jones Industrial Average in just those two days—40 to 50 percent of its value.

And because the 116 various bearish leveraged derivatives bets "Charles Stone" had arranged with foreign banks and investment houses would become "in-the-money," billions of American shareholder wealth would be transferred to entities controlled by the partnership. And in the course of those two days, the American stock market would suffer a paper loss roughly equivalent to the entire gross national product of France. "And that's what the black-box system will do tomorrow morning," Colbert concluded.

"Christ," Jermyn mumbled.

"The gross national product of France," Zull echoed in genuine shock.

"I believe another bottle of wine is in order, gentlemen." Colbert grinned. "And in honor of the gross national product of France, perhaps another Château Haut-Brion Bordeaux is appropriate. What do you say?"

Forty-six

NERVES JANGLING, Hansen returned to the offices of Wolcott Fulbright at quarter past midnight. He found Freddie Zaraghi right where he'd left him a few hours ago. The kid was hunched over the keyboard of the desktop computer as if in prayerful communication with the machine, decoding Bingham's encrypted files and printing them out.

Freddie barely looked up from his typing when the lawyer appeared in the doorway. "If you're back at the shop, I guess that means it must not be baby time yet."

"Freddie."

The lawyer's tone caused the kid to whip around. "Yes?"

Hansen beckoned for him to come outside. Wordlessly, Freddie complied. Hansen led him away from the office.

"What is it?" Zaraghi asked.

Quietly, the lawyer relayed the events of the last few hours—the suspicion that his apartment might be bugged, the relocation of his wife to a nearby hotel, just to be on the safe side.

Zaraghi palmed his chin stubble as Rick spoke. After Rick finished, he mused, "That means your office could be wired too."

"Well, that's exactly right. That's why we're having this conversation right here rather than in there."

"Don't you think we should find out for certain?"

"I suppose I could call Security—" Before Rick could complete the thought, Freddie Zaraghi turned around and reentered the office. The kid purposefully circled around the desk and unplugged his 200 MHz Gateway 2000 laptop computer from its charger. The ten-pound device was now running on the lithium-ion battery, untethered by a power cord. The *Star Trek* screen-saver function was up. The image of Mr. Spock with his world-famous spread-fingered, live-long-and-prosper greeting filled the LCD display panel.

Hansen stood at the threshold of his own office and hissed, "What the hell are you doing? Didn't you hear what I just said?"

"Loud and clear." Inexplicably, the college dropout lifted the humming laptop up from the desk, and held it out in front of him as he would a tray of hors d'oeuvres at a cocktail party. He moved deliberately about the office, positioning the back of the device until it nearly touched the wall. He slowly rotated it around.

"What are you doing?" Hansen demanded.

"I'm using the computer to detect EMI emissions."

"Run that by me again?"

"EMI, meaning, electromagnetic interference." Freddie Zaraghi spoke conversationally. "Assuming arguendo that there's some sort of surveillance device in your office, then by the very nature of the device, it will emit some sort of radio frequency waves, right?"

"If you say so."

"Of course I say so. A bug is a *transmitting* device. That's its purpose, to transmit our voices to a remote location. Now, this portable computer that I now hold in my hands? This laptop emits radio waves of its own. Did you know that?"

"No, I didn't."

"Well, take my word for it, it does. The FCC has classified laptops like my Gateway as a Class B computing device, meaning it is an unintentional radiator of electromagnetic radio waves. Following the bouncing ball?"

"Shouldn't we have this conversation somewhere else?" Hansen worried that their every word was being monitored. The cyber-brat was tempting the fates.

Zaraghi continued, "That's the reason the airlines don't let you use computers or cell phones or CD players during takeoff or landing. Computers emit a shitload of electromagnetic radio waves, which interfere with the airliner's navigational equipment. Therefore, it follows that if there is a surveillance device here in your office, transmitting our every word to the bad guys, well, the EMIs from that listening device are going to interfere with my laptop's functioning." In a theatrically loud voice, he added, "Isn't that right, bad guys?"

"That's not humorous, Freddie," Hansen said.

"You're right, it's not humorous," Zaraghi agreed. "Corporate espionage is a fucking outrage, a federal fucking offense." As Zaraghi now moved the portable computer above his head, levitating it toward the ceiling, the digitized image of Mr. Spock flickered noticeably.

"Getting warmer," he singsonged.

Hansen was still a nonbeliever. "Could be some electrical interference from the light fixture."

"Could be," Zaraghi muttered distractedly. He moved the LCD display panel of the laptop around the ceiling like a divining rod homing in on moisture. Then it became obvious: the closer the device came to the water sprinkler, the more the on-screen image throbbed with distortion. When Zaraghi moved the device away, the image of Spock stabilized. With a chill racing up his spine, Hansen conceded to himself that the kid might be on to something. Now Zaraghi lightly touched the back of the computer to the stem of the water sprinkler. The screen display turned unstable, interference bars roiling the quality of the picture.

Freddie smiled in self-satisfaction. "Come to think of it, ever wonder why your sprinkler is located directly *above* your desk, rather than the center of your office?"

Numbed, Hansen uttered, "I never even noticed a sprinkler before."

"I'll bet you didn't. That's the beauty of it." Zaraghi drew the wheeled chair over and stepped cautiously onto the seat. He positioned his head as close to the fixture as possible, while keeping the laptop in contact with it. In a robust monotone, Zaraghi recited, "Mary had a little lamb, little lamb, little lamb."

Each syllable he uttered caused a violent interference spike in the LCD display panel.

"Fuck," Hansen blurted in stunned disbelief.

Zaraghi whistled. "You were right, chief, your office is *hot-wired*. Bad guys, this is Radio Free America signing off. Good night, Mrs. Calabash, wherever you are." Zaraghi yanked the fixture from the ceiling with a vicious tug. The device easily pulled away from the perforated ceiling panel, a tangle of tiny wires sprouting out from its base. Zaraghi inspected it. "Jeeze-louise, lookie here! It's a fucking camera, a pinhole camera with a wireless microphone. Hope you didn't pick your nose in the privacy of your own office, chief, they could have some incriminating video footage of you, you ever decide to run for public office."

Hansen snapped, "Would you shut the fuck up?"

The kid went wide-eyed at the outburst.

"This is not a game, Freddie." Hansen said. "It's not a game. They're fucking deadly serious. They bugged my home and my office. They've killed people. And you're doing Henny Youngman."

Zaraghi murmured, "Okay, okay. You're right, I'm sorry."

Hansen rubbed his eyes, tried to clear his head. "I don't need to hear you're sorry. Let's just find someplace else and keep working."

Forty-seven

VIKTOR ALEXEYEV strode down the plushly carpeted corridor toward Colbert's suite in the St. Regis, dreading his imminent encounter with the financier. The Russian had grown to dislike Colbert intensely, and found it increasingly difficult to suppress the iceberg of jealousy that rose within him. *A hard man living a soft life*, he thought bitterly. *A week in a hotel like this must cost tens of thousands.* Colbert had more money than God himself and, accordingly, thought himself superior to that higher deity.

Alexeyev knocked at the gold-leafed door to the financier's suite. Even at the early hour, Colbert answered the door dressed in suit and tie. There was coffee on his breath and a tenor of irritation to his voice. "Yes, what is it now, Viktor?"

"There are some things to discuss."

"Apparently they can't wait until morning."

"No."

Colbert sighed. "Come in."

The opulence of the Presidential Suite was unlike anything Alexeyev had ever encountered. Even as he was overwhelmed by the money taunting him from every corner of the room, he maintained his glacial exterior. "Zaraghi is in town."

"Zaraghi. The name is familiar."

"Zaraghi was Gammage's business partner, the college student who developed your computer program." Alexeyev pointed to LINDA on the large monitor screen. "He is meeting with the lawyer at the office right now. They're going through Bingham's papers and it seems they will be at it all night."

"Which lawyer? You mean Kilmartin?"

"No, Kilmartin's still in Florida. The other lawyer, Hansen." Alexeyev paused. "The lawyer and the programmer have discovered our surveillance devices at two locations. Hansen is frightened enough that he has moved his wife to a hotel."

Colbert absorbed this, his mind working to process its implications. "Do we know which hotel?"

"The Millenium."

Colbert nodded, gratified to know of a vulnerability to exploit. "In reality, we're in the eleventh hour, Viktor. Is there a quantifiable threat to the initiative at this very moment, or are we simply overreacting?"

Alexeyev analyzed the situation for Colbert's benefit. On the positive side, he said, the risk that the scheme would be brought to the attention of the authorities was minimal. Time was the lawyer's enemy; it would run out well before he could call the initiative to the regulators' attention. More to the point, the lawyer and the programmer had not yet been able to piece anything together directly linking The Contrarians to Bingham. Still, Zaraghi was a renowned expert in computers. He had decoded hundreds of pages of encrypted documents, and who knew what information those papers contained? Disturbingly, they had uncovered a flowchart of fictitious shell companies Bingham had created for Stiletto. And LINDA was *Zaraghi's* creation after all, so, conceivably, the computer programmer could pose a threat if he gained access to the Wolcott computers running the software program. Worse, the Russians no longer had the ability to monitor the activity of the lawyer and the computer programmer. They were now effectively flying blind.

Colbert mulled all the information, then said pointedly, "Yes, it was most unfortunate that the lawyer came into possession of the contents of Bingham's hard drive. We're still paying the price for that, aren't we?"

Alexeyev stiffened. The statement was a blatant slap at the Russians for their world-class screwup. Colbert was right, of course: it was unforgivably sloppy to presume that *all* of Tom Bingham's possessions had been removed to his new apartment. That the dead lawyer planned to maintain the rent-stabilized apartment for his lover Oberlin should have occurred to them. Granted, it was a fuckup. Still, Colbert had no right to withhold $250,000 in fees due to TCI. Calling Ilyutovich to badmouth the Gargoyle did not put Colbert in good favor with Alexeyev. Alexeyev maintained his poker face as he conceded, "Yes, it was unfortunate, but what's done is done, eh? We now need to contain the situation."

"So what do you need from me?"

"We need access to the secret facility."

Colbert checked the clock. 1:32 A.M. He smiled. Actually, it would be his pleasure to wake Stiletto. By Colbert's estimation, the Wolcott insider was still a long way from earning his $40 million payout. "That will be arranged. What else?"

"I need to know that we have all options at our disposal."

"All options?" Colbert raised an eyebrow. "You mean, can you *kill* them if you have to? Of course you can. But you tell Gagarov not to do it for the sport of it. It is a measure of last resort. And for crissakes, it is not to be done anywhere on the premises. Take them somewhere else, take them to the water. Got that?"

"Yes." Viktor Alexeyev regarded the financier with a dispassionate gaze.

"Good. I'll make arrangements for you to access the facility." Colbert returned to the flickering computer screens surrounding him. "Now, if we're done here, I need to get back to work."

Alexeyev said, "Yes. We're done here. Thank you." He left.

———•———

1:52 A.M.

The security guard looked as though he'd been awakened from a fitful sleep to respond to the incident on the thirty-seventh floor.

Much to Rick's outrage, the guard barely reacted when informed that a secret surveillance camera had been planted in the ceiling of the lawyer's office. Mechanically, the guard pulled out a pink "Security Incident Report" form, smacked his lips sleepily and wrote HIDDEN CAMARA FOUND IN OFFICE in the scattershot penmanship of a third-grader. Hansen couldn't believe the guy didn't know how to spell "camera."

Once the guard shambled off to the lower floors, Zaraghi shook his head. "Same as NASCIA," he muttered. "Night-shift security sucks."

After filing the report, the pair moved their operations to the War Room, that windowless space on the other side of the floor. It was highly unlikely that the out-of-the-way conference room would have been wired. Hansen and Zaraghi found an audiovideo cart in the legal library area. The computer was disassembled and moved to the War Room on the A-V cart. Once inside, Zaraghi put the machine together and they were back in the conspiracy-detecting business.

Over the next hour, Zaraghi decoded the rest of the documents, printing them out on the maddeningly slow dinosaur of a laser printer Felicity had stuck Rick with when he joined the firm. In total, over seven hundred pages of printouts from Bingham's computer needed to be examined by Hansen for clues. Before Rick got down to that, he went through the archives boxes he had called up last month to pull key documents for Zaraghi's review. Hansen suppressed an urge to check in on Stephanie; she needed the rest.

After 2:00 A.M., they swapped documents. Zaraghi looked at the memos Bingham had archived; Hansen scanned the decoded documents Zaraghi had produced.

They often lapsed into silence as they read the pages. All at once, Zaraghi snorted out an ironic laugh.

"What is it?" Rick asked.

"This memo that your man Bingham wrote on the inevitability of stock market crashes?"

"What about it?"

"That's *my* freaking research he's critiquing. I remember Gammage asking me to look into it for a prospective client, and I did it in a forty-eight-hour supercaffeinated jag in the CMU libes. Now to see the guy passed it off as his own? Beautiful. I know how to pick business partners, huh?"

"No comment," Rick said, turning back to his reading.

Time crawled while they sifted through the stacks of word-processed documents. Nearly an hour passed. Hansen yawned. He was shot for any work tomorrow. *Them's the breaks,* he thought sleepily. The lawyer sipped some weak machine-brewed coffee and picked up a document. Instantly, he squawked triumphantly.

Zaraghi's head shot up from his reading. "What is it?"

Hansen looked up at him, beaming. "The mystery of BEACON is solved!"

"Better not be funning around." Zaraghi came around to where Hansen was seated, looked over his shoulder.

CONFIDENTIAL

TO: MAX SCHOMBURG
FM: ROBERT M. WOLCOTT III, CHAIR
BEACON PROJECT EXECUTIVE COMMITTEE TASK FORCE
RE: THE BEACON PROJECT—DISASTER RECOVERY INITIATIVE

"Ho-lee shee-yit," Zaraghi yodeled. "Disaster recovery, you know what that is?"

"It's corporate-speak for a backup plan in case of disaster."

"Right. I've done some consulting on this type of thing, a so-called 'massive disruption event' like an information terrorist attack, a fire, an earthquake. You guys in the financial services business especially, you rely entirely on electronic communication of data. There has to be a series of backup plans in case a disaster disables the primary facilities. The BEACON Project is your firm's backup plan in case a disaster of some sort knocks out your primary systems—"

"Exactly," Hansen said, eager to get Freddie off his cyber-know-it-all soapbox. "The BEACON Project is Wolcott Fulbright's backup plan. Let's read on."

Executive Summary:

Wolcott, Fulbright & Company maintains two critical facilities for the efficient conduct of its global business lines in the Americas, Europe and the Pacific. These two critical locations are 44 Wall Street and Parsippany, New Jersey.

A disaster or emergency is declared when a force majeure or other event disables a critical component of the data stream. If primary-site contingency plans prove ineffective, the Disaster Recovery alternate-site recovery procedures would be initiated. The primary thrust of the BEACON Project, then, is to retain partial or full control of vital business functions in a disaster scenario to protect the firm's proprietary and customer accounts from sustained losses in the case of a disaster/emergency event scenario.

Risks:

In the event of a Level 1 or Level 2 Disaster Scenario, customer and proprietary accounts could be subject to undefinable losses because of paralysis in the effectiveness of the firm's trading facilities.

Recommendation:

The task force recommends that two alternative sites should be established.

Geographically Remote Mirror-Architecture ("Shell Site"): One would be at a site at least 150 miles away from the epicenter of New York City to be located safely away from the disaster/emergency event—Camden, New Jersey, or Framingham, Massachusetts, are under consideration. This is for LEVEL 1 DISASTER SCENARIOS, which would disable the firm's ability to conduct normal operations for a full business day or longer (earthquakes, acts of God, etc.).

Backup Facility On-Site at 44 Wall Location ("Hot Site"):
At the same time, in case the event is limited to Wolcott's facilities and not New York City Metropolitan area (e.g., power outages, telecommunication equipment failures, sabotage, flood, fire, etc.), a miniature "Hot Site" should be constructed on-site inside 44 Wall with a "mirror-architecture" to ensure seamless performance of local-area network (LAN). This facility would be equipped with the minimal software and hardware resources to continue managing securities and derivatives inventories despite facilities failure. This is for LEVEL 2 DISASTER SCENARIOS, which would be reserved for temporary, contained emergencies that would impact upon normal operations for only a matter of hours within a single trading day (i.e., temporary power outage).

Definition of Event:
Situation that results in a loss of all support services and disabling of existing business functions for several hours, one business day or an indefinite period of time.

Risk Management:
The risks appurtenant to a disaster/emergency scenario may be minimized by maintaining a number of redundant architectures at alternative "hot sites" dispersed in distinct geographical locations.

"Ah-ha," Rick said. "It's code-named BEACON because when the lights go out, the backup contingency plans are switched on, acting like a BEACON in the darkness."

"Cute," Zaraghi said, tearing the wrapper from a Snickers bar. "I like that. But what does it have to do with Tommy Bingham?"

Hansen exhaled in frustration. "Maybe Tom was just a legal consultant to the project. Maybe BEACON doesn't mean anything in the scheme of things."

"It's got to mean *something*. Remember, in his PDA, he constantly made references to it. 'Visit BEACON.' 'Do programming at BEACON today.' 'Meeting on BEACON floor.' The BEACON entries figured prominently in his PDA during his last three months of life." Zaraghi spread his hands as though to say, the facts are the facts.

Hansen stared at the memo. He reached into his canvas bag and pulled out the envelope that Bingham had marked simply "BEACON." He pulled the electronic security key out of the envelope and stared at it, as if willing it to give up its secrets. Where was BEACON?

Then a fraction of a smile came to his face. "I wonder if—" His voice trailed off elliptically.

"What?" Zaraghi asked.

"Follow me."

Forty-eight

2:16 A.M.

THEY WENT OUT into the hallway. Hansen stabbed the call button for the elevator. It lit up, indicating the car was on its way. Hansen said, "There's always one thing that's intrigued me since I joined this firm. About the elevator, specifically."

Zaraghi gave him a puzzled look.

In the next moment, the elevator arrived and its doors parted. Zaraghi followed Hansen inside. The doors closed, but the car remained stationary, awaiting the selection of a floor.

"Yeah?" Zaraghi said. "You were saying?"

"See what happens when I press this?" Hansen repeatedly jabbed the B button at the bottom of the panel.

"Absolutely nothing," Zaraghi shrugged.

"That's right." Hansen held up the white plastic security keycard. "Now let's see what happens when I do *this* first."

Hansen swiped the keycard along the electronic slot.

Then he pressed the B button again.

This time, it lit up.

"Hey," Zaraghi smiled, "you now have control of the board."

With a lurch, the elevator began its straight-line journey to ground level, then beneath the surface of Wall Street.

———————————●———————————

The doors opened on the basement level, revealing a dimly lit area of concrete and chain-link fencing. At first sight, the B level seemed to be nothing more than a neglected subterranean facility for the storage of junk. Toolboxes and wood planks were stacked haphazardly against the far wall, and the sharp tang of acrylic paint filled the damp air. Zaraghi peered around in the semi-darkness. "Nothin' doin' down here."

"Then why the high-level of security?" Hansen asked.

"How would I know?"

Hansen led them farther into the belly of the beast.

They came to a windowless drywall with an imposing metal door in its center. Next to the door was a keypad with a red LCD display. Zaraghi groaned, "Ah, bummer. Dead end."

Hansen grunted. The lawyer leaned forward in the darkness and squinted at the display panel. "I've never seen a security display like this before."

"Without a SmartCard, it's impenetrable." The kid absently punched some digits at random and hit the ENTER key. It emitted an angry red light of denial. "Yeah. Like Fort Knox."

Hansen turned to Zaraghi. "What did you say? A 'smartcard'?"

"Yeah, an Ace SmartCard." Zaraghi framed an area the size of a credit card with his fingers. "It's a tiny computer about yay-big that generates a different, disposable pass code every two minutes. The pass codes are created by your firm's central security system and updated by radio waves. Anyway, the technology limits access to a small group of authorized personnel, so rogue employees and outsiders can't hack into high-security sites. Designed to keep out curious riffraff like us, I guess."

Hansen closed his eyes and smiled beatifically. *Thank you, God.*

Zaraghi gawked at him. "Why the game-show-host face?"

"Because I've got Tom Bingham's SmartCard."

Zaraghi grinned. "Chief, you're full of surprises. How'd you pull that off?"

"Tom Bingham bequeathed it to me. Stay here. I'll be back in less than five minutes."

———————●———————

As a point of fact, it took Hansen over six minutes to get up to the War Room on thirty-seventh and race back down to rejoin Zaraghi at the subterranean facility. He had Tom Bingham's datebook clutched in his hand. Positioning himself in front of the security keypad, he opened the datebook, flipped to the back. He withdrew the Ace SecurID electronic device from the back pocket.

The current pass code was 067-455. In the next several seconds, it reset itself, displaying the next disposable passcode: 898-010. Hansen poked the new code number into the keypad. A green light appeared, and the sound of a lock disengaging echoed in the expanse of the subterranean location. *Access granted.*

"Open sesame," Zaraghi said.

Hansen twisted the knob to the windowless steel door and it opened.

As they stepped inside, the fluorescent lights overhead automatically flicked to life, one after the other, triggered by the motion sensors detecting their presence.

"Infinitely cool." Zaraghi's voice boomed out in the expanse of the facility.

In the next moment, they jumped at the sound of a combustible-engine generator kicking on, its low rumble filling the silence. Backup power had automatically kicked in.

"Christ," whistled Hansen. "That scared the hell out of me."

"Me too."

Wordlessly, they walked through the facility, absorbing the ambiance of the firm's top-secret disaster-recovery location. BEACON was indeed a fully functional duplicate trading floor, just as described in the internal memo. The site was equipped with banks of telephones, direct lines, hoot'n'hollers, market data feeds, broker screens via networked and stand alone systems, PCs, UNIX workstations, output devices, cellular phones, connectives to the mainframe in Parsippany. Fax, telex machines, copiers and calculators. The temperature was noticeably cooler than the other office space in 44 Wall, largely because of the subterranean location. The ceilings were less than half as high as the regular trading floors in the Manhattan sky, but then again, this was a temporary site, to be used only in the event of some catastrophe that might disable the trading floors. The seating capacity was just two hundred, meaning many of the firm's sales and trading personnel would have the day off in the event of a Level 1 catastrophe. In a true belt-and-suspenders security measure, the computer keyboards were locked away in sliding drawers beneath the desks. The mini-towers that powered the Pentiums, NeXT machines and the Sun SPARCStations were also locked in metal cages beneath the desks to prevent theft or sabotage. No doubt, the Disaster Recovery Assessment team leaders were entrusted with the keys needed to unlock the cages. The security measure was clearly overkill. *Ninety-nine percent of the firm didn't know this place even existed,* Hansen thought.

Each mini-department was marked with an overhead sign. The fixed-income products were: EMERGING MARKETS, GOVERNMENTS, CORPORATES, HIGH-YIELD. Then the equity businesses: BLOCK TRADING. EQUITY OPTIONS. COMMODITIES. OVER-THE-COUNTER. Two- and three-man turrets only. Apparently, the fortunes of the firm would rest in the hands of two hundred people, who would continue to trade away even in the face of some crippling disaster that may befall New York City. Hell, if they detonated an atomic bomb in Lower Manhattan, Wolcott Fulbright could keep trading with Chicago, London and the over-the-counter markets without skipping a beat.

Echoing Hansen's thoughts, Zaraghi marveled, "It's like a fallout shelter. Hey, like, 'It's World War III, baby, get me short one thousand shares of Coca-Cola.' Spooky."

"Yeah." Hansen's attention had already turned elsewhere. "Hey, you notice that all the computer screens are black except that last one?" Secluded at the back end of the equity area was a single workstation that was flickering kinetically.

The two approached it quietly, as though trying not to scare it into inactivity. They stood silently over the machine, watching the screen display rapidly scrolling lines of characters. The data rolled up the screen almost too quickly for the eye to see.

Something familiar on the floor caught Hansen's attention. He stooped over and picked it up from the carpet. A yellow-and-black cigar band . . . Rick gasped as he saw the words: Liguito No. 2 . . . the rare Cuban cigar he'd sampled his first week in McGeary's office. Hansen frowned. McGeary had been here? Was he part of the BEACON project? Rick deposited the cigar band into the front pocket of his suit trousers.

"Oh my fucking God," Zaraghi blurted, startling Hansen.

"What's wrong?"

Zaraghi couldn't pull his eyes off the screen. "This computer's running LINDA. It's fucking running *my program!*" He whirled on the lawyer. "Your firm's computers are running *my* program. *Wolcott Fulbright* is the one hacking LINDA."

All at once, Hansen found himself reeling. Right before his eyes was evidence that Gil McGeary and Tom Bingham had conspired to pirate Freddie Zaraghi's computer software for modeling stock market trends. Zaraghi would have grounds for a multimillion-dollar lawsuit against Wolcott Fulbright for misappropriation of intellectual property. *And Hansen had foolishly brought the plaintiff onto the premises of the firm!* The defendant's own legal counsel had compromised the firm's position in future litigation. "Freddie, I don't know what to say. But if you and I are going to be on separate sides of a lawsuit, we're going to have to leave the premises—"

"Wait a minute." Freddie Zaraghi wheeled on him, his dark eyes feral. "Wait a minute. What's tomorrow?"

"What? Tomorrow is Saturday."

"No. Jesus, I mean *today*. Today's Friday, I know, but what's the *date?*"

Hansen consulted his watch. "March nineteenth."

"March nineteenth." Zaraghi spoke in a robotic monotone. "The third Friday of the last month of the quarter."

LINDA – AUTOMATED ELECTRONIC ORDER SCREEN – STATUS REPORT

File Connections Orders Layout Format Tools Formula Font Help

LINDA   Execute   Clear   Load   Simulator   DOT OTC ITG POS DC

Side	Size	Symbol	Order Type	Account		Reports
Sell	4000	S	MKT OPN			0 T @ 71.5000
						0 GM @ 70.5000
						0 GE @ 75.1250
						Sld 0 MMM @ 74.3750

Buy: 0/0   Sell: 0/0   SS: 0/0

=F1/G1   Σ Σn

A / AD	B / TICKER	C / SIDE	D / SIZE	E / STATUS	F / LONG/SHORT	G / ORDER TYPE	H / % LOADED	I / % FILLED	J / AVG PRICE
1	ALD	SELL	610,400	LOADED	LONG SALE	MKT OPN	100%	0%	81.50
2	AA	SELL	712,500	LOADED	LONG SALE	MKT OPN	100%	0%	101.25
3	AXP	SELL	545,000	LOADED	LONG SALE	MKT OPN	100%	0%	87.50
4	T	SELL	457,900	LOADED	LONG SALE	MKT OPN	100%	0%	88.375
5	BA	SELL	768,900	LOADED	LONG SALE	MKT OPN	100%	0%	89.8733
6	CAT	SELL	660,100	LOADED	LONG SALE	MKT OPN	100%	0%	55.75
7	CHV	SELL	710,500	LOADED	LONG SALE	MKT OPN	100%	0%	97.00
8	KO	SELL	560,200	LOADED	LONG SALE	MKT OPN	100%	0%	91.125
9	DIS	SELL	610,800	LOADED	LONG SALE	MKT OPN	100%	0%	76.000
10	DD	SELL	567,700	LOADED	LONG SALE	MKT OPN	100%	0%	50.500
11	EK	SELL	780,000	LOADED	LONG SALE	MKT OPN	100%	0%	71.55
12	XON	SELL	670,900	LOADED	LONG SALE	MKT OPN	100%	0%	70.333
13	GE	SELL	760,000	LOADED	LONG SALE	MKT OPN	100%	0%	62.765
14	GM	SELL	670,400	LOADED	LONG SALE	MKT OPN	100%	0%	61.50
15	GT	SELL	575,700	LOADED	LONG SALE	MKT OPN	100%	0%	74.375
16	HWP	SELL	557,800	LOADED	LONG SALE	MKT OPN	100%	0%	37.75
17								MKT VALUE: $9,716,375,800	

All Page   ripken_1   list10

list10   System Layout*

"Yes," Hansen confirmed. The two men uttered the next four words at the same time. "Triple-witch expiration Friday."

"Right," Hansen said. "So what about it?"

Zaraghi fastened his bloodshot eyes on the computer screen. "In connection with that stuff on stock market crashes I did for Gammage? Well, Gammage asked me if it was theoretically possible to program LINDA in a way that it could crash the stock market. I told him, of course it was possible, not just in theory, but in reality. I mean, if you could hack into the flow of money, create a disruption, LINDA could just . . ." Zaraghi's voice fell off; then he said, "LINDA is an expert system, programmed with all the known events and circumstances surrounding Black Monday, October 19, 1987. It has access to every trade ever executed on a national stock exchange . . ."

"What are you saying?"

Zaraghi face drained of color. "This computer, the stuff it's setting up. It's different from the program I created. The activity on the screen . . . it looks like it's preparing to . . . sell a shitload of stock."

"A shitload? How much is a shitload?"

"Dollar terms, ten billion dollars."

Hansen couldn't believe what he was hearing.

Zaraghi pointed to the screen of the monitor. "Look."

"I don't understand what's happening," Hansen said.

"It's loading up all of the stocks in the major indexes. And it's preparing to blow them through all the stock exchanges. Someone's modified my program to do what Gammage proposed. LINDA's going to start a crash of the stock market when the exchanges open this morning."

"You can't be serious."

"Death-row serious. *That's* what this is all about."

Hansen eyed Zaraghi closely, looking for some deceit. He detected none, and a novocaine numbness coursed through his body. Much to his horror, the kid was starting to make sense, and the picture that was emerging was mind-boggling. "All right, all right, what do we have to do to . . . shut this thing down?"

"I don't know how we can." Zaraghi frowned helplessly at the computer screen. "The keyboards and the systems are all locked up. I don't have control of the device. Rick, I swear to God, I don't know if I can stop this thing from happening."

Hansen stared at the computer, then stared at Zaraghi. "That's the wrong answer," he said, flatly. "*You* created this fucking monster, Freddie. Now *you* have to kill it."

Forty-nine

4:53 A.M.

COLBERT WATCHED LINDA PERFORM its functions in an awestruck daze. *This is good*, he said to himself, *this is so good*. The columns of numbers marched up the screen in an endless progression, digits signifying *value*. Wealth distilled to its raw form, numbers denoting winners and losers. Colbert was fascinated by the sheer volume of information unfolding before his eyes. While the financier considered himself a man of the world, until now he hadn't a clue that there were so many stock exchanges engaged in frenetic trading activity while North America slept. In a small window on the right side of the screen, a Reuters feed provided a real-time tally of the stock activity in Tokyo, London, Frankfurt, Paris, Milan, Madrid, Amsterdam, Stockholm, Zurich, São Paulo, Sydney and Hong Kong. Even the lesser-known stock exchanges were represented in the data window. Colbert was mildly surprised to learn that there were trading bourses in locales he'd have difficulty finding on a globe: Bangalore, Gauhati, Guayaquil, Ljubljana, Maebashi, Pernambuco. Perhaps LINDA could be modified to crash those Third World markets as well, Colbert thought to himself with a smile. Ah, the world provided so much *opportunity* to create wealth from nothingness.

As he waited for 5:00 A.M. to arrive, he amused himself by calling Stiletto's home in Connecticut one more time. The busy signal made him smile. Finally, Stiletto's wife had taken the phone off the hook. All night long, Colbert had called every hour inquiring of her husband's whereabouts. "At late-night compensation meetings," she had replied. "I'm not certain if he's going to come home or stay in the city tonight." Stiletto had failed to respond to his pager messages, and he did not answer calls to his cellular phone, leaving Colbert little choice but to ring his residence in Connecticut ritualistically in search of his highly compensated lackey. The wife had finally taken the phone from the hook, and Colbert realized Stiletto was not coming home at all.

Possibly with a lover, Colbert thought. No matter.

In five minutes, all would be moot. The Russians would have nothing to concern themselves with. The cartridge was loaded in the chamber; Colbert was set to pull the trigger. The financier sipped his coffee and waited as the minutes melted away irreversibly.

———●———

After forty minutes of tearing through the archives boxes in the War Room, a bleary-eyed Rick Hansen returned to the BEACON facility to check on Zaraghi's progress. He found Freddie hunched over the keyboard of his laptop computer like a concert pianist, furiously poking at the keys, trying to make something happen.

"Any luck?" Hansen asked him.

Zaraghi jolted upright. "Whoa, Jesus, you scared me." He shook his head. "Without direct access to the Sun SPARCStation itself, it's rough sledding. I've got a Hekemian auto-dialer hooked up to your phone lines, trying to dial every extension at Wolcott Fulbright. Soon as I connect, I've got a password sniffer to gain access. Even then, we're talking another eight, nine hours."

"Freddie, the market opens in *less than five hours.*"

"Well, this would go much faster if you had some keys for these locks," Freddie replied tersely. "Otherwise the process is gonna be like giving birth. Sloooow and painful."

Hansen shook his head. He'd searched the BEACON facility and Bingham's archives boxes, but turned up no keys. "I've called Security countless times and all I get is voice mail."

"Then let me do what I gotta do."

Absently, Hansen reached into his pocket and pulled out the cigar band. McGeary . . . maybe McGeary had a key. Maybe McGeary had some *answers.* But it wasn't even five in the morning yet, and the trading floor population would not be in force until seven. Hansen rubbed the glossy paper loop between his thumb and forefinger. "Freddie, I've been thinking about all this gloom-and-doom stuff, and I don't see how any single computer could crash the stock market."

Zaraghi stopped typing and turned around. "This one can."

"The markets are *gargantuan,*" Hansen said, shaking his head. "It would take like a hundred billion in capital to move the S&P 500 in a way that would crash the market. One computer couldn't do that much damage."

"You're not thinking about it the right way. Think about the Dow Jones Industrial Average. How many stocks are there in that index?"

"Thirty," Hansen replied immediately.

"Thirty stocks. *Three-oh.* Imagine if hundreds of thousands of sellers just came in from the sideline and hammered away at those stocks all day long, just selling the crap out of those. Imagine what that would do to the Dow Jones Industrial Average? People get a whiff of panic in the market, they panic themselves. No one wants to be left holding the bag. It's like someone shouting 'fire' in a crowded theater. There may not be a fire, but do you really want to stick around to find out? Imagine if—" Zaraghi stopped. His eyes fixed on the activity on the screen before him. Wordlessly, Hansen followed his gaze.

An ominous prompt had been generated by LINDA.

DO YOU WANT TO SEND THE FOLLOWING SELL ORDER "DARTMOUTH BASKET TRADE ON LONDON STOCK EXCHANGE"?
YES   NO

"What does that mean, Freddie?"

"I don't know," Zaraghi frowned. "It's a different trade."

- - -

It was the moment Colbert had spent the night waiting for. With prickles of an almost sexual excitement racing over him, Colbert drew the arrow of the mouse over the YES icon and clicked the left button. The screen prompt immediately disappeared from view and was replaced with the following:

CONFIRMING . . . CONFIRMING . . . CONFIRMING . . .

- - -

"Confirming?" Hansen asked. "Confirming what? I thought your system was fully automated."

"It is, but I built a threshold safeguard into the protocol. Any time there's an order created that exceeds the largest trade in dollar-volume in LINDA's memory, it asks the user to confirm that it's all right to send it. That's what just happened now. And the asshole who stole my program just went ahead and confirmed the order."

McGeary?

CONFIRMING . . . CONFIRMING . . . CONFIRMING . . .

"What's happening now?" Hansen asked.

"LINDA is working the order on London's SEAQ system. Waiting for the trade to be executed with counterparties on the London Stock Exchange."

The Stock Exchange Automated Quotations system, Hansen knew, was the electronic trading system linking dealers to the London equity markets via computers. SEAQ permitted users to trade U.S. stocks overseas on the London Stock Exchange, which was frequently done by large institutions during the hours the New York Stock Exchange was closed.

Helplessly, they watched the stocks loading up on the system one by one, and the dollar volume ratcheting up. All blue-chip stocks that were components of major stock indexes. A chill raced through Hansen's flesh as he realized that the total of the executions so far were quickly running up into the billions of dollars. A window calculated the value to be over ten billion dollars' worth of stock. *Ten billion dollars.*

In another half-minute, LINDA flashed a message:

YOUR TRADE(S) HAS/HAVE BEEN CONFIRMED AS EXECUTED.

"They're done," Zaraghi said flatly.

"Done?" Hansen demanded. "What does that mean?"

His answer came not from Zaraghi, but from the machines surrounding them. All around them, blackened computer screens began to light up, one after the other, flickering with activity. Within seconds, nearly two dozen Sun SPARCStation screens had lit up, each whirring industriously.

Zaraghi stood up and whipped his head around, cursing softly as the machines came to life.

"Freddie, talk to me, what the hell's happening?"

Zaraghi screwed his face up in frustration. "Phase two. LINDA's loading itself onto other computers. It's preparing to flood the stock exchanges with sell orders when the market opens at nine-thirty." Zaraghi turned to Hansen and said sarcastically, "Hey, maybe you were right. One computer can't crash the stock market. But maybe twenty-two of them can."

McGeary. They had just over three hours to get to McGeary.

Fifty

THE WORKDAY PILGRIMAGE to the southernmost tip of Manhattan was in full gear that Friday morning. Commuter trains converged on the city from the grassy suburbs of New Jersey, Connecticut, Long Island and Westchester, packed standing-room-only with bond traders, securities research analysts and stockbrokers. Subway trains brought the secretaries and receptionists in from the outer boroughs. The young analysts shared cabs down the FDR from their one-bedroom co-ops on the Upper East Side and the West Side. By the time the equity markets opened at 9:30 that morning, Wall Street would be populated by 237,000 workers, a virtual city roughly the size of Norfolk, Virginia, or St. Petersburg, Florida.

At 44 Wall Street, a handful of early-bird Wolcott Fulbright employees filed into the main entrance of the building, reporting to their posts for the upcoming trading session. Gil McGeary was among them. The desk head gulped down a scone from a vendor's cart and chased it with gulps of coffee. Last night's meeting had gone on into the wee hours of the morning; they were reconvening at 6:30 A.M. McGeary had his game face on and was prepared to do battle.

7:07 A.M.

"Personally, I still think a crash is in the cards," Joe Money was saying. "And this Dartmouth thing could be the beginning of the end."

The morning call was conducted in the Kuala Lumpur conference room without McGeary. In satellite offices around the world, everyone was buzzing about the desk head's marathon negotiating sessions with the Risk Management Task Force, which was also the final arbiter of this year's discretionary bonus pay outs. Final "comp" numbers had to be in to Accounting by noon today in order to hit the month-end paychecks. McGeary's hard-line stance for the Derivatives group was threatening to disrupt the entire process worldwide, no doubt a bargaining chip he was using to his advantage. Accordingly, Magilla was tied up in a final closed-door session with the brass, completely inaccessible until the markets opened at 9:30 A.M.

In the Kuala Lumpur room, the talk turned to the overseas markets. Everyone was adrenalized by the big trade done by Dartmouth Funds Group on the floor of the London Stock Exchange through the SEAQ electronic trading system. Nigel Playford, the derivatives trader in London, reported that Dartmouth's move was a clear sign to the market that at least one widely respected investment management institution was bailing out of U.S. blue-chip stocks in a big way.

"According to the whisper circuit," Julian Stainsby reported, "the Big Three car company pension plans are studying the Dartmouth move. They may follow into cash."

There was a murmur of concurrence. True, most of the people in that room had been pimple-faced Nintendo addicts when the Crash of 1987 decimated the stock markets over a decade ago; their brief careers on Wall Street had bracketed the $5 trillion increase in Americans' wealth since the bull market began in the winter of 1991. Still, they had the sense to know the bubble had to burst sometime. A downturn was an historical inevitability. The question was whether it would be a "healthy correction" that played itself out over time, or a vicious nuclear meltdown that caught millions of investors with their pants down.

"Like trying to catch a falling knife."

"I'm a big buyer of short-dated volatility."

"The captain has turned on the fasten-your-seat-belt sign. It's gonna be a bumpy ride."

The meeting broke up after twenty minutes and the troops returned to their desks to prepare for the quarterly triple-witch expiration. The consensus was that it would be a wild session.

———◆———

Chicago, 7:47 A.M.

Trader Vic arrived at work at his booth on the trading floor of the Chicago Mercantile Exchange to find his sleep-deprived associate Andy Studd in a spectacularly foul mood. Andy's runway-model girlfriend from Kansas, a notorious gold digger, had dumped him unceremoniously for a government bond trader at PaineWebber. Hey, what could Vic say?

He offered some shopworn platitudes about there being plenty of fish in the sea, yada-yada, Andy would know when the right one came along, yada-yada, the only thing in a man's pants that Miranda really cared about was his wallet, and so forth. When this failed to raise his spirits, Vic grabbed him by the shoulder and said, "Andy, listen to me. Yeah, it hurts, but you just got to suck it up. It's freaking triple-witch expiry and we got work to do. Now let's get some color on this trade Dartmouth did in London."

Over the next fifteen minutes, Trader Vic and Andy plugged into the buzz on the Merc trading floor. According to the phone clerks from Refco and JP Morgan, big sellers were prepared to blow out substantial stock inventory at the opening bell, which would place enormous downward pressure on stock-index futures. Of course, on the Merc trading floor, you had to be careful about the veracity of such rumors, which were often disinformation calculated to fake out the upstairs traders in New York. But the Refco guy was a drinking buddy of Vic's, and had never steered him wrong before. Vic hopped on the hoot'n'holler to broadcast his findings to his New York audience. "Good morning, Apple, greetings from the Windy City. Lots of whispers that Dartmouth's big sale, make that capital B-I-G sale, of blue-chip stocks in London this morning has severely weakened an already very nervous market. Others are expected to move in from the sidelines. We're expecting a very fast market for equity futures when the market opens. Over and out for now."

———●———

Long Beach, California, 8:17 A.M. EST.

His spirits soaring, Eddie Slamkowski arrived at the modest offices of Infinity Technology and flicked on the overhead lights. The predawn surf had made for spectacular surfing—totally tubular, as Derf had called it. On top of that, things were coming together for him back in Chicago. Trader Vic had scored him a cheap two-bedroom apartment not too far from the East Bank Club. Vic put a deposit down on the place as Slam's proxy, and Eddie was free to move in anytime after April 15. The Merc membership people predicted that his floor trader badge would be approved by May 1—thus, Slam would be trading in the S&P pits in just over a month's time. *Back where he belonged!*

The Mr. Coffee was brewing in the tiny kitchen alcove, and as he waited, Slam realized he was not going to miss these crappy Kilroy Airport offices. Nor would he miss the irrational tirades of Chuckie Stone. *Weird*, Slamkowski thought, weird that he would never meet the man for whom he worked for five months. Then again, *so what?* Slam's brief stint with Infinity would just be a quirky footnote on the résumé anyway, brushed over as just a way he'd paid the light bills while he went through the *surfer phase* of his life. Sayonara, Mr. Stone.

Slam fired up the trading systems to see what mischief had transpired in the overseas equity markets while he slept. *Holy crow!* Stone's biggest customer—Dartmouth Funds Group—had done a big-ass transaction in London just a few hours ago. Ten billion dollars of sell orders, mostly in the thirty component stocks of the Dow Jones Industrial Average!

The phone rang. It was Trader Vic. Vic wasted no time on small talk when he was on the hunt for market color. "Hey, Slam, Dartmouth is your customer, isn't it?"

"Yeah, Stone's biggest."

"Inquiring minds want to know. What's up with that humongous trade they did in London last night?"

"Damned if I know," Slam replied. "It went over SEAQ as an electronic trade while I was in REM mode. But the ripple effect on that one could be nasty."

———•———

The Russians wore the standard-issue navy blue uniforms of Wolcott Fulbright's third-party internal security provider. They carried Wolcott Fulbright identification credentials. Accordingly, no one questioned them as they conducted a floor-by-floor search of the premises for the lawyer and the computer programmer.

The search failed to locate them. They regrouped in the lobby of the building. The Gargoyle voiced his belief that they were now in the BEACON facility. The thought unsettled Alexeyev. He extended the telescoping antenna of the cellphone to its full length and called the financier. "We need immediate access to the facility. Have you contacted Stiletto?"

"I can't raise him. Await further instructions."

Colbert hung up before Alexeyev could protest.

———•———

Bedminster, New Jersey, 8:35 A.M.

Senior manager Ray Nysinger had already put nearly two hours into the workday when the shift change brought Ed Savage, John Certo and Wayne Bernier to their posts at the phone company's Network Operations Center. As chief systems security officer of the NOC, it was Ray Nysinger's mandate to ensure that the telephone switcher systems were perpetually on-line, that any glitches to the hardware or software were contained or repaired without disruption to service.

The general public had ridiculously high expectations of flawlessness in phone service. In truth, the teleco company had no one but itself to blame for that. Because of its phenomenal quality control standards and vast investment in technology, ordinary people had come to expect that when they picked a phone up off its receiver, there would be a dial tone. Punch in a number, and the call would go through, someone would pick up on the other end, and a crystal-clear dialogue would commence. Phone service was just there, like the air you breathe, the sun that rises each day. Under Ray's watch, that virtually impossible standard had largely been met.

Dirty job, but somebody has to do it, he often told friends. *Namely, somebody with three daughters about to enter private colleges.*

"Morning, Ray," Savage said as Nysinger drifted past. "Still having trouble sleeping, huh?"

Nysinger nodded warily, worried that his middle-age insomnia was so evident to his underlings. He turned his bleary eyes toward the bank of seventy-five Sony high-resolution video screens along the wall, one hundred feet wide and one story tall. The NOC was the cinematic replica of the Pentagon's most visually stunning war-situation room. Cryptic alphanumeric status reports skidded across the screens, which, as a contiguous unit, was a glowing map of the United States, Canada, Mexico, Europe and Asia.

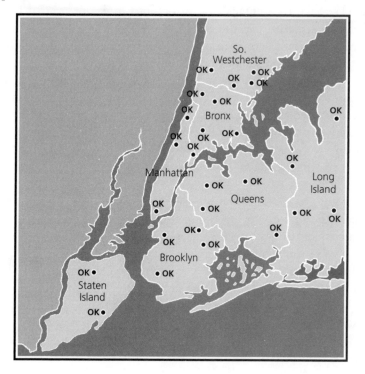

"How're we looking today?" Nysinger asked.

Savage pecked at a single hot key and an instant status report flickered on his screen.

"Business as usual," Savage replied around a Dunkin' Donut. "They repaired the glitch in Queens and everything is smooth sailing. See, nothing to lose sleep over." He winked at the boss. "Now tell me about the oldest. Has she picked a school yet?"

———•———

8:42 A.M.

That morning at the cavernous icon of global finance—the floor of the New York Stock Exchange—the molecules were bouncing off the wall. *Something was going on*, according to the buzz of the specialists and market-makers in the brightly colored jackets who populated the floor.

The fabled exchange floor itself was actually reminiscent of a high-school gymnasium. It was constructed of narrow planks of polished wood and had a worn blue stripe dissecting its length (meant to help guide first-time visitors to the floor to their destination). The massive air conditioning systems recessed into the ceilings blew an arctic chill over the throngs collecting in the trading posts below. The posts were sprawling, podlike structures that served as a kind of convenience store for stocks. Like the tentacles of an octopus, poles protruded from the trading post structures, at the end of which was a liquid-crystal Hewlett-Packard Pixelvision screen displaying the latest trading data. The specialists and market-makers stood behind the posts, providing liquidity to buyers and sellers of the stocks. IBM Thinkpads were used throughout the floor for entering data. The old technology (clattering keyboards and color-coded trading tickets) meshed with the new (the high-tech computers of prominent NYSE-listed companies like IBM and Hewlett-Packard).

The talk that morning centered on predicting the behavior of the markets, a daily ritual.

"You guys hear about that big-ass trade Dartmouth did in London?"

"Yeah, ten billion worth of blue chips."

"The arbies are going to wade in today," predicted one of the specialists, "raise the level of the ocean."

"This is the point where the U.S. markets decouple from the European markets."

"When it happens, the correction is gonna be ugly. You heard it here first, sports fans."

———

8:54 A.M.

The screen of the SPARCStation suddenly displayed the following:

WELCOME TO WOLCOTT FULBRIGHT'S
SECURITIES TRADE ENTRY AND PROCESSING
SYSTEM (STEPS)
PLEASE ENTER PASSWORD NOW.

Zaraghi jumped up from his chair and pumped his fist in the air triumphantly. "Yessssss."

Rick Hansen hung up on Kilmartin's voice mail and raced over to the kid. "What happened?"

"A breakthrough. The Hekemian box found a back door to your firm's UNIX protocol. I've gained access to the system."

Finally, some good news! "You're in? That's great."

"Don't uncork the champagne yet, kemo sabe. Now I have to crack the password to Wolcott's electronic trading system."

Hansen's euphoria instantly deflated. "Is that doable in just a half-hour?"

"No money-back guarantees, but I'm sure gonna give it the old college try." Zaraghi pulled a floppy disk from his bag. The disk had a crude drawing of a skull-and-crossbones on it and the words THE PHRACKER'S TOOLKIT. The kid inserted it into the floppy drive bay of his laptop, and activated a "password-sniffing" utility. The screen filled with indecipherable computer-speak that signified an attempt to crack the STEPS system password.

Hansen felt queasy as he watched it go to work. He wondered what was going on in the head of LINDA's creator. "How you holdin' up, Freddie?"

"Me? I'm scared shitless," the kid replied with a grimace. "Scared shitless."

That was good. Zaraghi should not be as emotionless as the system he created. Hansen jotted down the number of the phone extension on a piece of paper. "I'm going to the trading floor to find McGeary, get the password."

"That would be awesome. When will you be back?"

"*Definitely* before nine-thirty."

Fully adrenalized, Hansen left Zaraghi by himself in the BEACON facility and sprinted for the elevator.

Pittsburgh, Pennsylvania, 9:00 A.M.

With the cold, detached precision that machine intelligence possesses, LINDA activated the Backbone network of supercomputers and prepared to devastate the global financial markets. The connection with the Wolcott Fulbright backup computer network and the Internet links with the electronic order routing trading systems of thirty-two financial service firms around the world had long ago been established. Now LINDA was prepared to prompt its user to confirm the next $10 billion in sell orders to occur on the opening bell of the stock exchanges.

There were two ways to sell stock on the stock exchanges—phoning the orders in to a real, live broker on the floor of the exchange, or entering them electronically through the "direct order transmission" lines of the stock exchanges. In the electronic method, the exchanges' systems accept the orders via computer, then routes them automatically to the appropriate specialist post. For customers, it was much faster than the human alternative; whereas it took an exchange floor specialist sixty seconds to turn around an order to buy or sell stock, it took the program trading wires an average of twenty-two seconds to receive, execute *and* report back the trade.

The electronic trading systems were far and away the most efficient way to get orders executed—in practice, 85 percent of each day's trading volume was conducted through the electronic trading lines of the public switched network of phone lines. More important, electronic orders were instantly and irrevocably executed. Once the genie was out of the bottle, you couldn't stuff it back in. Which was precisely what Colbert was banking on.

At 9:00:00 A.M., LINDA automatically blipped up its doomsday prompt for Colbert's consideration.

9:00:07 A.M.

With a breakfast of dry toast and lukewarm tea, Colbert scrutinized the machinery in his suite with an intense gaze. The tingle of anticipation was like none he'd ever experienced before. Colbert flipped on the television to watch *Squawk Box*, the early morning financial markets show on CNBC. The off-board Dartmouth sale was the top story of the hour, and had created enormous speculation on both sides of the ocean. *What was Dartmouth up to?* Everyone was wondering. Dartmouth itself was playing coy. A company spokesman would state only that Dartmouth believed a massive stock market correction in the immediate future was inevitable. The spokesman was identified as Charles Stone.

Colbert issued a guttural laugh at the mention of his doppelgänger on national television.

Suddenly, an insistent beeping erupted from the computer.

Colbert turned to the screen.

ARE YOU SURE YOU WANT TO SEND "SELL ORDER(S) TO STOCK EXCHANGE(S)"? YES / NO.

Oh, yes, yes indeed. *Click*. The machine whirred for several seconds. Then, the ungrammatical confirmation abruptly appeared on the screen. "SELL ORDER(S) TO STOCK EXCHANGE(S)" HAS BEEN CONFIRMED. Colbert grinned. This was too easy. With a single mouse-click, the fuse had been lit. Once the market opened for business, the real carnage would begin. The moment was hurtling toward him . . .

———•———

Zaraghi howled in anguish. The safeguard prompt he had built into the system blipped up tantalyzingly on the Sun SPARCStation screen before him. ARE YOU SURE YOU WANT TO SEND "SELL ORDER(S) TO STOCK EXCHANGE(S)"? YES / NO. But he had no access to LINDA, so he could not click the NO icon. The keyboard that accessed the Wolcott system was locked away in a cage under the trading turret, in full view but completely inaccessible. Meanwhile, the bastard who had stolen his program clicked YES, and LINDA began teeing up another $10 billion in sell orders. Freddie's creation was readying a devastating blow to the economy, and he was powerless to stop it.

Unless . . .

He thought about the disk loaded in his laptop. THE PHRACKER'S TOOLKIT. To be sure, there was evil embedded on the magnetic storage disk inside that square piece of gray plastic, pure evil. But now Freddie was viewing it from a different perspective. Considering the circumstances, THE PHRACKER'S TOOLKIT might contain a particularly *useful* evil . . .

———•———

9:06 A.M.

Once again, it was Joseph "Joe Money" Monetti who first noticed the news on the Dow Jones Newswire.

"Whoa, check this out," he yelled to the others, waving frantically at his computer screen.

9:06   DJN—AT&T Corp. Sell Imbalance: 546,900 Shrs

9:06   DJN—AlliedSignal Inc. Sell Imbalance: 313,700 Shrs

9:06   DJN—Aluminum Co. of America Sell Imbalance: 345,000 Shrs

9:06   DJN—American Express Co. Sell Imbalance: 412,900 Shrs

9:06   DJN—Boeing Co. Sell Imbalance: 441,700 Shrs

9:06   DJN—Caterpillar Inc. Sell Imbalance: 316,500 Shrs

9:06   DJN—Chevron Corp. Sell Imbalance: 446,700 Shrs

9:06   DJN—Coca-Cola Co. Sell Imbalance: 546,000 Shrs

9:06   DJN—Walt Disney Co. Sell Imbalance: 511,000 Shrs

9:06   DJN—DuPont Co. Sell Imbalance: 346,300 Shrs

9:06   DJN—Eastman Kodak Co. Sell Imbalance: 398,800 Shrs

9:06   DJN—Exxon Corp. Sell Imbalance: 426,400 Shrs

"They're all stocks in the Dow," Danny Partridge observed.

Julian's mouth flattened into a straight line. "What the hell's happening? Are those just sellers coattailing the Dartmouth trade?"

Joe Money said, "They're just early indications of sell pressure prior to the open. Big program trades. The specialists are asking for buyers to come in and offset the imbalances."

Danny Partridge shook his head. "The market's going in a straight line to Mexico at the opening bell, I can promise you that."

———•———

Detroit, 9:11 A.M. EST.

Pension manager Will Barclay peered at his Bloomberg trading screen and mutter-cursed to himself. What the hell was happening in the markets today?

As an investment manager responsible for a $32 billion piece of the pension plan for one of the Big Three American automotive manufacturers, Will's livelihood depended upon how well he shepherded the assets of several million blue-collar workers who were entitled to that pension money once they retired. Will had been in the game long enough to recognize that when the storm clouds gathered, the only prudent course of action was to seek shelter. It was time to go liquid.

He speed-dialed Jennifer Cleary, his relationship manager at Merrill Lynch. It was a special number dedicated to Barclay, and Cleary was trained to drop all other calls for his. "Good morning, Will," Jennifer answered brightly.

"Say, Jenn, any insight on this sell pressure?"

"All we know is that Dartmouth was a multibillion-dollar seller of blue chips in London before the market opened, and that the program trading sell orders are burning up the lines."

"We've hit the wall, Jenn, don't you think?"

"We just might have. I don't know, Will. Frankly, our analysts don't know what to make of it."

Barclay sighed. "Well, the bull market was good while it lasted, wasn't it? Okay, Jenn, I want you to begin reducing my equity exposure over the course of the day. I want to bring the portfolio down twenty percent, go to cash."

"Okay," Jennifer Cleary tried to keep her voice steady. "At market?"

"Use your discretion. I want it done with the utmost in confidentiality. I don't want people blaming Detroit for the carnage."

"I'll take care of it," Jennifer said. She meant it. Barclay's account meant hundreds of thousands in revenue to the firm and would prove to be her ticket to managing director at Merrill. Far as she was concerned, there was no greater calling on God's green earth than Will Barclay's account.

She prepared an order ticket to liquidate $6 billion worth of stock on the floor of the New York Stock Exchange throughout the trading session.

9:17.

Hansen arrived on the trading floor. "Anyone see McGeary? I need him *right now*."

The derivatives personnel did not pull their eyes away from their screens, waiting to see what would happen when the markets opened in thirteen minutes. "He's out of pocket until around nine-thirty," Danny Partridge said. "Comp meeting with the brass."

Hansen said, "I really need to speak with him *right now*."

Stainsby turned toward him. "Quite sorry, Rick, but he's not reachable. We don't even know where he is at the moment. Anything we can help with?"

"Do any of you guys know the password for the electronic trading system?"

Stainsby's eyebrows climbed his forehead. "You mean the password to STEPS? Only McGeary knows what that is. Everything okay?"

Hansen took a deep breath and let it out. "No problem. It can wait until he gets back." *No need to spread panic.*

The traders turned back to their screens and worked the phones.

For Hansen, the world had taken on a jerky, unreal quality. Was a nuclear winter really about to set in in just under thirteen minutes' time? It was . . . unimaginable. Rick picked up the phone at the trading turret and dialed Zaraghi's extension at the BEACON facility.

"Yeh," Freddie Zaraghi barked. "You got a password for me?"

"No. I can't find McGeary. We need to do something."

"What do you propose?" Zaraghi asked distractedly. The sound of furious keystrokes were heard in the background.

"I could call someone at the stock exchange."

"What would you tell them? That a computer system's rigged to crash the stock market? They'd laugh and hang up on you."

Hansen whirled around in the swivel chair and glimpsed the computer screen. Somewhere inside the Wolcott Fulbright computer network, an orchestra of circuits, wires and motherboards was cueing up a datastream of sell orders designed to destroy the American economy in the next seven hundred seconds. Hansen slammed his fist on the surface of the turret. "Goddammit! Do we have to sit back and let this happen?"

Zaraghi said in a tentative tone. "There is one option."

A last ember of hope. "What?"

"It goes against everything I believe in, you know."

"There's no time for philosophy, Freddie."

"It's a major computer hack. I mean *major*. Can you live with that?"

Hansen froze. What choice did they have? "Listen, just do whatever it takes. I don't care if it means tearing up the floorboards and ripping out the goddamned cables. Just do it."

"Gotcha. Rick, after all is said and done? This is not your doing, remember that. I'll take full responsibility." With that cryptic message, Freddie Zaraghi replaced the phone on its cradle.

What did he mean by that?

————◆————

Watch out what you wish for. The maxim popped into Freddie Zaraghi's mind as he prepared to commit the unthinkable. Maybe he should have come clean with the lawyer, told him what he had in mind. But what purpose would that have served? Zaraghi could not be dissuaded. Hansen was right; it was his monster, he alone had to destroy it. Better that the lawyer was not complicit in the act.

Like an electronic sorcerer, Zaraghi hunched over his keyboard and began scrabbling furiously at the keyboard. He activated a file named ESSSHELL.EXE on the floppy disk named THE PHRACKER'S TOOLKIT. The file began loading up.

Talk about ironic: Freddie Zaraghi had reverse-engineered the underground hackers' software in his fight against information terrorists. Now he was using it to commit one of their most heinous crimes.

But there really was no choice. A lesser evil was being committed to prevent a greater evil.

In the space of one hundred seconds, Freddie Zaraghi strung together a series of letters and digits that, though meaningless in appearance to the layman, would make headlines the following day.

At the end of the series of commands, the ring finger on his right hand casually but assuredly struck the ENTER key, sealing the fate, affecting the lives of 1.2 million people.

"Lock and load," he said, closing his eyes. "Lock and load."

Fifty-one

ZARAGHI'S KEYSTROKES PROMPTLY impacted Ray Nysinger's group in New Jersey.

Ray first learned about it from a brusque call from Ed Savage. Nysinger was in his windowless office upstairs, drawing up the preliminary budgets for the third quarter and working his way down a sixteen-ounce cup of cafeteria-awful coffee when the phone tweeted. "Nysinger."

"Ray, we got real trouble."

The frenetic tenor in Ed's otherwise calm, dispassionate voice immediately relayed the urgency of the matter to Nysinger. "What kind?"

"CMS is relaying a possible trunk-failure message."

Shit. "TERESA pinpoint the location yet?"

"Broadway 51 ESS," Ed responded. "Lower Manhattan."

The financial district, Nysinger realized. "I'm on my way down."

The teleco had an emergency task force of a dozen people staffing the NOC to monitor and control the millions of miles of phone lines, satellites, fiber optics and computers that comprise the network. Certo, Bernier and Savage were his go-to guys, the senior technical engineers.

When he got to the Situation Room, he saw the three engineers huddled around a workstation. "Okay, bottom-line me. Is it a roach in the kitchen, or an alligator in the bedroom? Temporary overload?" The guess he ventured was grounded more in hope than in likelihood.

"My hunch is that it's localized systemic failure," said Wayne Bernier.

"Hard or soft?"

Bernier replied without looking up from the keyboard. "Don't know yet. Doesn't appear to be physical. My first guess is that it's maybe a glitch in the Signaling System 7 software."

"Shit." Hands down, the NOC team preferred hardware problems over software glitches. Hardware problems were defined black-or-white physical situations, easily identified and, if not always easily repaired, at least always isolated. Phone service could always be rerouted to another, functioning 5ESS switching station. But software—software was the wild-card nightmare of the teleco engineer whose livelihood depended upon his ability to protect the integrity of the telecommunications network. "Well, people, let's not guess, let's do. Let's dispatch some bodies down there to goose-eye the circuit pack for damage."

"Already done, but it's not a hardware outage, boss," John Certo said, in his often-imitated high-pitched whine. "It's software."

"Why do you say that?" Nysinger said.

"It's replicating." He pointed to the illuminated map of color monitors along the wall. The colors in the Manhattan section of the map were changing from a placid blue to an alarmingly bright screaming magenta. "5ESS at White Plains is partially disabled now."

"My God." *Somebody's hacked into the X.25 protocol,* Nysinger thought, as his stomach collapsed into a ball. *Hackers!*

The number of ways the software-reliant public switching system could fail was infinite; it was impossible to fully duplicate conditions in the real world in anticipating catastrophic failure of the phone system. Yet the public had come to expect perfection from the phone companies. Anytime that reliability was threatened, the teleco faced an enormous public relations nightmare the following day. Hey, if Con Ed had something of a blackout for eight hours, it happens. The subway could get mucked up for hours, what can you do? But let the phone service be interrupted for even three minutes, people were writing their congressman, as if the teleco had committed treason against the United States of America itself.

The last time it happened was January 15, 1990. A fairly routine failure in a Manhattan switching center set in motion a chain reaction that froze AT&T's long-distance network, cutting calling capacity in half for eight and a half hours, knocking out telephone service completely for seven and a half hours and causing seventy million phone calls to go uncompleted.

A January fifteenth scenario was playing out, right here, right now. This was Nysinger's *Apollo 13* mission, his *Hindenburg,* his very own personal January fifteenth. Already he was imaging the scenes in his superior's office, the end-of-day assessment, the looking-over-the-shoulder analysis, Monday-morning quarterbacking. *Did you think to do it this way, Ray?* Nysinger dismissed it from his mind. There was work to do.

The team had figured it to be software—okay, fine, now they had to get to the nitty-gritty. "Hard fault or transient?" Nysinger barked.

"Normal fault recovery routine is engaged and it's a no-go," Bernier said. What Bernier meant was that the 5ESS station was trying to repair itself. Fifth-generation electronic switching stations used their own fer-rod scanners to check the condition of the lines and trunks, and would send a message through TERESA to the Bedminster team. It took only four to six seconds for a troubled 5ESS switch to drop all calls and reboot itself from scratch. In a less serious instance, the reboot would be enough to put the switcher back in operation. The reboots were not succeeding with the Broadway 51 switching system. "It's definitely hard."

"Has service been affected yet?"

"No, we're still alive, but barely."

"Long distance?"

"Unaffected. These are still local switches that have been infected."

"Okay, fellas, here's the million-dollar question. Bug . . . or bomb?"

The others did not answer right away. After all, it was *the* million-dollar question. If it was a bug, it could be isolated and repaired in short order. But if it was a logic bomb planted by some malicious hacker moth-erjumpers, there was no telling where it would end.

"Too soon to tell," Certo squeaked.

Before their very eyes, the maps changed color. Went from blue to green to yellow to red.

"It's spreading! We're in seizure mode."

That answered the question: it was a logic bomb.

"Can we reroute the calls to another switching station?"

"We're already doing that, but every time we do, it infects the new switch."

"Oh, no!" Certo cried out in genuine anguish.

"What is it?" Nysinger said, already knowing the answer.

"Local service is going down in Lower Manhattan."

Wall Street.

———◆———

All throughout the lower quadrant of Wall Street there erupted a chorus of "what the hell" as the phone system shut down, disrupting tens of thousands of calls between Wall Streeters and buy-side customers strategizing about the weakness in the equity markets.

An unprecedented silence overtook the floor of the great room of the New York Stock Exchange. The phones had simply *ceased ringing.* Con-versations had been rudely cut off in mid-sentence. Activity had ground to a screeching halt: no business could be conducted without the tie-lines tethering the NYSE personnel to the outside world. Everyone turned to the liquid-crystal display of the tickers to reference stock prices. There were no symbols displayed, no prices. Just ERR . . . ERR . . . ERR . . . Some wise-guy specialist shouted out over the pall, "I'm going short ten thou Ma Bell, any takers?" No one laughed.

———◆———

"Looks like the market's about to turn colder than a mother-in-law's kiss," Julian Stainsby was telling the trader at Tiger when there was an abrupt electronic click, then silence. "What the hell?" he said aloud, staring at the useless receiver in his hand.

Confusion reigned on the equity floor of Wolcott Fulbright, as traders and salespeople experienced the same disruption. They stabbed desperately at the two-hundred-button consoles, looking for a live line, all in vain.

"The phone lines are dead!" shouted Joe Money.

"Goddammit!"

"Someone call Systems!"

"The market opens in two minutes! We can't be closed out or we're going to get smeared!"

Waiting in a seat outside McGeary's office, Rick Hansen surveyed the chaos on the trading floor. Cutting off external phone service was like depriving the marketing force of oxygen; they simply could not live without it. Wolcott Fulbright had ground to a screeching halt. Hansen punched 44, the prefix for internal calls and found the in-house phone lines had been unaffected. He dialed up Zaraghi again. "Freddie?"

"Yeh." The kid's voice was melancholy.

"Freddie? Did you do *this*?"

"I'm sorry, Rick. There was no choice."

Hansen felt pinpricks in his midsection. "What choice did you make, Freddie?"

"In the words of Lieutenant Calley, to save the village I had to destroy it. I temporarily disabled local phone service."

"*What?*"

"Don't be mad. They can fix it in about fifteen minutes. It's just that we needed to buy some time to figure out the password."

Hansen buried his head in his hands. "What *exactly* did you do?"

"Um, I used an underground hacker's shell sequence to throw the telephone company's electronic switching network into an endless loop. But remember, it is reversible, Rick. Rick? Rick, you there?"

The horror raced through Hansen as he realized the enormity of the mind-bending act of sabotage necessary to save Wall Street from destruction. Hansen had aided and abetted a very serious federal offense. One that would cost him his job and his license to practice law . . . "Omigod," Hansen suddenly blurted.

"Chief? You still there?"

"I really have to hang up now," Hansen said. "Gil McGeary just stepped onto the floor."

———•———

"We've got to stop meeting this way," the senior-level guy from the Pacific Stock Exchange quipped.

No one laughed. Nothing about this situation warranted humor.

The fourteen participants from the national stock exchanges, the futures exchanges, as well as SEC, the CFTC, the Fed and the Treasury were connected by a special T-1 cellular satellite uplink, which had been established for an emergency such as this. There was no time for roll call to be taken.

The Chairman of the New York Stock Exchange cleared his throat and led the discussion. "As you know, there has been an unprecedented systemic failure of the phone lines in lower Manhattan. A delay in opening the markets for trading is unavoidable. At this time, we have no word on the cause of the outage, nor do we know when the glitch will be fixed. That said, we intend to open the market either at ten A.M. or fifteen minutes after service has been restored, whichever is later, of course. Any questions?"

There were none.

"Because we expect the cellular lines to be besieged, we will leave the cellular uplink open. We will reconvene as soon as there is any news to report. Thank you."

———•———

At the St. Regis, Colbert stared at his screen uncomprehendingly. The screens had blinked abruptly, gone black, then displayed the message: OPERATION INTERRUPT! After that, the activity on the screen simply died.

Colbert tried the phone lines. Dead. Two minutes before the orders were supposed to be executed? What sort of lousy luck was that? Or perhaps luck had nothing to do with it . . .

Alexeyev's words from the previous night came back to him. *Zaraghi could pose a threat if he gained access to the Wolcott computers running the software program.* Was it all a coincidence? Or did the computer expert have something to do with this?

The financier grabbed his cellular phone and called Stiletto's cell-phone. He was relieved to have not gotten an all-circuits-busy message. Once Stiletto picked up, he yelled, "Where have you been?"

"Comp meetings."

"Fuck that! The Russians are going to need access to the BEACON site. *Immediately*. Meet them in the lobby."

Rick followed the desk head into his office. As was the case with half the traders on the equity trading floor, McGeary had a cellphone pressed to his ear, talking to someone. He noticed Hansen frowned and said, "Listen, honey, I've got to go." He disconnected and faced Rick. "Morning, counselor, not much for a trader to do with all the phone lines down, huh? What can I do you for?"

"McGeary—"

"Yeah?"

"Who was that?"

"My wife actually . . . what's it to you?" McGeary said it playfully.

A surreal calm suffused Hansen. "The game is over, Magilla."

"Game? What game? I'm not following you, Counselor."

"I want the password to STEPS."

McGeary locked eyes with Hansen. "The password to *what*?"

"*You know what!* The electronic trading system."

"What? Why the *fuck* should I give that to *you*?"

"You know goddamned well why. Meltdown's gonna happen . . . *you're* behind it—"

"Goddamned right I am. I been saying all along the bubble's gonna burst. It's a Samhain full moon, Counselor, and I've got a boatload of short calls riding on this expiration—"

The bastard was playing cute. Hansen flashed him the black-and-yellow cigar band. "You left this behind in the BEACON facility."

Gil McGeary peered at the paper loop and seemed genuinely confused. "How do you know about BEACON?"

There was no time for conjecture. "Give me the password now or I go directly to Milgrim!"

"You threatening me, Hansen?"

Hansen yelled, "*Give me the goddamned password, McGeary!*"

The cold-blooded calm of the careerist speculator overtook McGeary. Confrontation always brought out the best in him. "I should say screw off, Counselor, but hey, you're the lawyer, right? You *must* have a good reason for asking for it. It's MUDHENS, all caps, no space."

Hansen scooped up the phone and dialed Zaraghi's extension. "It's MUDHENS, all caps, no space. Got it? Good. I'll be right down."

"You'd better know what you're messing with," Gil McGeary said ominously. "From this point forward, I disclaim all responsibility."

The lawyer jammed the phone back down on the hook and raced out of the trader's office.

Fifty-two

AT THE BEDMINSTER FACILITY, the engineers stood around the monitor for what seemed an eternity, like an emergency room team that, while still performing triage, watched the flatline of their expired patient in mute disbelief. *What did they expect from us?* Nysinger thought in that instant. *Miracles? Yes, that's what they expect.* But you live by the technology sword, you die by that sword. The more humans cede responsibility to machines like electronic switching systems, the more likely it was you ended up with a chocolate mess, like this one.

Certo adjusted his QuietKey QWERTY keyboard and viciously stabbed at the buttons. Within seconds, he launched an experimental countervirus program that he had been working for the last several months with Cheswick at Bell Labs. The electronic impulses carrying the code raced over the dedicated wires to the network of the ESS system, seeking out the programs that had been infected by the intruder's Trojan Horse virus. "Okay," Certo said to the chunk of software that had infiltrated the system. "You're there, safe and sound. Let's see you do the voodoo that you doo-doo."

This was the voodoo that it was expected to doo-doo—it would scan the ten million lines of code in the affected ESS software of each switcher, review the lines that had been altered in the last thirty minutes (which under ordinary conditions would have been none), perform an undelete function, and restore the corrupted lines of program to their rightful status.

For the next seventy-five seconds, they watched the status on the map.

"Something's happening," Bernier muttered.

And then, suddenly, abruptly, wonderfully, the ESS switcher in lower

Broadway flashed from red to green. The switcher was rebooting itself. Service was coming back on-line.

In the next instant Ed Savage shouted, "Broadway 51's alive!"

A huge cheer arose from the engineers in the Bedminster facility, as they slapped John Certo on the back. The squeaky-voiced lad from MIT had just attained instant-hero status.

———•———

Moments later, a huzzah arose on the trading floor of broker-dealers all over the southern tip of Manhattan as dial tones clicked back on in the turrets. They were back in business!

The Chairman of the Stock Exchange got on the cellular uplink and stated, "All New York securities exchanges will resume business at 10:05 A.M., Eastern Standard Time."

———•———

Hansen returned to the BEACON trading facility, hoping for the best. Running up to Zaraghi, he shouted, "Did it work?"

Zaraghi was too busy to reply.

Looking over the kid's shoulder, Hansen saw what was on the screen of the Gateway laptop. PASSWORD ACCEPTED. WELCOME TO WOLCOTT FULBRIGHT'S STEPS SYSTEM.

Hansen felt a ripple of delirium at the sight.

Within moments, Freddie Zaraghi intuitively stepped through the screen interfaces until he came to Wolcott's electronic trading screen. Hansen recognized it immediately.

"Hit Control-C," he told Zaraghi.

Immediately, the screen flashed the following:

ARE YOU SURE YOU WANT TO CANCEL YOUR TRADE(S)?

Two more keystrokes, and the immediate threat was eliminated.

"Okay," Zaraghi said, with a sigh of relief. "I've canceled all the pending sell orders that were going to go through the Wolcott Fulbright trading system to the exchanges."

"Fantastic." Hansen ran his fingers anxiously through his hair. "That means we're done, right?" It was more of a question, but Hansen expected Zaraghi to confirm it as a statement of fact.

"Not exactly."

"Not exactly? What does *that* mean?"

"They restored the local phone service, you know."

Hansen said, "But you've canceled the orders—"

"Within the next 120 seconds, LINDA will automatically cue up the sell orders again in Pittsburgh and attempt to transmit them to the stock exchanges. If that fails, it will reconstruct them and try again. It will continue to do so until it succeeds."

Hansen was chilled by the Sisyphean feat that now faced them. "So there's nothing we can do? What about accessing the stock exchanges' computers to block the trades?"

"No way possible. The computers at the exchanges are absolutely impenetrable to outsiders. The only way we have access is because of the Wolcott insider."

"So for all that, we just have to stand back and let it happen?"

"No." Zaraghi tapped the screen of his laptop. "Now that I've got access to the Wolcott server, I can reverse-access the Pittsburgh server. There is now a chink in the armor we can exploit with a DOS attack."

"DOS attack? You're going after the operating system?"

"Not that type of DOS. DOS, meaning 'denial of service' attack. The idea is to flood LINDA's server in Pittsburgh with literally millions of nonsensical streams of messages until it runs out of system memory."

"I'm not following you."

"Hope you don't mind if I work while we talk."

"Please."

Freddie began clacking away at his keyboard. "How to describe it? A DOS attack is . . . kind of like that episode from *I Love Lucy* where the conveyor belt at the candy factory kept speeding up and Lucy was forced to stuff her mouth to keep up? Well, I'm going to stuff the mouth of NASCIA with chocolate candy. Except my chocolate candy is actually packets of information. See, we spam the NASCIA server with a feedback loop of thousands of requests for service. The NASCIA system takes seventy-five seconds to verify improper e-mail addresses before rejecting them. It can usually handle about one-hundred packets at once. Well, my laptop will generate a hundred packets a *second*. It's a classic spam-jam—garbage in, garbage out. In theory, and in practice, it's a devastatingly effective way to paralyze a computer system."

"So do it."

"It's going to be a footrace to see if I can knock out Pittsburgh before LINDA can fire the orders through the system. It'll essentially be our machine against theirs."

"Shit. What are the odds that—"

"The odds suck, let's leave it at that."

Once again, Zaraghi went to work to activate the program that would generate the thousands of fictitious requests for verification intended to disable the NASCIA server.

———•———

At 10:05 A.M. the cheers on Wall Street turned to shocked gasps once the brief phone-line glitch was resolved and the stock market opened for business.

The pension plan's sell orders hit the floor of the stock exchange like shockwaves from an earthquake. Two big sellers of stock—Dartmouth Funds Group and the big seller out of Merrill Lynch sent the whisper circuit into overdrive. Prices were in freefall.

Even seasoned veterans on the floor of the New York Stock Exchange were stunned by the ferocity of the selling pressure on the morning of that triple-witch expiration. The NYSE specialists were directly in the path of the freight train.

Specialists are awarded, in effect, a monopoly right to make a market in that security on the exchange floor, in return for which the specialist undertakes certain responsibilities. Specialists were often described as air-traffic controllers. Just as air traffic controllers maintain order among aircraft aloft, specialists maintain a fair and orderly market in the securities assigned to them. The specialists act as catalysts, bringing buyers and sellers together, so that offers to buy can be matched with offers to sell. Specialists are required to maintain current bid and asked prices for stocks, and to buy or sell for their own accounts, against the trend of the market, when there is a temporary shortage of either buyers or sellers. This requires them to commit their own capital or inventory to sustaining the market.

In the case of the current hysteria in the market, however, the specialists were expected to step in and commit their own capital, since there were no buyers coming in to take the other side of the sell transactions. Orders came in so quickly that specialists could not keep up with the order flow.

Before the opening, the specialists were faced with sell imbalances of several hundred thousand shares. The imbalances forced delayed openings in a total of 183 stocks. Of the 30 DJIA stocks, 54 percent of the DJIA's price weight would not open because of the sell imbalances. In response to the imbalances, specialists moved down the prices of their stocks at the opening to the point at which other buying interest would supplement the specialist. Coca-Cola stock traded at the 9:35 A.M. opening with its price dropping 5½ points from the previous day's close. Eastman Kodak's opening price was 13½ points lower than the close on Thursday. Exxon was down 3½ points from the previous close. Fear seized the specialists on the floor of the NYSE that morning. If this kept up, their entire capital base would be wiped out by day's end. *It was Black Monday 1987 all over again!*

As the downward spiral continued, the Chairman of the New York Stock Exchange looked out over the trading floor from his vantage point on the balcony. Seventeen years with the Exchange and he'd never seen a panic like this one. He watched in mute horror as the market downdraft pushed past 300.

Outside the exchange, a fledgling young CNNfn reporter from Columbia Journalism School named Heidi Williamson thrust her microphone at passersby to get the man-of-the-street perspective on the meltdown. The first six people willing to go on-camera uttered variations on the same theme. *In my wildest dreams, I never thought I'd live to experience anything like this.* It was truly something to tell the grandchildren about. Then, in the blink of an eye, the market was down 422 points.

At the Charles Schwab branch in the concourse of the World Trade Center, retirees in their sixties, seventies and eighties collected inside the fishbowl office, gaping in disbelief at the financial carnage. Their retirement funds were evaporating with each passing minute. "Goddamned derivatives," Al Silverman, seventy-two, muttered to his companions. "It's all just computers selling to computers. All those guys with sixty-five credit cards and Porsches who think they're geniuses at age twenty-five, let's see what big shots they are after this." Then the Dow Jones was down 503.

On the West Coast, Eddie Slamkowski watched the proceedings with growing alarm. His father called on the other line. "I can't get out of the market," he told his son. "My broker won't take my calls." Slam sighed. "We're watching history in the making, Dad." "Yeah, and I'm gonna be eating Gainesburgers for the rest of my golden years." Within ten minutes, Slamkowski had sent a computerized trade of his father's stock position over SuperDOT. The market was down 565.

At the Chicago Mercantile Exchange's S&P index futures trading pit, a fistfight broke out in the middle of the trading crowd. The fighting spread and it became an outright free-for-all. Trader Vic stared at the scene as if he were undergoing an out-of-body experience. He'd never seen such chaos in his entire life. The stock market was now down 621.

In his hotel room, Colbert monitored the market with glee. The market was fast approaching 700 points down and already The Contrarians had captured millions and millions in profits. LINDA was performing superbly. The meltdown was happening as advertised.

It's a videogame, a fucking videogame, Hansen said to himself, one in which the graphics were beautiful—brilliantly colorful displays of words and numbers on a magical oracle of a cathode-ray tube. But the endgame here could mean a nuclear winter in the world economy for years to come. The whispery *snick* of mouse-clicks, ordinarily pleasant to the ear, now completely unnerved the lawyer. Hansen gnashed at a fingernail. He stayed back, helplessly watching the titanic struggle. Had it really come down to this? Machine versus machine, my computer versus your computer, let's see which one was the stronger of the two.

The screen of Zaraghi's laptop filled with the words: VERIFYING YOUR ACCOUNT . . . VERIFYING YOUR ACCOUNT . . . VERIFYING YOUR ACCOUNT . . . VERIFYING YOUR ACCOUNT . . .

The Sun SPARCStation screen in the BEACON facility flashed the prompt: ARE YOU SURE YOU WANT TO SEND "SELL ORDERS TO STOCK EXCHANGE(S)"? YES / NO.

———•———

Colbert perked to life. YES! Once this command was executed, the sell orders would be disseminated to all the broker-dealers and nothing could stop Colbert . . . He clicked the mouse repeatedly.

SENDING ORDER(S) TO EXCHANGE(S).

SENDING . . . SENDING . . . SENDING . . .

———•———

Zaraghi's laptop: VERIFYING YOUR ACCOUNT . . . VERIFYING YOUR ACCOUNT . . . VERIFYING YOUR ACCOUNT . . . VERIFYING YOUR ACCOUNT . . .

"C'mon, c'mon," Zaraghi urged, as if at a horserace.

Then. Then . . .

Simultaneously, the screens of Zaraghi's computer and Colbert's computer flashed an identical message:

FATAL ERROR—SYSTEM RESOURCES INSUFFICIENT TO COMPLETE OPERATION. TRADE(S) ABORTED.

Across town, Colbert screamed in frustration.

Zaraghi cheered in triumph. "It's done! We won!"

We won. The words rang in Rick Hansen's ears. *We won.* At last, it was over. Or was it? Instead of exuberance, Hansen felt a wave of dread washing over him. Was McGeary the one behind this? No, it was not over. Far from it; it was just beginning. "Let's get out of here, Freddie."

Zaraghi clapped down the lid of the laptop. Quickly, the lawyer and the computer genius tossed all the hardware into Freddie's Rollaboard suitcase. They strode swiftly to the exit of the facility, Hansen toting the bag. They said nothing to one another. They were too overwhelmed by emotion to discuss what had just transpired.

Outside the facility, they headed down the dimly lit corridor. Zaraghi automatically went to press the call button.

Hansen grabbed his arm. "Wait."

Zaraghi peered at him dazedly.

The lawyer pointed to the illuminated display above the elevator. He whispered, "It's already on its way down."

The lawyer pulled Zaraghi into the shadows. They pressed their backs up against the chain-link fence, scarcely drawing a breath. The elevator arrived with a *ding!* The doors opened. Two men in security guard uniforms jumped out. Hansen immediately recognized one of them—the man he'd encountered at Bingham's apartment. Unlike the typical security guards of Wolcott, however, both had guns in hand. The second one also had a SmartCard access computer like Bingham's. The men raced down the corridor to the door of the BEACON facility. They knew their way around, Hansen realized.

"Okay, now!" Hansen leapt from the shadows into the elevator. He stabbed the LOBBY button repeatedly, willing the doors to close. Zaraghi stumbled in behind him. The metal doors rumbled shut.

"Jesus Christ," the kid whispered. "They had guns." As the elevator lurched skyward, Zaraghi looked at him with wide eyes. "The people they work for must be super-pissed."

A very true statement, Hansen realized, and one that left the lawyer asking himself, *where do we go from here?*

———•———

With the cluster of supercomputers in the NASCIA network now disabled, LINDA was completely neutralized. Its ability to send electronic sell orders through the Internet to the order routing systems of brokerage firms throughout the financial community was completely shut down. Billions in pending sell orders created by LINDA simply disappeared from the computer screens of financial firms into the black hole of cyberspace. As a result, the artificial selling pressure that LINDA intended to maintain throughout the trading day simply evaporated.

Abruptly, the natural forces of legitimate buying and selling interest once again controlled the movements of the stock market.

Over the next half hour, the market immediately stabilized—which is to say, it was essentially just treading water. Volume tapered off slightly; there could be no doubt that the market was severely weakened, but now that the enormous sell pressure LINDA exerted on the market had been lifted, there was no longer a compass indicating the trend of market direction. Institutional investors sat on the sidelines indecisively, wondering what to do.

The machines were not as indecisive. In the next hour, as the value of the market indexes drifted sideways, the automated computer program trading systems clicked on throughout the corridors of Wall Street. Independently, the systems sifted through the up-to-the-instant pricing information, cross-checked it against their buy-sell current models, and identified innumerable buying opportunities. Most of the component stocks of the Dow Jones Industrial Average had been beaten down well below their fundamental fair value and were now trading cheaply.

The computerized models indicated BUY.

In the early part of Friday afternoon, program trading activity pushed the market up slightly from its 976-point trough. The market gained back 62 points.

By late afternoon, buying interest picked up.

In the last hour of trading, the market began *surging*.

When the closing bell rang at 4:00 P.M., the market had rebounded dramatically. At the end of the most volatile triple-witching Friday in history, the stock market had lost *only* 674 points.

———•———

It could have been a hell of a lot worse, the Chairman of the Stock Exchange assured himself as he rushed into an emergency meeting at a conference room in the 7 World Trade Center offices of the Securities and Exchange Commission at 4:45 P.M. *It could've been Black Monday all over again.* He entered the room just as a stern-faced Don Neufeld took the podium.

Within the next twenty-five minutes, all the participants in that meeting agreed that on the face of the facts currently available to them, it was appropriate to bring the Federal Bureau of Investigation into the loop. *Immediately.*

Fifty-three

8:51 P.M.

THE MEETING STARTED IMMEDIATELY after Maxwell Schomburg asked Freddie Zaraghi to leave the room. Once the large mahogany door closed behind the kid, Schomburg whirled around to face the rest of the participants. The CEO's forceful voice resonated in the expanse of the wood-paneled office. "Now then. At this moment, there's a joint task force of the Securities and Exchange Commission and the FBI on the premises conducting an investigation of our disaster recovery site, which seems to have been used by persons unknown to enter numerous electronic trades. Is that right?"

The executives in the room murmured their anxious consent.

Schomburg continued. "The SEC claims that those trades may have been responsible for this morning's market break. Is that right?"

"Yes," Irv Siegel said, nervously adjusting his glasses.

"As I understand it, both the Commission and the feds have asked to speak with some of our people immediately, but we've bought ourselves until tomorrow morning in order that our chief compliance officer—that being Mike—can be present."

Mike Kilmartin's voice warbled over the speakerbox from a pay phone in Miami International Airport. "Yes, Max, that's correct."

Max Schomburg drummed his manicured fingers on the conference room table. "What the fuck is going on here?" Schomburg turned to Rick Hansen. "What do you like to be called? Rich or Richard?"

Hansen cleared his throat. "Rick is fine."

Schomburg nodded. "Rick, you seem to be the only one here with a fucking clue. This is your meeting."

The truant voice in Rick's head said, *No, Schomburg, not in a million years is this my meeting.* The lawyer would have given a year's salary-and-bonus to not be seated before these dour-faced Wolcott Fulbright executives assembled in Max Schomburg's astonishingly gorgeous corner office on the sixtieth floor. Rick, badly in need of a shave and a good night's sleep, found himself squirming in the white-hot spotlight, the center of attention among the four most powerful executives of Wolcott Fulbright and his unseen boss, Mike Kilmartin, who was connected via the phone network Zaraghi had briefly knocked out just that morning.

As he sought to gather his wits about him, Hansen forced himself to look directly into the face of each man sitting around Schomburg's cherrywood table. Schomburg, Siegel, Milgrim, Bobby Wolcott—these men were most assuredly a different breed from him. Few successfully scaled the ultimate K-2 of American ambition—the New York finance community—yet these men stood at its very pinnacle. These were men who arose before five each morning, commuted to work by limousine or helicopter, possessed second wives who were referred to as "trophies." Men with three homes and mistresses in other cities. Each day, these executives yanked the big levers of global finance, giving birth to corporations and refinancing banana republic government debt. And now these incredibly powerful men were waiting to hear what this junior lawyer had to say about the presence of a small group of federal law enforcement officials in the BEACON site at this very moment.

Relax, Hansen, said the voice in his head. *Just think, you could kick the ass of any man at this table.*

That assuring thought calmed his nerves a bit.

Rick swallowed the knot of anxiety in his throat and began. "Well, thank you. Uh, as an internal counsel to the firm, I've asked to meet with you tonight to fulfill my obligations under Section 21(a) of the Securities Act." As detailed in SEC Release 92-30515, legal and compliance officers of securities firms were required to provide a complete report to senior management of apparent wrongdoing once it comes to their attention.

"We're well aware of the requirement, Rick," Schomburg stated tersely. "Now tell us just what the hell happened this morning."

And with that, Hansen told the story from the beginning. Bingham's datebook, the fictitious insider trading charges someone dummied up after his death, the mysterious memos on stock crashes, the Gammage connection, Rick's weekend trip to Pittsburgh to debrief Zaraghi, the surveillance devices found in his home and office. Relaying the chain of events of the previous evening and that morning, he felt his blood run cold.

When he signaled that he'd finished, each of the men clamored to speak at once.

Max Schomburg held up a silencing hand; his subordinates fell quiet. "I think we should give Mike the benefit of going first. Mike?"

Kilmartin's disembodied voice came out of the box. "Just for the record, this is the first I'm hearing about this entire thing. I'd known nothing about it until Max contacted me this afternoon."

"That's right," Hansen concurred, falling on the sword to protect his boss from undue criticism. "At no time was Mike advised and I take full responsibility for that."

Irv Siegel harrumphed, "When did this investigation of yours begin?"

"The first week of February."

"Seven weeks ago?"

"Yes."

"You mean to say almost two months passed and you never informed your direct supervisor of any of this?" Irv Siegel's bushy eyebrows were perched above his glasses incredulously.

Hansen sighed. He turned and peered out the huge picture window of the dining area for a reflective moment. Outside, the night had ripened in full and the city glittered in spectacular miniature. The lights of the Brooklyn Bridge glittered like a diamond trinket to the south. The avenues below were glowing rivers of white headlights and red taillights—vehicles transporting people to places on a carefree Friday evening, kicking off the weekend. Nightlife was going on while they were up here in this mahogany-lined room, discussing events that impacted the future of the firm; at this very moment, the people outside this window were eating, conversing, drinking, having sex. Life had come to a screeching halt for Hansen at this instant, yes, but it would go on after the instant passed. It was just that the life he had known was over and the new one was indiscernible.

He faced Siegel fearlessly. "Initially, I pursued the investigation only because I thought my predecessor had been killed under suspicious circumstances. Admittedly, that was outside the scope of my responsibility to the firm. Only in the last twenty-four hours did I come to realize that his murder was connected to an attempt to trigger a decline in the stock market."

From the other side of the table: "Proof?"

Rick Hansen turned toward the gruff voice of Alan Milgrim. "Pardon me?"

Milgrim cleared his throat and restated the question as a complete sentence. "I said, what physical proof do you have of this alleged scheme?"

Hansen pondered the question. He had Bingham's datebook and PDA, a bunch of disconnected memos and McGeary's cigar band. What did that add up to? *Squat.* In hindsight, the experience seemed surreal, dreamlike. "I can't point to anything specific. Much of it is . . . circumstantial. Actually, Freddie Zaraghi uncovered the attempt."

"Who is this Zaraghi?" Milgrim demanded. "That kid in here with the beard?"

"Yes."

Bob Wolcott growled, "Let me get this straight. This thing happened because of some disgruntled college dropout? *Who*, I might add, had been making noise about suing this firm for misappropriating his software."

Milgrim piled on. "Right. How can you be certain Zaraghi wasn't using some ploy to gain access to the premises, so he could gather evidence for a lawsuit?"

"You don't understand. It was *my* idea for him to come to New York, to help figure out Bingham's involvement."

Siegel said, "That it was your idea makes it even *worse*."

Hansen was on the ropes, dazed and staggering. His story was beginning to sound incredible even to him. "Look, guys, I know what I saw. I know how the firm's electronic trading interface works. I saw billions in selling orders cued up on our STEPS system. Someone in this firm was responsible for the market decline this morning."

"Who?" Milgrim demanded.

"I don't know," Hansen conceded. "Someone in upper-level management."

The audible gasps of several shaken executives filled the room. After a beat, Bobby Wolcott asked, "What leads you to *that* conclusion?"

"Several factors. Bingham had access to the BEACON disaster recovery hot site. He sent a memo to an unnamed executive on the likelihood of stock market crashes. He was given keycards, conducted meetings on the BEACON trading floor. None of that would have been possible without a senior-level executive holding his hand. Someone possibly connected to a group of outsiders who would benefit from the scheme."

"That's an astounding accusation," Schomburg mumbled as he stared into space.

Milgrim asked, "Have you drawn any conclusions as to who it might be?"

Hansen hesitated. The lawyer now found himself uncertain about Gil McGeary's complicity. The cigar band was not exactly a smoking gun that clinched the case against McGeary. Moreover, the trader certainly did not act like a guilty man when Hansen encountered him in his fishbowl office. Then again, the trader was legendary for being calm and collected at times of inhuman stress. He could have just been in poker-face mode with the lawyer. "No. I'm not certain who it could be."

Schomburg drummed the tabletop with his fingers. "I think we've got enough for now. Richard, I presume you will make yourself available at seven A.M. at which time we will meet with our outside counsel before preliminary discussions with the FBI and the SEC at eight. At that time, you can step us through your version of the events."

"Certainly."

"At that time, I think it would be appropriate to bring your computer genius acquaintance along." Schomburg spread his hands. "You did the right thing, Richard, bringing this to our attention. You're excused from the meeting."

Hansen scooted his chair away from the table, stood up and left the room.

"Okay, Mike," Schomburg said. "He's out of earshot."

Kilmartin's disembodied voice came over the box again. "Once again, I must apologize. I didn't have any advance knowledge that Richard Hansen was doing this. My secretary, Felicity, mentioned something about this fellow Zaraghi hanging around the office last night, but I had complete trust in Hansen." Mike Kilmartin was in cover-your-ass mode, a perfectly reasonable tack for him to take, given the circumstances.

"No one's pointing fingers at this stage of the game, Michael. Do you have anything to add?"

"Yes. Just that we should go easy on Hansen. His intentions were good, even if the results were flawed. For crissakes, who knows? Maybe his actions did prevent some wrongdoing from occurring."

"We shall see. You're on the red-eye?"

"Yes. I'll see you at seven A.M. tomorrow."

"Very good." Schomburg disconnected Kilmartin before he could hang up.

Milgrim shook his head skeptically. "Max, I debriefed McGeary myself this afternoon when I first got wind of it. I'm convinced he knows absolutely nothing about this alleged activity. He did tell me that Hansen demanded the password to the electronic trading system this morning."

"C'mon, Alan," Schomburg said. "McGeary's the obvious suspect, right? I know you're his direct line supervisor and *your ass* is on the line for this, but let's not whitewash reality."

Irv Siegel shook his head. "I *always* thought McGeary should be watched like a hawk."

Milgrim said, "I've asked McGeary to meet with us tomorrow at six A.M., before we meet with Hansen and this Zaraghi fellow."

"Good." Schomburg frowned. "It's imperative we don't rush to any uninformed conclusions. Hansen's made some very serious charges. I don't have to tell you that if the FBI and the SEC decide to proceed with charges against the firm, the initial public offering is dead on arrival.

But as I see it, until we have all the facts, there is nothing to be gained by pushing the panic button just yet."

"That's right, Max," Siegel said.

Realizing the weekend with his mistress in Washington was aborted, Bobby Wolcott ran a hand through his silver hair and sighed, "Looks like it's gonna be a long weekend."

"Yes, it certainly will be." Schomburg's eyes dropped to his watch. "I'm going to put in an appearance with the Feds downstairs. The rest of you are free to go."

With that, the meeting broke up.

Fifty-four

"GUESS THEY DIDN'T CARE to hear what I had to say, huh?" Freddie Zaraghi sat in a chair in Hansen's office, staring out his picture window.

"Nothing personal, Freddie," Hansen replied as he pushed papers into his briefcase. "It was a closed-door meeting with the senior brass. Believe me, there'll be plenty of questions tomorrow. And I promise you, it won't be much fun with the Feds there." Hansen shut his briefcase and sighed. "You know what frustrates me?"

"What's that?"

"I'm not entirely certain they believe me."

Zaraghi shrugged. "Look at it from their perspective. A) it's hard to swallow, and B) they don't *want* to believe it's possible."

Hansen nodded and yawned. He checked his watch. It was 9:25 P.M. All he wanted was to crawl into bed with Stephanie and grab ten hours of sleep. Already, that was shaping up to be just wishful thinking, considering the late hour and his early morning obligation with Schomburg tomorrow.

"So happens, I believe you, Richard."

The voice startled Hansen and Zaraghi. They turned to the sound of it and, to Rick's amazement, Alan Milgrim stood in the doorway to his office. *How long had Milgrim been standing there?*

Milgrim smiled grimly and stepped into the office. "You must be Mr. Zaraghi, the computer wizard. I'm Alan Milgrim." He extended a hand to Freddie, who shook it. Then he turned to the young lawyer. "Listen, Richard, I hope we didn't come down on you too hard in Max's office. With the severity of these charges and the involvement of the FBI, we're keen to get our arms around the problem."

Hansen said, "Certainly."

"As you know, McGeary is my direct report. If he's been involved in something that's not exactly kosher, well, Schomburg all but said it's *my* ass that's on the line. So I came down here looking for a little ass insurance. Can you come to a meeting in the Jakarta Room at six tomorrow morning to help me debrief McGeary?"

"Sure."

Milgrim smiled. "Terrific. I guess the first order of business is to get you guys home so you can get some sleep. Since it's all but impossible to find a cab at this hour on Wall Street, Max asked me to put you in one of the radio cars waiting downstairs. I'll sign the voucher so you don't have to worry about getting reimbursed."

Hansen was exhausted and wanted only to get home. "That's great, thanks."

"Think nothing of it. I'll go down with you, inform the driver. Come."

———•———

On the elevator ride down, Milgrim waited several seconds before he said, "This probably goes without saying, but let me just make it clear. If the FBI or the SEC gets the wrong idea on this, it could be devastating to the firm's initial public offering. Therefore, information is to be disseminated on a need-to-know basis only."

"Right," Hansen nodded, watching the floor numbers counting down on the lighted display.

"That said, have you told anyone else about the alleged incident in the BEACON facility?"

"No," Freddie said.

"What about you, Richard?"

"Just Mike Kilmartin."

"Of course, of course. Michael needs to be in the loop, he's your immediate supervisor and the chief compliance officer. But you didn't mention anything about this to your wife, did you?"

The lawyer hesitated. "About some things. Not specifically about what happened at the BEACON site this morning." It was true. He didn't want to scare her with it, not in her present state.

The elevator came to a stop on the ground floor and opened into the lobby. "That's good," Milgrim said, bobbing his head. "Please, need-to-know basis only."

"Need-to-know basis," Hansen agreed sleepily.

They stepped out of the lavish lobby of 44 Wall into the early evening gloom that had gathered in the nearly deserted financial district. A sleek black Cadillac Brougham idled at the curb twenty feet from the entrance. Milgrim made an angry gesture, beckoning the limousine to pull closer.

"Cool," Freddie burbled at the sight of it.

As it pulled in front of them, Milgrim handed Hansen a signed voucher. "Just give this to the driver, tell him to take you to the Millenium and have him drop Frederic wherever it is he's staying—"

Hansen became wide-awake. "Wait—how did you—?"

A confused look crossed Milgrim's face. He turned to the darkened windows of the black limousine, as if speaking to his reflection in the smoked glass. "Try to get some sleep," he said, staring at the car windows all the while. "We need you razor-sharp tomorrow."

"Alan?" Rick Hansen persisted. "How did you know my wife and I were staying in the Millenium?"

The back door of the black limousine opened. The Russian swung his legs out from inside. He dipped his head out into the pale light of the streetlamps. An ugly semi-automatic pistol rested menacingly in his lap. "Please get in the car," Viktor Alexeyev said.

———————●———————

Alan Milgrim watched the Cadillac drive off down Wall Street until it turned left on William Street and disappeared from view. Once it was gone, an involuntary convulsion brought the executive's head forward in a violent thrust. A half-digested stew of prime rib and vodka splattered against the curb. Milgrim jackknifed over the street a second, then a third time, vomiting up the contents of his acid-bloated stomach until there was nothing left to regurgitate. With great effort, he managed not to soil his suit.

Why did they do that to me? Why did they plan to cut me out after the public offering? Schomburg had no apparent rhyme or reason for it. The CEO muttered something about Wolcott Fulbright's *top-heavy infrastructure,* an infuriating catchphrase that meant, *no hard feelings, but we're giving you the gold-watch heave-ho. Thanks for the memories.*

For Milgrim, the whole "Stiletto" thing had started out as a game of sorts. *You-screw-me-I-screw-you.* But he should have known Colbert would take it too far, especially given the size of the payoff given to Milgrim. They killed Tommy Bingham, a decent guy, and his girlfriend, the paralegal. Then they did the professor when he got too demanding. Now Alan Milgrim found himself compelled to deliver over the lawyer and the computer programmer to Colbert's Russian thugs, raising the body count even higher.

He punched up the number on his cellular phone. "Stiletto here.

They're on their way . . . Yes, there's no traffic. You should see them in about ten minutes."

He clapped the phone shut and closed his eyes tightly.

Milgrim didn't want to imagine what would happen to them. The executive dipped his chin into his chest and began to weep quietly. It was all out of control. So out of control.

Fifty-five

RICK HANSEN'S SENSES WERE BUZZING, his mind was ablaze with terror. *What was happening to them?*

Wordlessly, the Russian sat stoically in the plush leather seat of the radio car with his weapon trained on Zaraghi. The first glimpse of his captor's face resulted in a flash of recognition; the Russian had been in the BEACON facility that morning, the same gun in his hand. At the same time, Hansen could tell from the partial reflection of the driver's face in the rearview mirror that he was the man Rick had encountered at Bingham's apartment. With a shiver of panic, Rick Hansen was certain his life would end that night.

A tense silence prevailed as the limousine threaded its way through the quiet streets of the financial district that Friday night. The driver took successive lefts on William, Pine and Broadway, before turning right onto Battery Place. Within six minutes, the Cadillac had circled around the perimeter of lower Manhattan and melded into the brisk flow of two-lane traffic on the West Side Highway, heading north.

Where are they taking us?

Outside the tinted window, the surface of the Hudson River glimmered with the reflected light of the buildings of New Jersey. Hansen cut a glance at Zaraghi. The kid's face was inscrutable.

In the next minute, Zaraghi muttered, "I can't stand this."

"What was that?" The Russian demanded with a scowl.

"I said, I can't stand the silence. Why are we here?"

Viktor Alexeyev's voice was cold. "Don't be stupid. You know why you're here."

"Where are you taking us?"

The Russian refused to reply.

Hansen jolted abruptly as his beeper went off with a shrill alarm. The Russian eyed Hansen warily as he drew the beeper from its belt-clip holster.

TRIED YOU AT THE OFFICE. NO ANSWER. WHERE ARE YOU? S.

"My wife," he said softly. "She's expecting a baby any minute now."

The Russian said nothing; he showed his teeth. His molars gleamed in the reflected streetlight.

———•———

Gagarov drove to Chelsea Piers.

The Chelsea Piers facility took up thirty acres of prime Manhattan waterfront real estate between Seventeenth and Twenty-third streets. At a cost of $100 million, the complex was a perfect symbol of New York City's breathtaking renaissance as a direct result of the billions of dollars of wealth generated by the Wall Street community during the longest bull market in history. Originally opened in 1910 as a port-of-call for ocean liners, Chelsea Piers was a world-renowned architectural wonder for fifty years until the popularity of air travel precipitated its rapid demise. By the mid-eighties, the structure had been abandoned and was crumbling; the state planned to demolish the rotting piers to build a highway.

Because of budget constraints, however, the plans for the highway were scrapped. In 1994, a consortium of private and public interests stepped in and created a vast, five-block-long entertainment complex from the long-neglected pink-granite facade that surrounded the four nine-hundred-foot piers. In the summer of 1995, the historic waterfront property reopened as a waterside resort with sports and entertainment complexes and a fully equipped Maritime Center for private boat dockage.

They're taking us to the water, Hansen realized.

The Gargoyle turned left at Sixteenth Street. He turned into an access to the five-block-long blue-red-and-gray headhouse. The Cadillac drove into the sheltered parking facility between Piers 59 and 60. Gagarov found a space between two blue-steel support beams and killed the engine.

"I am authorized to kill at will," Alexeyev hissed. "Stay quiet and follow my lead."

They disembarked from the vehicle. The sounds of the car doors slamming shut behind them were amplified monstrously in the cavernous parking facility. The lawyer was immediately struck by the dampness of the air. The world-famous spire of the Empire State Building pricked the evening sky to the east.

"Let's go," Alexeyev said, shoving the pistol into Hansen's ribs. Hansen flinched at the pain, and shuffled forward toward the ships docked at Pier 60.

———●———

Philip Colbert stood on the foredeck of the *Full Acquittal*, grasping the railing in a white-knuckled grip. He smoked his Liguito No. 2 and listened to the comforting slurp of the Hudson River against the hull of his yacht. When he saw the Russians emerge from the parking facility with their quarry in tow, he drew the cellphone from his blazer. He speed-dialed Milgrim. His eyes never left the two captives as he spoke. "Stiletto, they're here. I'll call you back with further instructions. Be prepared to take a trip."

Colbert closed the phone. He tossed his cigar into the spinach-green water, where it died with a brief hiss. Then he ascended the stairs to the bridge deck and walked into the pilothouse. He instructed his captain to prepare the crew for a brief trip to the Upper Bay. Then the financier went belowdecks to the stateroom to prepare for the arrival of the Wolcott Fulbright lawyer and the computer programmer. Colbert shed his blazer, spread a plastic tarpaulin on the floor of the stateroom and drew the venetian blinds on the full-height windows. Then he retrieved his pistol from the bottom drawer of the cherrywood cabinet.

He sat in a chair awaiting Hansen and Zaraghi. He was now ready for them.

———●———

The yacht was breathtaking in its size. Once Hansen spied the vessel, he began to fathom the unquantifiable wealth and power of its owner. They had unwittingly tangled with this power broker and had been abducted at his command. Hanson thought about his wife and choked back a sob of fear.

The Russians shoved them roughly onto the starboard side of the foredeck. The vessel listed slightly in the swells of the Hudson. Beneath his feet, Hansen could feel the mighty diesel-fueled in-board engines rumbling to life.

"This way," Viktor Alexeyev said, nudging them with his pistol toward the stairs. They descended belowdecks to the semidarkness of the stateroom.

In the next several minutes, the engines thundered at full throttle. The propellers churned up a boiling wake that slapped musically against the wooden piers, and the *Full Acquittal* glided sideways from its berth. With a vibrating rattle that shook its Kevlar laminate hull, the ship glided backward into the Hudson, then elegantly pivoted and headed south toward the tip of Manhattan.

———•———

Their hands were bound at stomach level with wire and they were instructed to sit next to one another on the tarpaulin.

Philip Colbert glared at Hansen and Zaraghi for a long while, as if committing their faces to memory.

"My wife needs to go to the hospital," Hansen pleaded. "Tell us what you want from us."

Colbert approached the lawyer, stood over him. Then he struck him viciously in the face with a closed fist. A spray of blood and spittle flew from Hansen's mouth.

"You can't give me what I want," Colbert hissed. "You've already taken it away."

"Leave him alone, man," Zaraghi said. "I did it."

Colbert turned to the kid. "It was you? You sabotaged my trades?"

"Yes, and *you* stole my program," Zaraghi retorted defiantly.

Colbert's voice was chilling. "Do you realize what you've done?" Colbert's lips were wet with saliva. "Jesus Christ, if only you went through the right channels, we could have come to an understanding, a deal. You would have been *set for life*."

"You mean, the same deal Gammage and Bingham got?" Freddie retorted sarcastically. "Strange definition of 'set for life.' "

Shut up, Freddie, shut up, Hansen willed him telepathically.

Colbert stared at the computer programmer. The cold dark orbs of his eyes narrowed into slits. A wave of nausea washed over Hansen. He was certain the businessman would not hesitate to kill them there and now.

At length, Colbert said, "Don't you understand yet . . . this is not child's play?"

Freddie remained quiet, but stared defiantly at Philip Colbert.

Enraged, the financier turned to Alexeyev. "Put his hands up on the chair."

The hulking Russian crossed the stateroom. He pulled Freddie's bound hands up. Zaraghi cried out in discomfort as Viktor Alexeyev maneuvered him over toward the table in the stateroom. "Ouch! The fuck you think you're doing?"

Alexeyev forced the kid's hands open against the padding of the chair. Then, Colbert came over to Freddie and pressed the barrel of the pistol against the back of his right hand. A small whirlpool of skin twisted beneath the silencer of the gun.

"Oh, Jesus, please," Freddie whimpered, his eyes widening, "you're not going to—"

The financier's gun jerked backward with a soft *kerchunk*. Zaraghi's hand exploded in a burst of blood and flesh, and the padding of the chair absorbed the bullet as it passed through his palm. Zaraghi screamed and jerked forward, yanking the mangled pulp of his hand away from the chair, as if from a raging fire. His face was a mask of disbelief, horror and agony. Zaraghi began sobbing, tucking the bloodied hand between his legs and rocking back and forth like a beaten child.

"Now maybe you'll realize what damage you did with that hand of yours," Colbert said dispassionately. Then he said to Viktor Alexeyev. "You know what to do."

With that, Colbert started up the stairs to the deck. Viktor Alexeyev stepped over to Richard Hansen and pushed the barrel into his temple. "Your wife is in Room 531 at the Millenium Hotel. She is nine months pregnant. After I kill you, I can kill them both with a single bullet. Unless you're willing to tell us what we desire."

Colbert climbed the spiral staircase toward the foredeck. In the next half hour or so, the Russians would interrogate the captives, using intermittent torture as necessary to extract the required information. After that—well, Alexeyev would do whatever he had to do. The bodies would be found floating in the Hudson tomorrow morning. . . .

It had been a magnificent plan, the initiative, one that would have been the achievement of a lifetime. Its failure was truly regrettable. With federal law enforcement involved as they were now, it would be impossible to reboot LINDA and try the initiative once again on Monday morning. But as a consolation, the GoldBridge derivatives were worth tens of millions. Was it safe to cash in on these in-the-money derivative instruments? That's what they needed to know from the lawyer. If so, Colbert decided that money would go to himself; screw the Partners.

Switzerland, he was thinking as he stepped onto the foredeck in the moments before the brilliant white light washed over him from above. *He would live out his life in Switzerland.*

Then his world suddenly disappeared a cone of blinding radiance.

What the hell?

Disoriented, Philip Colbert shielded his eyes against the glare and stared into the sky at the helicopter hovering just overhead, its rotor blades thundering at a deafening volume.

In the next instant, a voice boomed out over the aircraft's P.A. system.

"*Full Acquittal, this is the United States Coast Guard from Brooklyn Air Station. Federal law enforcement officials will be boarding your vessel momentarily. Repeat, we will be boarding your vessel.*"

Fifty-six

CONSPIRACY ON WALL STREET? was the headline blazed across page one of the *New York Post*'s early morning edition concerning the incident that occured in the financial district yesterday morning and the subsequent gunplay aboard the financier's yacht. By press time, the FBI and the SEC were still trying to puzzle through the events. Both were still in no-comment mode.

It turned out that while the Feds had agreed not to interrogate Hansen and Zaraghi until the next morning in the presence of the firm's counsel, that did not mean they had agreed to let them out of their sight. The Feds took no chances that these guys were in league with other co-conspirators and were therefore considered possible flight risks. In fact, when they tailed the limousine to the marina and watched the lawyer and the computer programmer board the yacht named *Full Acquittal*, the Feds flew into a panic. The pair possibly implicated in the massive market manipulation scheme were attempting to leave the country by sea!

The Brooklyn Naval Air Station of the U.S. Coast Guard was immediately called in to intercept. Within twenty minutes, the federal agents were shuttled by helicopter from Pier 59 to the *Full Acquittal*. Upon boarding, they found Hansen and Zaraghi bound by wire in the stateroom, held against their will. With that, the Feds' perception of the facts was completely turned on its head.

The financier in whose name the ship was registered was none other than Philip Colbert . . . now *there* was a blast from the past. Colbert had been one of the all-time great unindicted corporate raiders of the 1980s. In 1991, Colbert was fully acquitted on twenty-seven counts of securities fraud. Rumors of jury tampering were never substantiated by the frustrated prosecutors. Essentially, the bastard had gotten away with it. And he had the gall to call his yacht *Full Acquittal?*

What the hell was that sonuvabitch doing sending a pair of goons to abduct a Wall Street lawyer and a college dropout by gunpoint and terrorize them on board his yacht? They were certainly going to find out . . .

———●———

At around midnight, Max Schomburg received word of the abduction of Hansen and Zaraghi at his fifteen-room duplex on Park Avenue.

"That sonuvabitch," Schomburg said, when informed that one of his lieutenants, Alan Milgrim, had been implicated in the growing BEACON scandal. According to the Feds, several cellular phone transmissions had been documented between Milgrim and Colbert in the last forty-eight hours.

Desperate times called for desperate measures. Schomburg woke Artie Lefcourt from a deep sleep and asked Wolcott Fulbright's chief outside litigator, "Arthur, busy this weekend?"

"Max, I have a feeling I'm going to be," he said sleepily.

Lefcourt was fully awake once Schomburg told him what was happening.

In Schomburg's office at six-thirty the following morning, it was immediately conceded: the IPO was scuttled. There would be no need for further discussion on that subject.

Now on to the next order of business: how to salvage the franchise. On Wall Street, a reputation was a peculiar asset: it took years to establish, but only an instant to destroy.

Over bagels and black coffee, Lefcourt and the phalanx of young litigators from Wachtel, Lipton counseled Schomburg, Siegel and Bobby Wolcott that one thing was clear from the get-go: the SEC was to be kept at arm's length until Lefcourt's team conducted its own internal investigation of the firm's records with a fine-toothed comb.

"Preposterous," Schomburg said. Mighty Max would not be a party to stonewalling the regulators. In fact, the SEC would be brought up to date within the hour, and the CEO would not hear otherwise. The firm had to do the right thing. After all, Wolcott Fulbright was a *victim* of a rogue executive.

Schomburg himself personally placed the call to Don Neufeld's Brooklyn Heights residence. By coincidence, Neufeld had been classmates with Lefcourt at the University of Pennsylvania. None of them fooled themselves into thinking that meant special treatment, but it certainly couldn't hurt.

Neufeld's involvement meant that a well-oiled machine geared into action. Together with the stock exchanges, the SEC was charged with protecting the integrity of the public securities markets. Neufeld rose to the occasion, which was shaping up to be a once-in-a-lifetime opportunity for an ambitious career man at the Commission.

Late Saturday afternoon, he presided over a hastily called meeting in the great cream-and-gold conference room of the New York Stock Exchange, where the stern faces of former exchange presidents glowered over the attendees. Gathered around the enormous oblong table were representatives from all the exchanges and half a dozen from the New York branch of the SEC.

The action taken was swift and decisive. The electronic trading privileges of Wolcott Fulbright were immediately suspended pending an initial investigation by a team of regulators. (Schomburg had already voluntarily offered this, though Neufeld declined to mention that.) Also, the decision was made that in addition to the FBI, the Secret Service and the Justice Department would immediately be brought into the loop. After all, this thing went way beyond your basic, garden-variety stock manipulation scheme.

There was plenty of high-profile work to go around for everybody. Still, it was clear that Neufeld's people were running the show.

Sunday morning came, and the rude confrontation with Federal officers was the last thing Eddie Slamkowski would have expected.

Slamkowski had just caught a terrific break off the shore of Huntington Beach. It was the kind that jacks you up to the heavens and drops you straight to the bottom of the bowl. The kind that peels into a turbulent tube at the back of your board, propelling you into the shore with a distilled force unlike any other. And suddenly, there Slam was, in his Marvel Comics superhero-blue-and-yellow neoprene wetsuit, perched on his custom-shaped board, *throated* by this wave, man, alive with the joy of surfing, gliding along the clean rolling walls of the watery road, exhilarating in the electric-blue solitude, feeling sorry for all the others, the nonsurfers who didn't understand this life—the spray against your face, saltwater on your lips and the breeze whipping through your hair.

I am gonna miss this, he was thinking. After all, the waves of Chicago's Lake Michigan did not quite rival the singing, rippling roar of the SoCal surf. Ha ha ha. But as Slamkowski wrung out the final thrust of the wave and felt the crunch of the surfboard against the wet sand of the shore, he was stunned to find himself escorted roughly out of the boiling Pacific by some blue-jacketed federales wearing sunglasses before daybreak. Slam was roughly shoved face first to the wet sand, acrid and salty on his lips, abrasive against his sunburned face. "You are under arrest for suspected violations of the 1986 Computer Fraud and Abuse Act," some Fibbie screamed at him.

"And 10b-5 violations of the 1933 Securities Act," a young woman lawyer from the SEC added.

While Slam protested his innocence, he was pulled to his feet and dragged soaking wet along the sand dunes. He found himself thrown into the back of a good-enough-for-government sedan. As he was driven to a federal holding facility somewhere in Los Angeles in his surfing duds, he realized that when all was said and done, he would not be returning to Chicago after all. He didn't know how he would break it to his buddy Trader Vic, after all Vic had done for him. . . .

———•———

In Captiva Island, Florida, at 7:47 A.M. Eastern Standard Time, a group of Federal law enforcement agents waited patiently for someone to come to the enormous teakwood door at the residence known as Château-sur-l'Océan. They muttered to one another about the obscene opulence of the palace whose address matched the search-and-seizure affidavit. A woman wearing a chartreuse Chinese silk robe answered the door. She wore no makeup, but her beauty was unmistakable. "Can I help you?" she said in a tone that suggested anything but a desire to be helpful.

"Special Agent Stephen Cavanaugh from the Secret Service Computer Fraud division, ma'am." He crisply identified the others from the FBI and the SEC. Then he waved a signed warrant and affidavit authorizing them to conduct a search of the premises. Without another word, Mrs. Colbert slammed the door shut and engaged the deadbolt.

"Looks like we have to do this the hard way, people," Special Agent Cavanaugh said, unable to suppress his glee.

It was called "dynamic entry" in law enforcement circles and essentially it meant that a 250-pound battering ram was used to bash the door down. The Feds swarmed into the megamillionaire's mansion, seizing any piece of equipment that could have conceivably been used in the scheme.

The raid netted seven computers, two facsimile machines and twelve boxes of business records related to a company that the SEC had already been advised about—GoldBridge Capital Advisors and Infinity Technology Securities.

———•———

On Sunday night, when confronted by federal agents at his home in Southampton, Long Island, Alan Milgrim broke down and wept uncontrollably. With his lawyer present, he offered to testify against his co-conspirator Philip Colbert in exchange for leniency in his sentencing and dropping of several charges. Milgrim's personal attorney, a former Manhattan DA, dangled a promise that Milgrim would turn a letter over to the government that bore the legend TO BE OPENED IN THE EVENT OF MY DEATH. The attorney contended that his client—fearful that Colbert would have him killed once the deed was done—wrote down a detailed description of the scheme to be exposed if the Wolcott Fulbright executive was found dead. The government wanted the document badly, but not badly enough to cut Milgrim a sweetheart deal. Then one of the lawyers from the Justice Department realized that now they knew the letter existed, they could simply attempt to subpoena the letter. *No thanks*, they told Milgrim's lawyer. *See you in court.*

Milgrim and Colbert were taken to their arraignment in handcuffs and held without bail.

———•———

At around eight o'clock Sunday evening, Stephanie's water broke.

Fifty-seven

ON SUNDAY NIGHT while Stephanie slept, Freddie Zaraghi came to New York Hospital to see the kid. He came bearing flowers and primary-colored helium balloons.

Rick tiptoed out of the room with Freddie and his new daughter, bringing them to a visitor's lounge at the end of the hall.

"I've never held a baby before," Zaraghi said uncomfortably. He balanced the baby in the crook of his plaster cast. It was covered with get-well-soon graffiti, such as: HEY, DUMMY, ONLY SUPERMAN CAN STOP A SPEEDING BULLET WITH HIS HAND and OOPS! THERE GOES FREDDIE'S SEX LIFE.

"You're a natural," Hansen said.

"She's a good-looking kid," Zaraghi observed. "Must take after your wife's side of the family."

"Completely." Hansen took his newborn daughter from Zaraghi's awkward grasp and kissed her forehead. "How's the hand?"

"Hurts like hell. Thank God for the painkillers. I'm gonna have to hack into the hospital's computers and give myself a lifetime prescription to these jagged little pills."

Rick Hansen laughed. "The doctors still concerned about your prognosis?"

"They're feeling a little more positive about it than they were yesterday. I'm definitely going to have diminished abilities with it, but if it wasn't this, carpal tunnel syndrome would've gotten me anyway." Zaraghi issued a small ironic laugh. "I'll live. The shot went clean through, so thank God for small favors, right?"

Hansen bobbed his head. "By the way, I've been trying to figure out how to repay you for helping me figure out the Bingham thing, and, well, I think I've come up with a totally off-the-wall, senseless and ill-fated way to do that."

"Oh yeah? Hit me."

Hansen shrugged. "Maybe you and I could get LINDA patented, try to market it to the financial community. Could be a pretty hot commodity on Wall Street."

Zaraghi smirked. "I guess we wouldn't have to spend any money on publicity, huh?"

"Nah. But one thing you have to promise me?"

Zaraghi said, "What's that?"

"We only make the non-crash version available to the general public."

"You've got a deal." Then Zaraghi's face changed slightly. "Seriously, you mind if I think about it? As the monster's creator, I'm not certain it's quite ready to be alive."

"I can't argue with that."

They tossed the bull for another five minutes, then Zaraghi said the painkillers were kicking in and he needed to sleep. Hansen returned to the hospital room with his baby daughter, so her mother could nurse her.

Epilogue
Friday, March 26

ON FRIDAY, RICK HANSEN REPORTED to work at Wolcott, Fulbright & Company with two dozen H. Upmann Cuban cigars Paul Gelbaum had smuggled in from a recent trip to London. Rick had them retro-fitted with pink IT'S A GIRL bands.

"Congratulations," Gil McGeary said, accepting the cigar in his fishbowl office. "Baby girl, huh? Gonna be a daddy's girl, I'll bet."

"You got that right. Already is."

McGeary ignited their cigars. Hansen took a draw and contemplated his Upmann. Strangely, he found himself nostalgic for that first day they shared cigars in McGeary's office in January.

McGeary seemed to read his thoughts. "You know, those Castro specials were given to me by Bobby Wolcott."

"I know," Hansen said. "And Bobby had given a box to Alan Milgrim as well. I'm sorry I jumped to the conclusion that you were the one behind the scheme based on a lousy cigar band."

"Me as the suspect was too obvious, Counselor. That alone should have given you pause."

"You're right."

They smoked in silence for a few moments.

"This business." McGeary expelled a mushroom cloud of blue smoke, then continued, "This business we're in can be so all-consuming, you know? You liquidate your youth in the pursuit of the legal tender. And of course it's worth it, I wouldn't have traded away a moment of it to be anyplace else. But it's so all-consuming, you really do lose perspective on what's important. It's *not* this." McGeary made an all-encompassing gesture with his cigar that meant *this business*.

Hansen bobbed his head and dropped half an inch of ash into Gil's ashtray. "I know what you mean. Things are different once you have a kid. You care a lot more about things like life and death. Where you spend your time." It was getting a little heavy, so Hansen sought to change the subject. Hansen noticed the packing boxes with the Wolcott logo for the first time. He smiled. "Getting a new office, Gil?"

"Guess you could say that." McGeary's smile was grim.

The rudeness of reality pierced Hansen's feel-good vibe of new fatherhood. "They *fired* you?"

"And this is a surprise to you?"

"But it was Milgrim and Bingham. What did *you* do?"

"C'mon, Hansen, get with it. Read Scott Mendelsohn's memo—I pushed the GoldBridge trade. I crammed it down the throat of the firm, called in every favor I had in the favor bank. I'm the derivatives guy and I let GoldBridge bring the Trojan horse into the firm. That type of scandal requires a human sacrifice. You're looking at the human sacrifice."

"Jesus, Gil." Hansen felt numb. "I feel responsible, in some weird way."

"You *should* feel responsible, kemo sabe, because you *are* responsible. Responsible for exposing Milgrim and Colbert-slash-Stone, that is. And it's a goddamned good thing that you did. I mean, for crissakes, don't tell me you're having regrets."

"I don't know."

"Put another way, would you have done it the same way if you had a do-over?"

Hansen chewed his lip over that one. "Yeah. I think I would."

"Of course you would. You and that Carnegie-Mellon egghead averted a major stock market crash. Think of what could've happened."

Hansen smoked in silence for a moment. "What are you going to do, Gil?"

"Don't cry for me, Argentina. This is just the kind of kick in the ass a middle-aged man needs to reconcile his priorities in life, you know? What am I going to do? Nothing terribly original. I'm going to get about fifty million in other people's money and run me a hedge fund up in Greenwich. I mean, it's the day-to-day combat that gets me juiced.

"True, I'm going to the buy-side, but in my new life I'll be heading home five minutes after they ring the closing bell at the stock exchange. Yeah, it's a gear-down, no question, but I've always wanted to coach the kid's Little League team and now I'll have the time to do that. I mean, I'm thirty-fucking-six. Almost *half* my life's passed by."

"That's virtually retirement age," Hansen joked. Then he slipped into a trance of thought. "I guess Milgrim and Colbert were asshole buddies from the go-go eighties."

"Yeah, Milgrim did some sleazy takeover deals with Colbert in a previous life at some other firm. They've been in bed together ever since. As I understand it from Mad Max himself, Milgrim saw this Professor Gammage pitch the LINDA black box at some industry junket in London. Milgrim was getting screwed in the initial public offering, had a hard-on against the firm and finally approached his old entrepreneurial pal Colbert and said, 'Have I got a deal for you.'

"Colbert got the financing together, Milgrim got the systems together. Then I think it kind of spun out of Milgrim's control and he could do nothing to reverse it. I guess the good news is that at the end of the day, the firm is going to be okay. Not great, but okay. Full cooperation with the SEC may avoid some of the pain, but not all of it."

"Let's hope they're reasonable about it."

"Who? The SEC? Oh, they will be. The firm was a victim of one executive's fraud, right? The stock market has regained about a third of the loss already. History shows the SEC is tough but fair." McGeary exhaled a column of smoke. "What are *you* going to do, Counselor? As it happens, I could use a lawyer up in Greenwich."

"Thanks for the thought." Hansen expelled a breath. "I owe it to the firm to stick around long enough to see this matter resolved. Could be a couple of years before that happens. But I suppose I have job security as long as the interrogatories keep rolling in from the regulators."

"Yeah, tell me about it. You lawyers love papers." McGeary cast a glance at the boxes as he raised himself from his beloved racing car seat. "Well, Building Services will remove every last trace of my existence. Guess it's time to go gentle into that good night. You want to walk me out?"

"Sure. It'd be a pleasure."

"Good. That means you get to witness the last hurrah."

"The last hurrah?"

Hansen was amazed when McGeary picked up the microphone to the firm's worldwide hoot'n'holler, pushed down the button and began broadcasting. "This is Gil McGeary in New York." There was a whine of feedback, and Gil waited patiently until it subsided. Around the world, personnel connected to the hoot'n'holler network stopped what they were doing and listened in. McGeary plunged ahead. "Even Bruce Springsteen realized when it was time to say good-bye to the E-Street Band, go out and fly solo. That's the position I find myself in right now. I'm on my way out, and I just wanted to tell everybody how much I loved working here. It was a good run. Not the best finish, but a god-damned good run. It's been swell working with you-all. Good-bye, fare-well, amen. As always, kick ass, trade smart and have fun. I hope you'll always remember Gil McGeary as a guy who left you with nothing—"

The troops on the trading floor stopped listening and looked at one another uncomprehendingly. *Huh? What was that? Nothing?*

In the next moment, Gil McGeary brought out a regulation-sized basketball from his office. He stood at a chalk line that marked a regulation foul line in the NBA. He dribbled the ball on the carpeted floor a few times, as if to get a feel for the ball's heft. Then, in a moment of un-breakable concentration, he eyed the rim that had been affixed next to The Zipper, cocked his right hand over his head, and let the shot fly.

Whoosh.

Picking up the microphone, he said, "*—nothing but net.*"

As one, the sales and trading personnel on the equity derivatives floor rose up in a thunderous standing ovation. Acknowledging the applause, cheers and whistles with a brief salute, Gil McGeary strode off the trading floor for the final time with only the basketball tucked under his arm.

Watching the former desk head as he disappeared from view, Rick Hansen smiled as he said to himself, *See you around, Magilla.*

Afterword

This is a work of speculative fiction. None of these events ever happened, nor are any of these characters based on any living individual. LINDA is an invention of the author's imagination, as is Wolcott Fulbright. Virtually all global financial and trading firms deploy tremendous resources and capital to risk management of securities trading activity; nothing herein is intended to suggest otherwise.

Acknowledgments

Creating a novel is an exceptionally lonely process, but is often impossible without the contribution of many. Such was certainly the case with this project.

The inspiration for this novel was a January 25, 1993, article in *Wall Street Letter*, "MIT Study May Find Markets 'Forecastable' by Computer." Additionally, the work of *Wired*'s Kevin Kelly was influential, resulting in the title of the novel, among other things. For the current state of supercomputers and supercomputing technology, I'm grateful to the staff of the Pittsburgh Supercomputing Resource Center.

On the subject of technology and Wall Street, especially useful were works by Gary Weiss (*Business Week*, November 2, 1992), Michael Schrage (*The Washington Post*, January 3, 1992), and Lars Tvede (*Futures Magazine*, January 15, 1992). The sources for Tom Bingham's memo on the inevitability of stock market crashes included the scholarly works of John Kenneth Galbraith, Alan Greenspan, Charles Kindelberger, Charles Mackay, Burton Malkiel, Hyman Minsky, Allen Sinai, Randy Updike, Albert Wojnilower, and Martin Wolfson. For the inner workings of derivatives, John Greenwald's *Time* magazine cover story, "The Secret Money Machine" (April 11, 1994), was instrumental.

For perspectives on Information Warfare, the author is indebted to Winn Schwartau (who coined the term), the 1996 RAND study by Molander-Riddile-Wilson, *Strategic Information Warfare: The Emerging Face of Cyberwar*, and M. J. Zuckerman (*USA Today*, June 5, 1996). For his expertise on "denial of service" attacks, I'm thankful to Dr. Richard Power of the Computer Security Institute in San Francisco. On hacker attacks on the national phone-switching network, the following sources were essential: Dead Lord and the Chief Executive Officers, "Basic Concepts of Translation [of Electronic Switching Systems]," *Phrack* (Issue 26) ("*Want to throw the ESS Switch into an endless loop???*"), and Lou Dolinar (*Newsday*, February 26, 1990).

My personal gratitude to those who were responsible for bringing this project to print: William Clark of the William Morris Agency; my editor, Zach Schisgal; and Paul Fedorko at William Morrow—all of whom positively influenced the project from its earliest incarnation. Joe Gray, longtime friend and kindred, participated in countless late-night brainstorming sessions and contributed tremendously to the final product. Thanks also to Roseanne Farino who expertly converted my hieroglyphic handwriting into typewritten pages; Anne Cole at William Morrow; and Jessica Kaye at The Publishing Mills. For advice and support in the creative arena, I'm especially appreciative to Carole Sivin and Barbara Marks. I'm grateful, as well, to the "reading committee": JMGS, Adam Sifre, Rick and Jessica Steinhaus, Barbara and Robert Bangser, and Mike Faber. And gratitude to the Writer's Room in Manhattan for invaluable camaraderie and shelter, the equivalent of a Sundance Institute for the writers of Manhattan.

E-mail the author at VeloMoney@aol.com for a full bibliography of the resource material used herein. All errors of fact are attributable to the author.

—STEPHEN RHODES
New York

About the Author

Over the last decade, Stephen Rhodes has worked for several global investment firms in New York, London and Hong Kong, including Lehman Brothers and Salomon. He currently works in Manhattan for the asset-backed risk-arbitrage fund of an offshore money-center trading house. Rhodes has joint business and law degrees and lives with his family in Fairfield, Connecticut, and Stratton, Vermont.